Praise for Anna Castle

Murder by Misrule was selected ... ...us Review's Best Indie Books of 2014.

"Castle's characters brim with zest and real feeling... Though the plot keeps the pages turning, the characters, major and minor, and the well-wrought historical details will make readers want to linger in the 16th century. A laugh-out loud mystery that will delight fans of the genre." — Kirkus, starred review

"*Murder by Misrule* is a delightful debut with characters that leap off the page, especially the brilliant if unwilling detective Francis Bacon and his street smart man Tom Clarady. Elizabeth Tudor rules, but Anna Castle triumphs." — Karen Harper, NY Times best-selling author of *The Queen's Governess*

"Well-researched... *Murder by Misrule* is also enormously entertaining; a mystery shot through with a series of misadventures, misunderstandings, and mendacity worthy of a Shakespearian comedy." — M. Louisa Locke, author of the Victorian San Francisco Mystery Series

"Castle's period research is thorough but unobtrusive, and her delight in the clashing personalities of her crime-fighting duo is palpable: this is the winning fictional odd couple of the year, with Bacon's near-omniscience being effectively grounded by Clarady's street smarts. The book builds effectively to its climax, and a last-minute revelation that is particularly well-handled, but readers will most appreciate the wry humor. An extremely promising debut." — Steve Donoghue, Historical Novel Society

"Historical mystery readers take note: *Murder by Misrule* is a wonderful example of Elizabethan times brought to life...a blend of Sherlock Holmes and history." — D. Donovan, eBook Reviewer, Midwest Book Review

"I love when I love a book! *Murder by Misrule* by Anna Castle was a fantastic read. Overall, I really liked this story and highly recommend it." — Book Nerds

Praise for *Death by Disputation*

Death by Disputation won the 2015 Chaucer Awards First In Category Award for the Elizabethan/Tudor period.

"Castle's style shines ... as she weaves a complex web of scenarios and firmly centers them in Elizabethan culture and times." — D. Donovan, eBook Reviewer, Midwest Book Review

" I would recommend *Death by Disputation* to any fan of historical mysteries, or to anyone interested in what went on in Elizabethan England outside the royal court." — E. Stephenson, Historical Novel Society

"Accurate historical details, page turning plot, bodacious, lovable and believable characters, gorgeous depictions and bewitching use of language will transfer you through time and space back to Elizabethan England." — Edi's Book Lighthouse

"This second book in the Francis Bacon mystery series is as strong as the first. At times bawdy and rowdy, at times thought-provoking ... Castle weaves religious-political intrigue, murder mystery, and Tom's colorful friendships and love life into a tightly-paced plot." — Amber Foxx, Indies Who Publish Everywhere

Praise for *The Widows Guild*

The Widows Guild was longlisted for the 2017 Historical Novel Society's Indie Award.

"As in Castle's earlier book, *Murder by Misrule*, she brings the Elizabethan world wonderfully to life, and if Francis Bacon himself seems a bit overshadowed at times in this novel, it's because the great, fun creation of the Widow's Guild itself easily steals the spotlight. Strongly Recommended." — Editor's Choice, Historical Novel Society.

Praise for *Publish and Perish*

Won an Honorable Mention for Mysteries in Library Journal's 2017 Indie Ebook Awards.

"In this aptly titled fourth book in the Francis Bacon series, Castle combines her impressive knowledge of English religion and politics during the period with masterly creativity. The result is a lively, clever story that will leave mystery fans delighted.**—Emilie Hancock, Mount Pleasant Regional Lib., SC, for Library Journal.**

Also by Anna Castle

The Francis Bacon Mystery Series
Murder by Misrule
Death by Disputation
The Widow's Guild
Publish and Perish
Let Slip the Dogs
The Spymaster's Brother
Now and Then Stab

The Professor & Mrs. Moriarty Mystery Series
Moriarty Meets His Match
Moriarty Takes His Medicine
Moriarty Brings Down the House
Moriarty Lifts the Veil

The Jane Moone Cunning Woman Mystery Series
The Case of the Spotted Tailor

The Lost Hat, Texas Mystery Series
Black & White & Dead All Over
Flash Memory

NOW AND THEN STAB

A Francis Bacon Mystery — Book 7

ANNA CASTLE

Now and Then Stab
A Francis Bacon Mystery — #7

Print Edition | January 2021
Discover more works by Anna Castle at www.annacastle.com

Copyright © 2021 by Anna Castle
Cover design by Jennifer Quinlan
Editorial services by Jennifer Quinlan, Historical Editorial
Chapter ornaments created by Alvaro_cabrera at Freepik.com.

ISBN-13: 978-1-945382-44-4
Library of Congress Control Number: 2021901030
Produced in the United States of America

"You must cast the scholar off,
And learn to court it like a gentleman.
'Tis not a black coat and a little band,
A velvet-caped cloak faced before with serge,
And smelling to a nosegay all the day,
Or holding of a napkin in your hand,
Or saying a long grace at a table's end,
Or making low legs to a nobleman,
Or looking downward with your eyelids close
And saying, "Truly, an't may please Your Honour,'
Can get you any favor with great men.
You must be proud, bold, pleasant, resolute,
And now and then stab as occasion serves."
— Christopher Marlowe, Edward II, Act 2, Sc.

ONE

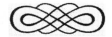

10 April 1593, Westminster

Here it came again: that basilisk glare laden with Her Majesty's displeasure. Francis lacked the courage to meet her eyes, but the glare, delivered in this most public of places, was part of his punishment. Dropping his gaze or turning his head would only arouse her contempt. His vision clouded — perhaps in some inward form of self-protection — but he managed to remain erect, with his face turned in her direction.

The Lord Keeper's nasal voice droned forth from his position at the queen's right hand. His rigid posture betrayed his anxiety that she might turn some of that simmering wrath on him. So far, she had ignored him, instead surveying the assembly, her gaze moving like a beacon from face to face, hardening only when it turned toward Francis. Or so it seemed to him.

Her throne dominated the Upper House at Westminster Hall, raised two steps above the common floor and sheltered by red brocaded hangings shot with gold. She'd come to observe the closing of her eighth Parliament. All the lords and commoners had crowded themselves into the hall. Not to hear the Lord Keeper's summary of the contentious session, but to be seen by Her Majesty fulfilling a vital role in her government.

His Lordship's voice, propelled by his portly frame, drove past the inner square of judges seated on red wool sacks and the rows of lords in ermine arrayed on benches. The monotonous drone even penetrated the throng of members of the House of Commons crowded into the back of the chamber. Whenever his speech returned to the matter of the triple subsidy — the overlarge tax to sustain the war against Spain in the Low Countries — both he and the queen turned their stony eyes toward Francis. Many heads among the seated lords turned his way as well.

His cheeks burned. He could only hope his beard might mask that visible shame. He had spoken against the tax, pointing out that it laid too great a burden on the people in a time of bad harvests and plague. He was right — he knew it still — but his objections had earned Her Majesty's wrath.

He'd tried to stand at the back of the hall, fearing this public censure, but had been inevitably pushed toward the front ranks of the commoners. At least he was spared the sight of his fellows' stabbing glances. His objections had added many days of heated debate to the proceedings. Still, he could feel their disdain burning into his back.

At last, the speech ended. Her Highness gave her royal assent to the bills passed by both Houses and so dissolved the Parliament. She rose. All men knelt as she paced the length of the hall. Francis lifted his head in hope as she drew near, receiving a final glower for his effort. The Lord Keeper, three steps behind her, added a touch of malice to his reproof, a sneer twisting his thin lips. Even the Earl of Essex, Francis's patron, could offer nothing more than a rueful shake of the head.

Francis lingered until nearly all had left, not wanting to hear what anyone might choose to say. He walked back to Gray's Inn alone to spare himself the jostle and gossip at the wharf. He crossed the yard without raising his eyes from the gravel and entered his own house, closing the heavy door behind him with a sigh of relief. He knocked once on the door of his brother's chambers and entered without waiting for a response.

He found Anthony, as expected, seated at the writing desk near the front windows. The desk had traveled home with him from France last year, its origins bespoken by the graceful carving of each polished walnut leg. Anthony always dressed as if about to pay a visit to someone important, although his gouty legs kept him confined to these two rooms. He'd been returned to Parliament as the member from Wallingford in Berkshire but had heard all the arguments at second remove and voted by proxy. Yet he'd dressed today as if he'd meant to go, in dark blue velvet with a ruff composed of several layers of nearly transparent white silk.

Francis dropped heavily into his favorite chair, positioned between the desk and the hearth. "She hates me."

Anthony set his quill in its holder and offered a sympathetic frown. "It isn't quite that bad."

"Yes, it is. She and the Lord Keeper kept scowling at me all through the closing speech. Along with half the lords and most of the commoners."

"I warned you," Anthony said. "She called this Parliament for the specific purpose of approving that triple subsidy. You should have taken the opportunity to demonstrate your willingness to comply instead of sticking at every little hitch."

Indignation warmed Francis's heart. "One enormous hitch, which no one else addressed. The people can't pay so much in so short a time. We've had two summers of bad harvests. The city is rife with plague. Add an extra tax to their burdens and we risk riot or even open revolt. There's enough resentment as it is, with refugees from the Low Countries filling the city and taking work from Englishmen."

Anthony shrugged that off. "She needs the money. We need it. The Duke of Parma has taken Brussels. He controls most of Brittany. He's scarce two hundred miles from where we sit. We can't allow him to advance, and we can't stop him without troops. And troops cost money, lots of money every week."

"I know that. I'm not opposed to additional funds. I just wanted them spread out to make the burden easier to bear. People won't pay taxes if it means taking food from their children's mouths."

"They can't put food on the table in a house that's been burned by Spanish invaders."

Francis growled. He didn't believe invasion was quite so imminent. The Dutch were doughty soldiers. They could hold the line without so much aid from England.

"It's a dangerous precedent," he insisted. "We can't allow this extraordinary rate of taxation to become the rule. I wanted the exceptionality noted as part of the measure. It's important to look to the future as well as the needs of the present."

"That may be so," Anthony said, "but sometimes our lofty principles must be set aside in order to maintain the good relations that enable us to press them another time. You can't always say what you think, Frank. Politics is the art of compromise — and discretion."

"I know." Francis slumped in his chair. "I'd do it again though. It's my duty to see through the exigencies of the moment to the deeper consequences. They know it as well as you do. That's why she keeps me dangling in her train."

"She may well cut the string this time. She expected unanimous support. You're lucky you haven't been confined to your house, like Cousin Edward."

"Edward insulted a Privy Council member to his face. And I have been expelled from court — again." Francis kicked at the brick floor of the hearth. "How long will it take to dig myself out this time, do you think?"

"Oof!" Anthony rolled his eyes. "I couldn't begin to guess. You've really done it this time, brother dear. She'll say you've sown seeds of dissension throughout the House of Commons and she won't be entirely wrong."

Francis gave him a bitter look. "Nobody pays that much attention to me."

"Everyone does. You underestimate your powers as a speaker. No, you'll have to grovel. You should seek out some wretched duty and perform it without complaint. Something grindingly dull. And then another one, and then another. By then, her temper will have cooled. But she won't forget. She never does."

"I could quit." Francis drew himself up again, placing his hands firmly on the oaken arms of his chair. "I could leave politics once and for all and retire to Twickenham to study philosophy."

Anthony laughed out loud. "You say that every time you put a foot wrong."

"I mean it this time." Desire for that life swelled in his heart as he spoke the words. "I'm wasting my time. I'm thirty-two years old and have accomplished nothing of importance. If I'm banned from court, I'll move to Twickenham." The mere thought of those eighty-seven acres of peaceful green parkland on the Thames, well west of the city's discontents, soothed his soul. "I'll study the workings of Nature and write down whatever I see, without fear of bruising a great one's pride."

"Nonsense. You'll weather this affront like the last one and the one before that. I give it three weeks." Anthony picked up his quill and returned his attention to his work.

Francis shot his brother a sour look, then addressed his next remarks to the fire. "Politics is inimical to truth. Truth is essential for science. Therefore politics is inimical to science. I am incapable of not telling the truth. Therefore I am better suited to philosophy than court."

"Have it your way," Anthony said without looking up. "But you'd better tell Lord Essex before you publish your first great discovery. He doesn't like to be kept in the dark."

TWO

10 May 1593, London

Tom counted the forty shillings one by one, dropping each silver coin into his purse. *Clink, clink, clink.* Such a satisfying sound. He smiled at the fishmonger as he tucked the purse into a deep pocket reachable only through the waistband of his round hose. He thanked the man and asked him to be sure to recommend Tom to his fellow guildsmen. Everyone needed a provable will in these perilous times. Then he turned away and began the long walk home.

Fishmonger's Hall stood west of London Bridge, a good three miles from Gray's Inn. In more plenteous days, Tom would have taken a wherry. Now he begrudged every unnecessary expense. He had two good legs, didn't he? And this light drizzle would do his cloak no harm.

He beguiled the walk by calculating his progress. He needed at least three hundred pounds, according to Mr. Bacon, to sue for his livery in the Court of Wards. He'd fallen prey to that notoriously rapacious court when his father died three months before Tom's twenty-first birthday. Most men in his situation would just borrow the money to get free, but Clarady Senior had hated debt. Tom meant to earn as much as possible before mortgaging his future.

He chafed at the indignity of it all. Legally, he was termed "the infant," irrespective of his actual age. His fellows at Gray's taunted him about it. "Look," some wit would quip, "here comes the infant. Shall we sop a bit of bread in milk for you, Tomkin?"

He was no helpless infant. He was twenty-five years old, six feet tall, and in prime condition. Better-looking than average too, or so he'd been told. He lacked only a year before passing the bar. If not for the most corrupt court in the kingdom, he'd be rich. Yet he had to walk through the plague-ridden city in the rain, being too poor for a wherry.

A man stood pasting a sheet of paper to the wall at St. Mary Somerset. Fresh news? Good news, he hoped. The city could use it. The streets were seldom swept these days; so many sweepers had died of plague. Thus the garbage piled up, attracting rats and starving dogs, creating the kind of stink that carried sickness. Tom stuck to Thames Street in hopes of a breeze and kept up a brisk pace.

The man walked away before Tom reached the church. Tom read the notice, then read it again, excitement rising through his veins like a strong drink. The Lord Mayor was offering a hundred crowns — one hundred! — to anyone who could identify the author of a libelous ballad which had been posted on the door of the Dutch Church last Saturday night. The libel had been taken down already, so there was nothing to be seen at the church.

How could anyone identify the author of a ballad they hadn't read?

Tom grinned at the proclamation. He had an advantage over the average churl. He'd wager a portion of that reward that Mr. Bacon could get his hands on a copy. He'd know who to ask, and his name would do the rest.

Tom could feel those big gold coins weighting his pocket already. He used his knife to slide the proclamation free of the wall and scrape off the worst of the damp paste.

Then he held it loose so it could dry and continued on his way. He would stop off at Lady Russell's house in Blackfriars to add his forty shillings to the chest she kept for him in her library.

Her Ladyship had won the auction for his lucrative wardship. His estate had been valued at some six hundred pounds per annum, so the competition had been stiff. But Lady Russell happened to be Francis Bacon's aunt, so she got her bid in early. She also happened to be the sister-in-law of the Master of the Court of Wards, who happened to be Francis Bacon's uncle. Favoritism made for a small world.

She had proved herself an able steward. Tom couldn't complain on that account. He lacked for nothing — except the right to spend his money how he chose. She paid his fees at Gray's and his tailor's bills directly, giving him an allowance meaner than a schoolmaster's wages. But once plague had closed the theaters and emptied the taverns, he had fewer demands on his thin purse.

Her Ladyship was confined to her bed, nursing her bad back, so he was spared an inquisition. He chuckled at the irony as he emptied his coins into the chest and locked it. The person from whom he strove to liberate himself was the only person he trusted to hold his money. No coins were safe at Bacon House. Money ran through the brothers' hands like water.

He reached Gray's and Bacon House at last. He went to his tiny room at the back of the ground floor to hang up his damp cloak and hat, then trotted up the stairs to Bacon's chambers. Pinnock, the pert young servant, told him his master had gone down to his brother's room. So Tom jogged back downstairs and knocked on the door.

"*Intro!*" Anthony called.

The brothers occupied their usual places — Anthony at the French desk near the windows and Francis slumped in the big chair by the fire. Anthony looked dapper, as always, with his thin dark moustache and neatly pointed beard. Tension around his eyes spoke of a difficult night.

Francis looked paler than usual too. He hadn't set foot outside this house for a month. He'd been lying on his bed most of that time, reading yearbooks of legal cases going all the way back to Edward the Second. He hadn't combed his mouse-brown hair or trimmed his shapeless beard in all that time, judging by the tangles. He'd been wearing the same doublet and slops for at least a week and had given up ruffs from the start. Tom and Anthony counted themselves lucky that Pinnock kept him in fresh linens.

No one could out-sloth Francis Bacon when he put his mind to it.

The three men exchanged greetings as Tom took his usual chair, a straight-backed one with a brocaded seat. It was a trifle slippery, but he liked being able to spread his legs a bit, especially when his stockings were wet. Jacques Petit, the strong young man who took care of Anthony, brought him a cup of beer without asking. After a long walk, it slid down his dry throat like the nectar of the gods.

Tom held out the proclamation. "Look what I found on my way back from the fishmongers'."

Francis sniffed in his direction, his nose wrinkling as if he detected an odor of spoiling seafood. "What is it this time? A two-headed whale or a brace of Spaniards trapped in a root cellar?"

"Neither." Tom took no offense. The queen's disapproval had soured his master's humor. This happened whenever Francis received any sort of shock or humiliation. Not uncommon occurrences, given his propensity for saying what he thought, whether or not anyone wanted to hear it. Giving unwanted advice required a certain artistry. Anthony had it. Francis didn't.

He handed the paper to his prickly master. "It's a proclamation from the Lord Mayor. He's offering a hundred crowns to the first person who can identify the author of a libel posted on the Dutch Church last Saturday night. A hundred crowns!" He looked at Anthony. "Have you heard anything about it?"

"Only the bare fact of its brief existence." Anthony laid a long hand on a stack of paper, which doubtless contained a note about the libel. He received a letter from everyone he knew nearly every day, from as far away as Constantinople and as near as Whitehall. Thus he continued to be one of Europe's most astute spymasters in spite of his crippling gout.

"Let me guess," Francis said, slumped so deeply his arse nearly slipped off the chair. "An offensive libel posted at the Dutch Church? Another tiresome incitement to violence against strangers, one assumes. Search among the apprentices in guilds related to cloth-making, if you have time to waste on fool's errands."

That made sense to Tom. Not searching among the apprentices — that was nonsense. What would he look for, fingers still inky after a week? The thing must have been handwritten or there would be more than one copy.

But an incitement to violence seemed likely. There had been riots against the inrush of Dutch, Flemish, and French Protestants fleeing the Duke of Parma. Many of them were skilled at weaving, lace-making, or printing. They weren't supposed to open their own shops, though many had. Their better-made wares took custom away from Englishmen. But where else could they go? Their homes had been overrun by Spanish troops.

"He must have some skill as a poet," Anthony said, shooting his brother a quelling look. "I'm told the libel took the form of a long ballad."

"A poet!" Tom clapped his hands together. "That's good. I know lots of poets. If I could get my hands on a copy, I'll bet Nashe or someone could guess the author."

"If you had a copy," Francis said, "your poets would solve the mystery and claim the prize themselves. That proclamation is fatuous. How can anyone identify the author of a document that has been suppressed?"

Anthony laughed. "It's a riddle, isn't it? Sometimes the authorities tread on their own cloaks and wonder why they can't move. But someone must have a copy. The sheriff, certainly. And he would've sent one to the Privy Council before sending another to the Lord Mayor."

"Privy Council, eh?" Tom grinned at Francis, whose eyes narrowed, though he refused to look up. "Or the sheriff, if you're still feeling raw. He'd give you a copy in a minute if you asked."

Everyone gladly gave copies of documents to the Bacon brothers in hopes of getting their considered opinions on the matter at hand. No one could analyze a report like Francis, who read everything in the world and remembered all of it.

Francis scowled at the fire. "I've had enough futile endeavors to last me a lifetime."

He meant to be stubborn, did he? No doubt he feared a rebuff if he approached any of his usual sources. Besides, withholding his services was the only form of revenge he could exact.

Ah, well. Let him sulk. Tom had another friend at court, now that he thought of it. Trumpet wasn't usually privy to political documents, but there was no reason she couldn't lay her hands on one if she tried. She could claim her lord husband had taken an interest. And since Tom had steadfastly refrained from murdering the said husband for two long years, she owed him an endlessly renewing favor.

Francis stirred, hoisted himself up a little, and gave Tom a weary look. "If I have any part in it, they'll deny your prize as a rebuke to me. Let Anthony help you if he wants."

Tom turned to Anthony, giving him his best dimpled smile. He knew the older brother found him appealing, though both understood that their tastes were opposite in that domain.

Anthony set his velvet-clad elbows on the desk and steepled his long fingers. "I might be able to conjure a copy. No promises, mind. And I'd want a share of those hundred crowns."

"How much?"

"Forty percent sounds fair, don't you think?" Anthony's dark eyes twinkled.

"Forty! All you'll do is write a letter."

"Ah, but it's the knowing who to write and how to ask that adds the value," Anthony replied.

"I have other means," Tom countered. "I'll give you thirty if you get there first, but not a penny if your copy comes in last."

"Fair enough." Anthony grinned. Tom had the sinking feeling he'd just been cozened.

Ah, well. One way or another, he'd have that libel in a matter of days. The poets wouldn't ask for more than a few jugs of wine. And then he'd have seventy more clinking coins to lock away in his livery chest.

THREE

"What about this one, then?" Lady Alice Trumpington Delabere, known to her close friends as "Trumpet," plunked a leather-bound volume with a title pricked out in gold leaf on the library table.

Christopher Marlowe picked it up with a broad smile. "Ah, the *Zodiacus*! An old friend, my lady. You'll enjoy it." He'd dressed for today's lesson in fine broadcloth of a subtle shade of brown that brought out the red tints in his hair. Brass buttons glinted on his doublet, but his ruff was small and bore no lace. Kit's handsome features were decoration enough.

Trumpet shook her head. "I meant, what's it worth? Is it valuable?" She had a chronic need for ready money. As Lady Dorchester, both the daughter and the wife of earls, she had unlimited credit nearly everywhere. But she couldn't bribe a servant to silence or treat the lads at the tavern she shouldn't be visiting, especially not disguised as a man, by having the bill sent to her steward. Blending her old and new lives was proving more challenging than she'd anticipated.

Kit shook his head. "Not very. Any book this nicely bound is worth something, of course. But no, my lady. This is taught in grammar schools. Everyone's read it."

"I haven't." Trumpet knew a fair bit about property law and could plumb the weightiest yearbooks with confidence. But now that her position demanded seasons at court, she found herself woefully behindhand with respect to the arts. Queen Elizabeth's courtiers made constant references to literary works, showing off their erudition to the highly educated queen.

Trumpet required a tutor, so she'd hired Kit. He held a Master of Arts degree from Cambridge University and wrote plays riddled with classical elements. Better, he was an old friend of Tom's and thus of hers. He knew about their special relationship and could be trusted to keep that knowledge to himself. And his view of Roman literature was unlikely to be dull.

They'd been meeting two afternoons a week in the library in her new house on the Strand. Oak shelves covered each wall from floor to ceiling, except for the expanse of windows facing the garden. Each shelf groaned under stacks of books. Trumpet and Stephen had bought the house with its furnishings intact, including the extensive library, to serve as their London home. She'd only recently come to regard the collection as a quiet source of funds.

Kit opened the book. "It might not be valuable, but it has its merits. Let's read it together, my lady. When's your birthday?"

"I'm an Aries." She perched on a stool next to him, her skirts pooling around her. She'd dressed for him as well, seeking a balance between patron and friend. Today's red wool skirt and doublet brought out the green of her eyes. The crisp white of her lace-trimmed cap accentuated the blackness of her hair.

She leaned forward to plant her elbows on the table and rested her chin on her hands. "What does my future hold?"

"It isn't that sort of zodiac, my lady. It's more of a metaphysical disquisition on the relations among scientific knowledge, religion, and happiness."

She gaped at him. "That sounds boring in the extreme."

"Oh. Perhaps it is. I loved it as a boy though." He closed the book, giving it a little pat. "Well, you can read this on your own, my lady. It isn't difficult. We should probably go back to Tacitus today. Sir Walter tells me that's a favorite at court."

"That's history, isn't it?"

Kit nodded.

"I like history," Trumpet said without enthusiasm. She'd begun to realize that she didn't want to study literature in the usual sense. She could produce wise little grunts and hums when the topic at court strayed beyond her capacity. She clapped both hands on the table. "In truth, what I really want is to become a patron of the arts."

"Bless you, my lady!"

She waved off the praise. "My lord husband and I have agreed that we will host brilliant supper parties, inviting leading poets and playmakers to mingle with our friends. The sort of parties people talk about for a month. But who? How do I choose them? Must they live here? Must we be able to converse with them? Stephen won't read anything. He's made that clear."

"I will gladly help you choose, and no, they don't have to live here. Although you might provide houseroom for a select few at your home in Dorset during the winter or plague summers. They would dedicate everything they wrote to you."

"I like the sound of that."

Kit grinned. "Patrons always do. As for the dinners, my lady, you don't have to do much. Gather the poets and keep the wine flowing. You'll be lucky to get a word in edgewise." Kit cocked his head, offering her a half-smile. "Dare I hope that I might be among this fortunate group?"

"You'll be the first. You'll get used to Stephen. As long as he isn't left wholly in the dust, he's happy. But who else can I invite? Thomas Nashe?"

"If we clean him up a bit. He's unpredictable, but he does make people laugh. There are others more fit for a lord's table. Mathew Roydon, for one. George Peele."

"Do I know them?"

"Tom does."

Trumpet frowned. Her role as an emerging Woman of Influence kept her busy. She seldom had time to go rowdying about the taverns in Shoreditch anymore. It was harder to get free too, especially when Stephen was in town. "I could invite Francis Bacon. He's brilliant, and he can carry on a conversation when he wants to."

Kit hummed a caveat. "Separate parties, then. I doubt Mr. Bacon would appreciate being seated at a table with the likes of me."

"Why not?"

"He's a Calvinist. I'm an atheist."

Trumpet clucked her tongue. "No, he isn't. And neither are you. Even if you were, you shouldn't say it. For some reason, everyone's up in arms about atheists all of a sudden. They're saying they're as dangerous as Catholics."

"More!" Kit cried. "We believe in nothing. We accept no restraints. We murder babies and bugger devils, didn't you know?" He leaned back and crossed his arms, lifting his chin in mock defiance.

Now she blew out a rude breath. "Fiddle-faddle. You play it up for the drama, but there are people who take you at your word. I've heard rumblings at court about you, Sir Walter Ralegh, and the Earl of Northumberland."

His lip curled. "They rumble about anyone with a curious mind."

"Curiosity killed the cat, remember? Why can't you write something lighter? Something Romanish, why not? What about Julius Caesar?"

"Caesar was murdered by his closest friends. If that's your idea of entertainment, you're going to love my current work. It's about James the First."

"First of what?"

"Scotland. A few hundred years ago, he was murdered by his councilors. Thirty men chased him all around a monastery, finally trapping him in a sewer." He rubbed his hands together in glee. "I'm already spinning out rhymes and metaphors."

Trumpet pursed her lips. Courtiers whispered the word "Scotland" behind gloved hands. And murder committed by Privy Councilors? Unlikely to win favor among those who mattered. "I don't know how you pass the censors."

Kit grinned, unrepentant. "It's a narrow line, but I know how to walk it."

The narrow line between fame and infamy. She hoped he could maintain his balance.

"My lady?" A footman in Stephen's tawny-and-saffron livery appeared at the door. She'd left it open to preserve the proprieties. "You have another visitor."

"Who?"

"Mr. Thomas Clarady, my lady."

"Send him in. And bring us refreshments. Cool beer and something savory."

"Yes, my lady." The footman disappeared, his tall figure soon replaced by Tom, dressed in his everyday lawyer suit of black broadcloth with gray silk linings. He looked well in anything — and even better in nothing — but she didn't like his hair hanging down over his ruff. It might be the fashion, but the extra length dragged out his golden curls.

Trumpet bounded up to clasp his hand. "Kit's here." The poet rose and tilted his head by way of greeting.

"So I see." Tom gave her a special smile, then grinned at Kit.

"You missed Stephen," she said. "He's taken William to an armorer."

"The boy is scarcely a year old!" Tom scoffed.

Trumpet laughed fondly. "Stephen likes to look at the wares. He loves armor; it's so shiny and it makes him feel invincible. Naturally, he wants his son to follow in his footsteps."

Tom's mouth tightened. William was his, in origin if not in name. He rarely even got to see the child for fear of Stephen noticing a resemblance when the two heads came close together.

The footman brought a tray with a jug, three cups, and two plates of small pies. He unloaded it onto the long oak table, neatly avoiding the books strewn across its surface. Then he bowed and left without so much as raising an eyebrow at his mistress's guests. Trumpet had learned long ago that servants who were well-treated and fairly paid could be relied on to keep their observations to themselves.

The men sat down without ceremony and tucked into the refreshments. Trumpet poured herself a cup of beer before returning to her stool. She watched her guests devour the pies, gabbling at each other through full mouths. She loved them both unreservedly, but the ease with which they left her aside nettled her. Worse, Tom had made no effort to see her recently. Stephen presented no obstacle. He slept on the other side of the house and spent most of the daylight hours shopping. Tom could slip in any afternoon for a spot of dalliance.

"What brings you here today?" she asked, a trifle tartly. "I haven't seen you in a week."

"More like a fortnight," Tom said with a little tartness of his own. "Time flies when you're busy, doesn't it? But I have a new case, and you can help me with it."

That perked her up. "Murder?"

Kit laughed at her enthusiasm. He gestured toward her with a flat hand. "This is the lady who thinks my plays are morbid."

She clucked her tongue at him. "Real murders are different. For one thing, the violence is over by the time we get there."

"Sorry to disappoint you," Tom said, "but it isn't a murder. It's a riddle. Who wrote the libel posted on the door of the Dutch Church last Saturday night?"

"A libel? Who on earth could possibly care?" Trumpet's shoulders sank.

"The Lord Mayor, for one," Tom said. "He's offering a hundred crowns for the author's name."

"That's a handsome sum," Kit said. "It must've been powerfully offensive. What did it say?"

"I don't know," Tom said. "That's the ticklesome part. The authorities took it down almost the minute it went up."

Kit burst into laughter so contagious they all fell prey to it. Every time one caught the gaze of another, the laughter began again. Finally, after many deep breaths and gulps of beer, they regained their composure.

"It's a wonder all plays don't mock the government," Kit said. "Who but the English would offer a reward for finding the anonymous author of an unread work?"

"That's my advantage," Tom said. "Of course there are copies. The Privy Council must have a few, don't you reckon?" He grinned at Trumpet, showing his dimple.

She loved that dimple beyond all reason but didn't like to be played. She lifted her chin. "I'm not privy to the deliberations of the council."

"They'll have it," Kit said, shooting her a wink to acknowledge her justifiable pique. "One per member, so none has an advantage. The sheriff and the Lord Mayor must have copies as well. I'll wager that reward isn't meant to be paid. The proclamation just shows the public that the authorities take such things seriously."

"No." Tom looked as if they'd snatched the coins from his hand. "You don't think he'll pay?"

Kit shrugged. "It's a lot of money. I doubt they expect anyone to succeed. Who would look if they can't read it?"

"No one." Tom squared his jaw. "That's my advantage." He gave Trumpet a pleading look. "I was thinking you might be able to lay your hands on a copy if you tried. If you want to help."

"Why not ask Mr. Bacon?" She hadn't forgiven him for a fortnight's absence, although she did like the idea of being a source of coveted information. An important role for a Woman of Influence.

"If you mean Francis, he's still sulking." Tom explained to Kit, "He offended the queen during this last Parliament. She glared at him. It'll take him at least a month to recover." He turned back to Trumpet, clasping his hands before his breast. "You're my only true friend at court, Trumplekin. Do you think you could manage it?"

"I don't know." She pursed her lips, considering her options. "I doubt I can just ask. Stephen's not on the council, nor is he ever likely to be. He hates meetings. I doubt anyone would believe I wanted it for him. And everyone still thinks I'm a bit of a tickle-brain."

"They do?" Kit sounded gratifyingly incredulous. "Are they deaf? Blind? Stupid?"

She giggled. "It makes things easier. No one suspects me of odd things that might happen when I'm out doing something I shouldn't be doing in clothes I shouldn't be wearing."

"I understood that," Kit told Tom. They both chuckled.

"I suppose I could steal a copy," she said.

"That's my girl," Tom said with pride.

She gave him a catlike smile. "Most of the councilors are old men with old servants. And they're still in Whitehall, though the queen is in Croydon, I think, at the archbishop's house. Things will be quieter here with her gone. We might be able to manage it. No promises, mind."

"Dress up as servants, go about with brooms?" Kit asked.

Trumpet nodded. "Rags, more like. They're easier to get rid of. My maidservant is very clever. She'll know what to do." She turned to Tom. "Mr. Bacon would extract a fee. I won't cut into your savings, but I should have some reward. What do I get if I bring you this libel?" She batted her lashes at him.

Tom shot her a leer that made her heart dance a jig. "How about another baby?"

FOUR

Francis Bacon lay on his bed in his stocking feet, propped up by a mountain of pillows, reading Henry Savile's recent translation of the *Histories* by Tacitus. He'd read them in the original, of course, more than once. The works of Tacitus were an evergreen topic in Her Majesty's court. This translation wasn't bad. Francis would have made different lexical choices here and there, but on the whole it was well done. And much needed. Women like Lady Dorchester had a poor grounding in Latin, being barred from the universities where one spoke the ancient language day and night. Perhaps he would recommend this book to her, as a small favor.

Then again, why bother? He was leaving the court and its favor-mongering. He no longer had any reason to cultivate connections among the great.

While part of his mind critiqued the book, another part considered a plan for creating a vast table displaying the progress of knowledge through the centuries, with special emphasis on progress in the crafts. Lenses, for example, and other devices for extending the sight, merited a column of their own. Most philosophers neglected the practical arts, essential to everyday life. He would grant them a more central position.

A tap sounded on his door, and Pinnock entered waving a folded letter. Francis recognized the seal from where he lay. It bore the blue wax Lord Essex preferred. He sighed as he accepted the letter and a knife from his servant. Butterflies tumbled in his stomach. He must inform His Lordship — or no, not inform, that would be presumptuous — advise or suggest or, better, intimate that he intended — or rather, wished or felt inclined — to disengage himself from political activities and devote himself to scholarly pursuits henceforward.

He opened the letter. It was a summons, as expected, couched in the courteous form of an invitation. His Lordship wanted to share some thoughts with his counselor. Francis sighed. It could be anything from a discussion of poetics to plans for subduing the Irish. He hoped for the former, given his new decision.

Francis wriggled himself off the enormous bed, built wide enough to accommodate several of the sons of Sir Nicholas Bacon. The older ones had London houses of their own and never stayed at Gray's, so Francis had grown used to the luxury of having the expanse all to himself. Pinnock slept on a narrow bed in the study chamber.

Francis pulled off the shirt he'd been wearing for the past some-odd days and scrubbed his torso briskly with a towel. As he donned a clean shirt, he caught a glimpse of a disheveled vagrant in the mirror. "God's mercy! I can't go out like this. Quick, Pinnock, find a pair of scissors."

He ought to go to the barber on Holborn Road, but he begrudged the delay. The letter hadn't mentioned a time, but one didn't keep a nobleman waiting.

He drew up a stool and attempted to comb his hair, though he soon gave up. The tangles had developed layers, like an untended hedge. This wouldn't do; not at all. He couldn't let himself return to a state of Nature, however much he might like to study it. He vowed to scrub his body from scalp to sole and comb his hair every morning, even if he only hopped right back onto the bed to read.

Hair and beard now neatly trimmed, Francis dressed in his best black doublet and hose, choosing gray silk ribbons for garter and hat. He dabbed on a little civet for good measure and popped some fennel seeds into his mouth to chew as he walked. "Tell Anthony where I've gone," he instructed his servant. If he delivered the message himself, ten minutes would be lost to speculation as to the earl's intent.

At Essex House, an usher led him to the library, His Lordship's favorite room. Robert Devereux, the second Earl of Essex, exhibited all the traits of the well-bred man. Tall, with clean limbs and handsome features, he was the portrait of health and good breeding. He wore his ruddy beard longer than the current fashion, but what did he care for the common taste? At the ripe age of twenty-seven, he had proven himself as a general, having led men on land and at sea in defense of the realm many times. And yet, for all his martial qualities, he preferred a good book above all other company.

Francis bowed low. "How may I serve Your Lordship?"

"By joining me." The earl gestured to a cushioned seat not far from his own.

Francis sat with a straight back and folded his hands in his lap. "Your letter said you'd been thinking. About what, my lord?"

"About atheism. What are your views, Mr. Bacon?"

"I disapprove of it, my lord."

As expected, the earl grinned at that pert response. Francis granted himself a small smile.

The earl said, "I've been considering this recent *Act Against Puritans*. How can we use it to combat the full range of religious dissent? To my mind, Puritanism stands at one end, being an excess of religious fervor. Atheism, the rejection of religion, stands at the other. Shouldn't we therefore consider them two sides of the same coin?"

Francis thought of his mother, who would be called a Puritan if she weren't the mistress of a great house and the sister-in-law of the Lord Treasurer. Her Calvinist faith infused her every word and deed. "Not quite, my lord, though you sail very near the mark. Puritans believe much the same as you and I do. What they dispute are the forms of religious practice. Dispute over practices disrupts the peace of the realm. Worse, to my mind, such disputes are a principal cause of atheism. Given a multiplicity of beliefs and practices, what is the truth? Atheism is as much a condition of lawlessness as of religious disdain. They must be restrained, but they should be treated with pity for their confusion rather than with harshness."

The earl nodded. "I commend your charity, Mr. Bacon. I can see you've given this matter some thought as well."

"I've written an essay on the subject of unity in religion, my lord." The spark of interest in the earl's eyes made him add a hasty amendment. "Or rather, a draft of an essay. Far too rough to share. I have so little time to write. Which brings me to a topic I want —"

"Do you agree with Sir Walter Ralegh that exile is an excessive punishment for dissent? The new Act would require it."

Francis blinked to cover his relief at the interruption. He could answer such questions all day. "I doubt it can be enforced, my lord. Juries will look at the man's wife and children and decide the parish can't afford their maintenance."

"That point should have been raised."

"Sir Walter touched upon it, my lord, but was overruled."

The earl grunted his disdain for the efforts of his chief rival. "Then he failed to make his case. You should've spoken up. I'm sure you would have been far more coherent."

"I had already done myself enough damage, my lord." Francis blanched at the thought of siding with Sir Walter, now entering his second year of Her Majesty's displeasure. He had married without permission, going so far as to have a child in secret. After a stint in the Tower, he and his wife had been banished from the court. "Which brings us to the topic that I —"

"I'm intrigued by your connection of religious disunity with civic unrest," the earl said, leaping ahead. "Take these refugees, for example. We welcome them, of course. We have an obligation to assist them. But we must be certain they're not importing dangerous points of view." He shook a finger in the air. "On the other hand, as you remind me, we would be wise to exercise restraint. Excessive restraint inspires resistance. Zealotry offends our sense of common decency and thereby stimulates dissension."

The earl grunted, pleased with his argument. He beamed at Francis. "I find your mere presence stimulating to the mind, Mr. Bacon. I look forward to many fruitful discussions in the gardens at Nonsuch. When will you go? I'll move with some of my staff this week."

"Ah, Nonsuch." Francis steeled himself. It was now or never. The butterflies began battering the inside of his chest with frantic wings. "I fear, my lord, that I will not be going."

"Not going? Why not?"

"I doubt Her Majesty would countenance my presence this summer."

"Nonsense. Surely you aren't discouraged by that little hurly-burly over the triple subsidy. She'll get over it." He winked. "I'll see that she does. We can't afford to lose so valuable a counselor as you. Not in these perilous times."

Such airy confidence! Francis didn't share it. He couldn't face the earl's penetrating brown eyes, so he turned his gaze toward the rush matting on the floor. "It's different this time, my lord. I understand her perception of my objections. Yet I remain convinced that they were, and are, valid. They had to be made. I must speak the truth as I know it, or my counsel is without value. Given that fundamental conflict, I am forced to conclude that I am not suited to politics. I will always err in this way and will thus always fall afoul of Her Majesty's will. One day, the consequences might be greater than her mere disapproval. I haven't the courage to wait for that axe to fall."

He risked a glance and saw the earl's eyes go flat. Francis hurried on to what he hoped would be a more favorable argument. "Besides, my lord, I have other work for which I am better suited. My experiments in natural philosophy, for example. If I spent the legal vacations at Twickenham instead of putting my feet wrong at court, I would have time to clarify my ideas about the proper foundations of scientific inquiry. That would benefit mankind in the long run more than any speech I might make in the House of Commons."

"Would it? Would it really? That sounds like a supposition to me, Mr. Bacon." The earl's tone was icy.

Sweat prickled Francis's brow. He resisted the urge to wipe it off. "Of more immediate benefit, perhaps, my lord, is my study of the common law. I don't mean to leave Gray's. I might even take a few cases here and there, especially those testing principles of particular interest." He forced a note of hope into his voice. "I've undertaken a comprehensive review of the yearbooks going back to Edward the Second, drawing out the essential principles in several areas —"

"You have a present duty *here*, Mr. Bacon." The earl spoke in the clipped tones of a man restraining his wrath. "Do you mean to abandon *me*? Your brother relies on your assistance in analyzing the intelligences he receives. You're an essential part of that service, which *I* rely upon to make *my* decisions. To say nothing of the favors I've done for you and your brother already. Loans, for example, never called in. Have you forgotten those?"

Francis shook his head, clasping his hands together to stop their trembling. His throat closed, but he managed to whisper, "No, my lord." He didn't even know how much he'd borrowed to ready his house for his invalid brother. A hundred pounds? More?

Essex regarded him for an excruciating eternity, then blew out an exasperated breath. He stood and walked over to a cupboard, where he poured red wine into a Venetian glass cup. He thrust it at Francis, who took it in both shaking hands, murmuring his thanks without looking up.

He gulped down a large swallow and let the unwatered drink do its work. He cradled the costly cup in his sweaty hands and breathed deeply. Then he looked up, his gaze reaching to the earl's ruff. "Naturally, I will continue to serve Your Lordship in whatever way you see fit. Your friendship means more to me than anything, even my life."

Essex nodded and resumed his seat. Lesson delivered. He gave Francis time to drink a little more wine, perhaps watching for his color to return to normal.

Then, as if nothing had transpired between them, a coy smile curved on his noble lips. "I have something special in mind for you, Mr. Bacon. Something worthy of your talents. I won't say what, not just yet. I'd like to test the waters first. But keep reading those yearbooks." The smile hardened. "We'll discuss it further at Nonsuch. Next Friday, shall we say?"

"I look forward to it, my lord." Francis drew his own lips into a smile, though he had to grit his teeth to do it. He drained his cup and set it carefully on a small table. He rose and bowed from the waist, regretting it immediately as the drink rushed to his head. Half-blind with wine and shattered dreams, he made his way out of the house.

He had no choice but to comply. He didn't dare risk Anthony's position. His brother had no other employment. Nor could Francis advocate for reform of the common law without the support of a powerful patron. He'd never find another man like Essex. Essex, for all his pride and vaunting ambition, understood the true value of men with minds like the Bacon brothers.

Francis had boxed himself in with debt and obligation, trapped himself like a rabbit in a hutch. He'd lost the freedom to choose his path the day Anthony came home and they threw in their lot with the mercurial earl. Francis's destiny was no longer his own. Perhaps it never had been.

FIVE

Tom leapt out of the path of yet another cart piled perilously high with household chattels. Another tradesman fleeing the city with his family before summer's heat fueled the plague. Many shops were already shuttered, even on this Monday morning. Other houses had been boarded up by the city authorities to trap their infected inhabitants inside until they got better — or died.

A horrible fate and a good reason to avoid the city as the days grew longer. But Tom wanted those hundred crowns, and that meant investigation. He'd find that libeler and maybe write another will or two, then bar himself from the city.

It would be a hardship. He loved these crowded streets, in rain or frost or baking heat. He'd loved them from the first day he and his friends had skipped out of Gray's to go exploring. He loved every resident of the most wonderful city in the world. Men, women, and children of all classes, wearing all manner of garb, hurrying or dawdling, shopping or selling, gawking or scolding. He even loved the cozeners eyeing the passersby with hawk-like intent. Every time he passed through Newgate, he felt a thrill rise from the thick soles of his street shoes. Adventure waited around every corner.

His target today was the Dutch Church, properly known as Austin Friars. It dominated Broad Street Ward, its yellow bricks gleaming through gaps between the tall houses around it. Some years ago, the sexton had been an older man who lurked near the front steps angling for gossip, like a heron fishing at the edge of a stream. Sure enough, he still manned his post. His belly had grown rounder and his beard longer, but his eager welcome hadn't cooled a bit.

"Good morning, Sexton," Tom said as he approached.

"*Guten morgen*, Master," the sexton replied. "Have you come to see our church? We don't get so many visitors in this sad year."

"Some other time, perhaps." Tom had the feeling he'd said those very words the last time. The sexton's narrowed gaze suggested something tickled his memory too. No matter. "I'm here about the libel that was posted on your door. I'm hoping to find —"

The sexton's face crumpled in disgust. He flapped the words away with a broad hand. "Vhy can't they think of some other place to post their monstrosities?"

"It must be a great nuisance to you," Tom said. "The author must be caught, so he never does it again. I intend to find him and bring him to justice."

"And win those hundred crowns in the bargain, *nicht wahr*? Well, good luck to you."

"Did you see it?"

"Me? *Och* no. I am sleeping in my warm bed at that hour."

"Who found it, do you know?"

"*Natürlich.*" An impish smile creased the old man's cheeks.

Tom chuckled, playing along. He looked from side to side as if checking for eavesdroppers. "Would you mind sharing it with me?"

The sexton held the impish smile long enough for Tom to wonder if he'd forgotten the question, then burst into a series of harsh caws. "Haw! Haw! Haw!"

Tom's own smile stiffened. How long could this clay-brained fustilarian drag out his game? Better to prowl the streets in search of the constable who'd taken the libel down.

He shifted his weight, and the old man relented. "*Och,* I jest with you, no?"

"A small jest," Tom allowed. "That libel wasn't funny though, was it?"

"*Och* no. I didn't see it, but you know they put these rude ballads on our door here" — the sexton jerked his thumb over his shoulder at the tall oak doors — "so good folk, hardworking, honest folk, will see that filth when they come to church on Sunday morning. This is not the first time. So we keep an eye open. Printer Younge" — now he pointed southwest with his chin — "saw a fresh paper on our door on his way home from the tavern on Saturday night."

"A printer?" That sounded hopeful. Printers could read. Younge had surely read the verses before summoning a constable.

"Yah. He prints ballads. Not that kind, mind you! But he saw how bad it was, so he took it down. Then the constable happened by, so Younge gave the foul paper to him. And so, no one of us ever read a single word of it." The sexton sounded disappointed. Rumors about a vicious libel were far less satisfying than the thing itself.

Tom sympathized. They parted in good accord. The sexton gave him directions to Younge's shop, which lay just south of Lothbury. Most of the shops on that street were copper- and tinsmiths, so no one minded the noise and smell of a busy print shop. He would know it by the candlestick on the sign over the door.

He found it easily enough. He didn't even have to stuff his fingers in his ears against the constant tapping of mallets on metal. Judging by the lack of clamor, a good quarter of the smiths had either died or fled to the country.

If things kept going at this rate, Cheapside would soon be as quiet as Drury Lane.

The shutters were raised at the shop, but no counter had been placed across the sill. People didn't buy ballads in a shop. They bought them from sellers crying on street corners. Tom hated to walk straight in, given the probable lack of custom, so he knocked twice on the front door. He heard a woman's voice call something inside, followed by firm footsteps. Then the door swung wide open.

There, just across the threshold, stood Clara Goosens, the love of his life for three weeks — maybe four — some six or seven years ago. Tom gaped at her and she at him. He'd only knocked on two doors in Broad Street Ward in all his life. He'd found her inside both times. It gave him a weird sense of dislocation for a moment.

"Tom," she said, in the same round Flemish tones that used to make him swoon.

But his wits held steady. Good. Those embers had gone out. She'd lost her ethereal golden glow, though she remained a beautiful woman.

"Clara," he managed at last. "I didn't expect to see you."

"No? But this is my home." She cocked her head to study his face as if she meant to draw it. Which she might well do. She'd earned her bread as a limner when they'd met. "Your hair is darker and your beard more ruddy. And your cheeks are more thin. More strong, I mean." She stroked her own as if testing her description.

"Yours are rounder," he countered. And she'd gained a touch of softness under the jaw. "But you're still beautiful."

She accepted that with a smile. "You are more handsome, I think. Age is the friend of men. But a little sad, no? Here, around the eyes." She gestured to the corners of her own eyes, which bore a few faint lines. "Is my golden boy gone forever?"

"Not quite." Tom gave her his cockiest grin, and she laughed happily. Once he would have done handsprings down the filthy street to win that laugh. Now it brought only a sweet memory.

She nodded to signal that the moment had passed. "If you did not come for me, you must be here for Martin. My husband." She stepped back to give him room to enter.

"Husband?" Tom followed her inside. "There's a lucky man."

She let that pass. Beautiful women grew accustomed to compliments. As she moved, her skirts shifted, revealing a small girl. The child gazed up at Tom with wide eyes.

Blue eyes in a round face framed in blond curls. Tom's stomach clenched. "How — how old?"

Clara laughed merrily. Her daughter giggled along with her. "This is Hanna. She is five. I would have told you, silly man."

Tom blew out a breath. "I'm an idiot. It's just the surprise, that's all."

"You have no children?"

"Not that I know of." He hadn't given a thought to bastards in those halcyon early years at Gray's, when he'd had a full purse and all London at his doorstep. Now he wondered. Perhaps there was a child out there he could claim for his own. The cuckoo he'd planted in Stephen's nest would never know him as anything more than an old family friend.

Clara clucked her tongue at that unseemly response, then spoke to her daughter. "Run and tell Papa we have a guest."

The girl skipped away, crying, "Papa!" in a high, clear voice.

Another child toddled up clutching a wooden doll. His free hand patted at his mother's skirts. She bent to hoist him onto her hip. "And this is Gerrit. He is two."

"Good morrow to you, Gerrit." Tom took the infant's free hand to give it a shake, regretting the action when he found it damp and sticky. "A fine fellow indeed. This one doesn't look like you." The tot's straight brown hair curtained his light brown eyes.

"He takes after his father."

"Who have we here?" A deep voice heralded the appearance of the said father. A man with broad shoulders and a genial expression strode forward with an outstretched hand.

Tom gave a quick wipe to the seat of his slops and stepped forward for a hearty shake. They exchanged names and pleasantries, then Younge raised an eyebrow. "Are you here to commission a ballad?"

"No," Tom said. "I'm searching for the author of the libel posted on the Dutch — er, on the door of Austin Friars a week or so ago. The sexton told me you were the one who spotted it and took it down."

"Oh, that." Younge sighed. "I can't tell you much." He caught his wife's gaze. "Have we some ale to offer this gentleman?"

"*Ja*, sure." Clara moved toward a square table at the back of the room.

A long narrow table covered in stacks of paper dominated the front room. Ballads waiting to be picked up by street sellers, no doubt. The room smelled of ink in spite of the open windows, an acrid tang one soon got used to. As Tom stepped toward the family end of the long room, the fresh scent of tansy rose from beneath his feet. The whole room gleamed with cleanliness. Wholesome herbs dotted the floors; tables and chairs shone with wax. The Younges took a risk, hanging on in a city riddled with plague, but Clara was doing everything she could to keep her family safe.

Ballad-printing seemed a prosperous trade. The furnishings included two straight-backed chairs to flank the oak table along with two backed stools and a large cradle. A handsome cupboard displayed pewter plates and two candlesticks and a variety of cups and bowls made of green-glazed pottery. A slanted drawing table with a tall stool stood near the front windows, where it could catch the best light.

"Is that yours?" Tom asked. "Are you still doing portraits?"

"Not so many. I draw the illustrations for our ballads."

"Do you?" Tom strolled over to the long table to admire the ballads. One had a sketch of a man in fashionable garb with two feathers springing from his cap, so lifelike and individual he wondered if he might know the model. "These are excellent."

"Thank you." Clara gestured toward the family table, taking a stool and setting Gerrit in her lap. Tom took one of the chairs.

Younge poured out cups of ale and passed one to his guest. He sat in the other chair, pulling up a stool beside him for his daughter. She leaned against her father, wide eyes fixed on Tom.

"I can't tell you much," Younge said. "Just that I saw something new on the church door as I walked back from the Black Swan. I had my lantern, you see, so I went to take a look. If it had been the usual sort of foolery — bawdy hints and winks, you know the sort of thing — I would've burned it on the spot. But this was different."

"How so?" Tom took a sip of his ale, then a longer swallow. It was earthy and delicious. They must buy it from a neighbor. Clara couldn't have time to brew ale as well as producing those fine illustrations and tending to the children.

Younge said, "Well, it was longer than usual, for one thing, and better written."

"You had a chance to read it, then."

"Well, I had to, didn't I? I wouldn't call the constable for a bit of bawdry."

"Can you remember what it said?"

"The gist, not word for word. It was a wicked piece of work, I'll tell you that. Clever and plainly aimed at rousing up anger against newcomers." Younge pushed his cup aside to reach for his wife's hand. His voice grew angrier as he spoke. "They bring us nothing but good, these people. New skills, new methods, and a willingness to work hard. All they want is a safe refuge. They just want to do their jobs and live their lives in peace. Is that too much to ask?"

"I don't think so," Tom said. "It must have been pretty hot for the authorities to react so severely. They've put out a reward, you may have heard."

"I've heard," Younge said. "I don't have time for such foolery. We get along well enough, don't we, sweetling?"

Clara beamed at him in answer. Their loving gaze left Tom quite alone for a minute.

He pretended not to feel it. "This sort of foolery is in my line, you might say."

Younge cocked his head. "What is your line, if you don't mind my asking?"

"I'm a lawyer. A member of Gray's Inn." Tom flicked a glance at Clara. "I expect to pass the bar next year."

"Hey-ho!" Younge leaned back in his seat. "An Inns of Court man, at my table!" He grinned at his wife. "Bit of the old days for you, eh, sweetling?"

"Perhaps a little." Clara pointed her chin at Tom. "I have met Mr. Clarady before. He is the one who got me into jail that time, in all that trouble about my first husband."

"*Into!*" Tom couldn't let that injustice stand. He tapped himself on the chest as he faced Martin Younge. "I'm the one who got her *out*." Spending all the coins in his purse to make her week of confinement as comfortable as possible, he refrained from adding. "It was bad luck for Clar — for Mrs. Younge. She got swept up in a larger case. But that's the sort of thing I do, finding people who don't want to be found — in between writing wills and suchlike."

"Wills, eh?" Younge said. "Must be a market for those this year."

"Sad but true."

The baby stirred on Clara's lap. She gave him a tiny sip of her ale. These people had better things to do than idle about at ten o'clock in the morning. Tom asked, "Was there anything distinctive about the ballad? A style, a turn of phrase . . ."

Younge shrugged. "It wasn't one of ours, I'm sure of that. We don't deal in political matters. Too risky. We like miracles, curious events, court gossip — that sort of thing. I can tell you it wasn't written by a novice. The rhythm was regular and the rhyming competent. Written out by hand, probably by a scrivener. You wouldn't learn much from the original, if you could find it."

Tom grunted. "No clues as to the author?"

"Well, he signed it 'Tamburlaine,' if that tells you anything. Maybe Christopher Marlowe wrote it in between plays." Younge laughed, patting the table for emphasis.

Clara looked at her husband with so much affection Tom could hardly bear it. He longed for a table like this, with a family gathered around it.

"It couldn't have been Marlowe," Tom said. "He likes strangers; I've heard him say it. He likes hearing other languages as he goes about the city. He says they tickle his ears."

"He's a rarity, then," Younge said, sobering. "If I hadn't stepped out for a drink with the lads that night, it might've been seen by a hundred churchgoers next morning. That would've been a rude shock. God's hand guided me that night."

"I'm glad you caught it." Tom gave Younge a rueful smile. "Although I wish you'd made a copy before surrendering it."

The printer grunted. "I wouldn't let such evil in my house. Here's what I can do for you. Whoever wrote that ballad has written others. He's had practice. If so, someone's printed those ballads. There are members of my trade who like the rude stuff, sad to say. Libels and scurrility — you know what I mean." He laid a hand on his daughter's head as if to protect her from the mere mention of such verses. "I'll ask around, poke my nose in here and there. In truth, I'll be as glad as you to see the man caught."

"I'd be grateful for anything you can learn."

The men rose, their business done. Clara handed the baby to her husband before standing. "I'll see you out, Mr. Clarady."

Younge bade him good-bye and went to tuck his son into the cradle. Clara walked with Tom to the door and opened it. "You should have a family of your own, Tom. You must have a sweetheart."

A vision of Trumpet's heart-shaped face rose in his mind, with her emerald eyes and sable hair. He couldn't explain any part of their secret life to anyone, though Clara would be as safe a confidante as any. Who would she tell?

"Yes and no," he said. "I could never marry her, or rather, she couldn't marry me. And now she's wed to another. It's messy." He gave her a sad smile, putting on a brave front.

Her wise eyes saw right through it. "I am sorry. That must be painful. But there are many women within your reach who would be glad for so handsome and loving a husband. You will find her, once you start to look."

Tom shook his head. Even standing here, gazing at the beauteous Clara Goosens, his heart saw only Trumpet. "I'm glad you're happy."

"Very happy." Clara glanced behind her. Younge was walking toward the shop at the back, holding his daughter's hand. Clara rose to her toes and dropped a swift kiss on Tom's cheek. "Be well, Thomas Clarady."

He walked into the street. The door closed behind him. He searched his feelings as he turned his feet toward home and was pleased to discover that he didn't envy Martin Younge, at least not for having Clara. He envied them both for having each other, along with the house and the two bonny tots. A sudden lust for that domestic bliss rose up in his chest so powerful it nearly choked him. He spat bitterness into the street.

He could support a family on forty shillings a month. That was probably twice as much as Martin Younge brought in, when all the bills were paid. But he hadn't spent six hard years at Gray's to become a pettifogging writer of tradesmen's wills. His father, God rest his eternal soul, had wanted more for him.

Tom wanted more too. He would pass the bar before he sued for his livery, and he would win that livery before he thought about a wife. But then he would find one and make a home. Let Trumpet howl her fury to the moon.

Trumpet had a son — his son, never to be acknowledged, much less bounced upon his knee. She had a husband and two palatial houses. She shared the work of a courtier with her husband, the way Clara and Martin Younge shared the ballad trade. They were partners, each pair, pulling together toward a common goal, building a future for their children.

Where was *his* partner? He wanted a daughter to lean against him and a son to tuck into a crib. He wanted to sit by the fire in the evening with a witty, comely woman who understood the law, or something of it.

Not like Trumpet did, of course. There could only be one Lady Alice in the world. But she wasn't Queen Elizabeth, and he wasn't Sir Christopher Hatton. He hadn't sworn eternal bachelorhood in exchange for lands and titles. He had hurdles to jump, certainly. Money to earn, strings to pull. But he'd do it. He'd find that woman who could pull beside him. He would marry her and put a baby in her womb.

The bar. His livery. And then he'd find a wife.

SIX

"A letter, my lady." The usher bent at the waist as he extended a silver tray bearing a square of paper with a black seal.

Trumpet, seated at her writing desk, thanked him. She waited until he had gone, then examined the seal more closely. "It's from Tom," she informed Catalina Luna, her maidservant and most trusted confidante.

Tom and Trumpet wrote each another almost daily, changing inks and wax colors to mask the frequency. Tom used an old seal of Stephen's left behind at Gray's when the young lord had tired of law books and dull clothing. Stephen wouldn't notice unless you held the thing right under his nose. Besides, he followed the restless Earl of Essex on every campaign, which kept him out of the country for months on end.

Trumpet slit the seal with her ivory-handled penknife and unfolded the paper. The message was brief. "It's about the libel," she told her servant. "He says it's a ballad, long enough to fill a page. The libeler signed it *Tamburlaine*. It calls for violence against strangers, according to the printer who took it down."

Tom hadn't signed his note. Why bother? She knew his handwriting at a glance.

"A single page filled with verses. That should be easy enough to spot."

"If you say so, my lady." Catalina shook out a tattered gray apron, laying it next to a much-patched kirtle. She'd expressed a low opinion of the present plan but hadn't come up with anything better.

They were going to Whitehall to steal a copy of that libel. Tom needed it, and it gave Trumpet a role in his new investigation. She hadn't investigated anything in ages. Her life had become more restricted since she married. She loved being back on the Strand, which she couldn't have achieved without Stephen, but she had to cope with so many more servants. Many of them came from Dorset and gave their primary loyalty to their lord. She'd been replacing them little by little with her own partisans, but it took time and a delicate touch.

The queen and half the court had gone to Croydon Palace in Surrey, home of Archbishop Whitgift. He didn't have room for everyone, so most of the Privy Council remained at Whitehall. Stephen also had a chamber at Whitehall, which he'd taken while negotiating for their house. He'd spent a few nights there, hoping to be invited to a late-night card game with the queen and the Earl of Essex. No luck so far.

But palaces were crowded and smelly. They now had a comfortable house not half a mile down the Strand. He'd decided to not keep the room when Her Majesty returned from her summer progress. Trumpet thus had an excellent excuse for a visit — arranging for her lord husband's chattels to be removed. Once inside, she and Catalina would transform themselves into cleaning women, find some rags and buckets, and prowl the corridor where the Privy Council members lived. No one was more anonymous than a lowly woman with a mop.

They found what they needed behind the kitchens. They scurried across the central courtyard with their heads down and climbed a back staircase to the first floor. Trumpet knew the Privy Council met in a large chamber overlooking the court. She'd gone with Stephen once to call upon the Earl of Essex, who always kept a room near the seat of power wherever the court might be, so she knew the councilors had chambers along the corridor behind the council chamber. The rooms overlooked the Privy Garden and were thus highly favored.

Before they could enter the first one, a gentleman in secretary black popped out and snapped, "There you are. Get in here and clear up this mess. How am I supposed to work with this stink?"

The two women traded grimaces, but what could they do? They followed his pointing arm into a spacious chamber that reeked of puke. The secretary offered no explanation for the mess. "I'll wait outside," he said and left.

"Must we, my lady?" Catalina asked.

"I'm afraid we must. Otherwise our game is over before it's begun." Trumpet scouted about for something like a rag. The best she could find was a pair of linen breeches with a dark streak down the back. She held them up, wrinkling her nose. "Someone has a large arse and messy habits." She tossed them to Catalina.

"This is fine cloth, my lady. He will miss them, this large-bottom man."

"Not until after we're gone."

Catalina approached the pool whence arose the stink, turning her face away as she knelt and swabbed up the puke. "What do I do with it?"

"Throw it out the window." Trumpet dunked her mop into her bucket and slapped some water over the affected area. It left a substantial puddle. There must be some trick to this mopping game. Ah, well. It would dry. "Let's take a quick look around."

She set the mop and bucket near the door and skipped over to the table where the secretary had been working. Here she found a plate with a half-eaten serving of fish in sauce. The cause of the vomiting, no doubt. She left it and leafed briskly through all the papers she could reach. They seemed to be mostly letters, signed on behalf of Sir John Fortescue. Not a scrap of poetry and nothing like a page-long ballad. She opened the writing desk sitting on a side table and searched it too.

Why wouldn't Sir John have a copy of the libel? Surely every member of the Privy Council had been given one to examine. Or did he not concern himself about riots in the city?

Trumpet's opinion of the councilor sank, though she'd never met him. She hoped she never did, now that she'd had a look at his napery.

"How long does this take?" The secretary cracked the door and glared at them.

"All done," Trumpet said.

They grabbed their tools and slithered past him, scuttling down the corridor. Trumpet glanced over her shoulder and saw that he'd gone inside and closed the door. "Let's try this one." She opened a door without knocking. A woman's voice shrieked, and she hastily closed it again.

She frowned at Catalina. "Napping at nine o'clock in the morning?"

"Perhaps not napping, my lady. I heard a man make a grunt."

Most of the councilors were married. Most of them were also well past fifty.

Trumpet cocked her head at Catalina. Her servant had passed her thirtieth birthday last year. She'd spent her youth traveling with a troupe of actors performing *commedia dell'arte* in Italy. She had a lush figure and the exotic coloring of her gypsy ancestors and very much enjoyed the company of men. Trumpet regarded her as an expert on sexual matters. "Do old married couples often make love at this hour?"

"No, my lady. But old men like young women, and young women like powerful men." Catalina produced one of her articulate shrugs.

"Hmph. Let's try the next one." This time they found a man dressed in the muted yet stylish manner of a valet. He stood near the window brushing a black velvet doublet.

"It's about time," he scolded. "You should've emptied these pots while we were at breakfast." He draped the doublet over a chest and set down his brush. "Don't leave any dribbles, now. I hate that. I'll be back in a few minutes."

"Chamber pots." Trumpet's stomach lurched. "I hadn't reckoned on that. I thought we would dust a bit and give the floors a swipe."

"Should we empty them into our buckets, my lady?" Catalina sounded resigned.

"Ugh, no. Then we'd have to carry the stuff downstairs." Trumpet peeked around the corner screen at a lidded pot. She tilted up the lid, revealing its ample contents. She hastily dropped the lid and turned to cough away the stink. "Let's throw them out, pots and all. But let's search first because someone's bound to notice chamber pots flying out the window."

This room belonged to Sir Thomas Heneage, the Vice-Chamberlain. By the documents stacked neatly on the table, this councilor was thickly involved in the pursuit of radical Protestants and atheists. Most of the letters were addressed jointly to Sir Thomas and Lord Keeper Puckering. They must be partners in zealotry. Trumpet found a few pages with snatches of poetry and a pamphlet titled *Strange News* by Thomas Nashe. She vowed to warn the satirist that he might be attracting the wrong kind of attention.

She found no long page of verses signed "Tamburlaine." No ballads whatsoever. You'd think a man eager to catch dissenters would pay more attention to the popular press.

She plopped on the edge of the bed, releasing the smell of some astringent ointment — an old man smell. "This plan isn't working, Catalina. The work is too disgusting. There are something like fourteen Privy Council members. We'll be puking ourselves before we do half their rooms." She sighed. "We'll have to think of something else."

"Thank you, my lady," Catalina answered fervently. She held up a second chamber pot. "Shall I throw this out the window?"

"No. God's teeth! Put it back where you found it. Let's get out of here."

Trumpet peeked out the door, saw an empty corridor, and led the way back to the service exit. They abandoned their mops and buckets under the stairs and hastened into the labyrinth of houses behind the Stone Gallery. Dorchester's rooms lay on the first floor overlooking the garden. They slipped inside, locked the door, and stripped down to their chemises, kicking their servant rags into a heap. Catalina bundled them back into a sack to bring them home again.

"They smell like puke," Trumpet objected.

"They can be washed. We'll want them again someday."

"I hope not." The laundry women at home were Trumpet's people, brought from Suffolk. They'd long ceased to wonder at the contents of Her Ladyship's buck-baskets.

She went to the sideboard in hopes of a cup of wine. No luck. The cups were theirs though, silver ones embossed with Stephen's crest. How had they not been stolen by the real chambermaids? "I'll send the steward back at once to collect these things."

She took a quick survey of the flotsam her lord husband had left behind. One beautiful shirt, two mismatched sleeves, a kidskin slipper under the edge of the bed, and two books. Some three or four pounds, not counting the silver, left to the mercy of the palace staff. She'd have a sharp word with Stephen's manservant that afternoon too.

They dressed in their proper garb, helping each other lace things up. They'd grown accustomed to these quick changes and had established a routine, building each other's costumes side by side. First the bodices, which they'd shed to achieve the shapeless figures of laboring women. Then their farthingales, laced to the bodice to keep them from shifting around. Trumpet added a bum roll to extend her fuller skirts in back. Then skirts, partlets, doublets, sleeves, shoulder rolls, and ruffs.

Catalina wore black broadcloth with gray silk linings and a brocaded forepart. Trumpet wore dark red taffeta with white linings and buttons wrapped in gleaming black silk. They'd twisted their long locks into knots at the base of their necks. Catalina donned a stiff white attifet trimmed in black velvet, then fixed a man-styled hat trimmed in black feathers at the perfect tilt on Trumpet's head. Trumpet added a long rope of pearls, knotted just above her breasts.

She'd had been gazing out at the garden as Catalina added the finishing touches to her costume. She laughed when the trick fountains spurted up, splashing a couple who strolled unwittingly past the sundial. They sprang apart like a pair of tumblers and hurried away from the hidden jets.

Stephen loved those fountains, which sprang up out of seeming nowhere to drench the unwary. Perhaps she could surprise him with some later this year. The gardeners might be at work today, with so few notables in residence. And they could both use some fresh air after the stenches they'd faced this morning.

She locked the door behind them, tucking the key into her small, tasseled purse. They walked along the Stone Gallery to the stairs that led down to the garden. Then they hovered a few yards from the sundial, wondering how to get close enough to examine the jets without being splashed.

While they dithered, Sir Robert Cecil appeared on the path leading to the Holbein Gate. Had he been in the Privy Council chamber while she and Catalina were scampering up and down that corridor? Trumpet shuddered at the thought. She doubted even her best disguises could deceive that hawk-eyed man.

He altered his course when he saw her, walking toward her with his quick, short steps. "Good morrow, Lady Dorchester. What brings you to Whitehall this morning?"

"Sir Robert! What a pleasant surprise!" Trumpet held out a hand for him to bow over.

He puffed out a fake kiss, then straightened with his smile already in place. Their eyes met nearly at a level. Sir Robert stood only a few inches taller than her five feet. She wasn't used to conversing with men without tilting her head back.

He arched an eyebrow. She hadn't answered his question. "I've come to see what my lord husband left behind in our chamber here." She rolled her eyes. "His servant did a poor job, I must say. Though no doubt His Lordship was in too great a hurry to allow him time to pack everything."

Sir Robert chuckled. "My lady wife lays the same offense at my feet, I fear."

"Busy men care nothing for lost slippers and cuffs, however long it might have taken to embroider them." Trumpet gave a little laugh. As she smiled into those alert hazel eyes, it occurred to her that courtiers had other ways of obtaining favors. But how to broach the subject?

Court gossip said Sir Robert was devoted to his wife. It also said his friendship with Lady Derby was warmer than it ought to be. A little mild flirtation might serve her turn. She batted her lashes at him and saw his expression change from routine courtesy to a more personal interest.

"I wonder, Sir Robert, if you could help me."

"Nothing could please me more, my lady." He gave her a wry smile. "If it doesn't take too long. Her Majesty is expecting me at Nonsuch this afternoon."

"It will only take a moment." She took his arm and turned him toward the sundial. "You must know *all* about these clever fountains."

He rolled his eyes. "Such a hazard for silks and velvets. But Her Majesty enjoys the effect."

"So does my lord husband! He finds them most amusing. And though I share *your* sensible view, it would be fun to surprise him with one or two in our garden at Dorchester House. But I haven't the least idea where to start." She gave his arm a little squeeze, and the warmth returned to his smile.

"I have a book about water features. I'll have it sent to you this afternoon. And I'll have my secretary find the man who fashioned these. If he's still in London, I'll have him call upon you at your convenience."

"Oh, Sir Robert!" Trumpet leaned toward him as if to kiss him on the cheek, then caught herself and pulled back with a coy little smile. His eyelids drooped as his eyes darkened. She might be playing it a bit too strong. "I *knew* you'd have the answer!"

"It's nothing, my lady." He placed his hand over hers and smiled into her eyes. "Is there anything else I can do for you?"

She stifled the urge to pull her hand away, casting her gaze to one side. "There is one small thing — the tiniest of things."

"Oh?" ·

"Well, if you're going to send me a book, perhaps you could send me a copy of that libel everyone's talking about."

Sir Robert withdrew his hand and took a step back. "If you mean the one taken from Austin Friars two weeks ago, no one should be talking about it."

Trumpet painted surprise on her face, shaping her lips in a round O. "It was only my lord husband and my good lord of Essex. You know they are such *close* friends. My lord wants to take up his share of the burdens of government. Not like his father, who hid in Dorset all his life. My lord, to his credit, recognizes that high station brings responsibilities as well as privileges."

"Admirable." Sir Robert's eyes grew wary. What did he think she wanted? Ah! The plum of plums.

She simpered at him. "He doesn't want a seat on the Privy Council. That would be *too* much. To be frank with you, he finds meetings terribly dreary. Yet he wishes to stay abreast of current affairs. *You* know what I mean better than I do, I'm sure!"

Sir Robert gave a relieved chuckle. "I don't suppose it could do any harm. He won't spread it about."

"Certainly not!"

"And of course Lord Dorchester's opinion will be highly valued," he added, as if by rote.

Trumpet managed not to snort at that. She usually pretended to be Stephen's match in wit and education, which was to say, weak in both areas. "I don't suppose you could send it this afternoon along with the book?"

"I'll write to my secretary at once, my lady, before I leave." He patted her hand, which she had kept pressed upon his sleeve. His eyelids drooped again in that lidded gaze men seemed to think seductive. His tone softened. "I'm delighted to be able to perform these little services for you, my lady. Please don't hesitate to ask if you have any other desires I might satisfy."

Trumpet batted her lashes again, bleating a high-pitched laugh. She hadn't expected so bold a response to her maneuver. She withdrew her hand from his arm, offering it for a more genuine kiss as he bowed and bade her farewell. He stumped off toward the privy wharf with his awkward gait.

She felt sorry for him with his dwarfish stature and hunched shoulder, especially considering Her Majesty's taste for tall and comely men. What must it be like for twisted little Robert Cecil to stand next to the magnificent Sir Walter Ralegh day after day?

Sir Robert might have her sympathy, but that was all he would get. Both her husband and her lover were well above average in terms of masculine beauty. Besides, she could never betray Tom to that extent. Sleeping with Stephen to produce a legitimate heir was one thing; trading sex for favors at court was another thing altogether.

However, she had learned something new today. Sneaking about in servant's garb was the old way — the troublesome way — of stealing secrets. Courtiers used flattery, flirtation, and insincere promises to get what they wanted.

She only hoped she hadn't just made a promise she could never bear to keep.

SEVEN

Francis sighed when he saw the blue seal on the letter Pinnock dropped atop his desk. Another command from Lord Essex. A thrill of pride once coursed through his veins at the sight of that seal; now a great weariness weighed upon his shoulders. He had failed to foresee this sense of burden or the time lost to his scholarly pursuits. He'd only thought, *At last, a nobleman who truly values what I have to offer.*

The earl's regard had lifted Francis up, even in his own esteem. His Lordship had flattered him by asking his advice on sundry matters. He'd given him books — expensive, but lacking the usual odor of bribes. He'd lent him money to get through last summer's royal progress, always a monstrous expense — the travel, the tips, the exorbitant fees for every little service.

Out of such minutiae, the chains of obligation had been forged.

Francis slit the seal to find two sheets of paper. The first contained a note from His Lordship asking Francis to cast his eyes across the enclosure — a copy of the Dutch Church libel. His Lordship keenly desired to beat Lord Keeper Puckering to the author's identity.

Francis cast quick eyes down the pageful of verses. The intent was clear enough. The ballad urged London's apprentices to rise up and drive all strangers from their city, by violent means if necessary. He reached for a sheet of paper to jot down a few observations, then decided to take it downstairs to discuss with his brother. In fairness, this sort of thing fell into Anthony's bailiwick, not his.

He rapped on Tom's door on the way. He hadn't promised him a copy of the libel, but now that he had one, he might as well enjoy the credit.

"I have my own." Tom waved a sheet of paper covered with Trumpet's neat scribal hand. "You're not the only one with friends at court."

Francis twitched his lips. Tom might well exceed him in influence one day. He had no other ambitions to impede him — no desire to change the world through the reformation of natural philosophy, for example. And he possessed the unfair advantages of height and good looks. He could probably surpass Francis simply by standing about and smiling.

Anthony welcomed the interruption. "I can't get used to these bitter spring days. In the south of France, sunshine means warmth." He directed Jacques to fix spiced wine for everyone.

Francis held out his copy of the libel, but Anthony forestalled him by holding up another one. "Thomas Phelippes is on Puckering's committee. They were warned to keep a tight grip on copies, but he had no compunctions about sending me one." He laughed as his gaze fell on the paper in Tom's hand. "It appears you didn't need my help after all, Mr. Clarady. May I ask the name of your benefactor?"

Tom hesitated. Anthony still didn't know about his special relationship with Lady Dorchester, at least not openly. But the spymaster spent his cloistered days intuiting nuances and deducing connections. He had probably worked out the essentials for himself. Francis kept mum. It wasn't his secret to tell.

"My friend prefers to remain anonymous," Tom said.

Anthony smiled, accepting that reply. Then he cocked his head as if trying to read Tom's ballad sideways. He held out a hand. "Do you mind?" Tom handed the paper to him. Anthony took one look and gave a soft laugh. "That's Robert's secretary." He flicked his eyebrows at Francis. "I've seen reams of his writing."

"Sir Robert Cecil?" Tom took his ballad back and frowned at it. "What did she — I mean, why him?"

Anthony smiled at his slip. "I'm sure Her Ladyship struck a shrewd bargain."

So much for secrets.

Tom scowled, doubtless recalling what commodity ladies most commonly traded to men of power. The jealousy of a lover proclaimed itself across his burning cheeks.

Francis caught his brother's twinkling eyes and shook his head. *Don't tease him, not on this score.* He breathed a rueful sigh in Tom's direction. The man made an able intelligencer when working with men he didn't know or didn't care about, but he was painfully vulnerable to people he trusted.

As was Francis, in all honesty. He'd trusted Essex to value his dreams as well as his talents. He'd been wrong. He was just another tool to further the earl's ambitions.

Francis and Tom took their accustomed seats near the fire, turning their chairs toward Anthony at his desk. Jacques delivered mugs of hot wine. Francis inhaled the rising steam, savoring the spicy fragrance of nutmeg and orange peel. He and Tom both accepted small mince pies from the plate Jacques extended.

Anthony had turned his gaze to the libel. Now he looked up and said, "I can see why they suppressed it. It's quite incendiary."

Tom said, "The man who found it knew at once it meant trouble. That's why he gave it to the constable."

"You've spoken to him?" Francis asked.

"He's a printer of ballads in Broad Street Ward," Tom said. "I reckoned he'd live somewhere near the Dutch Church, so that's where I asked. How else would he happen to pass that door at midnight?"

"Good work," Anthony said. "Did he see who posted it?"

Tom shook his head. "He was coming home from a tavern, walking with a lantern. He noticed it because the sheet was still white. He stopped to read it because he's caught other nasty bits posted there from time to time. Usually, they're just ill-written bawdry. He burns them on the spot. This one was longer, better written, and blatantly political, so he thought the authorities should see it."

"Did the original document have any features of interest?" Francis asked.

"Not that the printer noticed. It had been copied out by a public scrivener. They're trained to make their hands as uniform as possible."

Francis nodded. No point in searching for the scrivener, who had probably been paid to hire a street urchin to paste the libel up. "Is there any reason to speak to the constable?"

"None I can think of," Tom said. "He would've taken it straight to the sheriff, who would've taken it to the Lord Mayor, who would've taken it to the Privy Council. No one would want this burning a hole in their pocket for long."

"And here we are with three copies!" Anthony laughed, waving his like a stiff flag.

"Shall we turn to the matter?" Francis had to write a report to Lord Essex today. He wanted to get the onerous chore over with as quickly as possible.

The others responded to his crisp tone with patient looks and readied their copies for a discussion.

"The principal theme," Francis said, "is the call to violence against strangers. Note the last lines. 'By letting strangers make our hearts to ache; For which our swords are whet to shed their blood; And for a truth let it be understood; Fly, flee, and never return.'"

"The rhyming isn't very good," Tom said with the air of an expert. He had doubtless read more ballads than Francis and Anthony put together. "But he isn't shy, is he? 'Death shall be your lot.' 'We'll cut your throats.' No shilly-shallying about."

Anthony chimed in. "'Not Paris massacre so much blood did spill.' Do you think he's referencing the historical event?"

"The play, more like," Tom said. "It ran for a few weeks in January before they closed the theaters."

"You skipped over the part about praying in a temple," Francis said. "That's the second theme — religious dissent, or rather, deception. It's less prominent but equally alarming."

"He calls them Jews," Tom said. "Right up at the top. 'And like the Jews, you eat us up as bread.' But there can't be many Jews in the Low Countries, can there?"

"A few," Anthony said, "but less likely to be among those seeking refuge here. Other charges are sharper. Toward the end here, he accuses refugees of counterfeiting their religion to gain entrance to England in order to send intelligences back to Spain."

"So they're not just taking bread from English mouths," Tom said. "They're also spying for the Duke of Parma."

Anthony said, "This fellow wants to stir up as much trouble as possible."

Tom nodded. "He's poking every sore spot, isn't he? Here he's blaming the refugees for bringing the plague. But that can't be right, can it? Or not the only cause. Ships come here from every corner of Europe. Venice, Constantinople. It could come from anywhere."

"Originally, it might have done," Francis said. "Now it seems to be native. We've had intermittent plague in

London for as long as I can remember. It isn't caused by these recent incomers."

"They do take work from Englishmen though," Tom said. "Weavers, especially, but also others. Printers, papermakers, goldsmiths . . . I've heard more Dutch on the streets in the past year than usual. You'd think they could at least make an effort to learn English."

"They're our allies in the desperate battle for our independence from Spain," Anthony said. "Their cities burn so ours can remain whole. We owe them shelter, at the very least."

"I know that," Tom said. "I agree with it. But I can understand why some folks would be angry. The newcomers are supposed to take jobs with English masters, but they don't. They open their own workshops and even sell their own goods at retail."

Francis said, "They're not allowed to do that."

Tom laughed. "And yet they do it." He plucked at his round hose to display the fabric. "This is some of the new drapery, as they're calling it. It's a wonderfully lightweight serge. Perfect for summer. I like it even now, if I'm indoors most of the day. This came from a shop in Blackfriars owned and operated by one Robbe Mertens, late of Antwerp."

"You shouldn't shop there," Anthony said, though he licked his lips as he peered at the fine gray cloth.

Tom snorted. "You speak as if I had a choice. Your lady aunt does the choosing for me. The better I look, the better my wardship reflects on her."

"She does have excellent taste." Anthony chuckled. "Still, she should know better."

"That illustrates a key point," Francis said. "These newcomers contribute as much as they take. The trades will find a new balance in time, provided the city isn't set on fire by rioters first."

They all fell silent. Debate among those who agree served little purpose. Each sipped at his wine and reread the ballad.

Anthony spoke first. "I suspect the Privy Council was more outraged by the last theme. Near the end here, the author accuses some upstart nobles who 'wound their country's breast for lucre's sake.' These nobles, whoever they are, are allegedly taking Spanish gold in exchange for helping Catholic infiltrators enter our country."

"I noticed that," Tom said. "Who's the upstart, I wonder?"

"Lord Burghley, I would guess," Francis said. "I believe his barony is the most recent creation on the council."

"Is he?" Anthony turned his gaze toward the plastered ceiling, moving his fingers as if counting off the names. "I believe you're right. Well, he's been called worse."

The brothers shared a knowing chuckle. They'd used some harsh terms to describe their uncle over the years. Never "upstart," however. That seemed oddly specific. Could it be a clue? "More than one was postulated, to be precise. '*Upstarts* that enjoy the noblest seats.'"

Tom wagged a finger at him. "Wasn't Sir Robert knighted right before the queen appointed him to the council?"

Francis groaned. He hated to be reminded of that event. Yet another personal humiliation. Why couldn't he have been knighted at the same time? Stupid question, to which he knew the answer — because his father died years ago, leaving him to flounder on his own.

"Well, then," Anthony said. "Who wrote this? Any clues to the author's identity in the text?"

"He signed it 'Tamburlaine,'" Francis noted, "though I doubt that means much. It was a popular play."

"Still is," Tom said. "But Kit never wrote this."

"There are other references to his plays here," Anthony said. "The Jew, perhaps, refers to *The Jew of Malta*. And we've agreed that 'the Paris massacre' most likely refers to Marlowe's play rather than the actual event."

"Both of which packed the Rose day after day," Tom said. "All that tells us is that the author likes to see a play now and then. So we've narrowed it down to half of London."

"Marlowe's work is deliberately challenging," Francis said. "This could be seen as consistent with his work." He disapproved of Marlowe's plays. Violent, cruel-minded, almost atheistic, they lacked any redeeming moral messages. Plays and poetry should be uplifting. Their themes and characters should support the highest moral standards so as to instruct the public while entertaining them. Marlowe had a God-given talent for producing poetry of astounding beauty, but he squandered his gift on cynicism and disbelief.

Tom rolled his eyes. They'd had this debate before. He always defended his friend with vigor. "Kit never wrote this, I tell you. First, it's too clumsy. He dreams in iambic meter. He told me so. And he couldn't botch a rhyme if his life depended on it. Besides, why would he paste a single copy of a bad verse on a door where it would surely be removed by morning? He could write another play and reach a thousand people in a single afternoon."

"That's almost a good argument," Anthony said. "A play inciting violence would never pass the censors. But no, the author of *Tamburlaine* isn't fool enough to implicate himself by signing it with that name. I think we can rule him out."

Francis wasn't so sure. "A play would be attributed to him publicly. Perhaps he wanted to stir up animosity and chaos in secret."

"He wouldn't," Tom said. "I tell you, I know the man. He likes foreigners. He finds them interesting. That's an important quality for Kit. It's what he likes best about intelligence work — traveling and meeting people of other countries."

"A common motivation," Anthony said. "Along with the pay." He tapped a finger on his desk. "The author could be trying to implicate Marlowe with these references."

"Or borrowing the luster of his name," Tom said. "Perhaps he lacks the schooling to throw in classical figures, so he reaches for a university-educated playmaker to elevate his verses."

"Or his works were chosen to add atheism to the list of dangers," Anthony said. "He is notorious on that count. You might warn him that his name is being bandied about in unsavory contexts."

"He's all right," Tom said. "He's living with a friend — a gentleman — in Kent. I doubt he was even in London last Saturday night and can prove it."

Francis sniffed, impatient with the whole discussion. He had nothing to report, which meant he'd have to keep digging. Or keep Tom at the task. "We're no closer to a solution. If it wasn't *Tamburlaine*'s creator, which I agree isn't likely, then I see nothing to indicate any individual. We're at an impasse."

"Not necessarily," Tom said. "We don't recognize this style, nor did the printer, but someone will. I'll take this to the Goose and Gall this evening and show it to whoever's there. Thomas Nashe knows everybody. He might recognize something right off." He scratched his beard — a signal of impending thought — then asked, "What happens to the whoreson knave when they catch him?"

"He'll be sent to jail," Anthony said. "Probably Bridewell."

"That's not so bad." Tom had spent three nights in Bridewell a few years ago. He'd rebelled against his wardship, which he'd imagined would simply dissolve on his twenty-first birthday. Francis had to explain the process of suing for one's livery in the Court of Wards, emphasizing how long it took and how much it cost. Tom had stormed off to rack up a mountain of bills in his favorite brothel, impudently sending them to Lady Russell. She'd had him arrested to teach him a lesson, letting him stew a while before bailing him out and dropping the charges.

Francis smiled at the memory. "Your experience was of the mildest nature."

"Not in the olfactory sense." Tom pretended to blow a stink out of his mouth. His cellmates had been vagrants and drunkards picked up off the street.

"Bridewell has other uses," Anthony said, "including several cells equipped for the manacles. The libeler will likely be racked to elicit the names of his co-conspirators."

"God's bones," Tom said. "That's cruel. Who says he has a co-conspirator?"

"That tends to be assumed. Anthony shrugged as if apologizing, though he bore no blame. Torture had been part of the criminal justice process for centuries.

Tom grunted in disgust. "I want those hundred crowns, and I don't want folks attacking Flemings in the street. But I wouldn't wish the manacles on a Spaniard, much less an English poet — however rotten his verses may be."

EIGHT

Tom had supper in the hall that evening. Then he went back to his room to change into his least costly outfit, a brown worsted doublet with linen-paned galligaskins. He preferred not to advertise his status as an Inns of Court man when whiling away an evening in a tavern with a bunch of poets. Some of them might be gentlemen, but none could afford silk linings.

He tucked a candle stub and tinderbox into his pockets. A full moon would shine that night, but it might not make it over the rooftops before he headed home. He rolled up the libel and tucked it into his doublet. With luck, Nashe would be holding court at his usual table.

He chose to walk the roads north of the city walls with open fields on at least one side. He would have ridden his horse to keep his nose above any lurking miasma, but then he'd have to pay for stabling. And if one of the poets put him on the scent of the libeler, he wanted to be able to follow the trail without worrying about Tristan.

He breathed deeply as he passed Moorfields, filling his lungs before diving into the warren of houses spreading out from the city wall. Boarded-up windows punctuated the rows, and rubbish clogged the streets. He'd find a different way out.

He made his way across Bishopsgate to Norton Folgate, where many poets and players shared cheap lodgings. The liberty lay close to the theaters and a little distant from London's moralizing authorities. He turned up Ivy Lane and entered the Goose and Gall, to be met by a gust of tobacco smoke and peaty ale. So much for fresh air.

Ah, well. No plague could survive in this reeking fume.

He found Nashe, as expected, seated at a round table near the front window. The window was closed, and there was nothing to see but the house across the street, but it did get more light than the rest of the room. And it saved friends from having to walk upstairs to seek him out.

"Tom!" Nashe called, waving a hand. "I was hoping to see you before I left."

Tom pulled up a stool and signaled the wench for a pitcher of ale. "Where are you going?"

"To my parents' house in Norfolk. The city won't be fit to live in this summer."

"Wise man," Tom said. "Lucky I came today, then. I have something to ask you. Have you heard about the Dutch Church libel?"

"That cursed libel!" Nashe spat into the rushes. "Have you heard about Thomas Kyd?"

"I don't know the man. What about him?"

"He's been arrested. They took him to Bridewell."

"On account of the libel?" Tom asked. "Are you sure?"

"That's what I've heard." Nashe shrugged. "I believe it, for what's that worth."

"Did he write the libel?" Tom fought his disappointment. Losing the reward was nothing compared to prison.

"Kyd? Never! He's as straight a middle-way man as you could hope to find. Kyd wouldn't agitate for a pot of ale. He wouldn't rouse the apprentices to do so much as change their linens on a daily basis. You've never met a less offensive man, whatever you might think of his *Spanish Tragedy*."

"Then why did they arrest him?"

"No one knows." Nashe folded his arms on the table and lowered his voice. "No one's seen that cursed libel, have they? But rumor says it had something to do with Kit."

"Not much." Tom pulled out his copy and unrolled it with a flourish. "See for yourself."

Nashe's jaw dropped. "You slippery rascal! Give me that thing." He snatched the sheet of paper and held it to the fading evening light. Like every writer, he could read like the wind. When he finished, he slapped his hand against the sheet. "It's the signature, I'll warrant. Though signing a boiling pot of fevered verse like this 'Tamburlaine' is about as revealing as signing a love song 'Cupid.' It's not even particularly original. Every whoreson groundling with a penny and a sack of hazelnuts thinks he's Tamburlaine nowadays."

"Agreed," Tom said. "Kit never wrote this. But why arrest Thomas Kyd?"

"Who can say? Our best guess is that someone informed on Kyd, denouncing him as a former chambermate of Marlowe's."

"That's a stretch," Tom said. "Longer than the tenter frames in Moorfields."

"Nice image," Nashe allowed.

Tom took his ballad back. "I mean to find out who did write it. I want that hundred-crown reward. And now I want to get Kyd out of jail, if I can. And warn Kit while I'm about it, if that's the way the wind is blowing."

"He should leave town," Nashe said. "Go home to Canterbury."

"He's safe enough. He's riding out the plague in Kent. A place called Scadbury."

"Thomas Walsingham's house? Lucky fellow! I hear it's idyllic." Nashe sighed. His scrawny frame, straw-like hair, and gag tooth — to say nothing of his unruly wit — barred him from most gentlemen's tables.

Two men approached them, mugs in hand. Both were a good ten years older than Tom and Nashe, who were the same age. The short one had red hair that clashed with his tawny doublet. He thrust his face toward Tom, squinting at his features. The taller one showed better taste — or a deeper purse — wearing a light brown doublet that might have been made of the new drapery. He carried himself with the confident air of a man who mixed easily in all levels of society. Tom cultivated that air himself and appreciated a good model.

The newcomers seated themselves without asking permission, proclaiming themselves familiar friends. The red-haired man peered at Tom again. "Who's this?"

"Thomas Clarady," Nashe said. He tilted his head toward Tom as he introduced the others. "That blind bat is called George Peele. You've probably seen *The Battle of Alcazar.*"

"I loved it." Tom extended a hand and gave the bat a hearty shake. "My father was a privateer."

Peele's eyebrows rose, but Nashe moved on before he could reply. "The handsome one is Mathew Roydon. He's an able poet and a gifted comedian, but more germane to the present topic, he's a friend of Kit's. Are you sure you haven't met him?"

Tom shook his head. "I'd remember."

Roydon smiled. "Kit keeps his friends in different pockets, like other aspects of his life." He tossed his head to shake a lock of brown hair from his eyes. "So the topic is Marlowe? Any connection to Kyd's arrest?"

Tom nodded. "I'm trying for that reward they're offering for the author of the Dutch Church libel. Looking for people who don't want to be found is what you might call my by-work."

"What's your usual work?" Peele asked.

"I study law at Gray's Inn." Pride warmed Tom's breast as always, even after seven years' residence at that august institution.

"His tutor is Francis Bacon," Nashe added. He never minded basking in Tom's reflected glow. "The Parliamentarian. We've all heard him speak."

The others murmured, impressed. Many writers attended sessions of the House of Commons. They had the time and also the education to appreciate the rhetoric.

Nashe added, "Tom tells me Kit's out of reach, in Scadbury."

"Lucky man," Roydon said. "That's a beautiful place. What's he writing?"

Tom spoke up, pleased to be the one with news. "I saw him last week. He's tutoring a friend of mine in Roman literature." That drew a round of guffaws. "He said he was writing a play about James the First of Scotland. Apparently, the poor churl was trapped in a sewer by twenty angry noblemen."

"Irresistible," Peele said, shaking his head. "For Kit, I mean. Did they run him through with hot pokers or boil him in a vat of oil?"

Roydon chuckled. "Never known a poet as bloodthirsty as our Marlowe. Why can't he write a comedy? I'd be willing to collaborate."

"Oh yes," Peele said, nodding sagely, "a comedy by Christopher Marlowe. It's about a clown who goes mad and massacres a theater-full of people by pissing plague on them."

"Ugh!" Tom waved that away. "No one would go see it."

"Everyone would," Roydon said. "The poetry would be sublime, and we'd have deep philosophical themes to debate in the taverns afterward."

They all grunted at the truth in that. Marlowe had the magic, no question.

"He's a fool," Nashe said bitterly. "He should at least write something without religion in it. Julius Caesar died a bloody death. What's wrong with that? Romans are safe."

Tom agreed. "He probably doesn't know about Kyd yet. When I see him next, I'll tell him." It would give him an excuse to visit Trumpet too.

"It makes me sick to think about it," Nashe said. "And that libel barely mentions Marlowe."

"You've read it?" Roydon asked. He tossed his lank hair back again and made a futile attempt to tuck the offending lock under the brim of his cloth cap.

Tom handed him his copy. "I have a friend with influence."

"Indeed you do." The older man acknowledged the status with a flick of his eyebrows. He read the ballad quickly, let out a low whistle, and handed it to Peele, who had to go find a candle to hold in front of the lettering.

"It's hot all right," Roydon said. "But Kyd didn't write it."

"Nor did Kit," Nashe said. "If he wanted to write a thing like that, which he wouldn't, it would be beautiful. Every verse would thrum with Marlowe's mighty line. We'd be quoting it already, pointing out favorite passages."

"This isn't the worst I've seen," Peele said, "in terms of ballads. The author's written a few, I'd wager. See how he keeps up the rhythm of an extra phrase every twelfth line? It's not bad work. Not good, but not at all bad." He handed the paper back to Tom.

"Foul stuff though," Roydon said. "I can see why the authorities whisked it out of sight. I can see a band of weavers' apprentices marching up the street crying, 'We'll cut your throats. We'll cut your throats.'"

Nashe shuddered. "Glad I'm leaving. But what about Kyd? Did they really arrest him because he shared a room with Kit once upon a time?"

"It can't be that alone," Roydon said, "although that may be why they went to him in the first place."

"They may think he's closer to Kit than he admits," Peele said. "They don't listen to protests, however true, when they're in the torturing mood."

"They won't torture him!" Tom cried. "Will they? From what you're saying, Kyd has no connection whatsoever to this libel."

"We don't know what's happening to him," Nashe said. "But why Bridewell, if they don't mean to hang him in the manacles? They take seditionists to the Marshalsea, as a rule." The satirist's eyes were bleak.

The others reflected the same fear. If the authorities were rounding up friends of Marlowe, who would they come for next?

"I'll find him," Tom said. "I'll try to visit him and see how he's being treated. I'll do what I can. It might not be much."

The others nodded, looking slightly relieved. An Inns of Court man had a louder voice than a poet in some places — and more coins to spread around as well. Tom vowed to extract a few from his treasure chest in Lady Russell's library. Prison guards lived on bribes, after all.

"If you're serious about finding this libeler," Nashe said, "you might try the Angel on Maidenhead Lane near St. Paul's. Balladeers go there to drink while they're waiting to make a sale. I've seen some of them scribbling away in there, hoping to profit from some fresh scandal."

"Thanks." Tom had guessed Nashe would point him down the right trail. He glanced out the window. Not quite dark yet. "I think I'll go now." He rose, rolled up his ballad, and tucked it back into his doublet. He glanced at the large jug of ale he'd ordered and grinned. "I'll pay for that on my way out."

"Be careful," Roydon said. "If the authorities find out you're showing a copy of a suppressed libel around, you might be sharing a room with Thomas Kyd yourself."

A wise caution. Tom considered it as he made his way down Bishopsgate into the city. But he couldn't think of another way to identify the author. He detoured down Broad Street to pass the Dutch Church — out of general interest, not hoping to see Clara. He wondered if the Lord Mayor hadn't offered that huge reward knowing full well it couldn't be won. They might not even have the money.

There was a sobering thought. Here he was, walking through a plague-ridden city, risking his very life — for what? A chance at a prize that might not even exist.

He turned up Cheapside and realized he had another reason now. He loved the theater — the poetry, the spectacle, the actors, the costumes. The flirting gentry in the galleries, anxious women clutching handkerchiefs, scoffing men shouting ripostes at the players. He even loved the odiferous groundlings crowding the pit and throwing nutshells at the stage.

The theater was one of London's greatest glories. He couldn't go back to scribing wills while playmakers were arrested merely for knowing Christopher Marlowe. A shiver ran up his spine that had nothing to do with the east wind. If friends of Marlowe could be tortured, what would they do to the man himself?

He found the Angel easily enough. The sign actually had an angel on it. Most shops and taverns in London had changed hands so many times over the centuries that their signs bore no relation to their present function. It wasn't much of a place though. Four stories tall, but so narrow three square tables spanned the width.

He walked to the back and ordered a beer, which turned out to be decent. He leaned an elbow on the counter and surveyed the crowded room with interest, making sure the counterman noticed. He nodded to himself as he spotted a man in a worn doublet hunched over a sheet of paper, writing at speed with a short quill.

"Haven't seen you before," the counterman said.

"Not my usual haunt." Tom turned to the wiry man with a grin. "I'm looking for a balladeer. I'm told this is the place to find one."

The man nodded. "What kind of ballad are you wanting?"

"Something with a bite. I've a friend with a grudge. We won't name names, though you'd recognize it. Someone who could use taking down a peg or two."

The counterman frowned. He was called away by a wench with orders before he could answer, but a man sitting on a stool against the wall turned toward Tom. He had a long face with sharp cheekbones and lank blond hair.

"An Inns of Court man should know better than to solicit a libel." His voice had a rasp in it, like he'd just come from a shouting match or lived in damp lodgings.

"Is it that obvious?" Tom didn't have to pretend to be chagrined.

"It's that air of dominance," the man said. "You think you can walk in anywhere and get whatever you want."

"Not always." Tom caught the counterman's eye and pointed at the sharp-faced man's cup. After it had been refilled, he flashed a grin at his new friend. "Know anyone who can write a catchy libel?"

The man laughed at his impudence. "I might. But you don't want a new ballad, do you? You want the man who wrote the libel posted on the Dutch Church a fortnight ago."

Tom's grin vanished. The man smirked. "The Lord Mayor's proclamation has stirred up a herd of men wanting ballads. You're the third one today asking the same sort of question."

"Competition, eh?" Tom doubted many could lay their hands on the work. He shrugged it off. "It's a lot of money." He shot the man another cocky grin. "Any guesses?"

"You're a bold one, I'll give you that. If I knew who wrote that libel, I'd tell the Lord Mayor instead of you. Get those hundred crowns for myself." He took a long draught of ale, then studied the interior of his clay mug as if reading something on the surface of his drink. He turned to Tom with a sly smile on his lean cheeks. "You're looking in the wrong place, Mr. Lawyer. You'll find the knave who had that ballad made at Whitehall."

NINE

On Friday morning, Francis sent a note to Lord Keeper Puckering requesting a brief audience. He'd decided to ask for a seat on the Dutch Church libel commission. His reasons were three. First, Lord Essex had asked him to identify the libel's author. His best hope of success was to be privy to the commission's discoveries. Second, Anthony had advised him to seek out such humdrum committees to work his way back into the queen's good graces. His best hope was to prove himself all over again through diligent service. Two sound political reasons; sufficient for most men.

His conscience supplied the third reason. Tom's report this morning included the news of Thomas Kyd's arrest — an egregious abuse of power. *The Spanish Tragedy* had been performed at court. Francis found it too exciting for his taste, but in no wise offensive. The playmaker had no discernible political views as far as anyone knew.

If Francis could help free Kyd by apprehending the real libeler, he had a moral obligation to do so.

Puckering responded within the hour, granting the honor of a visit that morning at eleven o'clock. Francis arrived at York House a few minutes early. He'd been born in this house and spent much of his childhood here since his father had been Lord Keeper for twenty years. He and Anthony had loved the ancient manor on the Strand, sneaking out from lessons to watch the boats traveling up and down the Thames.

Three other Lord Keepers had occupied York House since Francis's father died in 1579. He hadn't been inside since. Now every plaster rose, every marble mantelpiece, and every view caught through a diamond-paned window caused a pang.

The usher led him into the large chamber that his father had used as his principal place of business. The smell of the special beeswax used to polish the linenfold paneling brought a tear to Francis's eye. How he longed to turn and see his beloved father standing at the bookshelf, searching for a book to supply the perfect reference for whatever he was writing! Instead, the bland features of Sir John Puckering awaited him behind the gleaming oak desk.

Sir John had dark hair and eyes, with a short growth of beard around his fleshy jaw. His features lacked all distinction. He looked like the middling sort of grocer, though his father had been a gentleman. Sir John had climbed the legal ladder up to this high seat. He'd made his name trying Catholics for treason, arguing on behalf of the crown. He'd been a Member of Parliament for twenty-five years and had been elected Speaker.

For all his achievements, he failed to compete with his more personable predecessors for Her Majesty's favor. She regarded him as merely a useful servant. He had to acknowledge that distinction every time he faced her.

Francis stopped a yard from the desk, removed his hat, and bowed.

"Be seated, Mr. Bacon," Sir John said, indicating a chair in front of the desk. Francis had favored that very chair when he sat with his father, practicing his letters.

Francis swallowed back the memories and sat. "Thank you for seeing me on such short notice."

"How may I accommodate you?"

Straight to the point. Why waste time on courtesies? "My lord of Essex asked me to look into the matter of the libel posted at Austin Friars. I thought I might best serve the council by joining the commission which I understand you have formed for the same purpose."

Sir John frowned. "Did His Lordship request that you seek a place on my commission?"

His commission, was it? Not an action of the whole council? "No, not directly. But it makes sense to combine our efforts." He smiled to show his willingness to add his proven abilities to further the Lord Keeper's objectives.

"Hmph. I disagree. I think a small group can focus more intently on the task at hand. Less debate. Less confusion."

Sir John's abrupt refusal surprised Francis. Stifling debate allowed grievous errors like the arrest of Thomas Kyd. And he'd never been refused a seat on a committee before. "Who comprises this small group, if I may ask?"

"It's headed by Dr. Julius Caesar, Master of the Court of Requests." Sir John's raised eyebrows indicated that he considered that choice unassailable.

Francis could dispute it easily. Caesar was a great striver who claimed a seat on every commission he could find. Then he contributed next to nothing, claiming press of work from the Court of Requests. A valid excuse, but then why insist on being named? To his credit, he did keep excellent records. Nor had he ever shown any signs of zealotry, unlike the present Lord Keeper.

"A capable gentleman," Francis allowed. "Who else?" He refrained from adding, *Who will do the actual work?*

"Thomas Phelippes, whom I believe you know, and William Waad."

William Waad was a clerk of the Privy Council who also served on many commissions, supplying eyes and ears for Lord Burghley. Thomas Phelippes was the most brilliant cryptographer in Europe and England. He'd joined the Earl of Essex's service when Sir Francis Walsingham died.

Francis could have guessed at Waad. He'd known about Phelippes too, through Anthony. But why include a cryptographer? "Mr. Phelippes is an interesting choice. Do you suspect some hidden message encoded within the verses of the ballad?"

"Not at all. But Mr. Phelippes might be able to deduce the identity of the author through a close analysis of language and style."

Francis could do that better than Phelippes, being far more broadly read. But never mind. "I should think another balladeer or a printer of ballads might do better."

Sir John offered him a smug smile. "I did manage to think of that, Mr. Bacon. Edward Allde is the fourth member of my committee."

"I know the name."

A prolific printer, Alde had a shop near Cripplegate. He published a little of everything: chapbooks, playbooks, songbooks, as well as more serious literature. And ballads. He alone might contribute something of value to this otherwise incapable commission.

Sir John's closely set eyes took on a crafty gleam. "I suppose you've read the libel, since Lord Essex has asked you to look into it."

"I have." Francis suppressed a laugh. Sir John wanted his opinion without having to give him credit. "I saw nothing to suggest a hidden meaning."

"As I said, I don't believe there is one. The overt intention is offensive enough."

"It is provocative," Francis said. "You were wise to suppress it. These strangers are refugees. They're our guests, in a sense. We can't have hotheads assaulting them."

"Indeed not. But in my view, that was not the most disturbing element."

"Wasn't it?" The theme of murdering strangers had dominated the work.

"Perhaps you missed the subtleties," Sir John said. "I perceived a call to atheism and religious dissent."

"Atheism?" Francis skipped past the sneer about subtleties. "I remember one slur against Jews and one or two vague references to counterfeit religion and Spanish gold. I understood that as an attempt to cast the refugees as covert Catholics."

"The word 'Catholic' does not appear in the libel, Mr. Bacon. Not once. Instead, we see advocacy of the sort of violent chaos promoted by the author of the play identified in the signature."

"Tamburlaine," Francis said. "The most popular play of the past five years. The name was obviously chosen to associate the author with that heroic conqueror." Another objection occurred to him. "But the author chose badly. Tamburlaine conquered foreign nations. He didn't rise up against an invading force in his own country."

Sir John glowered at him. "The name points at the author, the notorious atheist Christopher Marlowe. I should think *that* would be obvious." Pink spots flared in his cheeks.

Francis countered the Lord Keeper's heat with cool calm. "I don't believe Marlowe is truly an atheist. He writes provocative plays, but they contain more simple brutality than religious conflict. Sad to say, that's what makes them popular. They pass the censors, I must remind you. They've been performed at court. That's where I've seen them."

Sir John's eyes flashed at the reminder that Francis was a frequent attendant in Her Majesty's court and had been since his youth.

"Marlowe is a known atheist and suborner of atheism," Sir John said, clipping each word through gritted teeth. "The fact that's he's clever enough to fool the censors makes him all the more dangerous. Atheists foment chaos. They're worse than Catholics, who at least submit to some authority. But atheists shake the very foundation of society." Spittle formed on his lips as his speech grew faster and more fervent. "If we allow it to prosper, we'll be drowned in civil disobedience, social breakdown, and utter anarchy. Church and State are one in England, need I remind *you*. Atheism is a crime against the state, the most heinous form of treason."

Francis sat back in his chair, stunned into silence. Now he understood. Sir John had formed his useless commission because he had already determined the author of the libel. He'd twisted the words of the ballad into a call for the destruction of England and cast himself as her sole defender.

Francis found his voice. "With all due respect, Lord Keeper, I must disagree. I saw neither atheism nor treason in that ballad. Violence against strangers, yes. One disturbing charge against the government, yes. The implication that councilmembers are accepting Spanish bribes should be addressed. I also saw a clumsy attempt to implicate Christopher Marlowe — far too clumsy to have been made by so talented a writer."

Sir John grunted. "Talented." He spat the word as if were an insult.

Francis rose, bowed, and took a few steps toward the door. Then another thought struck him. "Atheism is caused by the confusion engendered by a multiplicity of religions. Harsh treatment only increases resistance. The best way to build sound religion in the populace is through example. Calm, consistent practice. Public sermons, for example, heal wounds and foster faith."

The Lord Keeper merely glared at him. He'd spent his wrath and had nothing else.

Francis turned on his heel and left. His advice was too simple for the frothing heretic-hunter behind the desk. Sir

John Puckering could never admit he provoked conflict rather than dispelling it. Francis wondered how genuine that zeal had been. The words had been hot enough, but the fire hadn't quite reached his eyes. They had continued to regard Francis with a measuring gleam, assessing the effect of his performance.

Many councilors and courtiers fought against Catholicism in England. Perhaps Sir John found that field overcrowded. He couldn't compete with the intelligence services of Essex or the Cecils. But he might stand out by devoting himself to the suppression of atheists. Never mind if innocent English playmakers were caught in his indiscriminate net.

Francis nodded his thanks as an usher opened the front doors to allow his exit. At the gatehouse, he glanced back for one last look. How far the Lord Keeper had declined since his father's day! Sir Nicholas had wanted to establish schools for civil servants, believing that education was the key to good government. His father had wanted Francis to use his talents to serve his country. But terrorizing poets didn't feel like service.

He missed his father in so many ways. Had Sir Nicholas lived to usher his youngest son into a suitable position, how different would his life be now? Francis feared he'd made a botch of things, choosing the wrong path at every fork in the road.

He sighed as he prepared to dash across the Strand. He couldn't abandon the search for the libeler, however futile or distasteful. He'd indebted himself to a great man — a pre-eminently great man — and would never be free to choose for himself again.

TEN

Tom waited until Monday morning to visit Bridewell to see Thomas Kyd. The Bacon brothers had argued against his going at all. They said he would accomplish nothing beyond drawing attention to himself. But Kyd's friends couldn't help him. Tom owed it to London's theatergoers to do what he could.

Noting his determination, Anthony had recommended the delay. On Saturday, Bridewell enjoyed a steady stream of visitors who came to watch vagrants and prostitutes receive their weekly whipping. With the theaters closed, there were bound to be more gaping thrill-seekers than usual, making it harder for Tom to make his case.

He dressed in his second-best clothes: black broadcloth with velvet trim, gray silk linings, and fine gray stockings. He tied a purple garter around his thigh and pinned a purple bow to his tallest hat with a silver brooch. Last, he tucked a handkerchief soaked in lavender oil into his pocket as a defense against the prison's noxious odors.

Clothes made the man; everyone said it. This costume proclaimed his standing as an Inns of Court man, which meant connections. Sometimes a mere visit from a well-dressed gentleman could lessen the harshness of a prisoner's treatment.

Guessing that he might be seen arriving, he took a wherry from the Temple Wharf, even though the trip downstream was much shorter than the walk from Gray's to the river. He wanted to make a show of his importance, should anyone happen to notice.

Prisoners saw him through the windows of the old palace. Arms thrust out and faces pressed between the bars to wave and shout at him. At least no one aimed a stream of piss in his direction.

He crossed a yard swept free of every pebble and clod. The front rooms displayed a similar degree of cleanliness, maintained by the inmates as part of their redemption. Tom didn't remember anything about the admitting procedure. He'd been drunk, for one thing, and in a towering rage, for another. The entry hall now seemed less terrible than his patchy memories.

The warden, summoned by a guard at the inner gate, denied Tom access to the lower levels, where Kyd was housed. "He's not receiving visitors at present."

That couldn't be right. Prisoners depended on friends to bring them food and drink. Prison rations could be nigh inedible.

"Why not?" Tom demanded, looking down his nose at the squat man before him.

"Orders," the warden said. His smirking manner bespoke confidence. In this place, his word was law.

Almost. Tom threw his best card on the table. "I'm here on behalf of a Privy Council member who prefers to remain anonymous. He wishes to confirm the information reported as issuing from the said prisoner." He offered a smirk of his own and hoped Anthony would find a way to back him up, if worst came to worst.

The warden glared at him, tongue in cheek, plainly considering his options. Deny this wealthy gentleman and risk offending a privy councilor, or yield and risk censure from whoever had Kyd arrested in the first place. He found a course between those rocky shoals. "You must have some proof. Some token you can show me."

Tom had prepared for this. He'd placed a smudged seal in the dark blue wax favored by the Earl of Essex at the bottom of his copy of the libel. If His Lordship found out, he might be furious. On the other hand, he would be pleased if Tom caught the Dutch Church libeler before any of his rivals. The prospect of success outweighed the risk of discovery.

He pulled out the libel, glanced over his shoulder at the guards to demonstrate his discretion, and displayed it so that only the warden could see. "Would I have a copy of this damnable tract if I weren't privy to the commission investigating it?"

The warden sucked at the fringe of his hoary moustache, then relented with a throaty growl. "Very well. But be quick about it." He pulled a guard aside and spoke to him briefly.

Tom couldn't hear what he said, but got the sense that hasty preparations had to be made before anyone could see the prisoner. He didn't wait long. The guard soon returned to lead him down to the basement.

Here the temper of the palace changed. No one had swept this dark corridor since Great Harry had been alive. The stink of piss and shit and human misery made Tom gag. He pulled out his handkerchief and pressed it over his mouth and nose. The guard sneered at the sign of weakness.

They passed several closed doors with bars set into small windows. Tom caught a glimpse of manacles hanging from a rope running through a pulley set in the ceiling. The room was empty, as far as he could tell, but the echoes of past screams lingered in the air.

Tom's stomach churned. He steeled himself but still let out a cry of pity when the guard let him into Kyd's cell. The chamber held nothing but a reeking heap of straw in one corner and a half-naked wretch in the other. They'd stripped Kyd to his shirt and breeches, leaving him to shiver bare-legged in the chill that rose from the riverbanks even in summer.

"Leave us," Tom told the guard, who shrugged disdainfully.

"Mind your manners, Hieronimo." That was the hero of Kyd's famous *Spanish Tragedy*. The guard gave the wretch a vicious nudge with his booted foot and left.

Tom's heart skipped a fearful beat as the key turned in the lock. He reminded himself that the sons of Sir Nicholas Bacon knew where he was and when he had left their house.

Kyd struggled painfully into a sitting position. He leaned his head against the seeping bricks, breathing as if that mundane effort had cost him what strength he possessed. He'd been here for little more than a week, but he was filthy. His rank odor filled the cell. He sat limply, shoulders folded inward, arms dangling in his lap, huddled into himself like a man in constant pain.

Tom had seen Kyd acting in *The Spanish Tragedy*. He'd played Balthazar, the Viceroy's son, with vigor and verve. He'd looked so gallant, tall and handsome, clothed in blue satin with his brown curls streaming behind him as he leapt and pivoted in a thrilling sword fight. Now the hair hung lank against his hollow cheeks, and straw crusted his beard. He seemed exhausted, almost too weary to turn his defeated gaze toward Tom.

"Who are you?" he rasped.

"You don't know me." Tom squatted beside him. There wasn't so much as a rough stool to sit on. "I'm Thomas Clarady, a member of Gray's Inn. I'm investigating the Dutch Church libel. Thomas Nashe told me you'd been arrested for it. He doesn't believe you wrote it, and neither do I. Can you think of any reason for your arrest?"

"Reason?" Kyd coughed a painful laugh. "They don't need a reason. Someone informed on me. I don't know who."

"He must hate you to do this. A hate that strong must have a cause or at least an origin. Can you think of anyone you've offended or obstructed?"

"A rival playmaker, you mean? We don't do this to each other." Kyd tried to sit up a little more but couldn't support his weight with his hands enough to push. Tom rose, then bent to help him. Kyd cried out at the pressure under his armpits.

He'd been hung in the manacles, by the nature of his pain. Tom had seen a woodcut illustration of that torture on a ballad once. They locked your wrists into the iron rings and tied weights around your feet. Then they cranked the pulley to haul you up a few inches above the floor. The height didn't matter. The weight of your body and the blocks under your feet gradually pulled your shoulders out of their sockets. It was like the racks in the Tower, only cheaper and more portable.

Tom squatted on his heels again. "Who signed the warrant, do you know?"

"Lord Puckering," Kyd said. "They came to my lodgings. I didn't think they wanted me at first. They kept asking where Marlowe was. They searched the room, tossing papers on the floor, spilling ink, crushing quills. They made a mess. It's still there, I suppose, waiting for me — if they ever let me out."

"What were they looking for?"

Kyd puffed out a sour breath. "Evidence of Marlowe's atheist conspiracy."

"No such thing. Kit doesn't conspire with anyone about anything."

Kyd's black eyebrows lifted in the shrug his ruined shoulders couldn't make. "Maybe not, but he's uttered some vile blasphemies. Too loudly and too often. If he isn't an atheist, he does a good job of pretending. He lodged with me for a while, you know. I had to listen to his scoffing every blessed day. He enjoyed taunting me, jabbing at my faith. I'm a good Christian, I tell you. I hated his noise, but I had no control over him."

His voice took on a plaintive rhythm. He'd probably said those words again and again, pleading for mercy.

This wasn't the time to argue in Marlowe's favor. He could be cruel, in certain moods, tossing shrewd taunts like darts at your tenderest beliefs. He could also be generous and kind. For the most part, his better angels won out over the angry ones.

"Did they find anything incriminating?" Tom asked.

"I don't know if they found it or brought it with them, but yes. A copy of an Arian heresy. It wasn't mine. Kit left a pile of papers I'd been using for drafts. Paper's expensive, you know."

Tom nodded. He'd ask the Bacons what an Arian heresy was. It sounded bad. Such a thing could have been Kit's. He read widely concerning religion, filling his head with ideas for his plays. Possessing a tract didn't mean he believed its argument. "Why arrest you if it's Kit they're after? It doesn't make sense."

"I stopped looking for sense around the time my shoulders popped. It's hard to think when you're howling in agony."

Tom grunted. What could he say? He vowed to have this man released if he had to fight his way into the Earl of Essex's library and beg the lord on hands and knees to intervene.

"Who's questioning you?" It couldn't be the Lord Keeper himself.

"They don't introduce themselves," Kyd said. "One's a gentleman, by his clothes and speech. The other's a monster, by the pleasure he takes from my screams."

Tom heard shame and terror in that confession. He forced himself not to look away. The least he could do was listen and let the man know he'd been heard.

"They mentioned a churl named Cholmeley," Kyd said. "They asked me how long I'd known him. I've never heard of the man. They must not have cared much because they let it drop. I'm not sure they care about any of it anymore."

Kyd coughed, and Tom looked about for a jug of water. Of course, there wasn't one. He kicked himself for not bringing a bottle of wine.

Kyd sagged into himself with a soft groan and rested for a moment. Then he tilted his head to look up at Tom from under a lock of filthy hair "You start out thinking you have pride. You have substance. You're a man of honor. Then they go to work, and in a matter of minutes — so few minutes — you're telling them everything you know, babbling like an idiot. You start making things up, trying to guess what they want to hear. Mostly, these men want to hear about Marlowe. Warn him, won't you? If he's in town, he should scuddle."

"He's in Kent, avoiding the plague at a friend's house. He's safe enough, I hope."

Kyd nodded. His head sank down again. "I'd like to lie down, but I'm not sure I can manage it."

Tom gently laid him flat on the hard floor. "I'm going out, but I'll be back."

Kyd gave a breathy grunt, whether agreeing or disbelieving, Tom couldn't tell.

He banged on the door, which opened promptly, to his relief. "I'm coming back," he told the guard. He said it again to the guards upstairs. They offered no argument, and he didn't wait for the warden. He strode out of the palace grounds as swiftly as he could, breaking into a jog as he reached Fleet Street. He fairly ran past St. Paul's and up to Cheapside, jumping and twisting through the plodding throng, ignoring the curses hurled at his back. He veered onto Bucklersbury and slowed his pace, looking for the sign with the blooming mugwort that marked the shop of Mr. Bacon's favorite apothecary.

Tom breathed deeply as he entered the shop, filling his lungs with the wholesome scents of medicinal herbs and tangy oils. He'd have to rub himself raw with warm towels tonight to rid his skin of prison stink.

"Is he out of it already?" Henrik Verboom, the apothecary, asked. Tom had been coming in every week for the past six years to pick up Mr. Bacon's supply of theriac, the opium-laced concoction he stirred into a cup of wine every night before bed.

"It's not for Mr. Bacon. I need something for aching joints. Something strong."

Verboom grinned. "What have you been doing to yourself, Mr. Clarady? Too much dancing?"

"It's not for me either." Tom leaned an elbow on the counter and lowered his voice nearly to a whisper. "It's for a friend in Bridewell."

The apothecary frowned. "I see." He turned around to study his crowded shelves, humming as he moved slowly along. "Ah, this should help." He chose a fat jar with a canvas lid tied with twine.

Tom picked it up and gave it sniff. "Smells like garlic."

"Mm-hmm. Also bishopwort and wormwood. But you don't need the recipe. Is there anything else?"

"Some poppy juice would help, wouldn't it? The man's in pain. Do you have any mixed in wine already?"

"Of course." Verboom brought out a good-sized bottle. "Two good swallows, twice a day. No more, mind."

"I don't know how long he can hang on to that bottle, but we'll hope for the best. Can you add these to Mr. Bacon's bill?"

"Why not?" Verboom sounded resigned. Who knew when that bill would be paid?

Tom hated being in debt, unlike most men in his position. But he'd been reared by a ship's captain, not a lord. He knew the value of money. "I'll pay for it by the end of the week," he promised, then sped out of the shop.

He stopped at a stall on the way back to buy meat pies and a pail of beer with a cheap wooden cup. He wasn't sure how much Kyd could stomach, but he hoped he'd be allowed to take his time with the provisions.

Tom gave each guard one precious shilling to encourage leniency on that score. "I'll know if you cheat me," he warned them. "And so will my master on the council. This man wasn't meant to be treated so harshly."

"We just do what they tell us," one guard answered.

"Said every brute everywhere to excuse his brutality," Tom muttered as he walked away, half hoping he'd be heard.

Tom made Kyd drink two swallows of poppy wine, then gave him a pie to nibble on while he rubbed ointment into the bruised chest and shoulders. Kyd moaned with gratitude at the soothing touch. The clean scent of healing herbs overcame the stench of soiled straw.

The playmaker managed to get down a third of his pie, chewing each bite slowly. He set it in his lap for a short break and asked, "Why are you doing this?"

"How can I not?" Tom answered. "I loved *The Spanish Tragedy*. I've seen it four times."

Kyd laughed, groaning at the pain it caused. "You'll never pay the entrance fee again, I can promise you that."

Tom grinned and handed him a cup of beer. "Try that now."

Kyd took a sip and sighed with pleasure. "You're a good man, Thomas Clarady. But take heed. They've done this to me for nothing. You're asking questions, the wrong kind. You're telling lies too, I'll wager, to get in here with all this stuff."

"Not big ones." Tom chuckled, but Kyd reached for his hand and gripped it with surprising force.

"Listen to me! I'm doing you a favor. You may think you're safe, but they've racked gentlemen before, plenty of them. Informers are everywhere, posing as anything, willing to sell anyone for a few shillings. They call themselves intelligencers, but they don't care what's true and what's not. Cross the wrong spy, and you'll end up here. And then may God have mercy on you — because no one else will."

ELEVEN

"Sounds good." Stephen strolled into the music room to stand beside the table where Trumpet played the virginals. She'd had the beautifully painted instrument placed on a sturdy table covered with a Turkey carpet to quell the vibrations. "That piece is a good choice. Sprightly, but not giddy, with a sweet pastoral quality. Very suitable for Nonsuch, I should think."

Trumpet had chosen "Will You Walk the Woods so Wild" by William Byrd from her collection of twenty-three pieces by the popular composer. Stephen had commissioned the book for her twenty-third birthday in April. She hoped to play for the queen during her upcoming month at court. She'd bring the book too, in case Her Majesty asked for another, but this would be her centerpiece.

Her Majesty expected her courtiers to cultivate all the arts. A successful performance would enhance Trumpet's standing and earn a valuable modicum of warm regard. That, in turn, would ease her approach in the Privy Chamber, when she wanted to drop a word in favor of her husband or some petitioner. Neither she nor Stephen had petitioners as yet, but they would as their influence grew. The music, the patronage, the service in the queen's privy chambers were all part of her plan to transform herself into a Woman of Influence.

Trumpet had begun her music lessons as a means to an end, then surprised herself by enjoying them. She loved the dexterity and the enchanting sounds produced by her touch. She'd bought this fine instrument the day after she and Stephen had returned to London as lord and lady. When they acquired this house, they created a handsome music room in one of the ground floor reception chambers. Stephen's lute had its own carpet-draped table, while two others of different sizes hung on the wall for guests. An assortment of recorders stood ready too, though neither she nor Stephen had much skill with wind instruments.

They often played together in the evening while Baby William gurgled in his nurse's lap. Trumpet had never once imagined, in all her visions of the future, that she would enjoy such simple domestic contentments. And yet she did.

"When are you leaving?" she asked her husband. Stephen was taking the baby home to Dorset to avoid the plague. The queen wanted her subjects to produce heirs, but she didn't care to meet the offspring until they were old enough to converse politely.

"First thing in the morning. We'll take two days to get to Rye." Stephen pulled up a chair for a comfortable chat. "I'll be glad to get home. We've been back from France for months, but I'm still tired. I don't know why. I need to gallop across the downs and taste the sea breeze."

"It's William," Trumpet said. "He makes you want to revisit your childhood, to show him the things you loved when you were a boy."

Stephen laughed, light dancing in his tawny eyes. His aristocratic face was a shade too angular for classical male beauty, but laughter erased his habitual petulance. "That's true, isn't it? But he won't remember any of it for years yet."

"He might." Trumpet smiled at him with a fondness that had sprouted and grown over the two years of their alliance. Another surprise.

She'd been disgusted when the Delaberes' offer turned out to be the best of her few proposals. She'd known Stephen, though he hadn't known her. They'd studied the law together during her year at Gray's disguised as a boy. She'd gone by the name "Allen Trumpington" then. She, Tom, Benjamin Whitt, and Stephen had been inseparable until Tom and Stephen quarreled bitterly enough to break their friendship. Stephen had moved out of Gray's, throwing in with some other young noblemen at loose ends in the capital.

Those few months had left Trumpet with the firm opinion that her future husband was a pusillanimous oaf. An artless dewberry. A brabbling coxcomb with a brittle sense of self-regard and an interest in nothing but clothes.

She had not been wrong back then, but Stephen had grown up after his father's death. The late Lord Dorchester had been the severest sort of Puritan, keeping his oldest son pressed firmly under his thumb. When his relentless criticism was removed, Stephen expanded like a topsail filled by a fresh wind.

Seeking a new model, he'd followed the Earl of Essex to France. The earl, a wise employer of men, had recognized Stephen's gift for commodities and put him in charge of organizing provisions for the troops. By all accounts, he'd done a creditable job with limited resources. Being accepted in Essex's circle and becoming a friend of King Henri had given Stephen still more confidence, which made him less suspicious and less petty. He could be quite good company if nobody crossed him.

Trumpet would never love anyone but Tom — a truth as immutable as the stars in heaven. Stephen didn't love her either, not in that way, which made things easier. He had his mistresses, even in Dorset. He'd learned that habit from Essex too. But love had little to do with marriage. Lord and Lady Dorchester had formed a fruitful partnership, working together toward their mutual gain.

"Will you manage a whole month at court, do you think?" Stephen asked her.

"I'll do my best. I will miss the baby — and you, of course."

He let that pass with a smile. "We don't want her to forget about us."

"Never fear, my lord. I shall carry our standard high. I have the music. And now, thanks to my new tutor, I can hold up my end of a conversation about Tacitus or Plautus."

"Ugh! Better you than me." Stephen read as little as possible. He liked owning a well-stocked library because Essex had one. Essex, however, read his books.

Stephen licked his thin lips, a sign that he had something unpleasant to say. "About your tutor, Alice. I believe you should set him aside. You're leaving for Nonsuch in a few days. You can use that as an excuse."

"I hadn't planned on bringing him with me." Trumpet played a few chords. "What's your objection?"

"I've been hearing things about Christopher Marlowe. Disturbing things. They say he's an atheist who keeps a school for atheists."

"Nonsense." Trumpet slid her fingers off the ivory keys and turned on her short bench to face him. "He's a playmaker who loves an audience. He says outrageous things to provoke people."

Stephen shrugged, an elegant gesture in his dark orange velvet doublet. "They say rumors are only ever half-true. But the other half is still bad, isn't it? You don't want a tutor suspected of converting atheists."

"You should meet such gossip with a stern frown of disbelief." She modeled it for him.

He imitated the expression, then nodded. "That's what Essex does."

"Well, there you are." Trumpet turned back to her instrument and played another line. She stopped abruptly and turned back to her husband. "Marlowe is not an atheist. People must stop saying it. His plays pass the censors, remember, so they can't be seditious or blasphemous."

"I suppose not," Stephen said, "but there must be other tutors. Someone tamer, less likely to draw criticism."

And there was the rub. "If he's too tame, he won't add luster to our dinners. Patronage is an essential aspect of power, as we have discussed. I intend to cultivate a circle of the wittiest poets and philosophers in London. They'll impress our noble guests with our culture and learning. They can't do that if they're as mild as milksops."

"Must we really do that? I'm not sure I want to talk to poets and philosophers. What will I say?"

"You don't have to say anything. They do all the work. They know they've been invited to entertain the lords. Marlowe is the wittiest man alive. He'll stimulate lively discussions around *our* table which people will talk about for days."

The clock Stephen had brought back from Nuremberg chimed the hour.

"He'll be here in a minute," Trumpet said. "Ask him if he's an atheist, if you're so worried about it."

Stephen blanched at the suggestion. "He wouldn't answer me. Not truthfully."

"He won't mind." Trumpet cocked her head at him. "It would be good practice for you. A man of influence — a powerful lord — can ask anyone anything."

Stephen's eyes met hers, holding her gaze as if borrowing courage. Then he smiled. "I could make it sound as though I'm merely interested in his plays. I did love *Tamburlaine*."

"*Tamburlaine* is glorious," Trumpet said. "And just think — we could have its author regaling our friends at dinner."

Marlowe followed a servant into the room. His gaze went to her first as he offered a short bow. "Good morrow, my lady." Then he noticed Stephen sitting beside the virginals. "Lord Dorchester." He swept off his short-crowned hat and bowed deeply over a well-formed leg.

Stephen nodded, pleased. "Mr. Marlowe. Welcome."

"Thank you, my lord." Kit cast his gaze around the music room, letting his admiration show. "This is a beautiful room. Do you play all these instruments, my lord?"

"Oh no. My lady wife plays the virginals. I play the lute."

"A courtly art." Kit nodded, as if confirming something he'd long suspected. He continued to flatter Stephen with considerable artistry, to Trumpet's amusement. She hadn't realized Kit was so skilled at the art of pleasing prickle-tempered noblemen. But then Marlowe was a man of parts — parts which he usually kept well separated. He must have met many noblemen of a range of humors in the course of his confidential travels.

Stephen raised his eyebrows at Trumpet meaningfully. He wanted her to provide an opportunity for him to ask his burning question.

"We'll have our lesson in the library, Mr. Marlowe," Trumpet said, "but come sit for a moment. I'll play you a tune."

"Thank you, my lady." Kit found the humblest stool in the chamber and drew it up to a carefully calibrated spot between Trumpet and Stephen. He adopted the expression of a man ready to be delighted.

Trumpet bent to her music. His genuine smile when she finished was all the praise she needed.

"Well played, my lady," he said. "Will you perform that piece at court next week?"

"I hope so." She gave Stephen a now-or-never look.

He cleared his throat. "There is one thing I wanted to ask you, Mr. Marlowe. Things I've heard. Rumors about . . . you know." He cleared his throat again.

The sparkle in Kit's eyes went out. "You want to know if I'm an atheist."

"Well, yes." Stephen squared his jaw. Given the narrow point of his dark blond beard, the gesture gave him a goatish look. "Are you?"

"No, my lord. I consider myself a gadfly, like Socrates."

Stephen frowned. "Is he the Roman poet who wrote sonnets about death?"

Kit blinked at him, momentarily at a loss. "Ah. No, my lord. I believe that was Seneca. Socrates was the Greek philosopher who asked questions to make people to think about their beliefs instead of merely repeating commonplaces."

"Socrates," Trumpet said. "Isn't he the one who was executed by the state for stirring up doubts about the established religion?"

Kit gave her a wry smile. "Perhaps not the best analogy under the circumstances."

The servant reappeared at the door. "Mr. Clarady requests an audience with His Lordship."

"An *audience*." Stephen gave Trumpet a mocking frown, pretending to be impressed with his own importance. In truth, he loved these formal touches. Tom must want a favor to start the flattery before even entering the room. "By all means, show him in."

Tom strode in, tall and handsome as ever. He claimed to hate the endless black his guardian imposed on him, but it brought out the gold in his hair and the blue in his eyes. The sad color proclaimed his professional status while details like the translucent cambric of his ruffs and the pewter buttons running down his chest spoke of money. He looked every inch the Inns of Court man.

Stephen rose to clap him on the shoulder. Kit leapt up as soon as Stephen started to rise, backing out of the earl's sight to grin impishly at Tom.

"Mr. Marlowe," Tom said. "I'm glad you're here. I have bad news, I'm afraid. Terrible news. A villainous miscarriage of justice I'm hoping you can remedy, my lord."

"Me?" Stephen sat heavily back in his chair.

"Is this about Kyd?" Kit asked.

"You've heard, then."

"Only that he was arrested. What's happened?"

"Sit, please, everyone," Trumpet said. She didn't want to listen to bad news on her feet. She bade the servant to bring them some wine.

The servant moved chairs into a semicircle facing the virginals. She waited while he turned her short bench toward the circle, then shifted her skirts to bring them around. Tom and Kit waited for her to settle before taking their seats. The servant left to fetch the refreshments.

Stephen asked, "Who is Kyd?"

"Thomas Kyd," Tom answered. "A playmaker. He wrote *The Spanish Tragedy*."

"Oh, I love that play!" Stephen's eyes lit up. "Do you know, I saw it in French in Henri's court."

Kit smiled at him, then asked Tom, "Where did they take him?"

"Bridewell." That answer brought a crease to Kit's brow.

"Has he been —"

"Yes." Tom finished the sentence for Stephen's benefit. "He's been hung in the manacles, my lord. I saw him last night. He's in horrible pain, truly wretched. He's in a filthy cell with no water or rags to cover himself. I came to beg you to use your influence to make them release them."

"*My* influence!" Stephen looked aghast. "I've never done anything like that."

"I think you could," Tom said. "I hope you will."

"Why was he arrested?" Trumpet asked.

Tom shrugged. "The warrant came from the Lord Keeper's commission about the Dutch Church libel."

"What's that?" Stephen asked, sounding more fearful than curious.

Tom explained it to him. "It's signed 'Tamburlaine,' which is why they went looking for Mr. Marlowe."

"Well, that's just stupid, isn't it?" Stephen perked up a little. Trumpet beamed encouragement at him. "Anyone might sign anything that way to make themselves look grand."

"That's right, my lord." Tom pointed a finger at him, nodding as if he'd plumbed the depths of a complex riddle. "They knocked at Marlowe's old lodgings and found Kyd. They searched the place and found some damning documents and decided to arrest the man they had."

"What damning documents?" Trumpet cast a worried frown at Kit. He'd followed the conversation with acute interest but said nothing as yet.

"An Arian tract," Tom said, "whatever that is."

Kit answered, "It's a non-Trinitarian heresy." When Stephen's face darkened, Kit added, "A finely split theological hair, my lord. Arians believe that Jesus is the Son of God and also a holy God, but that the Son and the Father are separate beings. We English believe that the Son and the Father are aspects of a single being." He gave a self-effacing shrug. "I wanted blasphemies for my *Jew of Malta*. I never looked at that tract again. I left a pile of such trash with Kyd. He writes so many drafts that he goes through mountains of paper. I thought he might be able to use the back side."

"I knew it must be something like that," Tom said.

"Poor Kyd," Kit said. "It's horrible to think he's been tortured on my account. His religious views are as conventional as anyone could wish."

"The way you describe it," Stephen said to Tom, "that libel doesn't have much religion in it. Maybe Kyd has spoken out against strangers."

Kit said, "I doubt that, my lord. He has little interest in politics. And his father's a scrivener. His trade is not affected by the newcomers."

"They didn't even ask him about the libel." Tom's eyes flashed with anger. "He said they mainly asked about you, Marlowe."

"Why?" Trumpet asked. "On account of that signature?"

"That's only the excuse," Kit said. He leaned back in his chair like a man preparing to answer a great many questions. "I've become a subject of interest to the Privy Council."

"What? When?" Trumpet demanded.

"Yesterday. I was arrested in Scadbury by a courteous gentleman named Henry Maunder. He brought me to Whitehall to be interviewed by the Council."

"Not to jail, thank God," Tom said.

"Those were my very words." Kit shot a glance at Stephen. "Another proof for you, my lord. If they thought I was a danger to the state, they would've put me in prison."

"What did they want?" Stephen seemed calmer now that he'd successfully criticized an official act. He basked in the approval of these two comely and intelligent men who deferred to him at every turn. He always bloomed a little in Tom's company. Their youthful quarrel had long been set aside. They weren't friends, in the sense of men who went hunting or wenching together, but they knew each other with the depth of childhood familiarity. Stephen trusted Tom, and Tom understood Stephen.

Kit said, "They asked me the same question you did, my lord, only at greater length. Someone had found some actors' copies of my plays, so we walked through several lines that concerned them. All very civil. They let me go after a couple of hours. I'm to present myself every morning until further notice, but there was no talk of prison, to say nothing of" — he swallowed — "manacles." The sour twist of his lips betrayed the dread that word aroused.

Trumpet shivered. "I beg you to be careful, Mr. Marlowe."

"I am on my best behavior, my lady." Kit sounded as if he meant it, all trace of irony gone.

She met his gaze for a moment, thinking, then said, "You must flee. The risk is too great. Why don't you go to Dorset with my lord husband? He's leaving in the morning. You could meet the council one more time and be halfway to the coast before they miss you on Wednesday."

Kit and Stephen gaped at one another with identical expressions of alarm. Trumpet nearly laughed out loud. Their distress at the thought of spending the summer together far outweighed any concern for Kit's well-being.

Stephen, trained in courtesy from infancy, spoke first. "You would be most welcome, Mr. Marlowe, although I imagine you must have work or —"

"Work, yes," Kit said. "Endless, boring work. I'm locked in my room all day. I'd be a terrible companion for an active man such as Your Lordship."

Stephen wasn't listening. He'd found another path. "I fear we're hopelessly rusticated at Badbury House." This was a splendid mansion built in Great Henry's time, with every modern convenience. "And do you know, it's most awfully windy there."

"Oh, wind." Kit frowned with great seriousness. "Wind is a great problem for me, my lord, though I hate to mention it. I grew up in Canterbury, you see, a walled city in which there is very little wind, as a rule."

"It is windy on the downs," Tom chimed in. "A man can scarcely keep his hat on." He shot Trumpet one swift wink. It felt like a touch, though they sat six feet apart.

Tomorrow, the touch would be real. Stephen would ride off in the morning with the baby and an entourage of servants. A few would be left behind to close up the house when Trumpet moved to Nonsuch, but not many, and mostly hers. She wouldn't leave until Friday, waiting for the delivery of a coat of arms she'd ordered for the great hall. She and Tom would have three nights together — three bliss-filled, uninterrupted nights.

She had a new chemise of gossamer silk and new sheets of the supplest linen. She'd been preparing for these three nights for weeks. Now that the moment had almost come, she could hardly contain herself. She wanted to push Stephen and Kit out the door, lock it behind them, and ravage Tom right there on the rush matting.

The babble about the windy downs subsided. Kit leaned toward her with hands clasped in supplication. "I'm in no danger, my lady, I assure you. I'm quite safe with my friend at Scadbury. And in truth, the council seems to mean me no harm. They didn't even bother with me this morning. I waited on a bench for two hours without a summons. That may be all they want — to remind me that I am subject to their will."

"Let's hope so," Tom said.

Stephen offered a friendly smile. "We'll miss you in Dorset, Mr. Marlowe, but I'm sure you know what's best for yourself." They nodded at one another with evident relief. Some subtle bond had formed from their mutual desire not to spend time together.

"But we must help Kyd," Tom said. "We can't leave him in that hell. I don't think he has anyone else to speak for him. I promised I'd do what I could."

"I wish I could help," Kit said, speaking to Stephen. "He's a decent man and one of our greatest playmakers. It would be a grievous loss if he suffered lasting harm."

Tom met Stephen's eyes with a bleak expression. "You should've seen the poor knave, Steenie. Shivering, broken, lying in his own filth. It'd break your heart."

Stephen's brows furled. Imagining the playmaker's plight? Or annoyed at the boyhood nickname? Trumpet crossed her fingers, hidden in the folds of her skirt, willing her husband to take the higher road.

True to form, he found a by lane. "Why me? Why not ask Mr. Bacon?"

"I did," Tom said. "First thing. But he isn't high enough to overtop a Lord Keeper."

Stephen smiled at that.

Kit pressed the point. "Peers of the realm like yourself, my lord, are topped only by the queen. A mere functionary like the warden of Bridewell wouldn't dare to ignore a request from the Earl of Dorchester."

"It's not uncommon for peers to intervene in such matters," Tom added. "That's one of their vital functions in the workings of English justice — righting wrongs created by the misapplication of the law."

Stephen's thin lips disappeared as his chin jutted forward. He didn't like to be pushed.

But he rather liked to be begged. Trumpet left her bench to kneel before him, taking his hand in both of hers. "This is the perfect opportunity, my lord. That first step we've been waiting for. This is a chance for you to reach out and show your power. I doubt not that the mere sight of your seal — nay, the mere mention of your title — will have that grubby little warden scrambling to do your bidding. He'll carry poor Thomas Kyd out on his own back, huffing and puffing in his haste!"

Stephen laughed at the image she'd conjured. "If he doesn't, I shall have him whipped." Then he sobered and turned to Tom. "Should I go myself? Or will you go with me?"

Tom frowned, pretending to think about it. "I should hate for you to be kept waiting, my lord, if the churl isn't there at the moment we arrive. A letter would perhaps be a better instrument."

"An instrument." Stephen tasted the word and liked the flavor. "What would I write?"

Tom pulled a sheet of paper from his sleeve and opened it with a flourish. Trumpet sat back on her bench, fussing with her skirts to hide her admiration for her lover.

"Hoping for the best, my lord, and not wanting to waste your valuable time, I asked Anthony Bacon to draft a sample."

Stephen took it, read it, and smiled. "I can do this." He nodded at Kit. "Fear not, Mr. Marlowe. Your friend will be a free man again soon. In fact" — now he pointed a finger at Trumpet — "I shall delay my journey until he is safe at home with no further charges hanging over him." He grinned at her, sharing this first step toward influence.

Trumpet cast one fleeting glance of disappointment at Tom, then summoned up a smile to reward her husband for his newfound determination.

TWELVE

Francis gazed out his study window at the sky. He marveled at the shade of blue, always so much more pure after a week of drenching rain. Did it seem bluer in contrast to the days of gray, or did storms wash away some obfuscation that dimmed the essential color?

He shook that thought away and returned to his law book, dipping his quill preparatory to adding to his notes. Pinnock flung open the door with his usual superabundance of energy, waving a sheaf of paper. "Mr. Anthony wants you to read these and then come down to discuss them with him. They're from His Lordship."

In this house, that title given without a name always indicated the Earl of Essex.

Francis sighed and returned his quill to its holder. "Now what?" He accepted the papers and gave them a quick glance. The covering note from His Lordship's secretary identified them as documents presented to the Privy Council as evidence against Christopher Marlowe on charges of atheism.

"God's mercy." Francis sighed. How had the playmaker become the focus of such scrutiny?

The first pair of pages contained a list of blasphemies attributed to Marlowe. But Francis recognized most of them as commonplace barbs thrown at the Christian religion, such as the claim that Christ was a bastard and his mother an adulteress. Undergraduate stuff — daring for a seventeen-year-old; tiresome for wiser heads. While true on a certain crude level, it missed the whole point of the miracle.

The third page, titled "Remembrances," had little to do with Marlowe apart from two or three damning sentences. Most of the short paragraphs contained rants about prominent men, including Sir Francis Drake and the Lord Treasurer. The first one claimed the Privy Council consisted wholly of atheists and Machiavellians. That would make it difficult for Marlowe to stand out, one would imagine. Or that he was being persecuted by his peers.

What could Essex expect him to say about such vicious nonsense?

Francis stacked the pages with a rap on the desk, then went downstairs to his brother's room. He waved the sheaf at him. "What in the name of all that's holy are we to make of these? His Lordship can recognize lunacy as easily as we can."

"He doesn't have time to read everything closely. That's our job." Anthony set his quill in its holder — silver, as opposed to Francis's brass one — and rose from his desk. He gripped his ebony cane, rose, and paused. It always took a while for his legs to steady when he'd been sitting too long. Then he hobbled over to his armchair near the hearth as Francis took his own chair.

"Where do they come from?" Francis asked.

"Ultimately, from the queen's command to root out dissension by pursuing Catholics and atheists."

Francis shrugged that off. Hearing about the queen's opinions still wounded him. "I meant, how did the council come by these particular documents?"

Jacques pressed a cup of wine into his hand. Francis accepted it with a small smile. He loved the spicy perfume and the warmth of the drink, but today the refreshment felt like a bribe. Anthony didn't need his help to analyze these pages of drivel. He just wanted to ensure Francis's compliance with their lord's will.

If Anthony noticed the ill humor, he ignored it. "The one titled 'Baines Note' was submitted to the council by its author. An informant elicited the one titled 'Remembrances,' presumably in some jail. That's the usual place to seek confessions and names of accomplices."

"A common enough activity for intelligencers." Francis had a low opinion of that trade, on the whole. Some spies were gentlemen of knowledge and wit, but most were a mere step above the ruffian, whatever their education.

Anthony clucked his tongue but made no other response to that tired observation. "Both were solicited as part of the investigation of Christopher Marlowe. The *Baines Note* claims to be a list of direct quote. Shall we start with that?"

Francis raised one shoulder to signal his acquiescence — all the enthusiasm he could muster for the task. "It's signed 'Richard Baines.' Why does that name sound familiar?"

"You may have seen it in my reports over the years. He was one of Walsingham's men. Sir Francis recruited him from Cambridge and sent him to infiltrate the Catholic school at Rheims — oh, some twenty years ago. His job was to sow dissatisfaction among the English students, to draw them away. The master caught him and imprisoned him. He may have been tortured. The whole affair made him notorious in intelligence circles. I thought he had retired to a rectory somewhere."

"Evidently, he is still at work." Francis sipped his drink. "How did he come to write down so much of Marlowe's discourse? If that's what this is."

"I don't know," Anthony said. "His Lordship's secretary didn't elaborate on the source. I assume he heard the playmaker holding forth in some tavern. I don't even know who Baines works for now."

"Someone who considers Marlowe a greater threat than famine or plague."

Anthony gave him a weary look from under his dark eyebrows. "I agree it's an absurd use of official time and money. But I don't make those decisions, and neither do you. Dissension causes harm, as you very well know. Do you have nothing of substance to say about this *Note*?"

Francis sighed. "I've heard most of these blasphemies before. Baines probably picked them up in an alehouse near the university. Like this: 'That the apostles were fishermen and base fellows of neither wit nor worth.' I've heard that one here, from young gentlemen preening themselves about their position in society."

Anthony laughed. "Heaven forfend that we should learn anything from those beneath us! I've heard the one about St. John being Christ's bedfellow too — though perhaps that was in France. But some parts sound particular to Marlowe, from what I've heard of the man. Like this one: 'All those who love not tobacco and boys are fools.'"

"Which has nothing to do with religion," Francis noted. "It sounds like a man trying desperately to be shocking."

"Doesn't it? Who could take any of this seriously? How do you like the suggestion that the holy sacrament might better be administered in a tobacco pipe?"

"Now that is an original thought." Francis granted it a chuckle. "Had Christ been born in Virginia rather than Jerusalem, perhaps it might have been. It isn't blasphemy *per se*, though it's plainly meant to be shocking."

Anthony nodded. "It suggests to me that the original audience might have included Sir Walter Ralegh. Tobacco is his gift to England, after all. And Marlowe is known to be part of his circle." Anthony pointed a long finger.

"Ralegh could be the real target of this investigation, come to think of it."

"If so," Francis said, "the aim is poor. If you want to attack Sir Walter, why strike at a playmaker? Sir Walter does love to debate religion, though he's no atheist, and he's certainly not an enemy of the state."

"He's difficult to attack directly. Even when out of favor, he enjoys the queen's protection." Anthony tapped his finger on his desk, then shook his head. "Well, so much for the *Baines Note*. What shall we tell His Lordship?"

"That's it's blasphemy twice warmed-over. It should be burned and forgotten. But of course you spymasters must leap about pointing fingers at imaginary provocateurs."

"Frank." Anthony clucked his tongue. "Do you want to help or don't you?"

"I don't. It's absurd. These rude rantings are beneath us both." He grumbled in his throat and added, "But when our master calls, we must obey."

"Yes, we must. Hopefully, with more grace when you see him next."

Francis took a long drink of wine, struggling with his grievances. Then he said in a conciliatory tone, "My lord will find the notion of using tobacco as a sacrament amusing and recognize the rest as mundane. What about the other document?"

"The *Remembrances*." Anthony cast his eyes down the third page. "This one is far less coherent in both style and substance."

"*Remembrances against Richard Cholmeley*," Francis corrected. "Why against? And who is he?"

"I looked through my records and found enough bits and pieces to put together a sketch. He's the son of a Cheshire gentleman with connections to Lord Strange. Various members of the Privy Council have employed him from time to time to apprehend Catholics. He abused that position. Apparently, he would threaten his target, solicit a bribe to turn a blind eye, and then surrender him to the authorities anyway."

"Betraying both sides, then." Francis blew out a disgusted breath.

Anthony nodded. "He also informs on other informers. He's utterly corrupt. Even the compiler of these so-called *Remembrances* describes him as a loudmouth and a libeler."

"A libeler?" Francis quirked an eyebrow. "Could he be the libeler of current interest?"

"I wonder. If so, someone paid him to write it. Men like Cholmeley have no political views. I don't believe these *Remembrances* are genuine in the sense of true opinions or beliefs. Like Marlowe, perhaps, he's merely trying to be shocking." Anthony's eyes glittered with amusement. "You must have noticed the part about Cousin Robert."

"Indeed I did. He claims Sir Robert Cecil gave him a book to use to write verses praising Catholic priests, presumably to draw them out so they could be arrested." Francis shook his head. "I don't know how you and Robert can stand to work with these men. Or why you consider their results worth recording."

"A farmer casts a hundred seeds hoping ten will bear fruit."

Francis laughed. "We must pray for a better yield than that lest we all starve!"

"The minds of men are more difficult to cultivate." Anthony's flat gaze said he found the dispute tedious. And in fairness, intelligencers had uncovered grave threats to the crown and worked to forestall them.

"In any event," Francis said, "these *Remembrances* barely mention Marlowe. But here again, the poet and his alleged atheism are coupled with Sir Walter Ralegh. Cholmeley says Marlowe read 'the atheist lecture' to Sir Walter."

"Both documents link Marlowe to Ralegh," Anthony said. "Our Lord of Essex might welcome that connection if it helps discredit a rival."

"Perhaps, but that shouldn't be encouraged." Francis shook his head. "I don't like this solicitation of treasonous bombast, Anthony. It's too much like tricking men into putting a noose around their own necks."

"Their necks must be in the vicinity of treason to be hooked though, mustn't they?

"Like Thomas Kyd? All he did was share a room with a fellow poet. The Lord Keeper, if he's the one who solicited these documents, is overstepping the bounds of reason and justice." Francis paused, remember the spittle on Puckering's fervid lips. "Furthermore, Kyd has no connection with Sir Walter. His torture can only have been meant to frighten Marlowe's other friends into speaking against him."

Anthony nodded slowly. "I think you're right. Our Lord of Essex should be warned about Puckering's overreach. Dissension is harmful, as we all agree, but it can't be suppressed by terrifying the people."

Francis smiled at the small victory. He'd been advocating that position from the start. He returned to an earlier topic. "Do you think Robert could have hired this Cholmeley to write the Dutch Church libel?"

"Oh, isn't that a tantalizing thought?" Anthony sat back in his chair, rubbing his long hands together. "*Could* he have? Certainly. He and his father have solicited pamphlets and ballads to influence public opinion before. But I doubt he had this done. If anyone had read the thing, or God forbid, made copies and distributed them, it could have caused a riot. No Cecil would risk chaos on English soil."

"Agreed. But now I'm thinking someone did. There is a curious sort of circularity to the whole affair, don't you think? A ballad implicating a playmaker too clever to write it, posted where no one could read it, followed by a city-wide proclamation of a reward no ordinary citizen could claim. It seems to be an excuse for the Lord Keeper to investigate Marlowe. But why be so indirect? If he has reason to suspect Marlowe of spreading atheism, why not just call him in for questioning?"

"It's an occupational affliction, I'm afraid." Anthony gave one of his Gallic shrugs. "One desires to distance oneself from one's agents. Then that degree of distance seems insufficient, so layers are added until one risks losing control of the whole project."

"Sounds inefficient. All those layers want paying, one assumes." Francis took another sip of his cooling wine.

"Another motive could be to create a threat in order to be seen defending the realm against it." Anthony proposed that monstrous idea as if it were a common tactic. "Seen by the queen, most importantly. She doesn't much like Puckering, from what I hear."

"He's plain-looking and dull," Francis said. "He lacks charm. He's a useful servant, nothing more. That's a vile motive, however — stirring up trouble in order to put it down. Although I can imagine it being effective, if handled correctly. I would hate for Lord Essex to take it as a model."

"Then we'd be the ones doing the handling." Anthony grinned, his face lighting up with amusement. "I'd manage the affair, but he'd want you to write the ballad. You'd do a better job than Cholmeley, I'd wager."

That startled a laugh out of Francis. "Mine would rhyme properly, I can promise you that. But the whole thing does smack of the theater, doesn't it? Hiring a poet, then hiding his work, then pretending to search for him while prosecuting someone else. A play with a tortured plot, replete with violence. No wonder they're so interested in Christopher Marlowe!"

THIRTEEN

"I wish you could've been there, Wife. You'd have laughed to see that portly warden tripping over himself to please me."

Trumpet did her best to offer him an admiring smile, though she'd nearly exhausted her repertoire. He'd treated her to three versions of his adventure at Bridewell so far, augmenting his performance with each retelling. She couldn't even claim the press of household matters to escape, trapped as she was on the road to Nonsuch. They kept their mounts to a walk in consideration of the nurse and baby, who rode pillion behind a groom. At this leisurely speed, the twelve-mile ride would take six hours.

Time to tell that story many more times.

In fairness, Stephen deserved her praise and admiration. He'd never done any such thing before — bearding an official in his den to make what might seem an arbitrary demand. He'd carried the day with verve and dispatch, winning the immediate release of poor Thomas Kyd. Stephen had delivered the broken man to his former lodgings, not knowing what else to do with him. The landlady had nearly fainted with astonishment and pity but promised to look after the playmaker until he could tend to himself.

The affair redounded to Stephen's credit as a generous lord. But it did nothing for Trumpet's reputation, either as a Woman of Influence or as a patroness of the arts. Perhaps she should bring Kyd to Dorchester House to recover? He was one of the most popular playmakers, after all. But she wouldn't be there to bask in his glow. She'd go straight on to Dorset after her month at court. Kyd's luster had been tarnished anyway. Falsely, tragically, but there it was. His presence might drive people from her table instead of attracting them.

She should seek someone less controversial. She wanted Marlowe because she loved him, but wasn't he just as risky? More, apparently, since the authorities had been looking for him when they caught Kyd. She wished she knew more about the supposed charges against Kit and how they came to be levied. He would never tell her. If only that habit of reticence were as strong in matters of religion!

She caught the tail end of a joke and managed to produce a laugh. Stephen gave a soft chuckle, finished for now, and lapsed into a contented silence.

Trumpet let her horse fall back to check on William. He lay sound asleep in the nurse's arms, his rosebud mouth gaping open. He almost looked like Stephen in that pose. Trumpet nodded at the nurse but said nothing. She didn't want to wake the baby, and besides, she had other things to think about.

Between Stephen's errand of mercy and the torrential rains, she'd lost her chance for dalliance with Tom. Who knew when she'd get another? They could meet in Dorset — his mother's home was less than a day's ride from Badbury House — but by that time her belly would be unambiguously round. Tom could hardly fail to notice, and then be offended that she hadn't told him sooner. She'd just have to make some excuse to return to London before Tom left Gray's for the summer vacation. They could have their night of love-making. She'd tell him about the baby in the morning. He'd just have to understand that fair was fair. Stephen deserved his own true heir.

When they reached the palace, she'd go straight to the rooms reserved for Ladies of the Privy Bedchamber. Stephen would lodge in the chambers provided for visitors of rank, with his valet, the nurse, and the baby in adjacent closets. Trumpet could begin her campaign to make useful friends that very evening. She needed guidance, a counselor of sorts, to help her navigate the shoals of influence.

Men had it so easy! All Stephen had to do was don some costly garb and go gesticulate for fifteen minutes to gain a reputation as a compassionate and powerful lord. Gone and back in less than an hour. She had to juggle a husband, a lover, a baby, a dangerous playmaker, and a blended household on whose loyalty she could not wholly depend.

She needed a friend with similar goals and an equal number of balls in the air.

* * *

Wood struck wood with a satisfying smack as the black bowl kissed the white jack. "Mine again," Trumpet crowed.

"It's no fun when one person wins all the games." Two of the players, young ladies dressed for flirtation rather than sport, flounced off the green.

"Good riddance." Trumpet faced her remaining competitor, Mrs. Audrey Walsingham.

Audrey laughed. "They're more interested in Lord Southampton than bowling, my lady. You gave them the excuse they'd been waiting for to trot after him."

She tilted her head toward the knot garden beyond the rows of bowling greens. His Lordship had just set his satin-shod feet onto the gravel path between the herbs, with one inviting glance over his shoulder at the two girls.

"Bigger game," Trumpet said. "All they could win at bowls is a few pennies."

"You have been playing with, ah, considerable vigor, my lady."

"I play to win." But Trumpet recognized the truth in those words. She might have driven the other ladies' bowls into the ditch more often than necessary. But their prattling had scratched at her ears like an itchy lump in the band of a badly starched ruff. The peace of a perfect afternoon expanded in their absence. She could hear the birds singing again.

Audrey readied herself and released her bowl onto the clipped grass. It rolled swiftly out of the lane, bouncing off the green altogether. She gave a little shriek of frustration, then trotted after it. She met Trumpet's eyes as she returned to the pitch. "Since it's only the two of us now, Lady Dorchester, could we perhaps practice for a while instead of competing? Everyone plays this game, and I'm so bad at it. But you're so good. Perhaps you could you teach me?"

She made an appealing picture, standing on the bright grass in her green and yellow gown. She'd styled her light brown hair into a roll framing her white brow. The shape emphasized her neat eyebrows and alert brown eyes. She had a lively manner — not the least bit shy — which had made it easy to become friends in the space of a single day.

They'd met over Her Majesty's pillows that morning. Trumpet had been surprised to find a mere gentlewoman helping to gather up the royal linens. Her husband, Thomas Walsingham, hadn't even been knighted, although he was the nephew of Her Majesty's late Secretary of State. And it turned out that Audrey's great-grandmother on her father's side had been an aunt of Her Majesty's mother. Being pretty, witty, and eager to please enhanced her qualifications. When Trumpet learned her husband was

Marlowe's patron at Scadbury, she'd practically pounced on the woman.

She must know something about patronage, on the one hand, and about intelligencers, on the other.

Trumpet picked up her bowl and weighed it in both hands, seeking the heavy side. She prompted Audrey to do the same. "Find its center, the weightiest part. They're never precisely balanced. I like to have the center on the left side of my right palm as I prepare to pitch. Then keep your thumb up as you release the bowl, laying it smoothly into the desired path."

They worked on that for a while, enjoying the activity as well as the companionship. Birds twittered in the hazel branches, through which sunshine dappled the green. A light breeze stole under their ruffs to cool their necks. No one disturbed them. Nonsuch Palace held so many diversions when the queen was in residence. It was the perfect time for a confidential conversation.

"We have a bowling green at home," Audrey said, "but my husband doesn't play. Nor does our current guest, so I have no one to practice with."

"Your guest is Christopher Marlowe, isn't he?"

"Do you know him, my lady?"

"I do, as it happens. He's been tutoring me in classical literature for the past —"

A peal of girlish laughter cut her off. That choice had never made sense to anyone else.

"Let me guess," Audrey said, wiping a tear from her eye. "You started with the murder of Julius Caesar and went on to the rape of Lucretia."

Trumpet laughed in turn. "I did manage to steer him into some of Catullus's love poetry, but only for one afternoon."

"He's writing a love poem. That must be why. My husband says he can be supremely focused when he's working." Audrey arranged her bowl in her hand and stooped to roll it.

"Don't bend at the waist," Trumpet said. "You lower one knee into a kneel, only without touching the ground." She glanced around to be sure no one was watching, then gripped a middle hoop of her farthingale and lifted her skirts to demonstrate.

Audrey's mouth opened in an O. "That's the secret!" She tried it and came closer to the jack than ever before.

"Is it difficult having a poet living in your house?" Trumpet asked.

"Not particularly. Some days he locks himself up in his room. I have meals delivered to his door. Other days he wanders the estate from dawn to dusk. I don't mind that. But sometimes he keeps my husband up till dawn talking about old times."

"Have they known each other long?"

Audrey drew in a breath, plainly searching for an unrevealing answer.

Trumpet lowered her voice. "I know about Mr. Marlowe's other work."

"Do you, my lady?" Audrey sounded slightly alarmed.

"We have a mutual friend who has done similar work. I helped on one occasion. And I know your husband is the nephew of Sir Francis Walsingham, Her Majesty's greatest spymaster."

"Ah, well, then." Audrey relaxed. "My husband used to help his uncle in that work, supervising a few of the intelligencers. Mr. Marlowe was one of them. He enjoyed the work, he always says, but he gave it up when his father died and left him Scadbury. Then he retired and married me." That memory brought a smile to her lips.

"Does he miss it?" Trumpet asked. She would. Managing an estate could be demanding but never exciting. No intrigue, no danger. Just endless accounts of cows, bushels of grain, and barrels of ale. Deciding which tenants would live in which cottages provided the greatest drama of the year.

"Sometimes, my lady. A little." Her tone suggested he missed it rather more than that. "It isn't the excitement so much. He'd been glad to give up the traveling. But he liked being on the inside of great matters. Knowing about plots brewing on the Continent or, these days, in Scotland."

"I can understand that," Trumpet said. "I have a friend who says that knowledge is power."

"That's quite true, isn't it, my lady?" Audrey seemed pleased, as if she'd received a gift.

Trumpet had a sackful of quotes from Francis Bacon. She'd never thought of them as rewards before. She'd have to try using them here and there to test their value.

She took her position on the mat and released her bowl. A little off. The ground was still soft from the rains. "I suppose you know about Mr. Marlowe's trouble with the Privy Council."

"Oh yes, my lady. That has been a topic of much discussion at Scadbury lately."

"Do you worry about trouble arising for you and Mr. Walsingham from that association?"

"Well, yes, my lady, and also no." Once again, Audrey seemed uncertain about how much she could say.

"We are in the same boat, if that comforts you," Trumpet said. "I consider Christopher Marlowe a friend. And my lord husband extended himself so far as to have Thomas Kyd released from jail last week."

"Oh, thank God!" Audrey dropped her bowl to grasp Trumpet's lace-gloved hand. "That was a merciful act, my lady. We've been heartsick about it."

Trumpet smiled as she withdrew her hand. "I shouldn't think anyone would dare arrest the nephew of the queen's greatest spymaster."

"Someone might. These are uncertain times. We don't fear prison or, heaven forfend, torture, especially not with the mildness being shown to Mr. Marlowe. But there are other forms of censure, aren't there, my lady? Shunning, whispers, favors withheld."

Trumpet had endured shuns and whispers after her first husband had been murdered on their wedding night. She and Tom had been caught in their nightclothes. She'd been proved a virgin by eight women of good repute, but rumors had followed her until she married Stephen.

"Why is the council so mild, do you think?" she asked. "Thomas Kyd was racked to learn what he knew about his old chambermate. Yet when they arrest the man himself, they merely question him for a while and send him on his way."

"His master is on the council," Audrey said. "Or so we assume. And he's a very good intelligencer, according to my husband. Graceful, articulate, able to improvise. Not one to be wasted. If they racked him, he'd be useless."

Trumpet fought down the bile that rose in her throat. She couldn't bear to think of bold, handsome Christopher Marlowe being reduced to a cripple. She shook her head and moved on to her next question. "I've been wondering if my lord husband shouldn't employ his own intelligencers, like the Earl of Essex. To be candid, I would do most of the managing."

Audrey laid a hand on her arm. "Don't do it, my lady. That's my advice, if you'll forgive my boldness. It's horribly costly, for one thing. Sir Francis died many thousands of pounds in debt. He exhausted his wealth in Her Majesty's service."

A useful warning. Limits would have to be set. "Perhaps a less extensive enterprise?"

Audrey shook her head emphatically. "No, my lady. The money is only part of it. Mr. Marlowe is more couth than the average intelligencer, but if you know him, you know how unstable his humors are. Sunshine one day, thunderstorms the next. He can be quite cruel too."

"I don't see that side of him," Trumpet said, "but his plays reveal it. I often wonder how the man I know can invent such barbarous things."

"Most intelligencers, in my observation, are bitter men, ambitious and angry. They're gentlemen who've been to university — they must have been, for the languages and the manners — but they're not fit for decent company. They enjoy the deceptions required by their work, sometimes even when it causes real harm to their targets. Some of them like it *because* of the harm. They're easily bored and need excitement." She shuddered. "You don't want them idling about your garden, my lady. I pray daily that my husband will wake up one morning and say, 'Hold, enough,' and leave that life behind. We can further our aims by writing letters and cultivating connections. All we need for that are a few well-bred messengers."

What aims were these? Something involving plots brewing on the Continent or in Scotland? Trumpet could write letters as well as the next person, and they already had a stable of couriers, thanks to Stephen's travels with the Earl of Essex.

She tossed her bowl from one hand to the other and grinned at Audrey. "I'll just cross that off the list, then."

"A wise decision, my lady," Audrey said.

Bells tolled in the chapel tower. Time to go change for a turn in the Privy Chamber. Trumpet dropped her bowl on the green and took her friend's arm. "Tell me, Mrs. Walsingham, do you harbor any poets who aren't notorious for seditious views?"

FOURTEEN

"Here, put this on." Tom tossed Kit his spare legal robe. They'd met at the corner of the Holborn road, but he'd waited until they turned into the alley leading to Gray's before offering the disguise.

The poet shrugged it on over his velvet doublet, the one liberally sparked with brass buttons. He'd worn his best for this meeting with the famous Bacon brothers. "Isn't there a law against entering an Inn of Court under false colors?"

"You'd be surprised at the riffraff we get in here. False priests. *Real* priests. But your face is a shade too familiar to blazon across the yard. We're all theatergoers."

Anthony had asked Tom to bring Kit for a conversation, if congenial to both. Kit had leapt at the chance to meet the fabled spymaster. Francis wanted to ask the playmaker about his alleged atheism, to make up his own mind about the controversy roiling the Privy Council. He didn't trust rumors, not even when they came from Essex himself. His Lordship's observations were inevitably colored by his aspirations.

Tom leapt at the chance to bask in the reflected glow when he introduced London's most renowned playmaker — his close friend — to Westminster's most brilliant legal philosopher — his tutor. He could sell tickets to this conversation, if the others would allow it. Which they most emphatically would never do.

Kit's keen eyes took in everything as they entered the Chapel Court, from the raked gravel to the handsome red brick hall. "It's like a college, only richer."

Tom jerked his chin toward the long sagging building directly across from the hall. "That one's worse than the one we lived in at Corpus Christi. I spent two years in that moldering pile." He titled his head to the left. "But the sons of Sir Nicholas Bacon don't live in squalor."

He paused to let his friend take in the thick oak beams crossing the sand-colored plaster, both refreshed two years ago when Francis raised the roof to add two stories. He'd needed more room for Anthony and his stable of secretaries. The panes in the windows had been re-leaded and the floors and stairs repaired and polished. The poet inhaled deeply as they stepped inside onto clean floors strewn with tansy and rosemary. "No plague in this house."

"We're far enough from the city, I think," Tom said. "But Lord Burghley has canceled Trinity term. Most of the members will be leaving soon."

"Where will you go? Dorset?"

Tom nodded. "I could use the rest."

He knocked once and opened the door. They were expected. Anthony sat behind his desk, a position of authority, while Francis occupied an armchair by the glowing coal fire. Tom made the introductions, then stood back to watch as the three exchanged conventional greetings.

Kit's gaze traveled over the silk tapestry hanging on the far wall and the display of silver plate on the densely carved cupboard, lingering with interest on a set of shelves stacked high with books. Tom noticed Francis noticing and smiled. By that choice, Kit proved himself a scholar, not a grasper after costly objects.

Two straight-backed chairs had been placed to form a semicircle with Anthony and Francis at the poles. Tom gestured Kit into one and took the other. Jacques Petit served cups of rochelle, a white wine from France not commonly found in England. Kit tasted it and raised his eyebrows to show he recognized the rare treat. He thanked the youth in French.

"How did you know where Jacques is from?" Anthony asked.

Kit shrugged, though he seemed pleased to have scored a point. "He has French eyebrows. Something subtle in his manner. But everyone in our line knows you spent many years in Montauban. It's an easy guess that you brought your man home with you."

Anthony said, "I suppose you know why we asked Mr. Clarady to bring you here."

Kit nodded. "You want to know what I've been telling the Privy Council. One can hardly expect an earl to take notes." Another point scored, showing he knew for whom the Bacons worked.

Francis answered this time. "Nor to relate to us the parts that don't interest him."

"I fear I'm one of those parts," Kit said. "The Lord of Essex attended the first session but hasn't graced any of our subsequent meetings."

"The first one was, let's see . . ." Anthony consulted his calendar, on which he noted everything of interest every day. "A week ago yesterday. Was the full council present?"

"I don't know how many there are, all told. Perhaps a dozen on the first day. Never more than half a dozen after that. Most days they keep me idling on a bench for an hour or two before a clerk comes out to tell me I'm free to go." He shot a glance at Tom. "Those are the good days."

Anthony asked, "Who are the constant ones?"

"Sir Thomas Heneage asks most of the questions. Lord Keeper Puckering chimes in now and then. They seem to be working together."

"He's not on the council," Francis objected.

He'd been jealous of membership in that august body ever since his cousin had been installed. And lately he'd bristled at any mention of the Lord Keeper. Tom assumed his meeting at York House hadn't gone very well.

"I don't issue the invitations." Kit gave a short laugh. "It would be a very different body if I did. Lord Buckhurst attends each time. He always seems half-asleep, or perhaps he just finds me dull. Also Sir John Fortescue, if that's the one I'm thinking of. Old fellow with a sour turn of mouth." Kit drew imaginary lines from lips to chin.

Anthony nodded. "Has our cousin attended? Sir Robert Cecil?"

"Only the first day."

"What did he want to know?" Anthony asked.

Marlowe shook his head, a small smile on his lips. "He already knows enough about me."

From which they were meant to deduce that Sir Robert was Marlowe's spymaster. Tom had guessed as much years ago and had shared his reasoning with the Bacons.

Anthony let it pass. "Didn't you start out with Sir Francis Walsingham?"

"No," Kit said. "My first commission was carrying letters for Lord North. His servant recruited me soon after I took my Bachelor of Arts degree."

"You studied theology, didn't you?" Francis asked. "You must have, to win a second round of scholarship support."

"It made sense at the time, though I can no longer remember why. I would make a terrible pastor." Kit winked at Tom. "Can you imagine me behind the pulpit on a Sunday morning in one of the lesser wool towns?"

Tom barked a laugh, drawing a glare from Francis, who considered the quality of the English clergy a serious matter.

"That was the purpose of your scholarships," Francis said, a trifle crisply. "To fill England's need for educated priests."

"I never misrepresented myself," Kit said. "I came to university as a boy with no plan and left as a man with a play ready for the stage. Once I started writing, I knew I had found my destiny. I make full use of my education, you should note. Just not in the way originally intended."

"You can't make a living writing plays," Anthony said. "I suppose that's why you kept on with intelligencing."

"It's a perfect combination. The money affords me the niceties of a gentleman." Kit flicked one of his brass buttons. "The travel gives me time to think, and the places I go give me things to think about. I couldn't have written *Massacre* without having been to Paris." He paused as if waiting for some commentary on the play.

"They didn't see it," Tom said. "They don't go to theaters, and it wasn't performed at court."

Francis sniffed. "We don't have time for plays when Parliament is in session."

Anthony rolled his eyes at his brother's pomposity. "Did you never work for Sir Francis?"

"I did, for several years," Kit said. "Although I only met him once. Nicholas Faunt introduced me to Sir Francis's nephew, Thomas Walsingham. He oversaw my work during those years, which is how we became friends. He generously offered me a place to write this summer at his home in Scadbury." He glanced at Tom, who nodded.

"They know where you're living."

"I suppose Robert picked you up when Sir Francis died."

"Many skilled men went seeking new employment at that time," Kit said. "I couldn't tell you about any of the others, but I landed on my feet."

Tom grinned at the expression. Catlike images suited the poet's style — his physical grace and swift wits. He also noticed that the poet had not answered the question.

Kit and Anthony smiled at one another like two men who understood each other perfectly.

Francis spoke over the rim of his cup. "It's curious you're so reticent about your master — as you should be — and yet are so voluble on other themes."

That abrupt change of topic caught Kit off guard. He blinked, his mouth agape. Then he said, "It's a fair observation, but it misses the central fact that my life is composed of parts which rarely mingle. Duty demands reticence in one part, while art demands expression in the other."

Well said! Points to the poet. Tom turned his eyes to Francis, eager for the philosopher's response.

But Anthony hadn't finished his line of questioning. "What does Heneage ask you? Is he interested in the Dutch Church libel?"

Kit laughed. "He wanted to know why it had been signed 'Tamburlaine.' I had no answer for him, though he kept pressing. It might as well have been Charlemagne or Henry the Fourth."

"Another popular play," Tom put in. "That would've been more germane, wouldn't it? Since Henry the Fourth was an Englishman fighting against the French."

The Bacon brothers gave him that schoolmaster look that said they didn't require instruction from a tot. Tom shrugged off the censure. The analogy was perfectly valid.

"Do you know who wrote the libel?" Anthony asked.

"I do not."

Anthony nodded at the expected answer. "Could it have been a man named Richard Cholmeley?"

"Cholmeley?" Another surprise for the poet. "I haven't heard that name in a while. What makes you think of him?"

Anthony tapped a finger on one of the papers arrayed upon his desk. "The Privy Council received an informer's report about a knave called Richard Cholmeley. He claims you converted him to atheism."

Kit laughed heartily this time, tilting back his head. "Does he claim I gave birth to him as well? Because that's equally likely. Cholmeley doesn't believe in anything, though I can't take credit for it. He's the worst sort of scoffer, all insult and scurrility. I've met him here and there. He's a bore. And the most savage sort of informer. If he can't come up with anything else to earn his shilling, he'll throw out lies about other agents. Most of us avoid him, although I suppose he has his uses."

"He's done similar work for your unnamed master, I believe," Anthony said. "Writing ballads spreading falsehoods, that is."

"I wouldn't know about that. No one's ever asked me to write one. Perhaps I should feel offended." Marlowe offered a saucy grin.

"Could Cholmeley have written that libel?" Tom asked. "If so, I'll roust him out and turn him in to get my hundred crowns, however savage he may be."

"Ah, yes, your livery suit." Kit smiled at him. "In terms of the rhyme and rhythm — and the generally vicious tone — I would say yes. Cholmeley fancies himself a poet. I don't know where he lives, but if you want to find a balladeer, start with the printers. Someone will recognize his style."

"Thanks." Tom had managed to think of that strategy on his own.

Anthony said, "I doubt anyone on the council honestly thinks you had anything to do with that ballad, with the possible exceptions of Sir Thomas Heneage and Lord Keeper Puckering. Puckering, at least, seems to have quite an antipathy for you. Let us not forget he had Thomas Kyd tortured to find out about you and your associates."

Kit looked stricken. "I'll never forget — or forgive. Thank God Tom did what I couldn't and found help for him. I'd stop by to check in on him, but I'm sure my face is the last he wants to see. I can't for the life of me understand why they did it." He addressed those last words to Anthony, in a tone that begged for an answer.

"To make an example, I suppose." Anthony sighed. "From what Tom says, a few questions in the taverns favored by theater folk would've told them they'd picked up an innocent."

"Shoddy tradecraft." Kit's lip curled with disgust. "Cold comfort for Kyd."

Francis spoke up. "Cholmeley claims you read an atheist lecture to Sir Walter Ralegh and others. Have you written any such works?"

"No." Kit spoke without hesitation. "I wondered where that question came from. I may owe Cholmeley a visit when this is over. I don't write lectures, sermons, or tracts. I write poems and plays, none of which could be said to promote atheism. On the contrary, my skeptical heroes always die. Faustus was dragged off the stage straight into hell."

Answer that, Mr. Bacon. Tom grinned. A great ending to a magnificent play. He'd loved it so much he'd seen it three times.

Francis didn't respond. Everyone knew *Doctor Faustus* presented a formidable argument *against* atheism.

Anthony tapped his quill on the paper under his hand. "The mention of Sir Walter concerns me. Could he be the real target of all this hugger-mugger?" His words were aimed at Kit, but his gaze shifted toward his brother.

"That makes more sense to me than this sudden vexation of playmakers," Francis said.

Kit blew out a noisy breath. "I haven't seen Sir Walter in over a year. He hasn't been in London since he fell out of favor. Why look for more coals to heap upon his head?"

"Because he remains the favorite," Francis said. "Everyone knows this punishment is temporary. He's also an enormously useful man. He works harder than anyone but our cousin Robert. He'll be back within the year, mark my words."

"Then men like Heneage and Puckering will be lucky to get a word in edgewise," Anthony said.

"Or worse," Francis said, "they'll have to go through Sir Walter to reach the queen. Neither Cecil nor Essex would help them unless they committed to supporting their current schemes."

Tom soaked up the lesson in political influence, meaning to pass it on to Trumpet. Kit seemed to appreciate it as well, his quick eyes turning from one Bacon to the other as they spoke.

Now the poet sat back in his chair, stretching his long legs before him. "If they think I have any influence on Sir Walter's beliefs, they've never met the man. He possesses a rare intellect, powerful and questioning. I'm honored to count him as a friend. We've had many a rousing debate in which I barely hold my own."

"That's what they want to hear about," Anthony said, pointing his quill at his brother. "They want to find something smelly to hang around Sir Walter's neck."

"They won't get it from me," Kit said. "It's only talk, after all. Though we do explore everything in our circle. We range from heaven to earth, from the distant Orient to the Spanish Main. Nothing is out of bounds. Indeed, we oppose the very notion of bounds. We believe the Creator gave us our aspiring minds so that we might strive to comprehend the wonders of the world." He smiled at Francis like a man who had thrown down a gauntlet.

Francis picked it up, his eyes brightening. "I believe that also, to a point. But the laws of God are best left to God."

"I don't argue with the laws of God," Kit retorted. "I expose the hypocrisy in the practices of men."

Francis grunted.

And the poet scored another point! So far, Tom judged Kit to be well ahead in this verbal match.

Anthony regarded his brother with a patient look, waiting for a rebuttal. None came, so he continued to press his own interest. "I've wondered why they're treating you so gently, though I suppose your unnamed master is the reason. Still, if they tortured you" — he waved a hand — "forgive the thought, but they could make you say whatever they liked about Sir Walter."

"I hadn't thought of that." Kit cringed. "Thank God for my master! I was merely glad for the work when he recruited me. I didn't know I would need a bulwark down the road."

Anthony said, "You must be good at the work, or he wouldn't protect you. He wouldn't lift a finger to keep a man like Cholmeley out of jail."

"I like it, and I'm good at what I like." Kit's natural self-assurance re-asserted itself. He straightened up and drank some wine. "In fact, I'm hoping to be promoted soon to a more northerly field of endeavor."

"More riding, less sailing," Anthony said. "Your master must have confidence in your discretion."

That left Tom in the dust for a moment. A northerly field? Ah. Scotland. Carrying letters to and from King James. Delicate work, but doubtless better pay on account of it.

Kit offered Anthony a knowing grin. "I compose some of my best verses on the back of a horse. Something about the rhythm. And bad weather gives me days at an inn with no one to distract me, so I can write down what I've been thinking. I'm working on a new play about James the First, as it happens. I'd love to get the northern speech into my ears."

"The first of what?" Tom asked.

"Scotland," Anthony said. To Kit, he added sternly, "Don't do it."

Francis also seemed alarmed. "Under no circumstances should you write, speculate, or even think out loud about any king of Scotland."

"He lived over a hundred years ago." Kit sounded offended. Most people would be eager to hear about his current work.

"That doesn't matter," Anthony said. "One doesn't talk about the Scottish succession. The implications are too fraught."

Tom understood that part. King James the Fourth of Scotland was Her Majesty's most likely heir, but to speak of that transition amounted to speculation about her death. That was treason. It seemed overly nice to him, like refusing to write a will as one advanced in years. But there were folk who thought preparing for death summoned the reaper. Things were doubly ticklish when the estate to be inherited was the whole of England.

"Why not choose another English king?" Francis asked. "So many histories yet to be explored, and history has so much to teach us. Henry the Second, for example — another conqueror for you. Or what about a Roman emperor like Julius Caesar? There's a story that would play well on the stage."

Kit made a slicing motion with his left hand. A little rude, but he hated suggestions about what he should write. Tom understood that too. He'd been at the table when drunken gentlemen lurched up to tell the world's greatest playmaker all about his next work, from plot to themes, with plenty of spittle for emphasis. Kit only listened to his own Muse.

"You'd be well advised to choose another topic, Mr. Marlowe," Anthony said. "Have you told the council about this play?"

"Why wouldn't I?" Kit shrugged, a contemptuous gesture. "The man is long dead and rotted in his grave. They want details I can't supply since I haven't devised them yet. But don't worry. It'll pass the censors. I know how to play the game."

Anthony and Francis traded worried looks, but Kit set his jaw. He was a fool not to take good advice when it was offered. But then he didn't know the Bacons like Tom did. When they agreed, their judgment should be given serious consideration.

Anthony changed the subject. "Do you know a man called Richard Baines?"

Kit groaned. "Better than I'd like. I spent a few miserable months sharing three cramped rooms in Flushing with him and another man, a goldsmith."

"How did that come about?" Anthony asked.

"I was there on a project, trying something out. I won't go into it. The goldsmith was part of it. Baines came along and squeezed himself in. You know how things are there. Decent lodgings are hard to come by, especially for those who don't speak Dutch. I'd never met him or heard of him at that time, so I had no reason to object. But he's a mean one." Kit cocked his head at Anthony. "What brings him into our little drama?"

"He submitted a list of blasphemies you allegedly uttered in his presence to the Privy Council on Saturday. My Lord of Essex sent me a copy." Anthony selected a sheet of paper and held it out.

Kit sprang to his feet with his effortless grace to accept the paper. He sat down again and read it swiftly, chuckling now and then. Then he looked at Anthony with a grin. "The bit about the tobacco pipe isn't bad, is it? Can't you see the priest at Canterbury Cathedral holding a long-stemmed pipe for each kneeling communicant?"

"Smoke rises to heaven," Francis said. "In itself, it's apt. But there's nothing in the Bible about tobacco."

"And yet tobacco existed in the world," Kit said. "Indians have used it in their rites for thousands of years. That tells us the Bible is the work of men, with man's limited knowledge, not the word of God."

"Baines's *Note* isn't a list of themes for a disputation," Anthony said. "It's a set of quotes intended to condemn you with your own words. *Are* they your words?"

Kit shrugged. His lack of concern worried Tom. Anthony never scolded. If he thought the *Note* worth belaboring, Kit should take heed. This wasn't another debate at the Mermaid with no consequences for either winners or losers.

"I can't take credit for all of it," Kit said. "I picked up some of those witticisms in college. Undergraduate rot, pushing back against the endless diet of pious sermons. But some are mine. All the bits about tobacco, for example."

"What possessed you to say such things to a man like Baines?" Francis asked.

"I don't know." Kit shook his head. "But I remember that day. Nothing but sleet and a freezing wind, whistling into cracks and howling down the chimney, throwing the smoke back in our faces. You couldn't even go out for a walk without ending up on your arse. We were trapped indoors, the three of us, huddled around our smoky fire. By then, Baines and I had taken each other's measure. Both in the same trade, we knew, but I was going up and he was going down. Almost out, I thought. Now I see he's trying to get back in by abusing me."

He raised his cup with a hopeful look at Jacques, who took it away empty and brought it back full. Kit resumed his tale. "We were desperately bored, I remember that too. Baines entertained us with stories about his time at Rheims, where his task had been to foster discontent. His mere presence can do that, I assure you. I imagine he started this list there. He threw one out to start the game. I topped it with another." Kit slapped the paper with the back of his hand. "This list is evidence of the foulness of a winter on the German Sea. Nothing more."

"Someone solicited it," Anthony said. "Someone is compiling evidence against you."

"Evidence of what?" Kit demanded. "I'm a loyal Englishman. My deeds proclaim it, at least to those who know of them. Which the council does, or should. I love my country and revere my queen. No monarch in the world is as wise and generous as she. My plays are the proof of it. What other land allows such liberty of speech?"

"No other," Francis said. "And yet there are limits."

"It was ill-advised to engage in such talk with a man like Baines," Anthony said. "He's another of Cholmeley's type — always ready to throw another agent into the fire if it will gain him a few coins or credit with a great man."

Kit shrugged that off too. "A foul day stuck indoors. I suppose you would've been singing hymns."

"I would've been working." Anthony winked at his brother.

Francis merely flicked his eyebrows. He would've been reading in bed with a pan of coals at his feet and the covers pulled up to his chin. Tom could reliably find him in that position on any ugly day.

A silence fell while they sipped their drinks. Anthony caught his brother's gaze and gave him a nod. He'd asked his questions. Now it was Francis's turn.

Francis struggled out of his habitual slouch. "I wonder, Mr. Marlowe, that you can be so discreet about your master's projects and so incontinent about your own."

He'd said that before. Kit repeated his response. "Mine end up on the stage before a thousand people." He laughed. "What use is a reticent playmaker?"

"I mean the blasphemies," Francis said.

"I don't believe in blasphemy," Kit retorted. "All things should be questioned. That's why we have inquiring minds." He lifted his chin to quote himself. "I hold there is no sin but ignorance."

"I remember that line," Francis said. "*The Jew of Malta*, wasn't it? It sounds clever, but of course, there are many other sins. Murder, for example. Rape. Treason."

"Is treason a sin?" Kit dropped the *Note* on the floor and crossed his arms, leaning back in his chair. "I would deem it a crime against the state, not God."

Tom gave his friend a warning headshake. Kit should not attempt to argue law with Francis Bacon.

"When the state and the church are one, as they are in England," Francis said, "the difference is too fine to be more than a quibble."

Kit's eyes narrowed. A quibbler was a trivial man, a splitter of straws.

The philosopher had scored a hit.

Francis asked in a mild tone, "Are you an atheist, Mr. Marlowe?"

"It depends on what you mean." Kit's eyes glittered with challenge.

"I mean simply, do you believe in God?" Francis smiled at the light streaming through the window behind his brother's desk. "Speaking for myself, I had rather believe all the fables in the Alcoran than think this universal frame is without a mind."

"The Christian Bible has its share of fables," Kit said. "But I agree. I believe in a Creator who takes an interest in his creation. It's nonsense to believe otherwise. We didn't arise from the muck like tadpoles."

Francis flicked a wry glance at them. "I'm fairly certain tadpoles emerge from eggs." He'd grown up on an estate with ponds, among other enticements for a curious boy.

Tom and Anthony shared a soft chuckle. Francis could be counted upon to take such analogies literally.

"I wouldn't know." City-bred Kit sounded irritated by the digression. "Forget about the tadpoles. We — mankind — are born human, equipped with immortal souls by that selfsame Creator."

"That view isn't obvious from your plays," Francis said. "Your heroes challenge God in word and deed."

"And fail," Kit said. "But they fail grandly, after rising almost to the sun."

"Yes," Francis said, "but their striving is the meat of every play. They heap scorn on religion. Their co-conspirators agree with them. One could argue that the moral voice of your plays opposes religion of any kind."

"I could argue that better than anyone," Kit said. "My heroes disdain all religions equally, you might note — Jews, Muslims, and Christians alike. But their scorn is aimed at the absurd rituals that allow hypocrites to rule while serving their own appetites. Churches of all stripes have a lot to answer for. How many men have been murdered in the name of some religion?"

"Wars usually have other causes," Francis answered, unruffled by the poet's angry tone. "Your plays and your tavern talk foster disbelief, leading the sheep away from their shepherds."

"Men are not sheep, Mr. Bacon."

"But they do need guidance, Mr. Marlowe. The ephemera don't matter, I agree. Lighting candles or not lighting them serve equally well to turn men's minds toward God, in the right circumstances. But challenge and dissent encourage confusion, which drives men away from their spiritual shelters and encourages atheism."

"If that's atheism, then I deserve the charge. But I disagree. I think challenging men to think for themselves about the foundation on which they base their lives makes them stronger. Thinking men, not sheep."

"Yet history shows us the strife that follows religious discord," Francis said. "Unity of religion is vital to the health of a nation. Unity fosters peace, allowing men's minds to open like flowers under the sun. It kindles charity, allowing the calm forbearance that allows one man to make a little room for his brother's preferences."

Kit snorted. "That describes no religion known to humankind. At least I've never heard of one, and I studied theology for seven years. Men aren't flowers either." Kit spread his knees and placed a hand on one thigh. "But now that we've entered the garden, let's switch metaphors. My plays, or rather the questions they raise, are the spice that makes a man appreciate his daily bowl of stew."

Francis didn't miss a beat. "Rather say they're the nettles thrown into the pot to relieve an aching back, which distemper a man's bowels so that all the world seems bitter."

Kit laughed and held up his hands, surrendering. "Tom warned me about your mental agility. I appreciate a worthy opponent. You should join us at the Mermaid sometime, Mr. Bacon, when the plague has passed and Sir Walter returns to court."

Francis shook his head, but Tom could see that he was pleased by the invitation. Although if he ever walked into a tavern and saw his master drinking ale and smoking tobacco from a long pipe, he would haul the imposter off his stool and slap him until he confessed the reason for the deception.

Another silence fell. Anthony raised his eyebrows at Francis, who shook his head. No more questions.

Kit clapped his hands on his thighs. "I'm honored to have met you both." He nodded at Francis, the keen light of understanding in his eyes. "We start in the same place, you and I, with the Great Creator who watches over us. But you stand atop a high green hill, informed by a benevolent Mind greater even than your own, welcoming a future filled with light. You strive to shepherd men toward that light for their benefit, whether they know it or not."

"Well put," Anthony said.

Kit shot him a wry look. He was renowned throughout Europe for his ability to put things well. "I, on the other hand, prowl the dark alleys behind taverns filled with spies, the stink of offal in my nose and the echoes of lies in my ears. I seek whatever's new, always watching for a chance to pull another mortal out of the pit of mindless conformity. You guide people forward. I shake them awake." He let that sink in for a moment, then added, "As the painters would say, it's a matter of perspective."

Francis smiled beatifically. "Poetry without charity is mere sound. Perhaps you'll consider the lot of the men you meet as you make your long ride north. Consider whether peace would serve them better than discord." He glanced at Anthony. "And I hope for your sake you make that journey soon. You'll be safer out of London's reach. Out of sight, out of mind."

"On that, we agree." Kit rose and bowed to him. "Mr. Bacon." He turned and bowed to Anthony. "Mr. Bacon." He found his hat and donned it before nodding to Tom. "Mr. Clarady. Always a pleasure." He strode to the door, then turned to look back over his shoulder. "May we meet again under gentler circumstances. Perhaps at Lady Dorchester's table?"

And then he left. Marlowe always had to get in the last word, even if it meant idling in the hall while he waited for his escort.

"I'll see him out." Tom jumped up to follow his friend.

Sure enough, he found him in the entry, pulling on the spare robes he'd left draped over the bannister.

They went out but had to pause while a group of boisterous lawyers crowded through the passage alongside the house. Kit quirked his eyebrows at Tom. "You've done subtler work than I imagined, serving Francis Bacon all these years. He's a deep one. Doesn't miss much, does he?"

"Not unless he wants to."

Kit grinned. "He's taught you discretion, a valuable skill. I hope I've taught you to be bold when the occasion serves."

"I can be bold." Tom led the way around the house to the alley beside Fulwood's Rents. "But you, Kit. You must learn to be careful. Sir Walter can't help you if you get into real trouble."

"I know."

"And Sir Robert will only stick his neck out so far. You can't count on him either, not in a tight spot. Not against the queen or another powerful courtier."

"I know that too." Kit stopped to face him. "Don't worry, my friend. If I play my cards right tomorrow, I'll be on my way to Edinburgh by the end of next week." He gripped Tom's shoulder. "I appreciate your concern. And you're wise to stick with them, the Bacon brothers. They're nigh untouchable, thanks to their father."

"And their mother. She's a force in her own right. To say nothing of their aunt."

"That's good. That's important, Tom. You've made some powerful connections since we first met. Hold on to them. Kyd was tortured because he had no one to call on but a bunch of poets. We're less valuable than weavers' apprentices in the eyes of the Privy Council. One of these days, you may find you've gotten in too deep. Then the Bacons may be the only thing standing between you and the manacles."

A shiver passed through Tom's body that had nothing to do with the transition from sun to shade.

FIFTEEN

"Have you heard the news, Lady Dorchester?" Audrey Walsingham approached Trumpet on the path winding around Nonsuch Palace.

They'd parted only half an hour ago, after helping the queen rise and dress. While Her Majesty went for her morning ambulation in the palace garden, Trumpet liked to step out for a swifter stride outside the walls, where she could stretch her legs and get her arms swinging.

"What news is this?" She stopped and smiled at her new friend. They'd played bowls every afternoon that week, sharpening Audrey's aim and deepening their mutual accord.

Audrey's expression was grave. "It's bad news, I'm afraid, my lady. I've had a letter from my husband. Christopher Marlowe is dead. He was killed in an accident Wednesday night."

"Dead?" Trumpet blinked at her. "Kit?" She shook her head. "That can't be."

"I'm afraid it's true, my lady."

Audrey's voice grew faint as she faded into the distance. An empty wind echoed in Trumpet's ears, drowning out all sounds. The world stopped, or her heart did. "Kit is dead," someone whispered inside her mind.

A hand wrapped around her arm, startling her. Audrey loomed up out of seemingly nowhere. "Perhaps you should sit down, my lady."

Trumpet gave herself a little shake. "No, I'm all right. I just can't believe it. I saw him less than a fortnight ago. What happened?"

"My husband said an altercation arose in the ordinary where Marlowe and some other men spent the afternoon. Tempers flared, knives came out, and Marlowe caught one in the eye."

"God's mercy! How horrible." And yet believable. Kit had always had a short fuse. "Where did it happen?"

"In Deptford." Audrey shrugged. "Perhaps one of the men was waiting for a ship."

Trumpet stared blankly at the other woman. All pleasure in the glorious May morning had vanished. The light breeze lifted an irritating rill of lace under her left ear. The dappled light under the oaks confused her eyes. Birds chattered senselessly. The queen and all the workings of the court lost their meaning.

She didn't know what to do. Then she remembered Tom. Did he know? "Does everyone know?"

"Hardly anyone, I should think." Audrey's pale brow furrowed. "The inquest is this morning. They'll bury him this afternoon."

"I want to go." Trumpet's mind cleared at the prospect of action. "I should be there."

"My husband will be there."

"Good. We'll ride together. What time is it? We should leave at once. I just need to change clothes and write one letter."

* * *

The flurry of activity helped clear Trumpet's foggy wits, though she couldn't smile or understand much of what people said around her. Catalina dressed her in silence, like a doll. She'd brought black garb, fortunately, since the queen enjoyed the dramatic effect of a roomful of courtiers in black and white.

But drama had died on Wednesday and would play no more.

Audrey made their excuses to the queen, or rather to Lady Stafford, who managed the Ladies of the Bedchamber. Trumpet neither knew nor cared what excuse had been given. It was all she could do to wait for the horses. Her only concern was to get a message to Tom. As she pressed her ring into the warm wax seal, she hoped her letter conveyed a coherent message. She gave one of the queen's messengers a gold angel to get it to Gray's Inn as fast as he could. At a gallop, he could reach the river in two hours. Tom might reach Deptford before she did.

The bustle of clothes, letters, and horses kept her from thinking, but the long, plodding walk north churned up memories of Kit that played before her mind's eye like waking dreams.

They'd met in Cambridge, that spring when Tom had been sent to spy out a Puritan seditionist and Kit had decided to help, in his theatrical way. Naturally, Trumpet had leapt in to pull Tom out of trouble, as usual. She and Kit had understood one another from the start. They'd felt a spark, some kindred spirit. A fundamental sense of independence derived from singularity in childhood.

There would only ever be one Christopher Marlowe, however long the world might turn.

Audrey and the grooms who accompanied them insisted on stopping midway for refreshments. Trumpet stood beside her horse as she obediently chewed bread and drank ale. Some inner wisdom reminded her that her body needed sustenance, but the food lacked flavor.

She watched tears streaming from Catalina's wide brown eyes and wondered how that came about. Where were hers? Shouldn't she cry? Her eyes remained dry, although that distant ringing in her ears persisted, and her companions seemed shrouded in invisible veils.

She didn't have many friends. She never had. Her father's privateering and gambling had stretched the castle's resources to the limit, leaving nothing for gowns or county affairs. If there were any girls her age among the local gentry, she'd never met them. Just as well. They would have bored her.

Kit was a difficult friend, with his wild and secretive ways, but he was never boring.

They reached St. Nicholas Church in Deptford, a humble place with a tower built of flint and stone. An attendant handed them sprigs of rosemary as they entered. Trumpet's gaze ran up the central aisle to the plain box standing at the front of the apse. Two tall vases with white lilies stood on either side. A paltry display. But then, who would pay for more? Kit had no friends here. If they'd held the service at St. Botolph-without-Bishopsgate, near the theaters north of the city, the ranks of flowers would have turned the church into a garden, filling the air with perfume.

The rustle of clothing and hushed murmurs told Trumpet the service hadn't begun yet. Audrey led Trumpet to the front pew, where a gentleman in black sat alone. A long nose dominated his long face. His brown beard and moustache seemed as fine as the brown hair curling out from under his tall hat. Comely enough for an ordinary man, his looks wouldn't draw special attention. Useful for an intelligencer, one supposed. He must be Audrey's husband, Thomas.

Only three other people had been inspired to witness England's foremost poet being laid to rest. Trumpet noted each one as she passed. All were strangers to her, men in dark suits with closed faces. Too well-dressed to be church idlers. What had Kit meant to them?

A man in a dark red doublet made of quality cloth, cut in the latest fashion, sat alone in the middle of a pew. Silver streaked his black hair, cut to feather over a rising forehead. His silver-streaked beard obscured the jowls forming under his chin. His closely set dark eyes and beaked nose gave him the predatory look of a hawk. He'd been handsome in his day, but that day had passed. He met Trumpet's measuring gaze with equal assessment.

The other two men sat together in the second row on the right. One wore faultless black with crisp linens. A gold ring shone on one hand. He looked prosperous, plump and well-groomed, though hollows beneath his eyes betrayed a sleepless night. His flat nose and his stolid form made Trumpet think of a pig. Had he been part of the altercation that had stolen the breath from the Muses' darling? If so, Trumpet hated him. Perhaps her animosity showed. His gaze skittered away when she turned her eyes on him.

His companion looked to be the lesser sort of gentleman. He wore no jewelry, and his brown doublet was years out of date. He was the youngest of the three, by the lack of wrinkles and the full head of rusty brown hair. His pointed beard accentuated the narrowness of his face. He looked like a weasel, with round eyes and a pointed nose. He ducked his head as she walked past, as if to hide from her unyielding gaze.

She guessed these men had been at the inquest, which meant they'd played some role in Kit's death.

And that was all. The Walsinghams, Trumpet, her maidservant, and these three gloomy knaves. Mr. Walsingham must have assumed they would accompany him from the inquest to the service and had simply drawn them in his wake.

No poets. No actors. No publishers or theater owners. The news must not have reached London yet. Then again, the theaters were closed. Actors and writers had gone to wait out the plague in the countryside. They wouldn't know what they'd lost for weeks — perhaps months. People in Paris or Antwerp or wherever Kit had gone on his secret travels might never know what happened to the handsome man with the quick wit and quicksilver humor.

Trumpet took her seat as the priest began the service. She noted his white gown with its wide sleeves and sleeveless black mantle. At least it wouldn't be a Puritan service, though Kit would have wanted more pomp. Incense should fill the air instead of the dusty smell of cool stone. Candles, large and small, casting their yellow light. Monks should be chanting in Latin. He'd grown up in the shadow of Canterbury Cathedral, after all.

Her attention faded in and out as the priest droned on. Some part of her senses watched for Tom, though she never glanced toward the door. Apart from that, she felt empty, numb. Catalina continued weeping softly, holding a handkerchief under her veil. Audrey sniffled every few seconds. But Trumpet's eyes remained dry.

The priest intoned in a resonant voice, "I am the resurrection and the life, saith the Lord: he that believeth in me, though he were dead, yet shall he live: and whosoever liveth and believeth in me shall never die."

Had Kit believed in God? Any god? He'd scoffed and thrust barbs at every ritual and everything in the Bible. But then, he'd shone the fierce light of his agile mind into every corner of philosophy. Trumpet trusted that the God she loved would recognize the poet's gallant heart and welcome him to heaven.

One thing she knew without any shadow of doubt. Though his body might lie in that plain wooden box, Kit's words would live forever. As long as there was English and a tongue to speak it, his poetry would stir men's hearts and challenge their minds.

The service ended. Bells began to toll as the meager congregation slowly made their way outside. Trumpet waited with the Walsinghams, placid as a cow, ready to be led. Then a stir at the door resolved into Tom, pulling life and bustle into the church. Her heart began to beat again as he found her with his eyes. They held each other's gaze as he pushed some useless knave aside to reach her.

He took both her hands and looked down at her, his face taut with grief. "Are you all right?"

She shook her head. "I don't know."

He nodded. "Stupid question." He glanced down the aisle at the men he'd shouldered past. "Who're they?"

"I don't know."

He grunted. Thomas Walsingham cleared his throat, and Tom turned to meet Trumpet's companions. "I'm sorry I missed the service. I got here as quick as I could."

Trumpet introduced them. Tom greeted Audrey with his usual courtesy but shook Walsingham's hand with extra heartiness. "Thank you for giving Marlowe shelter these last weeks. It can't have been easy, with the Privy Council breathing down his neck."

"I wish I could have done more." Hollows shadowed Thomas Walsingham's eyes. He'd known for more than a day — almost two days. Almost since it happened. "It's a grievous loss."

"Unh." Too grievous for words.

Bearers came to carry the coffin up the aisle. They followed in silence out to the yard. The other three men had vanished, so only Trumpet and her small group stood around the open grave.

They listened passively as the priest said his last words. "Ashes to ashes, and dust to dust." A pause developed at the end, which Walsingham ended by taking a fistful of earth and tossing it into the grave. Trumpet did the same, watching each grain of gray soil break upon the box. She thought of what was in that box and closed her mind, reaching for another fistful of dirt.

As she reached for a fourth one, Tom's hand caught hers and held it. She looked up into the familiar, beloved face and remembered where she was. He drew her away from the hole toward the others, who had transported themselves onto a path leading out to the street. The Walsinghams stood close together, holding hands, speaking inaudible words.

Tom's eyes shone with tears, but he was master of himself. He nodded at Walsingham. "I don't know this place, but there must be a decent tavern nearby. I'd like to invite you both for a drink. Some supper, perhaps. I'd like to ask you what happened, if you know, but more — I just want to talk about Kit with folks who knew him."

Walsingham nodded. "I'd like that too. But not in a tavern. My wife and I would be honored if the two of you would come home with us to Scadbury. It's too far to ride back to Nonsuch today. Our house is only six miles. We could talk as long as we like, in private."

Audrey clasped her hands as if in prayer and spoke to Trumpet. "I told Lady Stafford we'd be gone for a night or two, thinking you might not want to go back right away. So much gossip and foolishness at court. They can be quite cruel sometimes." She cast a glance at Tom's hand, still gripping Trumpet's. "We've ample room. And we'd be grateful for the company. The house will feel empty without Mr. Marlowe. Come home with us, my lady, I beg you. Help us get through these first hard nights of grief."

Trumpet looked up at Tom, who gave her a half-smile and a one-shoulder shrug. A light in his eyes reminded her that they'd missed their three nights of love, thanks to the rain and Stephen's newly born conscience. And here was Audrey, a stranger only two weeks ago, offering to make up those lost nights with her ample rooms on her large estate in beautiful Kent at the height of spring. All it had taken to win this bounty was the loss of one true friend.

Kit had always known how to make a dramatic exit. She could see him walking into the aether with a swirl of his cloak and a wave of his hand, abetting their secret as his parting gift.

"Of course we'll come," Trumpet said. "We thank you for your kindness."

Something shattered in her chest, like a lump of clay breaking on a coffin. She looked up at Tom, drew in a shuddering breath, and burst into tears.

SIXTEEN

"Ah, there you are, Mr. Bacon." The Earl of Essex sauntered toward Francis, who sat on a bench in plain view of the windows in the Presence Chamber, through which one must pass to reach the Privy Chamber. Her Majesty sat there now, on the throne under the red canopy. It was as close as Francis dared to approach. He'd come to Nonsuch in hope of being invited back into the inner circle. It might not happen, he reminded himself every day. In fact, it was most unlikely. But it would never happen if he weren't here.

Out of sight, out of mind.

"My lord." Francis hopped to his feet and bowed from the waist. "I hope I haven't inconvenienced you." He'd been sitting here for nearly two hours, by the chapel bells. Courtiers looked the other way as they strolled past him. He had been allotted a third-share in a crowded chamber overlooking the stables — more than most Englishmen dared dream of, but still. Everyone knew he'd been denied access to the Privy Chamber and why.

Essex gave him that smile of genuine understanding that won men's loyalty on the spot. "It's the other way round, I think. I sent for you, forgetting that you couldn't come to me. And then I kept you waiting."

"Her Majesty's demands supersede all others."

"Don't they though?" Essex looked toward the green hills in which this prettiest of palaces nestled. Long shadows of the fancifully crenelated pinnacles stretched eastward from the lowering sun. Essex raised his face as if scenting the wind, closing his eyes briefly. Then he smiled at Francis. "Shall we walk? I've been standing indoors for hours and would love to stretch my legs and catch a breath of air."

"I would enjoy a walk, my lord." Francis kept himself half a step behind — easily done since the earl's long legs naturally propelled him at a swifter pace.

Essex clasped his hands behind his back. "Did you and your brother have a chance to discuss those documents I sent you?"

"We did, my lord. Both the Baines *Note* and Cholmeley's *Remembrances*. We concluded they were scarcely worth burning."

"Ha! That was my first thought. Those *Remembrances* seemed half-mad to me."

"We agree, my lord. Scoundrels repeat this sort of wicked nonsense to show their toughness and independence. Both Baines and Cholmeley hire themselves out as informers and troublemakers. Baines has been at it for years. Anthony remembered some of the items in his *Note* from another such work he produced a decade ago."

"Did he?" Essex grinned. "Worth his weight in gold, your brother. What a memory!"

"Thank you, my lord." Francis's mind threw out a vision of Anthony on a balance scale, rising well above the sacks of coin they'd borrowed. "We believe Richard Cholmeley is the worst sort of informer, my lord. The open hostility displayed toward Lord Burghley and the Privy Council betrays an unstable mind. He gains employment because he's willing to do anything for money, especially things that might harm a competitor. He may consider Christopher Marlowe to be one, for example, which is why he's mentioned in this recent rant. We recommend that you avoid retaining such men yourself."

"I leave such matters to your brother's good judgment." Essex slowed his steps to let Francis catch up as they crested a low hill. From the top, they could see miles of rolling countryside — green grass, shimmering under the sun, bordered by dark woods. A haze of purple marked a lavender field in full bloom.

"Speaking of Marlowe," Essex said, his eyes surveying the verdant prospect, "have you heard the news?"

"I have, my lord, but just the barest fact of his death. Wednesday evening, I understand. Do you know any more about what happened?"

Essex shook his head. "An altercation in a tavern, they say. A sorry death, but perhaps not unexpected, given the man's reputed character."

"I wonder at that reputation now that I've met him."

"Have you? I didn't take you for a theater-lover, Mr. Bacon."

Francis was nonplussed for a moment. "I enjoy many theatrical performances, my lord. I've written some myself, as you know."

"Oh, masques for the court. Yes, those. You've written some for me, come to think of it, which I very much appreciate. No, I meant the public theaters. Plays like Marlowe's."

"Ah. Well, no, my lord. I don't approve of the excitement such wild dramas induce, although of course I understand that is the reason for their popularity. But they inflame the passions and arouse distemper, which should never be the aim of art."

Essex wagged a chiding finger. "Passion has its place, Mr. Bacon. Strong feelings allow a public catharsis. Didn't the Greeks teach us that? But perhaps Marlowe supplied too much of it." Then he cocked his head. "And you dispute his reputation. Why is that?"

"I wouldn't say I dispute it, my lord. Rather, I consider it exaggerated, probably by the man himself. We invited him to Gray's to discuss the Baines *Note*. It was Anthony's idea since Marlowe is — or rather was — a friend of my clerk's, Thomas Clarady."

"I've met your clerk. I like him."

High praise! Francis wondered if he should pass it on. It might go to Tom's head, and he was cocky enough already. Then again, it might supply a balm against the hurt he must be feeling, assuming he'd heard the sorrowful news.

Francis sighed. "We discussed the conversation later, naturally, Anthony and I. He liked Marlowe better than I did, but we agreed that he was not at all in the same low class as Baines and Cholmeley. He did not spout sly hints and imprecations at us, for example. He conversed with knowledge and wit on difficult themes. He never lost his temper or even raised his voice."

"Difficult themes." Essex started down the other side of the hill. "I assume you mean atheism, the current theme of greatest interest on the council."

"Greatest interest, my lord? Surely there aren't enough atheists in England to warrant such attention."

"You'd be surprised at what occupies the minds of some of those exalted ministers." Essex sounded disgruntled. It must be hard to be one of only two young men around a table of old curmudgeons. And harder still when the other young one, Sir Robert Cecil, was your bitterest rival. "But atheism is a serious threat, Mr. Bacon. Or don't you agree?"

"I agree that it is serious, my lord. It draws men into skepticism, sometimes persuading them to give up on the very idea of truth. I don't believe it to be a widespread problem. It seems limited to a few would-be wits engaging in tavern talk. What little threat it poses isn't worth much effort in a time of plague, famine, and war."

"Ha! Put it that way, and one can only agree." Essex stopped to face him.

Francis said, "The torture of Thomas Kyd is an example of the sort of excessive zeal I mean. It served no purpose other than to frighten men who crucially support the good of the state, by whom I mean our English poets and pamphleteers."

"Yes, that was badly done," Essex said. "But I hear the Earl of Dorchester set that right, thanks to your clerk." He shook his head at the irony. "I wouldn't have thought Steenie had it in him. Perhaps I've had an influence."

"His Lordship has blossomed under your tutelage, I'm told."

Essex smiled smugly at the compliment, which he had earned. Francis could only imagine what it must be like to have such a beeswax of a man as Stephen Delabere at one's side day and night through a campaign filled with peril and frustration. But Essex was made of sterner stuff than most.

They walked in silence for a while. A fresh breeze cooled the sweat from Francis's brow, keeping him comfortable in spite of the sunshine warming his woolen doublet. The motion of legs and arms, combined with the peaceful beauty of the natural world, soothed his spirits as well. Following the queen on her summer progresses might be fraught with political hazards and the slights of courtiers keen to rise at another's expense, but it had its pleasures too.

Essex led him to a large pond. White clouds glowed on its blue surface, which formed a perfect mirror of the sky. They approached a stone bench under an elm tree. "Sit, Mr. Bacon. I have more news for you. Good news this time."

"My lord?" Francis lowered his bottom to the warm stone, looking up at the smile curved upon the earl's comely face. His chest tightened with anxiety. "Has Her

Majesty decided to allow me to wait upon her in the Privy Chamber once again?"

"Better than that, Mr. Bacon. Much better." Essex flicked his eyebrows. "I've decided to make you the next Attorney General. I proposed your name to her this morning. She agreed to consider it."

"Attorney General," Francis echoed. He patted himself on the cheek, earning a broad grin from the earl. "Won't it go to Edward Coke? He is Solicitor." Traditionally, when the Master of Rolls died, as Sir Gilbert Gerard had in February, the Attorney General advanced to that position, drawing the Solicitor General up to take his place.

"In my opinion," Essex said, "no man alive is better qualified than you are. I'm determined to seat you in that office."

"I'm honored, my lord. Astonished, as you can see. I never dreamed of this, not so soon." Landing in that seat of power and influence would transform Francis's fortunes. He could hold that post for the rest of his life and prosper, raising Anthony, Tom, and all his friends with him. Sir Thomas Egerton, now moving up to Master of Rolls, was an older man — some twenty years older. When he died, Francis would take his place. Given time and good health, he might one day climb into his father's seat as Lord Keeper of the Great Seal.

But the lowest rung on that long ladder was Solicitor General. Francis had yet to argue a single case in court. Not for lack of qualification. He simply hadn't had a reason to exert the effort.

"I'm honored, my lord," he said again, "and greatly flattered by your opinion. But wouldn't Solicitor General be a more palatable first step? Let Mr. Coke take the higher seat."

Essex frowned, jutting out his bearded chin. "I won't have it. He has experience, yes, but he's a petty clerk compared to you. I want the best legal mind in England in that position. I won't settle for anything less."

"Well, then," Francis said as his stomach tied itself in knots. "Attorney General it is." His mind whirled as he considered the work that lay before him, garnering supporters, preparing opinions on the most important cases of the past few years. And yes, finding some clients to defend when the courts convened again in September.

He watched the bright clouds drifting across the still waters of the pond, feeling almost as weightless and unbound. His mind whirled with visions of the possibilities. He could try cases that would affect the course of the common law. He would be regularly in Her Majesty's thoughts, if not her august presence, having every reason to discourse with her.

The news was the best possible news. The setting was the most peaceful and restorative of sites. The earl was a stalwart friend — and a stubborn man who lived to test Her Majesty's limits. Limits which only she defined.

Francis watched the snowy clouds upon the field of blue with the sense that it was all an illusion, a piece of scenery for a masque hiding the darkness of a gathering storm.

SEVENTEEN

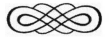

The mourners left the churchyard and walked together in silence to the King's Head, where Tom hired a horse for the next two days. Audrey Walsingham sent their escort back to Nonsuch with another message for Lady Stafford. The small party left Deptford without further fuss around half past three. England's greatest poet had been laid to rest in less than an hour with the minimum of pomp.

The weather was ideal for a late afternoon ride. Their route, as Walsingham explained, ran slightly east of due south. He set an easy pace since they had hours of daylight left and no need to hurry. He and Tom rode together with the ladies a few yards behind. Walsingham pointed out features of interest as they rode. They passed along the west side of the park surrounding Placentia Palace and then later, Eltham Palace. Otherwise, no one spoke.

The silence gave Tom time to think. He still didn't know what had happened, beyond Trumpet's terse words. "Killed in a brawl in an ordinary," she'd written. Such things happened. They happened every day. But till now, they'd only happened to men Tom didn't care about. He'd lost his father a few years ago, and his world had changed. This wasn't like that. His life would go on as before. But he'd loved Kit; more, he'd admired him. The thought that he'd never see that teasing smirk or those knowing eyes again weighed upon him like a sack of grain across his shoulders.

Shadows stretched across their path as they clopped along, though the sun stood high enough to warm their backs. Cool breezes slipped out from under the copses of oaks and hazels that dotted the hillsides. This country had the perfect balance of hills and shallow valleys, green swards and woods. No wonder the area boasted so many palaces.

Two grooms met them in the yard at Scadbury. Mrs. Walsingham led her guests to the first floor on a short wing running back from the central house. She pointed at a closed door. "That was Mr. Marlowe's room. We'll visit it in a minute, if you'd like."

"I would," Tom said. A chance to say good-bye. The wooden box they'd put in the ground had given him nothing.

She opened another door and led them into a pleasant chamber looking onto an orchard. The room was bare apart from a well-clad bed, a single chair, and a round table bearing a large bowl and pitcher. A stack of folded towels lay ready on the shelf below, and a small hearth had been laid ready for a fire.

"I thought this might suit you, Mr. Clarady," Mrs. Walsingham said.

"Admirably." Tom didn't plan on sleeping in that bed, but it did look comfortable.

"We'll give you a minute to wash your hands. You can borrow a nightshirt from my husband. We'll be just down the corridor in Lady Dorchester's room." She gave him a smile a trifle too bright, making a trifle too much effort to avoid glancing at Trumpet.

She knows, or she's guessed. They'd been unguarded at the church when they first set eyes on one another. He'd clasped her hand, hadn't he? An ordinary legal counselor wouldn't go that far to comfort a client.

They could avoid one another while staying here. He could sit up all night in the library as proof. But they wouldn't have another chance to be together for months. It would be pure self-castigation to resist the gift of these two nights. If that meant putting themselves in this woman's power, they'd just have to cope with the consequences when they arose.

The said coping would fall into Trumpet's domain. She'd manage it with her usual aplomb.

Tom went to wash his hands, but the pitcher was empty. How not, since they hadn't known this room would be occupied today? He dusted himself fore and aft as best he could, combing his hair with his fingers and peering into the small mirror to smooth his moustache.

Mrs. Walsingham knocked lightly on the door. She spotted the lack of water and promised to have it remedied at once. "But let's look at Mr. Marlowe's room. I'd like your help deciding what to do with his things."

Walsingham was already there. It was a handsome chamber, a good fifteen feet square, though four adults standing in the middle made it feel crowded. A wide window in front of the desk looked onto the orchard. If you lifted your gaze above the enchanting dance of sunlight on green leaves, your weary eyes could rest on rolling layers of green, light and dark, stretching to the horizon. No writer could ask for a more restorative view.

The bed had been made and the chamber pot emptied, but Tom suspected Marlowe had created the general tidiness. He had the self-contained habits of a man who traveled with secrets. He kept things — clothes, writing tools, saddlebags — where he could lay his hands on them at any moment. The desk alone showed signs of activity, seeming divided between two stacks of paper.

Tom and Trumpet moved together to see what their friend had left unfinished when he went to dinner in Deptford.

"The poem is called 'Hero and Leander,'" Walsingham said. He and his wife stood together near the door, shoulders touching. He topped her by only a few inches. "It isn't finished, but he had stopped at a good place. I thought I'd show it to a bookseller I know. But unfinished, perhaps it's better left unpublished." He sounded uncertain, recognizing that he had no authority over Marlowe's works.

"Do it," Tom said. "He wrote it to be read. People will want it all the more now."

Trumpet agreed with him. "This other one looks like a play. Is this his *James I?*"

"I'm going to burn that." Walsingham spoke without hesitation this time. "He shouldn't have started it. He shouldn't have thought about it, much less talked about it to the Privy Council. It's all about James's last days, when his kindred and his council struggled for power. He was assassinated, you know."

Trumpet said, "Thirty men chased him through the palace and trapped him in a sewer." Her lovely face wilted in sorrow. "Kit told me that. It sounded so much like his sort of thing."

"Too much so. He raised questions of succession and legitimacy that should never be broached. Not here. Not now." Walsingham sounded aggrieved or offended. He and his guest must have argued about that topic. But Kit had never listened to advice about his writing.

"Sounds like Kit," Tom said. "Always aiming at the center of contention."

Walsingham gave him a dark look. "It was a bad idea." The intensity behind that look sent a small shiver up Tom's spine. Bad, as in deadly?

"Burn it," Trumpet said. "No one but Marlowe could ever finish it anyway." She stroked the inky pages with her fingertips as if to commune with Kit's vanished spirit.

Tom reached for one of the ink-stained quills. "Can I have this?"

"Please," Walsingham said. He offered one to Trumpet, who accepted it gravely.

"I hate to be so mundane," Mrs. Walsingham said, "but what should I do with his clothes? He had a small chest of books too, and a rapier."

Tom and Trumpet cocked their heads at one another. Tom said, "Nashe?" She nodded. He turned to his hostess. "Give them to Thomas Nashe. He's Kit's closest friend. They met in Cambridge some ten years ago? He's poor as a church mouse. Nobody would mind seeing him in Kit's clothes. You could send them to me, if you like. I'll take charge of them until Nashe returns from Norfolk."

"If you have the room," Walsingham said. "Or we could pack the things and keep them here until you tell us where to send them."

Tom thought about his tiny chamber at the back of Bacon House. Three more chests would block either his entry or his light. "Come to think of it, I don't have room. I live in my master's house at Gray's Inn."

Walsingham tucked his chin in surprise. "Gray's Inn? I assumed you were another one of Lady Dorchester's poet friends."

Tom laughed at that, surprised he still had laughter in him. "I'm flattered, but no. I'm merely an Inns of Court man, working toward passing the bar."

Walsingham nodded, plainly taking his measure anew. "I know several members of Gray's. Who is your master, if I may ask?"

Here it came. "Francis Bacon." This nephew of the queen's greatest spymaster would recognize that name. He'd know still more about Anthony.

The name took Walsingham by surprise. He actually leaned back as if dodging a swipe of Tom's hand. He recovered, shooting a glance at his wife. "I've heard of him, of course. My uncle thought highly of both him and his brother. I hope we may meet someday."

Walsingham gave Tom another curious, sidelong look as his wife led them out of the room. He likely had questions about Tom's role in the Bacons' work. Tom had questions for him about Kit's. Perhaps they could sit down later and talk, just the two of them.

Mrs. Walsingham led them down the stairs and out into a garden backed by a red brick wall. "I thought we might have some refreshments out here. It's still warm enough. My husband thought you might want to hear about the inquest."

"We do," Tom said. "I mean, I do."

"Me too," Trumpet said. She'd been quiet since the outburst of tears at the church. She rarely cried. He couldn't remember the last time he'd seen it happen. His eyes had done some leaking on the wherry downriver, but he could feel unshed tears welling up at odd moments. They could have a good cry in each other's arms tonight.

They spaced themselves around a table already set with plates of savories and jugs of wine. Mrs. Walsingham filled cups and encouraged them to help themselves to the food. "Don't eat too much," she admonished them. "We'll have supper at seven. That will give you time to rest a little, if you like."

Trumpet roused herself to utter the courteous responses. She took a small pie and nibbled tentatively at a corner, then chomped the whole thing down in two bites and picked up another. Grief took folks differently from moment to moment, and she had ridden some fifteen miles today.

Nothing affected Tom's appetite. He'd held a feast after his father died and had eaten more than anyone else. But he was more thirsty than hungry at the moment, and thirstier still to find out what had happened to Kit. "Were you able to attend the inquest, Mr. Walsingham?"

"I was. My man Frizer was there on Wednesday, as it happens."

Tom's ears pricked at that last phrase. Bacon had taught him to pay attention to such small disclaimers. People used them to puff smoke over things they didn't want examined.

"This Frizer is a servant of yours?" Tom asked.

"He's a gentleman," Walsingham said. "He deals in properties. He's been living here while he helps me sort out some of my obligations."

"Properties" could mean anything from vast estates to barrels of oil. Vagueness piled on ambiguity. Tom nodded as if it made sense. "He must've ridden to Deptford with Marlowe, then, if they were going to the same place."

"They didn't ride together. Although it was Frizer who invited Marlowe to spend the day with him and another friend or two." Walsingham met his guests' blank faces and gave himself a little shake. "That's not helpful, is it? Let me lay it out as it was reported at the inquest." He paused for a moment and then began anew. "An acquaintance of mine named Robert Poley wanted to meet Marlowe, so Frizer arranged it. They met in Deptford for convenience."

"Whose convenience?" Tom asked.

Walsingham blinked at him. "Mr. Poley, I imagine. He travels a great deal. He may have been waiting for a ship."

"Wasn't that stated at the inquest?" Tom asked. You'd think they want to know what brought these men to that place at that time.

"I don't remember. It doesn't matter, does it?" Walsingham produced a weak smile. "Anyway, Frizer invited another friend, a Mr. Nicholas Skeres, to join them. He and Skeres work together sometimes brokering commodities. The four men spent the day at Mrs. Bull's house, a lodging house frequented by merchants and other travelers. Good food with a large garden backing onto the green."

"The whole day?" Tom asked. "What were they doing?"

"Talking, I suppose. Waiting for that ship, perhaps." Walsingham gave him another weak smile.

Tom now remembered Marlowe saying he had a meeting on Wednesday. If he played his cards right, he'd said, he'd be on his way to Scotland within the week. Poley must have been the one who would make that call.

Walsingham continued his patchy tale. "They had dinner around noon or one, then supper around six. By that time, they'd had rather a lot to drink and were doubtless a little weary of one another's company."

"I can imagine," Trumpet said. "I would've left hours before."

They hadn't concluded their business, Tom guessed. No decision taken. Kit would've argued his case for as long as he could.

Walsingham shrugged. "Mrs. Bull brought in the bill. Frizer regrets it now, but he asked Marlowe to contribute since he had insisted on sending to the King's Head for three bottles of better wine. Marlowe refused on the grounds that Frizer had invited him and thus should bear the full cost. His words had been insulting. You know how sharp he could be. They got into a ruffle about it. Next thing Frizer knew, Marlowe jumped up from the bed he'd been lying on, snatched Frizer's knife from the scabbard at his back, and pummeled him about the head with it."

"Three nasty cuts," Mrs. Walsingham put in. "I cleaned them myself. It must have hurt terribly."

Tom could almost see it. He could hear the sneering insults, especially if the day had failed to yield the hoped-for result. He could see Kit leaping up to beat the other man on the head. Tom had seen him do that very thing — an open-handed slap on the back of the skull. He'd felt it himself after some especially stupid observation. But he'd never seen Kit strike a man with the hilt of a knife or a mug or any other object. His words could be vicious, but his blows were seldom worse than humiliating.

"A struggle ensued," Walsingham went on. "Frizer got his hands on the knife. Somehow it pointed up as Marlowe was bending down. The blade went through Marlowe's eye, killing him instantly. The other three men were shocked, needless to say."

"As are we." Trumpet met Tom's gaze with a doubtful look. He returned with the slightest of nods. He couldn't quite credit the knife.

"Why didn't the other two stop the fight before it got so far out of hand?" Trumpet asked.

"One would assume they tried." Walsingham frowned at his wife for confirmation of that unfounded assumption. "Who wouldn't? At the inquest, they all said things happened too quickly for anyone to react. Poley and Skeres were trapped on the bench before the table, you see, on either side of Frizer. They couldn't get up. They must have been profoundly frustrated by their inability to act."

"Trapped," Tom echoed. Two grown men, unable to rise from a bench? And here came more "musts," "woulds," and "supposes." Those words evaded responsibility, leaving room for the speaker to deny any implications that might be drawn. But what did Thomas Walsingham have to hide? If he meant to lay their doubts to rest with that cryptic account, he'd achieved the opposite effect.

* * *

Tom washed his hands properly before supper. He'd been ready to accept a verdict of death by misadventure until Walsingham gave his account of the inquest. He'd raised questions Tom wouldn't have thought to ask. Those questions spawned others, and now he wanted answers.

Somehow he'd have to coax an invitation from his host for some private talk after the ladies retired.

The food was good, if plain, but then the Walsinghams hadn't been expecting company. They talked about the estate and its convenience to London. Walsingham recounted the history of the house, which had once been subjected to raids from bandits plying the road from London to Dover. "Hence the moat," he'd added with a smile. Tom loved the moat.

The weather got a thorough review, with competing prognoses for the coming week. After the history lesson, Tom and Mrs. Walsingham did most of the work to keep the conversation flowing. Trumpet seemed worn out by the strains of the day, and Walsingham turned his attention to his plate, picking through his meal like an invalid.

After the strawberry tart had been appreciated, Trumpet begged their forgiveness and went up to bed. She didn't so much as look at Tom. She didn't have to. If she were still sleeping when he crept into her room, he'd just slide into bed beside her. She could sleep on for all he cared, as long as he could hold her close and hear her breathing.

Mrs. Walsingham made her excuses as well, leaving the men to fend for themselves. Walsingham turned to Tom as they rose from the table. "If you're not too tired, Mr. Clarady, would you care to join me in the library?"

The invitation Tom had hoped for. He followed his host to a pleasant room with linenfold paneling, unpainted but well-polished. The windows looked out into the night, showing dark shapes of shrubs under a starry sky. Tall shelves lined the walls in the usual way but with many gaps between the books. Thomas Walsingham must not be a reading man. That seemed odd for a patron of literature, but perhaps Marlowe was the only poet he supported.

Jugs of wine and water stood ready on a cupboard along with bowls of sugar and spices. "I'll let you fix yours the way you like it," Walsingham said.

Tom filled his cup, adding a splash of water, then took a chair by the crackling fire. Walsingham set his cup on a table by the other chair, then took a box from the mantel. He sat and opened it, pulling out two long-stemmed pipes. "I've been thinking about this all afternoon. I thought we might take communion together in the true Marlovian fashion."

Tom barked a surprised laugh. "I hate the stuff, but yes. Let's do it for Kit."

They loaded their pipes with tobacco and lit them. They did their best for a few manly minutes, puffing and coughing, then set the pipes aside with rueful smiles.

Tom gulped wine to soothe his scorched throat. "Well, we tried. And wherever Kit is now, we've made him laugh."

"I hope so," Walsingham said. He'd seemed livelier, younger, while puffing away at the noxious weed, but sorrow overtook his features again. He stared bleakly into the flames.

Tom wanted to ask about Kit's intelligencing, especially his most recent commissions. He wanted to get this man's views on the Privy Council interrogations, which Kit would surely have discussed with his patron. Now he doubted he'd get any answers. The man seemed lost in grief. Besides, he'd been trained in reticence by his uncle.

But he had other questions. "I'd like to talk to the men who were there. At a Mrs. Bull's house, did you say?"

"The Widow Bull, yes. She's well-known and well-regarded in Deptford. But I've given you their testimony from the inquest. Why keep gnawing at it?"

"I'd like to get a better sense of Kit's mood that day. It isn't like him to strike a man for no reason."

"Not like him!" Walsingham nearly spat the words. "It was exactly like him. He could be wild, choleric. Mars must have ruled the heavens on the day of his birth. You would know that if you knew the man at all."

"I knew him well. Kit could be moody, certainly. Violent sometimes, but only in words. I never saw him strike anyone with anything other than his hand. He wasn't given to tavern brawls. In fact, I would say he considered that sort of thing beneath him."

Walsingham grunted, his burst of energy exhausted. "I don't go out to taverns much anymore."

Not an answer. Tom gave him a minute, then changed the subject. "You said Mr. Frizer lives here too, but he wasn't at supper. Doesn't he eat with the family?"

"Not tonight. Not with you and Lady Dorchester here. I imagine he's tired of talking about Wednesday. Not up to meeting any of Kit's friends."

"I can understand that." More imagining. Did this man know nothing for certain?

Tom determined to seek out the elusive Mr. Frizer tomorrow. "What about the other two? They were at the church, weren't they? A Robert Poley, you said, and a Mr. . . . Skeres, was it? Where could I find them?"

Walsingham blew out a noisy breath. "I have no idea. None whatsoever." He faced Tom squarely for the first time. "What difference does it make?" His raised voice sounded angry.

Why angry? There wasn't anything so unusual about Tom's questions. Most people worked through grief by picking at details — things done or not done. Tom resolved to stop in at the Widow Bull's establishment on the way home. Perhaps she would be more forthcoming.

"Ah, well," he said in a soothing rhythm. "Perhaps you're right. Best not to dwell."

Walsingham shot him a short look, then drained his cup and returned his gaze to the fire.

Tom rose to pour more wine for both of them. He added a little sugar this time. This tinto had been left in the cask too long. If — when — he had his own manor house, he'd stock it with a better class of drinkables.

His host drank off half the cup in one long swallow. Walsingham stared fixedly at the fire, the tears in his eyes reflecting the flames. Tom stared with him. Half his mind held a vision of Kit sitting in this chair, regaling his patron with improbable tales and mad philosophies. The other half poked at the holes in the story of the poet's death, wondering how he could get the answers he wanted.

Walsingham spoke softly, addressing the fire. "I should never have sent —" He stopped abruptly, his head jerking toward Tom as if he'd startled himself. "I mean, I shouldn't have let him go. I should've stopped him. Made some excuse, kept him home. Kept him safe."

Tom let the slip pass. It had revealed enough for now. "I've been thinking the same thing. I should've found a way to make him go back to Canterbury or stop writing that dangerous play. But once Kit made up his mind to do something, he could never be gainsaid."

Walsingham nodded, not looking at him. Firelight cast red shadows on his cheeks, picking out reddish glints in his beard. He pressed his lips together as if he meant never to open them again. He was hiding something; that much was clear. Deceiving someone, but whether himself or his guest, Tom couldn't tell.

* * *

He found Trumpet sitting by the fire in her bedchamber, bare toes stretched toward the heat. Her borrowed nightshirt swam on her slender shoulders. She'd draped a woolly coverlet across her lap. She smiled wanly when he came in.

"Couldn't sleep?" he asked, dropping a kiss on her head.

"I did for a little while. What time is it?"

"Not much past nine, I think."

"No long, revealing conversation by the fire?"

Tom shook his head. "A short, strange conversation." He bent to kiss her on the cheek.

She sniffed at him and shrank away. "You've been smoking tobacco!"

"Just a little, in remembrance of Kit." He made a sour face. "Nasty stuff."

She took his hands in both of hers so he could pull her to her feet. "Let's go to bed."

Tom wrapped his arms around her. "Shouldn't we talk? My gut says Walsingham's lying about that day at the Widow Bull's. I don't know why, or if they're his lies or the other men's, but I have a few guesses."

"Give your gut the night off." Trumpet placed a kiss at the base of his throat — as high as she could reach without standing on tiptoes. "I don't want to talk. I stare into the fire and see a great gaping hole in the world where Kit used to be. I can't stop feeling it, like a hollow in my own heart. I want you to make love to me and fill that hollow up again."

Tom scooped her into arms and carried her to the bed. He nuzzled her neck as he laid her down. "We've lost a life," he whispered. "Let's make another one. We'll call him Christopher."

She didn't answer. No hum, no giggle.

Ah, well. The lady said she didn't want to talk.

EIGHTEEN

Something itchy under her nose pulled Trumpet out of a dream into the new morning. Whatever the dream had been — something to do with the sea — it vanished as her eyes opened to a chestful of blond curls. She breathed in the warm scent of Tom and rubbed her cheek into the curls.

He stirred, sighed, and kissed the top of her head. "How's the hole in the world this morning?"

She closed her eyes to search for it, but her inner vision contained only Tom. "Better."

"Me too." He turned toward her, and they made love again.

This round was short, an early morning reminder of the night before. Soon she lay snuggled into his chest again, her heart restored, at least in part. She could grieve for Kit and still live her life.

A tap on the door announced the end of their reverie. Catalina peeked inside. "The house awakes, my lady. Mr. Tom must go."

"I'm out," Tom said, but he waited until the door closed to throw back the covers and get up. Trumpet leaned against the headboard with the covers pulled up to her chin to replace his warmth. She loved to gaze upon his naked body, tall and strong in the morning light. He hadn't gained an ounce of fat since she'd first met him, back when he'd been a youth of nineteen. He weighed more, thanks to years of dancing and fencing lessons, but that only improved the curves and angles.

She said as much. "A gentleman keeps himself fit," he answered, as if it were a law of nature. It didn't hold true for Francis Bacon, however. Or for Thomas Walsingham, who seemed about the same age as Tom but had already developed a little paunch.

He paused at the door. "We do need to talk. We have doubts. We have questions. Let's see if we can find some answers before we leave this place."

"Let's find Frizer, at least. And Audrey may know more about the other men, if you can't tease anything else out of her husband." She yawned, then added, "She's taking me around the estate this morning. She made the offer last night on our way upstairs. Come with us and help me tease something out of her."

Catalina entered the moment Tom left, her arms full of Trumpet's linens. She'd taken them with her the night before to be washed and ironed dry. The black kirtle, bodice, and sleeves had been hung on hooks or draped over chests to keep them from wrinkling. They smelled slightly horsey but would be fine for another two days.

"Have you met any of the servants?" Trumpet asked as they began the process of getting her into her costume.

"Yes, my lady. All of them, I think." Catalina met her gaze, her brown eyes filled with meaning. "There are not so very many."

"Oh? Understaffed, are we?"

"One cook, but no under-cook. You have two unders, my lady. She has one baker, one brewer, two assistants. But only two potboys."

"No wonder supper was so simple. I predict dinner will be eel pie, roast rabbit, and another strawberry tart."

Catalina hummed agreement as she laced farthingale to bodice. "Only one manservant, my lady. Mr. Walserham must dress himself." Her Spanish accent made a hash of some English names.

Trumpet nodded. Tom attended to himself as well. Stephen didn't even know how. Tom had done the honors of lacing him up during their years at Cambridge and Gray's Inn.

"The mistress," Catalina said, "she has a woman. From the same country, I think."

She meant the same county. "That makes sense. I don't believe they've been married for very long. A year, perhaps?"

"One year, yes, my lady. But do you know —" She bent to murmur in Trumpet's ear. "They do not sleep together."

Trumpet met her servant's dark eyes with interest. "Really? Are you sure?"

"The morning trays go up different stairs." Catalina raised her graceful hands to point in opposite directions.

"That is interesting." Trumpet turned back to face the mirror. Skirts next. "But perhaps Mr. Walsingham snores. Or *she* does." Women could snore, according to Tom. He claimed to have caught her at it once or twice, though she didn't believe him.

They finished dressing. Catalina remained to straighten the bedclothes, while Trumpet went downstairs in search of something to break her fast. She found Tom sitting alone at the long table in the hall, enjoying a plate of cold sausage and brown bread.

"Good morrow, Mr. Clarady," she sang out in case anyone was listening. Her voice echoed in the empty room.

"Good morrow, Lady Dorchester. I trust you slept well."

"As well as can be expected." He'd seated himself at the top of one long side of the table. She took the place of honor at the head. "Where are the others?"

He shrugged. "Perhaps they're early risers." He dropped his voice to a murmur. "I messed up my covers, thrashing around a bit to make my bed look slept in."

She bleated a short giggle, clapping her fingers over her lips.

"And I filled the chamber pot as best I could," he added, daring her with his blue eyes to giggle again. "They can think what they like, but the evidence shows I spent the night in my room."

"We'd make good swindlers, wouldn't we?"

"The best," Tom said. "In fact, I'm reserving that as our last resort if things ever go completely sour for us."

"Good plan." She reached a hand toward his plate, then pulled it back. "Where are the servants?"

"You have to serve yourself." He pointed at a sideboard with his knife. He waited until she returned with a selection of bread and cheese. She had to go back for a cup of ale. She sat down and stuffed warm bread into her mouth, suddenly ravenous. Yesterday had been a strenuous one, for both her body and her mind.

Tom watched her eat for a moment, then asked, "Do you think they keep a small staff to prevent blabbing? About intelligence matters, I mean."

Trumpet took a sip of ale to wash down the bread. The thin drink tasted too much of grain. Even the thrifty brewsters at her father's castle could do better. "I suppose that's possible. I think they're short of money."

"The wine wasn't very good last night. Too oaky." He gazed blankly at the single coat of arms hanging on the wall with his head cocked, the way he did when he was remembering a scene. "And there weren't many books in the library. Gaps on the shelves. Though not all gentlemen like to read."

"He's selling them. I'll bet you an angel." Trumpet pointed her knife at him. She knew all about pinching pennies to keep a household running. Her father, the infamous Earl Corsair, lost more treasure than he won chasing Spanish ships. She had learned at an early age how to keep her people warm and fed with whatever the estate could produce on its own.

"I'll join you on that tour," Tom said. "We have all day. I'll bet Walsingham avoids me this morning." He told her about the slip of the tongue last night.

"*Sent* him? To do what?" Trumpet tried the cheese. Tasty, if a little coarse.

"To meet with Robert Poley, I think. He may be another intelligencer. Walsingham said he's a man who travels. He could be one of those middling men, the handlers, like Walsingham used to be. And still is, for all we know."

"That could be why they're so poor," Trumpet said. "Audrey warned me about the expense of maintaining an intelligence service."

Tom gave her a wry look, guessing, no doubt, that she'd raised the subject. "It does look like he's been keeping his hand in. Perhaps he arranged that meeting, using his property agent as an intermediary. Maybe Poley asked for it. Maybe Kit did. The last time I saw him, he was expecting to win a commission to go north."

"Scotland," Trumpet said. "Everyone's thinking about it, even if no one talks about it."

"That's what Mr. Bacon said." Tom quirked his eyebrows. "Both of them. They told him not to write that play."

Trumpet gulped some more watery ale. She was so thirsty this morning. For a moment, the reason for that thirst transported her back to that well-built feather bed. They had tested its construction vigorously last night.

Tom gave her a smug look. He must have seen a smile fleet across her lips and took credit for it. "Anyway," he said, "the purpose of that meeting wasn't to while away the day while Poley waited for a ship. Kit went there to be interviewed, I'd bet money on it. The other two men were a property agent and a commodity broker, whatever that means. So Poley must have been the one to decide if Kit could be trusted with sensitive messages."

Trumpet shook her head. "Kit would have passed that test, don't you think? He must have been trustworthy. He'd been doing that sort of thing for years."

"True." Tom nodded slowly as he fed himself another slice of sausage on the point of his knife. "But everyone pales when you mention Scotland. It must be more ticklish than the ordinary sort of commission."

"Mmm." Trumpet lowered her voice. "They must all go to King James or his servants. Tricky stuff. No one on the Continent has claims to the throne."

Tom held a finger to his lips. With a quick glance around the still-empty hall, he said, "I can't believe Kit pummeled that Frizer fellow with his knife. I'd like to hear the story from him. He must have been there yesterday. Do you know which one he was?"

Trumpet cast her mind back to the men in the pews. "He could have been the plump one with the piggish nose. He looked like a property broker. Let's ask Audrey to introduce us after our tour. He must be around here somewhere."

"Walsingham came as close to saying, 'Leave him alone,' as a man can without being rude." Tom shook his head. "How could the other two sit there like lumps of clay with all that fury going on beside them?"

He got up to add more bread and a few hunks of cheese to his plate. As he sat down again, he said, "We talk to Frizer and get his side of the story. I'll try to track down the other two. Then what?"

"Let's see what Frizer has to say," Trumpet answered. "But I wouldn't mind reading that coroner's report myself."

"Neither would I," Tom mumbled through a mouthful of bread and cheese. He swallowed and gave her his best dimpled grin. "And nobody can get official documents from an official source faster than Anthony Bacon. I'll ask him tomorrow on the way to Twickenham. I promised to help him move."

* * *

They returned to their bedchambers so as to arrive separately outside the front door, where Audrey waited for Trumpet. Tom went out first, ostensibly to take himself for a salutary stroll. Trumpet found him chatting with Audrey on the brick path that wound through the small interior garden. Scadbury had been built in olden days when every manor had to defend itself. The brick-and-stone wings formed a square surrounding this sheltered space. One entered through a gatehouse set in the middle of one side.

Trumpet scorned the little garden. Hers had larkspur and Solomon's seal blooming in this season, among others. This one offered no color but green, though the shrubs were neatly trimmed and the path swept clean.

"I'm afraid my husband has work to attend to this morning," Audrey said. "He sends his regrets. Shall we walk?" Audrey gestured toward the gatehouse. She wore the same dark gray costume she'd worn yesterday. Perhaps she feared Trumpet would feel awkward wearing the same gown, sleeves and all, two days running.

They walked through the gatehouse and across the bridge. "This is a drawbridge," Audrey said with a laugh. "You don't see many of these anymore."

Tom asked how the bridge worked and learned it hadn't been raised in years. "Be fun to have it repaired, wouldn't it? You could play a trick on your guests some evening."

He'd taken up the role of a fascinated observer, delighted with all he saw. He pointed, asked questions, and clapped his hands at the answers. He swore he wanted a place exactly like this after he passed the bar. His handsome features supplied all the conventional responses, keeping their hostess occupied while Trumpet made a considered survey of the estate.

The bones were good, but the place looked half-starved. No flowers in the courtyard, for a start. A few bricks had gone missing from the outer wall. The moat held more weeds than water, by the stagnant odor. It should have fish in it to keep it clean and supply the kitchen.

Tom praised the weedy kitchen garden with its mossy walls so enthusiastically that Audrey stopped in the middle of the path to cock her head at him. "I swear, Mr. Clarady, I think you're ready to purchase an estate this very day. I'll do you a favor and introduce you to Mr. Frizer. He's your man, if you really are interested."

"That's very kind of you." Tom's mouth formed an O of surprised delight.

Kind indeed. It saved them having to devise a ploy for achieving that very thing. Trumpet had to turn full around to hide her silent laughter.

Audrey turned her pretty head from side to side as if expecting the man to be standing somewhere nearby. Then she wiggled a finger at Tom. "I know where he is — reading by the fishpond. He likes the bench there on sunny mornings like this."

They left the vegetable garden through a postern gate and followed a winding path to a round pond backed by lime trees. Shrubby willows crowded the banks. Lily pads spread into the center. Trumpet lagged behind to peer into the murky water, spying three or four silver-striped perch. A well-kept pond should be brimming in this season.

A gentleman sat on a stone bench in a patch of dappled shade — the man from the middle pew at the church, the portly one with the flat nose that made Trumpet think of a pig. He rose when he noticed their approach.

Audrey made the introductions. Ingram Frizer bowed deeply over Trumpet's hand, which she'd extended out of habit. He clasped it and planted a moist kiss on the back. She bore it without flinching. Had this hand struck the blow that killed her friend? She surreptitiously rubbed hers on her skirt.

He didn't seem to notice. He crossed his hands over his round belly and gave her a smirk. "May I say, my lady, that the color black suits you excellently well. In spite of the tragedy that occasions it, I should say."

She formed a curve on her lips but didn't bother to thank him. People expected a certain degree of rudeness from the nobility. It was a like an invisible shield she could raise whenever she pleased.

Frizer turned to Tom, extending his hand for a gentlemanly shake. Tom gripped it firmly, holding longer than strictly necessary. A glitter in his eyes told Trumpet he'd had the same thought — that this was the hand that had killed Kit.

Tom's genial expression grew somber. "Tell me, Mr. Frizer. What happened over there in Deptford? It's so hard to take in. I just can't comprehend it."

Frizer mirrored his demeanor, nodding as he pulled his hand free in little jerks. He proceeded to relate the same narrative Walsingham had offered them, with elaborations that added nothing. He started with the overlarge bill, owing to Marlowe's demand for costly wine. "It seemed only fair for him to help cover it."

"Mmm." Tom nodded shortly.

Frizer smiled, taking that for agreement. "We bickered a bit, and I'm sorry to say, things got a little heated. Next thing I knew" — the very words Walsingham had used —

"Kit leapt up, grabbed my knife, and beat me about the head with it."

He removed his short-crowned hat and bent double to show the wounds still visible through his thinning brown hair.

Trumpet studied them closely, going so far as to reach out and twitch aside a strand or two to get a better look. Round bruises, two still red in the center. She wanted to reach around the man for his knife and hold the pommel to the wounds for comparison but managed to restrain herself. Overt antagonism seldom aided an investigation.

She smiled at Frizer as he straightened up and restored his hat. "That must have been a great shock to you."

"Indeed, my lady. Thank you for your understanding." He told them how he had struggled with Kit for possession of the knife. "It was awkward, I can tell you, sitting on that bench, twisting half-around. I got the cursed thing into my hands at last, but as I tried to turn back, the point caught Mr. Marlowe in the eye. I believe his own downward movement drove the point home."

"How awful," Trumpet said. She couldn't think of anything to ask. She didn't want to believe that Kit had struck first, but this man had clearly been pummeled. If Kit hadn't done it, who had?

Audrey clapped her hands together. "Let's talk about something more cheerful, shall we?" She gestured from Tom to Frizer. "Mr. Clarady is interested in a property like this one. Not today, I don't think. Next year, I would guess, after he passes the bar."

"An important transition." Frizer switched in the blink of an eye from the sorrowful dealer of accidental death to the able broker of juicy estates. "And may I say, you're wise to be looking ahead. Properties that afford the peace of country life within easy reach of Westminster are hard to find at a good price. South of the river will give you the best options. Allow me to show you some of the features you might like to consider. With my mistress's permission, of course."

He bowed to Audrey, who twinkled at him as if enjoying some private joke.

She led the way around the pond. Trumpet remarked on the lack of fish. Audrey declared a preference for lily pads. Tom supported the aesthetic approach, at which point Frizer declared it the most modern method of estate management.

Arrant nonsense. A fishpond supplied food for both hall and servants at a minimal cost. Fish could be dried for soup in the winter. They also ate the tadpoles that produced noisy choruses of frogs. Every well-managed estate should have at least one well-kept fishpond. Either this Frizer was an ignorant fool or he was the sort of cozener who agreed with everything his current prospect said.

She'd bet the smallest manor in her dowry on the latter.

They visited a pigeon house devoid of birds and a large stable enjoyed by a mere half-dozen horses. They didn't pass a single gardener, though Frizer kept up a lively stream of excuses as they went. They were taking stock preparatory to launching a new approach. The gardeners — a family — had taken a few days off to visit relations. The pigeon house was in the middle of an annual cleaning.

Where had the birds gone, then? To the nearest inn?

They ended up in the herb garden, another walled enclosure near the house. This vital resource had also been neglected, but Trumpet liked herb gardens gone wild. The plants could take care of themselves, for the most part. The strongest grew rampant, while the weaker ones found shelter in odd places. They also bore a heavenly fragrance on a sunny day.

She twisted off a sprig of rosemary and handed it to Tom. "Rosemary is for remembrance." He nodded and held it to his nose.

To deflect suspicion, she tugged off sprigs for Audrey, Frizer, and herself. No one could resist that wholesome scent.

"We won't forget him, will we?" Trumpet said.

"No, we won't," Audrey answered.

"Although," Frizer said, drawing out the word to warn them of a contrary thought, "in time, we will be reconciled to the loss. We may even find a silver lining inside the tragedy."

Tom's eyes flashed. "How's that, Mr. Frizer?"

The broker held up his hands for peace. "A tragedy. I said as much. But you know Mr. Marlowe had become difficult to know. Difficult to claim as a friend. He was too outspoken, had too many dangerous ideas. The more his friends tried to restrain him, the wilder he became." Frizer frowned at Tom. "I can see this angers you, Mr. Clarady, so I won't belabor it. It's too soon for such reflections. But even mundane affairs like property transactions could be affected, you know. People don't want to be caught up in such trouble — the worst kind of trouble. They'll avoid the slightest association with a — well, with a blasphemer."

Audrey moved closer to the property broker, as if to align herself with his position. "I wouldn't have said it myself, not so soon. The grief is too fresh, and my husband can scarce — well, he's not ready to think about it yet. But he — we — will be better off without Mr. Marlowe in the long run. You will too, I suspect." She looked up at Frizer and nodded. He smiled down at her — a smile of praise for a clever partner, with just the lightest touch of affection.

Trumpet noted their accord while battling a fierce desire to scream at them. Better off without Kit! She might have grabbed Frizer's knife and put a few more dents in his skull if he were a foot shorter. She bit her lip hard enough to bring a tear to her eye.

Tom simply said, "Hmph," and turned his back on them to walk down the path toward the house.

* * *

Walsingham reappeared in time for dinner, which did include eel pie. Also roast tench and a pottage of fresh greens. Another strawberry tart rounded out the meal — a dish Trumpet never tired of. The host entertained his guests with tales about Kent in days gone by. It had been quite a lawless place, by his account, thanks to that London-to-Dover road. Bandits of all stripes, including Frenchmen, had prowled the hills looking for booty.

Afterward, Trumpet excused herself and went upstairs for a nap. She would leave at once if it weren't the chance of another night with Tom. They'd learned enough about the Walsinghams to support their first suspicions. It was galling to sit across a table smiling at people who might have conspired to murder their friend. Although perhaps they hadn't meant for things to go so far.

She slept for hours, waking groggy and disoriented until Catalina appeared with a cup of cool wine and a freshly brushed gown. She got through supper by chatting about fishponds and herb gardens with Audrey while the men discussed property values. Neither of them knew anything on the subject, but that didn't stop them from speculating.

At last, the Walsinghams went to bed. They left the hall together, wherever they might end up. Trumpet gladly shed her clothes one more time, handing her soiled chemise to Catalina in exchange for Audrey's nightshirt.

She left one candle burning on the mantel and climbed into bed, lying against a heap of pillows. She thought about all the things that would change because of Kit's death and how many people would be affected. Her heart broke again thinking about Thomas Nashe. When would he find out? Who would tell him? Kit had been like a brother to him.

She pondered the ways Kit could have caused trouble for Thomas Walsingham. People seeking advancement reached as high as they could. That was the nature of the world. Audrey had reached for Trumpet that day on the bowling green. She'd allowed it, being on the lookout for useful retainers herself.

But you didn't want associates who might end up on the rack. Everyone knew people would say anything under torture. They'd implicate their own grandmother, if they had one. What would they say about mere acquaintances? The mere threat of torture could frighten people into pointing their fingers at anyone who might draw attention from themselves.

A soft knock heralded Tom's arrival. He grinned at her readiness and began to remove his clothes. "I had an idea," he said, shrugging out of his unlaced doublet. "If we agree that Kit's death was not an accident —" He paused, waiting for her nod. "Then we should do this right. Let's get that coroner's report and review it with Mr. Bacon. Either one will do. Francis is at Nonsuch, and Anthony's at Twickenham, or will be. That can't be much farther for you than Deptford. Do you think you could get there on, say, Tuesday afternoon?"

"I'll find a way." Trumpet sat up, leaning forward with her hands flat on the covers. "But what about the other poets? Do they know? Who will tell them?"

"I will." Tom untied the drawstring holding up his round hose and let them fall. He sat on the edge of the bed to remove his long black stockings. He really did have the best legs in England, Sir Walter Ralegh notwithstanding. "I'll go to the Goose and Gall tomorrow or the next day. Someone will be there. We'll raise a few glasses and trade lines from Kit's plays. It isn't enough, but it's better than nothing."

"I'll be there if I can," she said. "Though it won't be easy."

"Here's hoping." Tom pulled off his shirt. And that was the end of talk for some time.

The candle had guttered in its dish by the time they broke apart. Tom lay flat on his back, sated but in a pensive mood. Trumpet felt it too. She propped herself up on one elbow to look down at him, tracing the edge of his beard with one finger. Tomorrow, they'd ride off in different directions. She'd see him Tuesday, but not alone. Not like this. It was now or never for her news.

Their eyes met, and they spoke at the same time.

He said, "I'm going to marry someday."

She said, "I'm with child again."

Tom sat up so abruptly he knocked her over. "What?" He propped himself on an elbow to smile down at her. "How is that possible? I mean, I know how it's possible, but how you can know so soon?"

She gave him a wary look. "It isn't yours."

"Not mine? Then whose?"

She swatted at him, outraged, catching him on the lip.

"All right, I didn't mean it like that. But *Stephen?*" Tom's whole body tensed with anger. He gripped her shoulder and gave her a hard shake. "You let him do *this?*"

"It isn't like this." She pointedly removed his hand from her body. She couldn't blame him for feeling hurt, but neither would she tolerate an angry touch. "I don't love him and he doesn't love me. We like each other, which makes things easier. We work well together. That's the main thing. As for the bed part, we're very restrained and respectful of one another."

"Ugh." Tom sneered. "What's that like?"

Trumpet rolled her eyes. "You'll find out if you *marry*. When will that famous event take place?" She made no effort to keep the jealousy out of her tone. She had as much reason to feel abused as he did — or she would, if he ever really did take a wife.

"After I pass the bar. Next year. Maybe next June. But one thing at a time. What caused this sudden urge to make restrained and respectful love to your spleeny, wart-necked husband? You went to great lengths to avoid him on your wedding night, as I recall. Can't you get through the winter without a poke anymore?"

He'd meant that to hurt and it did. Trumpet ignored it. "My wedding night was two years ago. Things change. He's changed. He's not the contemptible fool we knew at Gray's." She reached for Tom's hand. He allowed her to take it. "Once I saw how much you love Baby William, I knew I had to give Stephen one of his own. He's treated me with nothing but kindness and courtesy. It's only fair."

"Fair." Tom spat the word. "When did that become your first concern?"

She narrowed her eyes at him. Fairness had always been a concerns, if not always the first one. "Maybe I've changed too. Maybe two years with my new family in Dorchester has taught me something about the value of lineage. I'm happy for the next Earl of Orford to be your son. I consider that title mine to bestow. But Stephen is the eighth of his line. Who am I to break so long and distinguished a chain?"

"How do you know it hasn't been broken already? The third Lady Dorchester might have had a multitude of lovers, for all you know."

She had no answer for that. "I've thought this through, you know, from every angle. The last reason is the strongest. What if William starts to look more like you as he gets older? Stephen will notice, if no one else does. But if the second son is clearly his, I'll have room to bargain." She sighed. "This is the way the world works, Tom. We don't get everything we want. Sometimes we have to play the roles we're given."

Tom growled deep in his throat. He couldn't answer that. After a long pause, he said, "Then you'll understand why I have to marry. I want children too. Sons, daughters — I'm not fussy on that score. But I want a child I can claim as my own. Bounce on my knee and tell stories about my father. I have things to teach a child, you know."

"Like the law?" Trumpet regretted the pert tone as soon as the words left her mouth.

"Don't mock me." He sounded hurt.

She pressed his hand. "I'm sorry." Sorry about many things she couldn't change.

The candle hissed and went out. Starlight filled the room. Tom took his hand back, but only to shift her around so she lay against his chest. "When we started down this road — that night in the cellar in Cambridge, remember?"

Trumpet grinned into the darkness. "I remember. I'm surprised you do."

"I remember every minute that has you in it. I knew trouble might come to us, one way or another. But I only knew it in my head." He kissed her temple. "I thought we'd be caught and scolded. Separated. Maybe jailed for a little while."

"Which happened, including the scolding, if you count Mr. Bacon."

Tom chuckled. She could feel his chest move against her back. "I thought the trouble would be out there in the world, where it couldn't touch us. I never expected trouble here." He laid a hand over her heart. He sighed. "Didn't think it through very well, did we? And now it's too late."

"It was too late the day you threw me into that duck pond and I lost my boy's wig. But we'll get through it, won't we?" She didn't like the pleading in her tone. She tilted her head back sharply, cracking him on the chin. "As long as your wife isn't prettier than me."

"Foolish wench." He kissed her nose. "There are no women prettier than you."

He held her tight as he slid them both underneath the covers. They slept intertwined, cocooned in each other's breath and heartbeats, storing them up like grain in a silo for the long winter to come.

NINETEEN

Tom skipped church Sunday morning, certain no one at Scadbury would report him. He returned his horse to the King's Head but did not go straight down to the wharf. Instead, he strolled around the green until he found someone who could point out Mrs. Bull's house. He saw signs of life inside the front room and knocked on the door. It was well past ten o'clock. Any slug-a-beds inside deserved to be waked.

A servant answered the door and left him on the stoop while she fetched her mistress. Tom asked Mrs. Bull if she would mind answering a few questions about the day of Marlowe's death. She minded very much, if he cared to know it. She'd answered the questions they'd asked her at the inquest and did not have time to be showing every curious Tom and Tib around her garden. She all but slammed the door in his face.

Not the gossipy type, then. Doubtless her lodgers considered that an asset.

As Tom stood on the wharf waiting for a wherry going upriver, he remembered that Walsingham had referred to Mrs. Bull as a widow. A widow with property — thriving, by the neat look of her house and servant. What were the odds she belonged to the Widows' Guild?

He stopped at the Antelope Inn on his way through Holborn to have a quiet word with the proprietress, Mrs.

Sprye. She served the legal community with lodgings, private dining rooms, and a respectable public room. She'd been a good friend to Tom since he first arrived at Gray's. She was also one of Trumpet's co-conspirators, giving her a place to change from boy to girl — or vice versa — in case of need. She hosted the monthly dinners of the Widows' Guild, arranging a lecture from some member of the legal community on topics of interest to women managing their own estates.

Mrs. Sprye hadn't heard the news of Marlowe's death. That surprised Tom. It had been four whole days. Such a blow to English drama should have been shouted from the rooftops.

But she only frowned and tucked a strand of dark blond hair back under her frilled coif. "He's the one who wrote *Tamburlaine*, wasn't he? Oh my, how I loved that play! I saw it four times."

"He also wrote *Doctor Faustus*," Tom said, wanting his friend to be remembered for more than one thing.

"Oh no." Mrs. Sprye pursed her pink lips. "That one was too frightening for me. I only saw it twice."

Tom smiled. Kit would've loved both responses. "I miss him."

"A young man, was he? That's always hard."

"A few years older than me. I admired him enormously when we first met at Cambridge. That changed as I got to know him." Tom thought about Kit's infuriatingly opaque, taunting methods of teaching him spycraft. "He was a difficult friend, to be honest."

Mrs. Sprye patted his hand. "Sometimes those are the ones that most inspire us."

That simple remark — that homely truth — settled something in Tom's heart. It gave him a way to carry Kit in his memory with less grief and more gratitude. Being close to his mother's age but far more worldly-wise, thanks to her trade, the innkeeper always managed to guide him toward understanding.

She sent for paper and quill. "I'll gladly write you a note commending your honesty and discretion, but you won't need it. Just mention your guardian's name. Mrs. Bull will melt like butter on a hot bun."

* * *

Tom spent the rest of the day helping to move Anthony to Twickenham, the Bacon family's small property on the Thames. They boasted a pair of hunting boxes, simple two-story houses. Nothing grand, apart from being situated directly across from Richmond Palace.

They loaded a hired cart with the feather beds, the French desk, and other essential furnishings. Then came the chests, large and small, containing bedding, clothing, books, and any other oddments Anthony might want during his three months at the plague-free retreat. Thomas Lawson, Anthony's close friend, drove the cart down to Temple Wharf. Meanwhile, Tom and Jacques carried the invalid out to his coach and rode with him. The driver would take the long road west after depositing his master at the wharf.

It took four wherries to transport everything and everyone upriver. Anthony bore the upheaval with his usual good cheer, but the strain showed in the paleness of his cheeks. Still, his brown eyes gleamed with interest as Tom told him about Marlowe's death.

"Such accidents happen all the time," the spymaster warned him. "Men daring and dauntless enough for intelligencing tend to strike quickly and lie about it later." But he promised to have a copy of the coroner's report by Tuesday afternoon.

* * *

Tom went back Deptford on Monday morning, arriving around ten o'clock again. This time he introduced himself as a gentleman of Gray's Inn and the ward of Lady Elizabeth Russell, Dowager Countess of Bedford. He was admitted at once to the parlor, seated on a polished chair, and offered a cup of beer. Good beer.

Mrs. Bull frowned as she read Mrs. Sprye's note. She remained standing, slightly to one side, whether out of habit or so she could look down her fleshy nose at Tom, he couldn't hazard a guess.

"Lady Elizabeth Russell." The widow's voice held a note of awe. "My father was a Server of the Chamber to King Henry the Eighth. Mrs. Blanche Parry, Her Majesty's late Chief Gentlewoman of the Privy Chamber, was a cousin on my mother's side."

Tom frowned as if impressed. In truth, he was — a little.

Mrs. Bull raised her dark gray eyebrows at him. "You're Lady Russell's ward, you say?" Her steely blue eyes flicked across his beard, his size, and his lawyerly garb.

"My father died before I turned twenty-one, leaving lands that brought me under the jurisdiction of the Court of Wards."

She sighed, on his behalf, perhaps. "Well, you could've done a lot worse."

The universal opinion. Tom had appreciated it too at first. But that time had passed.

She folded up the note and tucked it into a pocket under her crisp green apron. "I don't know what I can tell you that you couldn't learn from the coroner's report."

"I haven't seen it yet," Tom confessed, "though I've asked for a copy. I suspect it won't go beyond the bare facts, however. Mr. Marlowe was a dear friend of mine. I know it may seem melancholic, but I wanted to know how he spent his last day. He arrived around this time of the morning, as I understand."

"He was the last. Mr. Poley was first. He came in, oh, perhaps half an hour earlier. He's one of my regulars, you see. He likes to be first on the spot, as he puts it." She crossed her wrinkled hands across her waist.

"Then Mr. Frizer and Mr. Skeres came next?"

"That's right. The girl led them straight out to the garden, where Mr. Poley sat with a nice cup of cool beer."

"This is excellent beer, by the way."

She granted that a small smile. She knew her worth. "I happened to be upstairs when Mr. Marlowe arrived. I noticed him striding down the street with his long legs. Probably coming from the stables at the King's Head. He was a handsome one, wasn't he?" She shook her head at the waste of youth and beauty.

Tom nodded. "I'd like to see the garden, if I may."

"All my gentlemen like walking in my garden. They're mostly merchants of the better sort, or travelers like Mr. Poley. They appreciate a chance to stretch their legs in a quiet green place."

The garden was indeed a pleasant place and quieter than you'd expect for being so near the shipyards and bustle of the port. Large enough for a small orchard and a neat herb garden, it extended to the village green at the back. A brick wall preserved its privacy. The advantageous position meant no tall houses crowded behind the wall with windows through which prying eyes might peer.

Flower beds brightened the scene with red, white, and yellow blossoms. Tom didn't know much about flowers. He would let Trumpet design his gardens, when he had some. He did like the zestful colors though. They refreshed the eye while enlivening the wits.

The span of time the four men had passed together made more sense to him now. "I could spend a day here with pleasure."

Mrs. Bull hummed her agreement. "They walked up and down, up and down."

"All four of them?"

"I didn't sit in the window and watch them. I have my work to do, you know. But I'd glance down when I passed along the corridor upstairs." She pointed to a row of narrow windows set at eye level. "Mr. Poley and Mr. Marlowe seemed to have a great deal to discuss. Every time I chanced to look out, they were walking and talking."

"What about the other two?"

"They spent most of the day sitting at that table over there." She pointed to a round table with four stools set beneath an oak tree. "Mr. Frizer brought a satchel of papers with him. He and Mr. Skeres kept themselves busy with those."

"I see."

Frizer must have arranged the day for the four men, at Poley's instigation — or Thomas Walsingham's. Poley had come to evaluate Kit. Frizer must have known they would spend most of the day in private conversation, so he invited Skeres to keep him company. Those documents were probably deeds or other contracts for deals in which the two men were collaborating.

"Did they stay out here all day?" He couldn't remember what the weather had been like.

"They came inside for dinner and supper." Mrs. Bull sounded as if she were explaining simple facts to a dullard. "I have a nice private dining room for the use of my day gentlemen." She gestured toward the house, correctly assuming Tom wanted to see that too.

They entered a clean room whose two windows overlooked the garden. Tom had been taught to measure spaces by extending his arms full out to either side. Mr. Bacon claimed that the distance between his fingertips equaled his height. He and Trumpet had tested it several times and found it true. He'd since learned to measure six feet by sight alone. This room was about twelve by fifteen, just large enough for a narrow bed pushed against the wall under the windows and a long table set flush against the inside wall. Two benches stood beneath the table, with a couple of stools nearby. The room had no fireplace. They must bring in a brazier on cold days.

"I suppose you pull the table out for meals," Tom said, though that wouldn't leave much room to move about.

"It's a bit small, I grant you, but I've had no complaints."

"Not with such good beer." Tom smiled, showing her his dimple. Her gaze lit on it, but she didn't smile back. "I'll bet the food is just as good."

"I've had no complaints."

Ah, well. Not every woman could be charmed.

"Did none of the men leave the house during the day?" If they arrived around ten and the accident occurred shortly after six, they'd spent eight hours in each other's company. No wonder tempers had grown a little frayed.

"No one left," Mrs. Bull said. "Although, now you ask, Mr. Poley did send for a messenger from the King's Head after dinner. Then he received a message from a man on horseback right before supper."

"What was that about?" Walsingham hadn't said anything about messages. He might not have known. Why volunteer information at an inquest? A man like Poley would doubtless answer only the questions asked and keep the rest to himself.

"I wouldn't know," Mrs. Bull snapped. "I don't pry into my gentlemen's affairs. They know they can rely on my discretion."

"I meant no offense, Mistress." Tom gave her another dimpled smile, but she was through with him.

His work here was done anyway. He thanked her for her trouble and left. As he walked back to the wharf, he calculated times and distances in his head. Poley sent a message after dinner. That would have been about one o'clock. The messenger had arrived around six, presumably carrying an answer. That gave five hours for the round trip: message sent, answer received. A good horse could carry a man at a trot about eight miles in an hour.

Tom ruled out the river because of the horse. What lay about sixteen miles from Deptford, land-wise?

Nonsuch Palace, for one. Five hours was enough time to ride there, wait for an audience, and carry back instructions. From a Privy Councilor, perhaps?

Tom nodded to himself. Likely; very likely. And now the question was, which one?

TWENTY

"Trumpet's coming," Tom announced by way of a greeting.

Francis gave him a wide-eyed warning look, tilting his head toward Anthony. The spymaster had not yet been made privy to the closeness of their friendship with Lady Dorchester, nor the reasons for it.

"Her idea," Tom said, turning to Anthony. "She wants to meet you."

"And I her." Anthony put down his quill. "The famous Trumpet, at last! Christened Alice Trumpington, now Lady Dorchester. It's a charming nickname."

"She's too short for anything longer." Tom flashed a grin. Now he turned back to Francis. "She shares my doubts about Marlowe's death. She wants to study that coroner's report as much as I do."

Francis pressed his lips together. Perhaps it was just as well. He'd agreed to come up from Nonsuch to discuss that report in hopes that his brother would help persuade Tom to let the matter drop. Grief took men in different ways. Many refused to accept the loss; others sought someone to blame. Tom fell into the latter category. He seemed determined to prove his friend had not caused his own death.

Trumpet doubtless shared his views. They always abetted one another's schemes, however ill-planned or poorly grounded. Better to treat them both together than to leave one free to re-infect the other.

Tom crossed the large room to peer out the window facing the road south. "They should be here soon. She planned to leave after dinner, once Her Majesty was settled for her nap."

"Shouldn't she be there when the queen awakes?" Francis asked.

"She says not," Tom answered. "She has the rest of the day free. She says Her Majesty will likely stay up all night playing cards with Lord Essex, so the maids of her chamber won't be needed."

"You're well informed." Francis heard the touch of bitterness in his tone. As an outcast, he knew nothing about the royal routine.

"We write every day. Sometimes twice." Tom pulled a ring from his pocket and tossed it in the air. "I have one of Stephen's old seals."

Francis gave him a chastening look that elicited only a cocky grin. That pair took far too many risks, but they were deaf to remonstrances. He only hoped to stay clear of the storm that must eventually descend upon them.

"Here's that report. You might as well read it while we wait." Anthony extended a roll of paper toward Tom.

He took it and looked about for a seat, choosing a backed stool near the stone-lined fireplace. No fire had been lit since the day had started mild and promised to grow warmer. The spymaster sat in the light of the two front windows at the long dining table, already covered with unfolded letters, rolled documents, and flat boxes containing more papers.

Francis used the French writing desk, sitting with his back to the side window. He liked facing his brother. They often paused in their work to trade observations.

He liked this room, with its lime-washed walls reflecting the daylight and the portrait of his father hanging amid bows and arrows. None of the Bacons hunted, but a guest would go out to stalk rabbits or birds from time to time. They always had more guests when Anthony was in residence.

Tom read the report twice, shuffling the pages. "This doesn't contradict what Walsingham told us. But it paints a different picture."

"In what way?" Francis had yet to be informed about the Scadbury visit. Anthony had told him that Tom had spent two nights with the Walsinghams after Marlowe's funeral, resulting in doubts about the cause of the poet's death. Hence the desire to consult the official report.

"Walsingham used a lot of those words you taught us to notice," Tom said. "Lots of 'mights' and 'coulds,' often introduced with 'I imagine' or 'I suppose.' He seemed reluctant to allow any actual thing to have actually happened."

Anthony raised his eyebrows at Francis, who returned a smug smile. He had trained Tom in intelligence work in his own fashion, inculcating an exquisite attention to detail. He'd trained Trumpet too, for that matter. This meeting would give him a chance to show Anthony the advantages of his methods by exhibiting his pupils' skills.

Tom noted the byplay with a flick of his eyebrows. "So there's the vagueness. Then, after many cups of wine, he slipped up. He said, 'I should never have sent him,' meaning Marlowe and that meeting in Deptford. He caught himself and changed course, but he shot me a glance that told me he knew he'd slipped. I pretended not to notice, but I take it as the truth. He arranged that meeting, using Frizer as the broker. The purpose, I believe, was for Kit and Robert Poley to talk. I'd like to know what Walsingham's interest is, for one thing."

"He may have none," Francis said. "Perhaps his only motive was to give his guest a little push to put down his quill and get out of the house." Tom had done that to him more times than he could count.

Tom shook his head. "Kit went out every day to attend upon the Privy Council. That would take hours, whether they were at Whitehall or Nonsuch. And that estate is large, with lots of good walking."

Francis noticed movement outside the opposite window. Two horses trotted into the yard. Their groom jogged forward to take the reins as two gentlemen in fashionable riding clothes swung down from their mounts.

Tom hopped up to admit the newcomers. The shorter one wore a suit of dark red with black silk trim, while the taller one with the Spanish coloring wore brown with cream linings. Both wore supple boots cuffed above the knee and wide-brimmed hats with brass brooches.

The saucy pair of minxes offered Francis short bows, then turned expectantly toward Anthony. Tom did the honors. "Lady Dorchester, may I present Mr. Anthony Bacon. Mr. Bacon, this other gentleman is my lady's companion, Mistress Catalina Luna."

Trumpet held out a gloved hand, palm sideways. Anthony hesitated, clearly not sure if he was meant to shake or kiss it. He touched the fingers tentatively.

Trumpet gripped his hand and gave it a firm shake. "Only treat me as a lady when I'm dressed as one, Mr. Bacon. It's simpler and preserves my disguise. Friends call me Trumpet in private and Mr. Trumpet in public."

"I'm delighted to meet you, Mr. Trumpet." Anthony inclined his head toward the other woman. "And you as well, Mr. Luna."

Mr. Luna swept off her hat and bowed. She had crafted a flawless illusion for them both. Unless you had reason to suspect, you'd never guess these booted and mustachioed young gallants were women. As always, Francis wondered how many such counterfeits — men or women — he had encountered in the ordinary course of his life. Men's and women's clothing were so different. They presented striking contrasts in profile even at a distance. Ruffs concealed chins and necks; hats could drape or draw the eye upward. Both sexes wore jewelry and painted their faces on some occasions.

"Did you ride here alone?" Anthony propped his cheek on his palm as he gazed at Trumpet with open admiration.

She returned his gaze with equal delight. "Of course. Surrey is hardly a wilderness, and it's only ten miles to Nonsuch. We took the ferry at Kingston-upon-Thames."

"Where do you change?" Tom asked. He touched his own hairy cheek. "Those beards are glued, aren't they?"

Mr. Luna nodded. "I have created a better glue. Easier and less itchable."

"We use a lodge. Something like this one," Trumpet said, looking around. "Smaller, with no books. It's a few miles from the palace. Stephen told me about it."

"Your husband knows about all this?" Anthony asked.

Trumpet flapped a hand at him. "Never. He was telling a funny story about arranging trysts with some of the queen's ladies without Her Majesty finding out." She flapped away Tom's scowl as well. "He pretended to be talking about a friend. I encourage it. His little frolics can be useful."

"I admire your resourcefulness," Anthony said. "Someday I would love to make use of your talents."

Trumpet treated him to a dazzling smile. "Someday I'll let you."

"Let's get on to the report, shall we?" Tom pulled up chairs for the women, then handed Trumpet the report before resuming his stool. "You'll want to read this first."

She scanned it quickly, then read it again more carefully, taking her time. When she finished, she asked, "Are we concerned about the composition of the jury?"

Anthony emitted a short laugh. Francis caught his gaze and flicked his eyebrows. Further proof of the excellence of his training. His intelligencers, unlike Anthony's, were also skilled in the workings of the common law. He couldn't have planned a more effective demonstration.

"I don't think so," Francis answered. "It looks to me like a representative sample of Deptford tradesmen. We'd be seeking signs of partisanship, but that isn't a factor here, is it?"

"What *are* we looking for?" Anthony asked.

"I don't know," Tom said. "Oddities. Discrepancies."

"Or too much similarity," Trumpet said. "Frizer and Walsingham used the same words. 'Next thing he knew,' although Frizer said 'I' instead of 'he.' They both said, 'It all happened so quickly.' And here those two phrases are again in the report. That suggests collusion to me. Someone concocted a story that everyone learned."

"Walsingham would've learned it at the inquest," Tom said. "How often do witnesses use exactly the same words?"

"Seldom," Anthony said. "It's usually that they've discussed their testimony in advance."

"I'm not so sure," Francis said. "These phrases are common enough. They could simply be words that apply. And we're not hearing the witnesses, remember. We're reading a summary written by a clerk. Perhaps the words are his."

"Walsingham wasn't a witness," Tom said. "And we heard Frizer utter them himself."

"Perhaps he was the originator and the others copied him." Francis held up a palm to stem the overlapping objections. "It's suggestive, but insufficient to prove collusion."

"Add it to the rest," Trumpet said, "and it's more than suggestive. Did Tom tell you that Frizer said we'd be better off without Christopher Marlowe in the world? That was enough to pique my wrath."

Francis started to point out that anger and reasonable doubt were two different things, but Anthony spoke first. "How would you be better off?"

"Not us so much," Tom said, "though he wanted us to think so. He implied that Kit being questioned by the Privy Council could cause trouble for Walsingham. By extension, for Frizer as well."

Anthony shook his head. "What sort of trouble?"

"Trouble selling or buying properties was my impression." Trumpet and Tom traded shrugs. "That's what Frizer does. He said buyers would think twice about a house tainted by scandal."

"That's nonsense," Francis said. "No one considers the poetry written in a house when assessing its value. And I can't think of a precedent of a gentleman being hindered for providing houseroom to a poet of Marlowe's stature."

"His plays passed the censor," Anthony said. "If anyone were liable for their content, it would be Lord Strange since his company performs them. If the authorities had objections, they could simply ban the plays. If Walsingham were hiding Anabaptists or Jesuit priests, that would be a different matter."

"The council seems to think Kit was an apostle of atheism," Tom said. "Isn't that the same thing as a Jesuit priest, in some sense?"

Francis and Anthony frowned at one another.

"To some," Francis said slowly, thinking of Lord Keeper Puckering, "that does seem to be the case." He grunted. "Very well. I'll grant some legitimate grounds for concern on that score. Though having interviewed Marlowe myself, I believe his intention was only to make men reflect upon the basis of their beliefs, not to shake them out of faith altogether. Not wise, perhaps, but not wicked either."

"Thank you," Tom said, as if his judgment had been vindicated.

Francis waved that off. "Besides, Mr. Walsingham could have limited Mr. Marlowe's stay if he were anxious about the ramifications of that association." He cocked his head at Anthony. "Where have I heard the name Skeres? It isn't a common one. I have the idea he is also some sort of broker."

Anthony pursed his lips, staring at the boxes of papers stacked at one end of the table. He used his hands to push himself back, then grabbed his cane and hoisted himself to his feet. Tom moved to help, but he shook his head. "It's just here. Notes of cases in Star Chamber. One of my friends keeps me informed."

"That's it," Francis said. "Star Chamber. A few weeks after I set my career in flames."

"A phoenix will rise, never fear," Anthony said without looking up. "Ah, here it is." He opened a flat wooden box and flicked through a few sheets of paper. "Yes, Nicholas Skeres. Brought before the court as a witness in the case of *Smith vs. Wolfall.* The latter stood accused of obtaining money under false pretenses." He gave Francis a knowing look. "He's a commodity broker."

"What's that?" Trumpet asked.

"A cheat," Anthony answered. "A cozener. He offers to lend you money, getting your signed bill of debt. Then he comes back claiming to be short of cash, offering you a 'commodity' instead. It's usually something worthless, like a heap of scrap iron. Then there you are with this load of trash, still liable for money you'll never see." He bent to read something on the page. "Skeres claims to have been forced into collaboration by Wolfall, but my informant notes that he's known for such tricks himself."

"Frizer's one of the same," Trumpet said, an avid gleam in her eyes. "I'd bet my horse on it. He smells like a coney-catcher." Francis clucked his tongue, but she defended her guess. "I don't mean literally, Mr. Bacon. I had the opportunity to observe his face and mannerisms closely while we walked around the estate, the way you taught us. He lies as easily as he breathes. He agreed with whatever Tom said, for one thing, however absurd."

Tom nodded. "I pretended to looking for a place like Scadbury. Which I will be someday, so it wasn't altogether false. He's an oily knave, is Frizer. I tested him by making sillier and sillier observations. 'Won't the fish eat the bees if the hives are too close to the pond?' Like that. He agreed with everything, flattering me for all he was worth."

"That's the sign of a cozener," Trumpet said. "They make you feel clever, so you trust them. And then they rob you blind. Robert Greene has written two books about it."

"An authoritative source," Anthony said with a chuckle. "The whole affair seems contrived, doesn't it?" He returned to his chair and folded his hands on the table. He had the infuriating air of a man who had noticed something important and was waiting for the rest to catch up. Francis reviewed the report in his mind but couldn't spot whatever it was.

"It isn't plausible," Tom said. "Things could not have happened the way they describe. Not unless everyone was a lot drunker than they admitted to being."

"Which is possible," Trumpet said. "No one's going to say, 'Well, I was cup-shot, Your Honor.' But I agree. How could the other two sit on that bench doing nothing while a violent altercation took place at their side?"

"They claim to have been trapped by the table," Francis said.

"That's the part I don't believe," Tom said. "Here, we'll show you."

He got up, and so did the women. Tom looked around, considering the space. "This room is bigger than the private dining room at Mrs. Bull's in Deptford."

"You've been there?" Anthony sounded surprised.

Tom shrugged. "That's my job — go around, look at things, ask questions. *Evidentia* and *testimonia*."

Francis caught his brother's eyes and gave him another eyebrow-flick of superiority. Then he asked his pupil, "Did the widow have anything useful to contribute?"

"Yes." Tom clapped a hand to his head. "God's bones! I've been chewing over the oddities in that coroner's report and forgot all about it."

Trumpet and her maidservant sat down again.

Tom remained standing. "The four men arrived around ten o'clock. Robert Poley came first, then Frizer and Skeres. Marlowe was last. She saw him striding up the street from the direction of the King's Head. Their stable seems to be the best one around. He would've been to Nonsuch to make his daily appearance at the Privy Council."

Trumpet put in, "That's four hours at a walk from Scadbury. He must've left before dawn and been dismissed almost immediately."

Tom pointed at her. "That's another factor, that immediate dismissal. You'll see why. They spent most of the day in the garden, which is quite pleasant. Mrs. Bull could see them from time to time through the windows as she went about her work. She said Marlowe spent most of the day walking and talking with Poley while Frizer and Skeres sat at a table working through a heap of documents."

"Property matters, I'll wager," Trumpet said. "That explains why Skeres was there — to keep Frizer company."

Tom nodded at her. "They had both dinner and supper in the private room. All fairly unremarkable, except for one thing. Mrs. Bull said Poley sent a message after dinner and got an answer just before supper. By my reckoning, the messenger could've ridden to Nonsuch, waited for an audience with someone, and then ridden back in that amount of time."

"That changes everything!" Trumpet jumped to her feet, the better to throw her hands about for emphasis. She tended toward excitability.

"Not necessarily," Francis said. "Frizer and Skeres conducted business during this long interlude. Why shouldn't Poley send and receive messages? They might have nothing to do with Marlowe."

"I'll grant that," Tom said, as if doing him a favor, "but it's one more straw on the camel's back. And here's another thing I forgot to tell you. Kit said — almost the last words he said to me . . ." Tom faltered for a moment but recovered quickly. "He said that if he played his cards right on Wednesday, he'd be riding to Edinburgh by the end of the week."

Francis glowered at him. "That alters the whole complexion of the meeting."

Tom shrugged off the disapproval. "I've had a lot to think about. But I think Kit went to Deptford to spend the day being interviewed by Robert Poley, who must be the agent of someone on the Privy Council. Poley came to some conclusion by dinnertime and sent to Nonsuch for approval or instructions."

Francis looked at Anthony, who smiled his cat's smile again, eyes twinkling. Francis clucked his tongue. Let him keep his secret. Francis's skilled investigators might very well work it out, in which case the victory would belong to him.

Tom said, "Let's have a look at those oddities. Things could not have happened the way the witnesses claim. If we reproduce the fatal event, you'll see what I mean. Just let me set the stage." He stretched out his arms on either side and wiggled his middle fingers. "This is about six feet plus an inch."

"Leonardo Da Vinci," Anthony said, smiling. "*L'uomo vitruviano*. Bravo, Brother."

Tom gave him a wry look. "They're *my* arms. Mr. Bacon never does this. Anyway, the room at Mrs. Bull's is only about twelve by fourteen. The bed Marlowe lay on was pushed against the wall opposite the table. We have about six and half feet of clear space between the two. Poley, Frizer, and Skeres sat on a bench in front of the table." He spotted one along a wall and moved it into place. "Now let's choose parts. Who wants to be Frizer?"

"I'm Kit," Trumpet said, moving toward the imaginary bed. "You be Frizer."

"I am Mr. Eskeries," Mr. Luna said.

Francis loved her Spanish accent. He seldom heard one these days, having been banned from the company of ambassadors along with everyone else in the Privy Chamber. "I suppose that makes me Mr. Poley."

"If you wouldn't mind." Tom gestured him into place. As he took his seat in the center of the bench, he said to Anthony, "The table should be flush against the wall. I guess that makes you Wall, Mr. Bacon."

"I shall give my utmost to the role," Anthony said. He seemed to be thoroughly amused by all this. But then he'd never seen Francis's team re-enact a crime before. It might look like foolishness, but it had proven revelatory on more than one occasion.

"Should we do the arguing, or start from the leaping up?" Trumpet asked.

"The leaping," Tom said. "I have no trouble seeing Kit refuse to pay a bill."

"Nor do I," Trumpet said. "All right, then." She gave a little hop to simulate leaping from a bed, then strode across the boards to stand behind Tom. "First question. Why wouldn't I do what I always do to express my contempt for a fool?" She proceeded to throw Tom's hat into a corner and use his head as a drum, beating it with flat hands. "Take that, you crook-pated knave!"

Tom hunched forward at first to duck the blows, then turned and grabbed her wrist. Neither of the others had time to react, other than to lean away from Tom-as-Frizer.

"That's what Kit would do," Tom said. "I've been on the receiving end myself. It's humiliating, but it doesn't hurt."

"Is it impossible that he would use a knife to pummel an opponent?" Francis asked.

"Impossible is a very large word," Trumpet said.

Tom agreed. "I've never seen him do it or heard of him doing it. And if he had done it, everyone at the Goose and Gall would know. They're a gossipy bunch, poets."

"All right," Trumpet said, "now let's try it the other way." She went back to her starting point and made her little hop. She jogged two steps and pretended to draw Tom's knife from the scabbard at the small of his back. Then she pounded her fist lightly on his head. A stream of curses more colorful than Francis would have expected a lady to utter issued from her cupid lips. Anthony laughed out loud before clapping a hand over his mouth.

"Ow, ow, ow!" Tom cried, this time rocking from side to side. He twisted toward Mr. Luna — or rather, Mr. Skeres — on his right, reaching up and back for his assailant's arm. He did a creditable job of pretending Trumpet was a man his own size, reaching higher and failing to catch a firm hold.

As he turned, his back pressed against Francis, who leaned away to avoid him. Then Francis pushed himself to the end of the bench. He pulled his legs free of the table, swung around, and lunged at Mr. Marlowe. He caught the left arm and cried, "Peace! Hold!"

Everyone froze. Mr. Skeres had also managed to get a leg free and grip Frizer's left arm with both hands, clamping it onto the table. Frizer had succeeded in grabbing the wrist that held the knife, though Marlowe still stood behind him. If Trumpet were a foot taller, her head would have been well out of reach of the blade.

The actors looked at one another, noting their final positions. Anthony spoke first. "Both combatants appear to have been successfully restrained without serious injury to either party."

The company disbanded, each returning to their original seat.

"They could've stopped it," Tom said. "Poley and Skeres. They're not small men. About average, I would say. They could've knocked the bench right over, tumbling Frizer to the ground, if they'd both stood up and pushed back at the same time. That would've knocked Marlowe over too unless he jumped away. We didn't feel a real threat here, but I can tell you, when a knife comes out, everyone's blood starts pumping."

Francis couldn't answer that from his own experience. Nor could Anthony. They relied on Tom for that domain of knowledge.

"That is true," Mr. Luna said. She had also enjoyed some of life's rough and tumble in her previous life. "You leap away. They will not care if they fall. From that bench, they fall on the back. One may grab Mr. Kit's legs and pull upon him."

"They could've stopped him by shouting and slapping at him," Tom said.

Trumpet nodded. "They could have done a number of things. It can't have happened that quickly either. Mr. Frizer had several wounds on his head. In the time it took to strike those blows, either Skeres or Poley could've turned and grabbed Kit's arm."

"I don't believe he caused them," Tom said, a stubborn set to his jaw.

"The inquest examined them at length," Francis noted. "Mr. Frizer must have been obliged to display his head to each of the fourteen jurors in turn. We must accept the wounds as described."

"I accept them," Tom said. "I saw them too. Frizer showed them to us. I just don't believe Kit did it. Take that away and the whole thing falls apart."

Francis leaned back in his chair, folding his hands on his stomach. "One man was injured and another man died. Three men tell the same story, which you dispute. What do you think happened?"

"Try this," Tom said. "Walsingham sent Kit to that meeting. He said Poley was a well-traveled man, implying he was some kind of merchant. I think he was the other sort of traveling man." He looked at Anthony. "Your sort, Mr. Bacon. An intelligencer. I think Poley's job was to decide if Kit could be trusted with messages to Scotland. Delicate work, everyone says. Poley had to send to Nonsuch to hear 'yea' or 'nay' from his master. The answer came back 'untrustworthy in the extreme,' or some such thing. Poley knew what that meant. He made the other two help him overpower Kit, who might have injured Frizer in his own defense. One of them —maybe Frizer, maybe not — took his knife and executed Kit with a thrust *alla revolta*."

"We learned that one in fencing class," Trumpet said. "I thought of it too."

"It's a killing stroke," Tom said.

"God's mercy!" Francis planted a hand over his heart. "You've both seen too many revenge plays."

"I'm not so sure," Anthony said. "I suspect Mr. Clarady may have put his finger on the truth."

"What do you know?" Francis demanded. "You've been sitting there like a cat with a private dish of cream all this time."

Anthony grinned. "I ceased to believe in the coroner's report the moment I saw the name Robert Poley. He's one of the most dangerous intelligencers I know of."

That raised some eyebrows.

"Who does he work for?" Francis asked.

"I don't know," Anthony said. "Not me, although I might use him if I needed someone utterly ruthless. He was one of Sir Francis Walsingham's."

"Ha!" Tom said. "I knew there was spy business lurking under the nephew's lies."

"Thomas may have thought he was doing Marlowe a favor," Anthony said. "Helping him to gain that Scotland commission he wanted."

"How is Poley dangerous?" Francis asked.

"He'll do anything," Anthony said, "to anyone, for a price. He was the projector for the Babington Plot."

"Oh," Francis said, understanding at once. Nothing more need be said about the man's capacity for deception.

"What's the Babington Plot?" Trumpet asked.

"A scheme to assassinate the queen," Anthony said, "back in 1586. The conspirators wanted to put Mary, Queen of Scots on the throne in her place. Sir Francis suspected correspondence was passing between Mary and the conspirators, but he couldn't catch them at it. Poley was sent to infiltrate the group. He succeeded beyond anyone's prediction. He became Sir Anthony Babington's most trusted servant for two years. Then he betrayed him, passing copies of incriminating letters back to Sir Francis. Poley spent some time in the Tower to preserve his disguise, where he managed to collect damning information on several other prisoners."

"Sounds like a valuable servant," Francis said.

"A clever one," Anthony said. "Clever enough to have commissioned the Dutch Church libel, which you seem to have forgotten about." That last was directed to Tom.

"Not forgotten. But Kit's murder comes first."

"They may be related," Anthony said. "It is well within Poley's scope to position that libel as an excuse to arrest Marlowe. He wouldn't care if an innocent like Thomas Kyd suffered in the process."

"But why?" Trumpet asked. "They'd been questioning Kit for weeks. Why suddenly decide he had to be killed?"

Anthony sighed. "I can only guess. He knew who had been questioning him and what questions had been asked. Marlowe was an acute observer and highly intelligent. Perhaps the questioner began to feel exposed by his questions. Perhaps, in his zeal, he became convinced that Marlowe must die, but he knew he could never gain approval from the rest of the council."

"They could never try him in Star Chamber," Francis said. "He was far too popular. Many courtiers would turn up to defend him. Sir Walter Ralegh, for one. Possibly even peers like Lord Strange and the Earl of Northumberland. Patrons of the arts like the Countess of Pembroke."

"I'd be there," Trumpet said, lifting her chin. "And I'd make Stephen come with me."

"The pamphlets would be full of it," Tom added. "And they'd favor Kit since most writers know him. Or knew him."

"There might even be a public outcry," Trumpet said. "That councilor might cause the very riots the fake prosecution of that fake libel was meant to prevent."

"Precisely why I argue against such aggressive prosecutions," Francis said.

Anthony nodded at him. "Riots, mocking pamphlets, nagging courtiers. So much simpler to murder the offender in some private house and tell a story plausible enough to convince the coroner in Kent. It was just his bad luck that Marlowe had friends trained in observation by Francis Bacon." He gave his brother a sad smile.

Francis shrugged, palms up, to signal his surrender. "I concede there is cause to investigate further. An over-rehearsed story, some powerful motives, and a notorious spy." He nodded at Tom. "I no longer believe your friend's death was an accident."

He blew out a weary breath as he sank back in his chair. So much for persuading Tom to reconcile himself to the official story and move on.

TWENTY-ONE

Tom left the Bacons' lodge shortly after Trumpet and Catalina rode off to Nonsuch. Much as she wanted to be part of the wake they'd planned for Marlowe, the risk was too great. She might not find a wherry when she needed it, or the ferryman at Kingston might decide to retire early that night. Better to show her face at supper in the hall, all things considered.

They'd shaken their heads at one another, bemused by their own maturity.

So Tom returned alone to the empty house at Gray's. He supped alone at his usual table in the nearly empty hall, idly watching three benchers gossiping in low voices on the dais. He ought to be on his way home, clopping along grassy roads through the English countryside in early June. He loved the peace of that week-long journey — no pursed lips from the teaching barristers, no finicky master to prod into work. No wagon-drivers shouting curses at the corner of Holborn and Gray's Inn Road. Just bird song, bridle bells, and the wind sighing in the trees.

He could go. Why shouldn't he? He would drink with the poets at the Goose and Gall tonight, remembering Marlowe with those who knew him best, then pack his bags and ride out in the morning. A great longing for home swelled his chest.

His mother's house would be full of people, as it always was. His two spinster aunts would try to fatten him up, clucking their tongues at his wasted condition. Tom's three sisters would descend upon them with their families, filling the rambling manor atop the seaside cliffs with the noise of women and children — a welcome contrast to somber, masculine Gray's Inn.

In a week or two, he'd ride out to visit his old chum, the Earl of Dorchester. Halfway home, he'd stop at a discreet inn to meet Trumpet for a few private hours. After a few more weeks, he'd be itching for the London bustle. He'd go straight to St. Paul's churchyard and buy up all the pamphlets he could find, eager for the news he'd missed.

This time would be different though. When he turned his back on the city, he'd be turning his back on an unsolved crime. Who else would pursue it? Kit's other friends lacked Tom's skills and his connections. The task had fallen to him. He couldn't stuff himself on plum tarts and fresh grilled mackerel or while away a jolly evening in the local tavern with his Uncle Luke, leaving Kit's death unresolved.

That long ride home would give him no peace. He couldn't leave without finding out what had happened in Deptford.

* * *

Tom stopped outside the Goose and Gall to draw in a deep breath. A mistake — the alley stank of piss — but he needed a moment to steel himself before entering. He had sad news to deliver tonight.

He found George Peele sitting alone at the front table. The poet peered at him, then grinned with recognition. The grin vanished when Tom told him about Kit. He stuck to the official story. Both Bacons had warned him not to speculate about deeper causes in public.

216

"A knife in the eye," Peele echoed, shaking his head. "God's teeth, what a way to go." He raised his cup. "But better than Robert Greene, eh? Dying in bed from a surfeit of rich food."

When the wench brought Tom's ale, Peele passed the news to her. "Christopher Marlowe is dead?" she wailed in a girlish pitch that carried across the room.

A general hubbub arose. Someone ran upstairs. Someone else ran out the door. The news spread like fire on a thatched roof. Soon the tavern was crowded with Kit's admirers. Tom told the story a second time and then a third. After that, it took on a life of its own.

Before a quarter hour had passed, he heard someone behind him telling someone else what happened. "He died with his rapier in his hand, cursing until the end."

The other man said, "He'll face St. Peter with that sword, daring him to keep him out of heaven."

The first one laughed. "Oh, they'll let him in. Angels will surround him and carry him to the softest couch. They don't make poets like Christopher Marlowe every day."

Tom looked at the crowd and mentally counted the coins in his purse. Could he afford to buy a round for this many people? Happily, someone beat him to it. A baritone voice boomed out, "Drinks for everyone, on me. Let's raise our cups to Kit. We may have lost a friend, but his works will never die. Here's to Marlowe's mighty line!"

"Marlowe's mighty line!" the crowd roared.

A silence fell, broken by a warm, low voice. A man with a sparse beard and a high forehead quoted Tom's favorite verse from *Tamburlaine*.

> "Nature, that framed us of four elements
> Warring in our breasts for regiment,
> Doth teach us all to have aspiring minds.
> Our souls, whose faculties can comprehend
> The wondrous architecture of the world
> And measure every wand'ring planet's course,

Still climbing after knowledge infinite
And always moving as the restless spheres,
Wills us to wear ourselves and never rest
Until we reach the ripest fruit of all,
That perfect bliss and sole felicity,
The sweet fruition of an earthly crown.

Silence followed, then came another quote. They went around the room, sharing favorite bits of Marlovian verse along with stories about Kit's mad humors and sudden generosities.

"Who was that, the first one?" Tom asked Peele.

"Name's Shakespeare. A newcomer. Another playmaker."

"Is he any good?"

"Kit thought so." Peele chuckled. "Greene hated him."

"That says it all." Tom raised his cup to the newcomer and received a smile in return. He turned back to Peele. "How's Thomas Kyd, do you know?"

"Home, thanks to you. His landlady's taking care of him. I looked in on him once to see how he fared." Peele shook his head sadly. "He's a broken man. He'll never be the same."

"I don't doubt it." Tom had nightmares about that cell in Bridewell.

Mathew Roydon pulled up a stool on Tom's right, laying an elbow on the table to lean toward him. "You don't believe that story you told, do you?"

Tom shot him a wary look. "Don't you?"

Roydon flipped that errant lock of hair out of his eyes. "Not quite. Nashe once told me you look into things like this. Now here you are, with the coroner's report on the tip of your tongue."

"I wanted to know, so I asked Mr. Bacon to request it."

Roydon nodded. "I assumed as much. What do you know about Nicholas Skeres?"

"He's a cozener of sorts," Tom said. "A commodity broker, I think."

Roydon snorted. "He helped a churl named Wolfall skin me for over a hundred pounds. I may never get out from under it. If there's trouble coming, I'd love to see it land on him."

"Do my best," Tom said. "Any idea where I can find him?"

"At his place of business — Duke Humphrey's tomb." Roydon gave him a dark look. "And, Clarady — whatever you find out, don't tell me. I know enough to know I don't want to know more. Besides" — his handsome face brightened — "I like the version with the rapier, where Kit curses in rhyming verse with his last breath."

* * *

Duke Humphrey had left his name to an aisle in St. Paul's Cathedral. He may have been an honest man in his day, but those who now loitered about his earthly remains fell short of that noble standard. Visitors to London invariably toured the great cathedral, so those who preyed upon such innocents lurked within its depths.

Tom found Skeres easily enough. He'd only had a glimpse of the man in the Deptford church, but Trumpet had referred to him as Mr. Weasel, which proved sufficient for identification. He still wore — or had donned again — the rusty-brown costume he'd worn at the funeral. Perhaps that was his best suit. If so, his trickery didn't pay very well.

"Mr. Skeres," Tom said, slipping around to approach the man from behind. He'd meant to startle him and succeeded. The man jumped right off the ground.

"Who are you?" he asked, taking a step away. "What do you want?"

Tom saw recognition in his eyes. Skeres had seen him at the church. Not surprising — Tom had barged right in, intent on reaching Trumpet. "I want to ask you a few questions."

"I don't answer to you."

"You could answer them in Star Chamber. But perhaps you had enough of that in April."

Skeres shrank away from him but didn't turn and run. "What do you know about that?"

"I know all sorts of things. For example, I know that you sat on a bench and did nothing while my friend Christopher Marlowe was killed."

Tom had expected that to rattle the man, but his words had the opposite effect. Skeres visibly relaxed, shifting his weight onto one hip. His small eyes took on a speculative gleam, as if he'd caught a fresh chicken and was wondering how best to pluck it.

Curious that Marlowe's name should inspire such calm. Tom didn't know what to make of it at the moment, so he pressed on with his original questions. "Why didn't you do anything? You could've grabbed someone's arm, knocked Frizer over. You could've stopped it."

Skeres shook his head. "It all happened so quickly. Next thing I knew, Marlowe was lying on the floor." His thin lips formed a smug smile, as if daring Tom to dispute that story.

"I've heard those very words before, and I don't believe them. I've read the coroner's report too. It doesn't make sense, not if you work through it step by step."

Doubt shadowed Skeres's narrow face. As it should — it showed Tom had access to someone who knew his way around the courts.

"You can't pester me like this," Skeres said. "I'll have you know I'm a servant of the Earl of Essex. I'm an Essex man through and through." Seeing the naked disbelief on

Tom's face, he bleated, "I am, I tell you. Ask His Lordship. He'll know me."

"I will," Tom said. "Next time I see him."

Skeres's mouth opened to fire out a retort, but he'd forgotten to load the shot. His jaw worked up and down, but nothing came out. Then he found something. His face took on a crafty look. "You'll stop asking questions if you know what's good for you."

Threats now? Not from this scrawny cur. He must have a bigger dog behind him.

Robert Poley, Tom guessed — the intelligencer Anthony Bacon considered so dangerous. If Skeres thought Poley could protect him, he must know where to find the man. "I never stop asking questions until I get the answers I seek. Where can I find Mr. Poley?"

Skeres's lips disappeared as he gave Tom a shrewd look. Then he grunted and said, "Go. Talk to him. Why should I care? Try your questions on him, if you're feeling lucky." He rubbed his chin. "I don't know where he lives, to be honest. But look for a wench named Joan Yeomans. A cutler's wife. If he's in London, he'll be with her." He crossed his arms, lips now curled in a toothy sneer.

Tom clapped him on the shoulder, hard enough to jolt him sideways. "Thanks, chum. I'll be sure to tell Mr. Poley you sent me."

That wiped the sneer off the weasel's face.

TWENTY-TWO

Another perfect June day at Nonsuch Palace, the most beautiful of all Her Majesty's residences. Another beautiful day to be gotten through with a minimum of humiliation or fresh gaffes. Francis had sat alone at dinner, the half-dozen other people at his table notwithstanding. Courtiers looked away when they passed him. And yet, in spite of those constant slights, Francis strolled the clean-swept garden paths with a spring in his step.

Attorney General! Attorney General! The title echoed in his mind, buoying his spirits. Yet that buoyance had its hazards too, as he knew from prior experience. He'd been lifted up before, only to be dashed on the cruel rocks of patronage and preferment.

He spotted his cousin Robert slipping under an arched opening in a garden wall. Would Robert support or oppose him? What about his uncle, Lord Burghley? The aging Lord Treasurer's opinion usually won the day with Her Majesty.

Francis dithered on the path. *Ask? Don't ask?* Then he chided himself for hypocrisy. He advocated experiment instead of speculation. Instead of wondering, imagining, and constructing fantasies based on fear, he should march into the fray and make the attempt.

He followed his cousin through the arch and found himself in a rose garden bursting into bloom. The vivid colors and heady fragrance rocked him back for a moment, stunned by Dame Nature's glory. He smiled at her gift and looked about him. Robert had found a bench in a nook under the striped shade of an arbor. He pulled a book out of his pocket and settled his crooked back against the wall.

Well, he could read later. This wouldn't take long.

Francis had planned to simply burst forth with his question. They knew each other well enough to obviate the need for preparatory chatter. Neither of them cared for social nothings. But as he approached, he glimpsed the title of Robert's book — *Tamburlaine, Parts I and II* — and altered his course.

Robert noticed him and slid to the end of his bench. "Join me, Cousin. It's a day to be appreciated." He seemed to be in an especially good humor. Had he prevailed in some small matter with the queen? Or won the favors of a lady other than his wife? Francis had heard rumors about the latter activity, or rather, Anthony had. Gossip was the core of intelligencing, apparently.

Whatever the cause, Fortune had smiled on Francis's adventure. "Nothing so lovely as a day in June, especially in a palace filled with gardens." He pointed his chin at the book as he sat. "An homage?"

"A reflection. Reminding myself of Marlowe's actual words instead of the mangled quotes being tossed about this week."

"I met him, as it happens, the day before he died. He was a friend of my clerk, Thomas Clarady."

"A problematical sort of friend."

"True," Francis said. "But not an atheist, in my view."

Robert grunted, accepting the value of that opinion. "His death is a loss to us all but, given his contentious nature, perhaps not a surprise."

"If you keep poking a bear, sooner or later you will be mauled."

Robert nodded. "I believe about half of what I've heard. For example, I sincerely doubt he died cursing and swinging a rapier. Why would he wear one to dinner at a quiet lodging house?"

"There was no rapier," Francis said. "I've read the coroner's report. We discussed it at length, in fact. Mr. Clarady believes his friend was murdered."

That startling news had no visible effect on the young councilor. Robert, at the tender age of thirty, had heard all manner of rumors, from the fantastical to the truly dangerous. "Intelligencing is a rough trade. I assume you consider that the cause rather than the poetry?"

Francis smiled. "Has anyone ever been murdered for the quality of his verse?"

"Only when the verse is vile."

They both chuckled at that despite the tragedy. Or because of it. Francis had noticed that men often told jokes to ward off sorrow.

"What aroused Mr. Clarady's suspicions?" Robert asked.

"Several things. Everyone told the same story in precisely the same words, for one. They sounded rehearsed. Then the scene they described made no sense. We tried it out at Twickenham the other day. It's unlikely the two onlookers would simply have sat on that bench like statues watching two men struggle over a knife. It would have been natural for them to push against the table and leap up to get out of the way. Even seated, they could reach the fighting men's arms to restrain them. Why didn't they?"

Robert raised his thin, arched eyebrows. "Then you agree with your clerk's assessment."

"I agree that there are oddities, which always pique my interest. The stabbing might have been planned — an execution. That would explain the well-rehearsed story. The obvious motive would be to stop Marlowe's undisciplined mouth, but who would want that? *Cui bono?*"

"Ah, well." Robert laid his book on the bench and laced his fingers over his black velvet doublet. "If we cast our net widely, we might come up with many who would benefit. Perhaps the Catholic circle in Brussels had it done to keep Marlowe from infiltrating their operations in the Netherlands."

Francis blinked. Could he truly believe such a preposterous thing? The flutter of Robert's eyelids betrayed the joke, startling Francis into a laugh. "So that was you. Anthony heard about Marlowe's aborted attempt to pass false coins in Flushing last year. He assumed the plan was to persuade the Catholics that he had more to contribute than a tenuous connection to Lord Strange."

He paused to let Robert confirm or deny, getting only a coy smile in response. Francis shrugged. It wasn't the worst idea, as such covert projects went. "Clarady thought Thomas Walsingham might have paid Ingram Frizer, who happens to be his property broker, to do the deed."

Robert tucked his chin, surprised. "For what earthly reason?"

"The idea seemed to be that Marlowe's reputation would stain his patron's good name, thereby obstructing his ability to trade."

"Ah, the patron." Robert's hazel eyes flashed. "I suppose he would be the first suspect, in the absence of a wife. But one would think Sir Francis's nephew could bear a fair deal of tarnish. If we're looking at patrons, I would nominate Lord Strange. His motive would be to rid his company of a controversial playmaker without angering his audiences."

Francis wagged a negatory finger. "Controversy sells seats. Marlowe's plays were hugely popular *because* of the controversy." His mind raced, seeking a theory wild enough to top that one. "Not a patron, *per se*, but another courtier with a reputation at risk is Sir Walter Ralegh. You know how haughty he can be about literature. He might have ordered Marlowe's murder in revenge for having had to listen to that mythical atheist lecture." He held the finger up to gain time for an amendment. "Or to prevent himself being tarred with that same atheist brush."

Robert chuckled, his merriment running on as if he couldn't bring it to a halt. He recovered with a sniff. "Sir Walter is still at Sherborne, although Deptford is a port and thus falls within his sphere of influence." He shot Francis an impish look. "I deem it more likely the plot was set in motion by the Lord of Essex. He's adamantly opposed to atheism. He says so at every opportunity. Implicating Sir Walter would be an added benefit. Such a complex plot would be child's play for Anthony."

They both laughed heartily at that. Robert patted himself on the chest as if encouraging the intake of air. Francis twisted a blossom from the eglantine covering their arbor and held it to his nose as a restorative. The sweetness almost made him giddy.

"I'm not privy to everything my brother does," he said, "but I'm fairly certain it wasn't us. The master plotter is more likely to be you, Cousin. You could've ordered the deed done by your man Poley, using Frizer as a screen."

Robert whisked that away with a flat palm. "Poley's not one of mine, I assure you. I've used him in the past, but I don't trust him. He's turned his coat too many times. I will grant that his presence is cause for suspicion. He's no idler. He went to that house with a purpose in mind. But tell me, Coz. What motive could I have for depriving myself of a useful agent?"

Francis smiled. "Clarady guessed Marlowe was one of yours. They've known each other since that commission Tom performed in Cambridge for your father."

"That's where we acquired Marlowe from Lord North. He accomplished his assigned tasks admirably, especially delivering messages. He was comely and well-spoken, with comportment perfectly balanced between deference and confidence. He was fluent enough to be witty in Latin and

French. He had a bottomless well of a memory and could report fine details of appearance and manners."

A eulogy of sorts. And a praiseful one, considering the source.

"But you'd advanced him into projections," Francis said. "The coining ploy in Flushing, for example."

Robert frowned. Rival services ought not to know so much about each other's stratagems. "We aborted that trial, partly because Marlowe seemed unable to moderate his talk. He was too easily baited into taking stabs at whatever religious authority happened to be available. He never spoke out of turn about his work, as far as I know, but he drew too much attention to himself. No one wants a notorious agent. A good intelligencer is a quiet man. An invisible man."

"It is a tragedy," Francis said, "that so great a poet wasn't given time to grow out of the distempers of youth. But it seems an early death — a violent death — was in his stars. Sooner or later, he was bound to provoke the wrong person."

"Poke the wrong bear."

"Just so." Francis inhaled the fragrance of his rose. Robert closed his eyes and turned his face toward the soothing warmth of the sun. After a few moments, Francis asked, "If Poley isn't yours and he isn't ours, whose is he? Anthony thinks him unreliable."

"Not in the short run," Robert said. "He can be bought and trusted for the agreed-upon terms. But he loves his own cleverness above all things. Worse, he has no loyalty. For me, that quality is paramount."

"I agree. I should think the best operatives share the aims of their commissions. That is, they are prompted by the safety of the realm as much as by their desire to earn a living."

Robert laughed at that. "Coin always comes first, Frank. The thirst for adventure second. Christopher

Marlowe illustrated that rule. He enjoyed the travel and the challenges of message delivery, but most of all, he needed money to support his writing. A steady income suited him best. That made him more reliable since you knew what he wanted. You also knew he wouldn't jump ship at the offer of a higher price."

"That seems to be what he was doing, however," Francis said. "Mr. Clarady believes Marlowe met Poley in order to talk about a commission carrying messages to Scotland."

Robert rolled his eyes. "Along with everyone and their favorite aunt." He shot a droll look at Francis. "Including our Aunt Elizabeth, I'll wager. She writes to everyone else on a weekly basis. Why not our friend in the north?"

"I probably shouldn't tell you this," Francis began. That opening tended to add value to what followed. "Anthony considers it possible that Poley was hired to project the Dutch Church libel." A stab pricked his conscience. Had he said too much? But one had to give information in order to get any. That was a fundamental rule of the game.

"Toward what end?" Robert's question sounded slightly disingenuous. No doubt he was fishing for more of Anthony's reasoning.

Francis saw no reason not to provide it. In his view, the sooner these troublesome questions were answered, the better. "The plan was to hire a balladeer to write something inflammatory and post it somewhere public. Poley would have been responsible for choosing both poet and place. The commissioner wouldn't risk a real riot, so Poley would have to arrange for someone to take the libel down before anyone saw it while making sure the sheriff and the Lord Mayor knew about it. Whether good luck or bad, a ballad printer happened by and performed that service for him."

"The printer wasn't in Poley's pay?"

That gave Francis pause. Had Tom asked that question? "Mr. Clarady — who wants the Lord Mayor's reward — spoke with him. He considers his story credible."

"It doesn't matter," Robert said. "It does seem like a lot of trouble for a negative result."

"Not negative," Francis said. "The goal would be to justify the formation of a commission to investigate the libel. They shifted so swiftly from anti-stranger riots to atheist conspiracies that I suspect those were the target all along."

"Still a roundabout method. Although perhaps not too devious for Poley. He enjoys elaborate deceits. But you'd think his masters could set a simpler trap for atheists, if that was their goal. Was it even mentioned in the libel?"

Francis had assumed Robert had read it. "Only indirectly, and only if you took Marlowe's characters as purveyors of his personal views. Do you think he was the target all along?"

"Why? To strike at me through my servant, perhaps?" Robert's long chin jutted forward in an aggressive frown.

"I hadn't thought of that one." Francis blew out a thoughtful breath. "Surely that's too tortuous, even for — for whoever Poley's master is. Lord Keeper Puckering organized the libel commission. But someone on the council ordered Marlowe's arrest. You must know who it is."

Robert smiled, tilting his head in lieu of a shrug. Shrugs drew attention to his crooked shoulder. "I could guess, but I won't. There's enough speculation flying around about Marlowe's death. Besides, everyone wants their own intelligence service these days. They see Essex doing it and think it's the path to influence."

"Nothing gets you credit at court like reliable information about the enemies' plots. Even if you have to invent an enemy yourself."

"Marlowe made himself an enemy. Or made himself an easy target for someone seeking to demonstrate his power. Someone bold enough, and ambitious enough, to murder a poet of Marlowe's stature." Robert gave Francis a warning look. "Tread lightly, Cousin. This is not the time for you to draw the enmity of influential persons."

The Privy Council, he meant. And the Lord Keeper. Then Francis heard the hidden message. "You're talking about my Lord of Essex's proposal. For me, as the next Attorney General."

Robert smiled. "Isn't that why you came to talk to me?"

"I'd almost forgotten. Your book distracted me." Francis cast his gaze around the garden, drawing strength from the profusion of blooms. Nothing stopped a rose from expressing its true glory, given a little water and sunlight. He licked his lips and glanced sidelong at his cousin. "Will you oppose me?"

"No."

Francis startled at the simple answer. He'd braced himself for a contest. "Nor your father?"

"Nor my father." Robert's face never gave much away, but his manner seemed kindly. "Edward Coke is more qualified in terms of experience in court. He has argued — and won — many cases, both before and after becoming Solicitor General."

That contest ended before it began since Francis had argued precisely none. "I plan to remedy that defect when the courts reconvene in September. But you — or rather, my Lord Uncle — backed Coke for the Solicitor Generalship last year."

"So did Sir Thomas Heneage, who suffered from the effort. Her Majesty didn't like the clients Coke defended."

"No, she didn't, did she?" Francis remembered her response that day. "She berated him about it so sharply he burst into tears." He laughed at the memory. She could be viciously witty — amusing, if you weren't the target. "That gives me hope. She may still be disgruntled by my stance in Parliament, but perhaps she could be persuaded that I'm the better candidate."

Robert's face transformed into an unreadable mask. "We are neutral in this contest. You would be an exemplary Attorney General, Frank. Everyone knows your knowledge of the law is unparalleled. As family, your advancement would also serve us better than Coke's. But I advise you to moderate your hopes." He caught Francis's eyes for a friendly warning. "Don't borrow money. Lord Essex is pushing you forward to demonstrate his influence with the queen. She knows that and may or may not allow it. Her will can never be predicted."

The central mystery at the heart of the realm. "I know. But he does me such an honor. I can hardly decline it." That was truth as well. He could no more refuse than he could retire to Twickenham to count stars.

"He would have done better to promote you for Solicitor General. Even that would not be assured, given your opposition to the triple subsidy." Robert sighed, as if lamenting a wayward hound. "It shows you're not conformable to Her Majesty's wishes."

"I have to speak my conscience, Cousin. If not, who am I?"

Robert's eyelids fluttered. "Not the Attorney General. That is precisely what I mean. Your first obedience belongs always to your monarch. Second comes your duty to the health and safety of the realm. Your conscience, Cousin, is at best a distant third."

TWENTY-THREE

"We still don't know what Thomas Walsingham was hiding," Trumpet said. She sat at the stool before her dressing table while her servant combed her long black hair. The sun had risen. Soon Her Majesty would too, and she would expect her ladies to be dressed and ready to serve.

"Is he a spy, my lady?"

"He was one. His uncle was a very famous spymaster."

"A spy may be always a spy, I think. Like a priest. Or a clown."

Trumpet held her servant's gaze in the mirror. "That is very astute. I believe you may be right. But Tom can't do much about it now. He has no excuse to go back to Scadbury to beard its master in his den."

Catalina used the tip of her comb to separate out another strand. "But the mistress is here. We may beard her, may we not?"

"Yes, we may. Let's do it today, as soon as Her Majesty goes out for her walk. I'd love to beat Tom to one suspect, at least."

* * *

There was no trick to finding Audrey Walsingham. She stood in her usual position in Her Majesty's bedchamber, shaking out pillows while two other ladies rubbed the queen's royal torso with linen cloths.

"Shall we have a game of bowls this morning?" Trumpet whispered.

"So early?"

Trumpet shrugged. "It might be too hot later."

They broke their fast together in the hall, sharing murmured observations on the garb and demeanor of the other courtiers. Some stumbled while others strode into the hall, betraying how they'd spent their evenings. Trumpet smiled at Mr. Bacon as they passed his table, but he didn't notice them. He could avoid looking at people better than anyone she'd ever known, even with his eyes wide-open. She guessed the world vanished while he studied whatever transpired inside his mind.

The grass was still wet with dew when they reached the greens — too wet for a good game. "Let's walk through the knot garden," Trumpet suggested. "The paths will be dry." There was little chance of being overheard since the ornately figured herbs rose only to the knees.

Everything seemed to be in bloom: lavender, chamomile, St. John's wort, and mallow. Trumpet bent to break off a dew-dappled sprig of rosemary, holding it to her nose to breathe in the clean scent. She handed it to Audrey, giving her a moment to refresh herself. Then she closed in and gripped her new friend's arm.

"I know your husband sent Marlowe to his death that day." Trumpet's voice tensed with implied threat.

"He never did!" Audrey flinched back, only to discover that Catalina had moved up behind her as silently as a cat.

"He's hiding something about that day," Trumpet said. "He told Mr. Clarady he sent Kit to that meeting. Why?"

Audrey's alarm abated somewhat. "To meet Mr. Poley, of course. To talk about a new commission carrying letters. Thomas meant it as a favor, knowing Kit wanted a change. He didn't know what would happen. How could he? He didn't know Mr. Poley, not well. He would never do anything to harm Mr. Marlowe. Never! He lov —"

Trumpet persisted. "Are you certain he didn't plot with Ingram Frizer to —" Then her wits caught up with ears. "He *loved* him, you say? Like a lover, do you mean?"

Audrey pressed her lips together and dropped her gaze to her feet. "I don't know anything about any such thing."

Trumpet bent a compelling glare on her captive's closed face, willing her to speak.

Audrey glanced at her, then lifted her chin and drew in a proud breath. "All right, then. I'll say it. My husband loved another man. Does that please you?"

"It isn't a matter of —"

"He was happier when Kit was around." Audrey sounded more defiant than ashamed. "Anyone could see it. He talked to him about everything, far more than he talked to me. His eyes lit up when Kit appeared on the stairs, in the garden, coming across the bridge . . . Kit liked him well enough in return, but he was always the loved one, wasn't he? Never the lover."

True. Very true. Kit always had that aloof, untouchable core. That was part of his appeal. People wanted him to notice them, to share some part of his magic with them.

Trumpet could see the problem. "You can't compete with that, can you? A new dress, a sheer chemise, a musky perfume. They're no good if you're the wrong sex altogether."

Audrey smiled, cocking her head with a curious gleam in her eyes. Trumpet hastened to add, "Not that I've experienced that particular problem myself."

Then a new theory of the crime popped fully formed into her head. She stabbed a finger at her friend. "*You* did it! You arranged that day in Deptford, to rid yourself of the cuckoo in your nest."

"I did not!" Audrey recoiled from the stabbing finger, bumping into Catalina and jolting forward again, wide-eyed with panic.

Good. Panic made people talk. Trumpet took a half step forward, closing the tiny gap between them. "It makes sense — perfect sense. You and your property broker, Mr. Frizer. You planned it together. You seemed very friendly last week. Perhaps *more* than merely friendly? He lives in your house; he eats at your table. He loves you, doesn't he? He'd do anything for you, wouldn't he?" She poked her finger into the other woman's chest, striking at the thin partlet between ruff and bodice.

Audrey emitted an open-mouthed squeal of fury. "Ingram would *never* —"

"Oh, it's *Ingram*, is it? I knew it! I have a nose for these things, you know." Trumpet stepped back, retracting the inquisitorial finger. "Funny sort of a household you have, Mrs. Walsingham."

Audrey glared at her with tightened lips.

Trumpet waited, smiling.

"All right, all right." Audrey crumbled like a damp biscuit. "I confess. I did form a special friendship with Ingram, but only after my husband fell in love with Kit. I was lonely. Can you blame me?"

Trumpet shook her head. "Not at all." She was in no position to cast that stone.

"But I wished Kit no harm," Audrey said, seeming eager now to get it all out. "To be honest, I liked having him in the house. Thomas and I get along well together without that part. The intimate part. Perhaps we lack the grand passion of Tristan and Isolde, but we share the same goals. We'll have a few children one of these days. I'm young. There's no rush. And we'll advance through my service and his. We're already corresponding with King James, if you care to know. He's quite genial, as it happens. When the time comes, he'll remember us. So what does it matter whom we invite into our beds? I can't offer you proof. How could I? But I ask you this. Why would I draw attention to my 'funny sort of household' by arranging the death of a man who made my husband happy?"

Trumpet frowned. She heard a reflection of her life with Stephen in that description of a dispassionate but effective marriage. Would she plot to murder Stephen's lover? Never. On the contrary, she encouraged them. And yet she regarded their marriage as a success.

"Very well," she said. "I believe you." She took a full step back, tilting her head for Catalina to do the same.

Audrey smoothed her partlet where the stabbing finger had left an invisible dent. Her face took on a crafty expression. "I know about you and Mr. Clarady."

Trumpet blew out a dismissive breath. "And I know your husband was in love with a notorious atheist. How genial would King James be about that bit of news?" She gave Audrey a disdainful shake of the head. "Let's not start something neither of us wants to finish."

* * *

Trumpet found a letter from Tom, closed with Stephen's old seal, on her dressing table when she and Catalina returned to their room. He'd found the weasel-faced varlet Nicholas Skeres haunting the aisles at St. Paul's. He'd told the same story in the same words as Ingram Frizer. He had also, however, given up one useful morsel of information. The elusive Robert Poley had a mistress named Joan Yeomans. She was a cutler's wife. Did Trumpet want to take that one on, if she could tear herself away from the pleasure palace?

He knew the answer well enough. Trumpet dashed off a note telling him she'd shake Poley's lodging out of the cutler's wife that very afternoon. She had news about the

Walsinghams as well and would send another note as soon as she reached Dorchester House.

Then she went back up to the queen's bedchamber to ask Lady Stafford if they could manage without her that afternoon. She claimed an urgent need to inspect the work of the tradesman crafting a new Delabere coat of arms for the hall. "It's a surprise for my husband, so it has to be perfect."

The queen's senior attendant approved the request. That meant Trumpet had all afternoon — and all evening — to do her part in bringing Kit's killer to justice. Or at least finding out what really happened. Her years with Francis Bacon had taught her that justice could not always be obtained.

The road from Nonsuch to Lambeth was so well traveled when the queen was at the palace that Trumpet and Catalina had no trouble finding the way. They traveled as themselves, so it didn't matter who saw them. Many courtiers had houses within a reasonable ride from the court and went home often, for a variety of reasons. Essex sometimes traveled all the way east to Wanstead just to have dinner with a friend in his own house.

The handful of servants left in Dorchester House were hers — men and women she'd brought from Suffolk. They were used to their lady's ways and thought nothing of her arriving in a gown and departing in galligaskins.

They would be pursuing a woman today, so they decided to dress as women of the middling sort. Good wool for skirts and doublets but with linen linings instead of silk. No velvet, no brocade, no pearls. Trumpet liked this costume best. Her belled skirt was dark pink with green guards. Catalina had thriftily composed the bodice of vertical stripes in the same pink and green wool. Add a short round hat with a plumed feather at the back and she looked an inch or two taller.

She raided the secret money box she kept atop the canopy over her bed. One needed cash, not credit, for paying bribes and buying tidbits on the street. She'd filled the box by selling the largest Bible in Lord Surdeval's library, fetching the satisfying sum of three pounds. She'd collected the fortune in small coins. Kit had assured her the Bible wasn't rare, so she could sell it in good conscience.

Did selling a Bible make her some kind of atheist? Who could she ask now that Kit was gone?

If it did, then so be it. The deed was done, for one thing. For another, she needed the money to resolve the mystery of Kit's death. God understood loyalty; in fact, he demanded it himself. She doubted He would hold it against her.

"Now," she said, inspecting herself in the long mirror. "How do we find the wife of a cutler? I'd rather not ask at the guildhall if we can avoid it."

"What is a cutteler, my lady?" Catalina had a little trouble with the new word.

"A person who makes knives."

"Knives for the killing or knives for the cooking?"

"Both, I should think."

"Then cannot we ask of your cook?"

"We can." Trumpet grinned. Her life had improved immeasurably when her uncle sent Catalina Luna to her. They'd understood one another at once and had formed a perfect partnership.

The cook dropped his spoon when she entered the kitchen. She hadn't been in here since they'd taken possession of the house. He crossed the expanse of stone-clad floor, wringing his hands in dismay. She reassured him that she wouldn't ask for supper that evening and would be gone well before nightfall. No need to alter his schedule in any way.

Thus comforted, he happily brought out his collection of knives, spreading them on his well-scrubbed worktable for her inspection. Some had iron handles, others wood. A few narrow, curved blades had ivory handles. They must be for special purposes. Together, they presented an astonishing variety of styles and functions.

"Were any of these made by a man named Yeomans?" Trumpet asked, lightly stroking the blades with the tip of her finger. She picked up one with an iron handle, hefting it to try its weight. She liked the smoothness of it.

"Yes, my lady. William Yeomans makes a fine knife. Like this boning knife here." The cook selected one with a long, thin blade and presented it to her on both flat hands.

She leaned forward to study it closely. "Is that his mark?"

"Yes, my lady. A *W* over a *Y*."

"Where can I find him?"

"Oh, well, now. Let me think." The cook set the knife back in its place and pushed up the rim of his puffy cap to scratch his forehead. "I suppose you might start at his shop, my lady."

Trumpet bit back a tart remark. He truly was an excellent cook. She schooled her voice to mildness. "Where is his shop?"

"Oh, well, now." More scratching of the head. "Well, he's up on Hugging Lane, isn't he, my lady? Just off St. Thomas Apostle."

"That's east of St. Paul's, isn't it?" Trumpet would wager this excellent cook that she knew London better than most women of her rank, but she fell far short of Tom's comprehensive knowledge. He could go out and prowl the streets whenever he liked, which gave him an unfair advantage.

"Yes, my lady." The cook beamed at her. "Will you be wanting more knives, my lady?"

"No, no. I just want to see his shop."

She thanked him. He thanked her. She thanked him again after accepting his offer of a glass of sweet wine and some warm honey cakes he'd let the undercook bake for practice. She asked for a glass for Catalina as well, to be served in the library.

Once there, she dashed off a note to Tom, telling him to meet her at the Temple Bar in half an hour. She sent that out with the young usher who brought the refreshments. "Let's hope this cutler knows where his wife is."

Catalina was less sanguine. "If she is the woman of Poley, she may not live with her husband."

"He still might know where she is. We follow the trail we have, my friend, until we find a better one." They finished their honey cakes, which were delicious, and left.

Tom stood in his usual spot on the west side of the southern arch. Trumpet's heart leapt when she spotted him, the same way it leapt every time she saw him since the very first time.

"What's afoot?" he asked, falling into step with them.

"A cutler named William Yeomans. A good one, according to my cook."

Tom grinned at that. "I wouldn't have thought to ask a cook. I would've gone to their guildhall."

"Then they'd know someone was looking for him. Which might not matter. But then again, it might. This way we can surprise him."

"Not sure I want to surprise a man sitting in a shop full of knives."

Trumpet clucked her tongue at him. It felt good to be out on the street with her two favorite companions. The jostling, the noise, the blobs of shit waiting for unwary feet — London was always full of life, even in a bad year.

Tom led them unerringly to Hugging Lane. The cutler's shop stood right on the corner. Customers crowded the place. They had to wait their turn just to go inside. The blue-clad youth at the counter frowned when Trumpet said she only had a question.

"Sure you don't need a new knife, Mistress?" He gestured at the display behind him. "Finest quality in all England, right here at Yeomans'."

"Perhaps another time. Today, we have an urgent message for Mrs. Yeomans, only we can't remember where she said to meet her."

He blinked at her, his mouth turning down in an oddly froglike expression. "At Browne's, I expect. She's there most of the day."

Trumpet snapped her fingers at Tom. "Browne's, that was it. Where is it again?"

"Round the corner, isn't it?" The youth started to turn toward a woman craning her neck to look at a cleaver hanging high up on the wall.

Tom plucked his sleeve. "On Trinity?"

"Bread Street. I thought you knew her." He gave Tom a suspicious look, shaking off his hand. "Browne's lodging house. It's Mrs. Yeomans's now, but they still call it Browne's, after the old woman."

They thanked him — or rather, the back of his blue doublet — and left. As they turned the corner, the heady aroma of baking bread made Trumpet's mouth water. "Let's buy some buns when we're through here."

"Cinnamon," Tom said, "with lots of raisins." He popped his head inside a bakery to ask for Browne's lodging house. Trumpet caught him extending his nose for a snootful of yeasty air.

They found the house at the corner of busy Thames Street. The substantial four-story building seemed well kept, with smooth yellow plaster gleaming between strong oak beams.

Tom pointed across the street. "Go around that row of houses there and you'll find yourself at Queenhithe." That

Anna Castle

wharf was large enough for masted boats bringing corn and other goods from far up the river.

"A convenient location for an intelligencer." Trumpet studied the front windows of the tall house, seeking a gap between the pale curtains. Anyone might be inside — or no one. She tossed a grin at Tom and knocked on the door.

Nothing happened. Tom reached over her shoulder and knocked again, louder.

"I'm coming! I'm coming! Don't pound the house down!" A woman of some thirty-five years, judging by the tiny lines around her mouth, opened the door. She'd been pretty once, with thick fair curls teased out at the front of a dark green snood. The green brought out the blue of her eyes, which were too closely set for beauty. A sprinkling of pockmarks spoiled her otherwise fair cheeks. Large breasts surged under a plain partlet. Either she employed a poor dressmaker or she'd deliberately had her bodice made to create that display.

She stood in the doorway with one hand on the jamb and one on her hip, the pose of a woman accustomed to bartering with strangers at her door. She gave Trumpet a quick up-and-down look, lingered a little on Catalina's southern features, then lit on Tom with a smile — the same smile every woman always gave him. Trumpet swallowed her jealousy. Someday, he'd be gray and stoop-shouldered. Then she'd be the only woman who smiled at him like that.

"What can I do for you?" The landlady addressed the question to Tom.

Trumpet answered. "We're looking for Mrs. Yeomans — Joan Yeomans. I'll hazard a guess that's you."

"I won't deny it." An odd answer for an honest woman. "What do you want with me?"

"We have a question," Trumpet said. "Where can we find Robert Poley?"

The woman startled but recovered quickly. Her eyes narrowed. "I don't know anyone by that name."

242

She did; she absolutely did. Trumpet would bet her hat on it, and she loved this hat.

"Nicholas Skeres says you do." Tom had the bland, genial look on his face that usually made people trust him. "I'll hazard a guess Mr. Poley lives here. Looks like a nice house."

"It is a nice house," Yeomans said. "Ask anybody."

"Don't you know who lives in it?" Trumpet did not want to play guessing games with this harlot. She wanted to find Poley, then go home and play indoor games with Tom.

"Why should I tell you?" Yeomans set the other hand on the other hip in a challenging pose.

Trumpet adopted a ready stance. "I fail to understand the difficulty in answering a simple question. Does a man named Robert Poley live here or not?"

"My lodgers like their privacy," Yeomans said.

"What, none of them receives visitors?" Trumpet scoffed. "We only want to talk to the man."

"I've given you my answer."

"You've given me no answer at all!"

Yeomans took a step toward Trumpet. She stood a good six inches taller and took advantage of that height to look down her nose. "I don't have to answer your questions. And I don't think I like you blocking my doorway." She flapped her hand in Trumpet's face. "Be off with you."

Tom muttered, "Oh no."

What ailed the woman? Someone must have put too much salt in her porridge, aggravating a choleric temper. That, or she'd been born a quarrelsome scold. No wonder her husband lived elsewhere.

"It's a public street," Trumpet said, not flinching one jot. She put her hands on her hips, squaring off. "I'll stand where I please."

Yeomans's lip curled. "Not if I budge you. Puny little clog like you, it won't take much." She reached out a hand and pushed Trumpet on the shoulder, rocking her back a little.

Tom took a step forward. "Now, now, my good women, let's just —"

"I'll handle this." Trumpet stopped him with a flat palm. "Puny, am I? You'll find me harder to budge than you think, you poxy old scold."

"*Old!* You meddlesome minnow! Get your prying, spying, cheese face out of my street!" Yeomans used both hands this time, shoving Trumpet hard enough to knock her back a few steps.

"I'll stand here as long as I like, you brabbling harridan." Trumpet grounded herself on both feet, the way Tom had taught her for wrestling a larger opponent. She bent her knees and drove up through her legs, using her full weight to push the harpy back.

"That's my girl," Tom said, laughter in his voice, as Yeomans fell down on her oversized arse.

Alas, the harpy clutched at Trumpet's sleeves on the way down, pulling her on top. The steel hoops in the harpy's farthingale bounced, sinking, but not breaking, under Trumpet's weight. They made a springy pad with the layers of fabric bunching on top. The ropes in her own farthingale simply collapsed, making it easy for her to dig a knee into the mass of skirts below.

Catalina had insisted on ropes for their tradeswoman's garb, claiming they were more authentic. It would seem they had other advantages as well.

Trumpet's knee hit flesh and bone under the wriggling mass, making the harpy squeal. She pressed her hands against the woman's shoulders to lever herself up. Yeomans bucked and rocked, trying to roll Trumpet off. But the steel hoops had spread sideways and refused to give way. So Yeomans pressed her palm under Trumpet's chin, pushing her head back. Trumpet slapped wildly at her with her right hand, unable to see well enough to land a worthy blow. She coiled her hand into a fist to make the blows that landed count more when a strong arm wrapped around her waist and lifted her, still kicking, straight up into the air.

"You take the little one," Tom said, handing her to Catalina.

"Little!" Trumpet screamed, but the Spanish woman outweighed her by a stone, and she'd lived a harder life. She tugged her mistress out of reach.

Yeomans yowled like the devil she was, lunging forward onto her knees, stretching her hand out to yank on Trumpet's skirts. Tom caught her around the waist and pulled her up and off her feet, twisting his head back as she tried to butt him and enduring her kicking heels. She couldn't hurt him much that way, with her skirts muffling the blows, but that didn't keep her from trying.

Trumpet glared at her erstwhile opponent. "What ails you, you pox-ridden whore?"

Yeomans bared her teeth in reply. But before she could open her mouth, a tall cart pulled by a stout horse rumbled into the street, stopping a mere arm's-length from the combatants and their restrainers.

Two burly men jumped down and began untying the ropes that held a tall cupboard-shaped object wrapped in canvas. The shorter man turned to the quartet, looking from one pair to the other, scratching his rusty beard. At last, he grunted and spoke to Tom. "This here's for Mr. Robert Poley. Which floor d'ye want it on?"

Yeomans withered in Tom's grasp as Trumpet pumped both fists in the air. "I win!"

TWENTY-FOUR

Tom ordered a couple of pies — one cheese and one mince — to go with his second mug of ale. He'd been sitting by the window in this alehouse on Thames Street for a good couple of hours, watching for Robert Poley. He couldn't think of another way to catch up with the man, given the shrewish temper of his landlady. He could only hope the knave wasn't tucked up in bed nursing a cold in the head.

He'd been flirting with the tavern wench to pass the time and to keep his hand in. He didn't get many opportunities these days. Luckily, she was pushing forty and had a laugh like a wheezy donkey. The pretty girl she once had been still showed through the sagging jowls and bags under her eyes though, every time she smiled. She enjoyed the game as much as Tom and expected nothing more from him.

Miriel brought his pies, hot from a bakery on Bread Street. He poked a couple of holes in them to let out the steam. "Ever met a woman named Joan Yeomans? Has a house around the corner here."

"Met her! Joan Yeomans! Well, I should say so!" Miriel crossed her arms over her round belly and shook her head. "Or I should say, I try *not* to meet her. I go around the other way to get to the bakeries. She's a scold, is what she is. There've been complaints — many of them. Not that anything will change her tune."

"What's her story?" Tom asked. "She inherited that house from her mother, I hear."

Clearly not the interesting part. "Why wouldn't she? And anyone would keep their lodgers, if the lodgers are good. But Joan lives there too now, with that Mr. Poley, leaving her husband in the rooms above his shop. Not alone though, is he?" Muriel's thinning eyebrows flicked meaningfully.

"Does he have a mistress?" Tom tested the edge of his mince pie. Still too hot, but hunger drove him to nibble around the crimped crust.

"He has a journeyman." Miriel gave him a broad wink. "Not that it's any of *my* business. *I'm* never one to pry. But working in an alehouse on a busy street like this, you see things."

"You hear things." Tom nodded at her with a knowing look meant to encourage the sharing of those sights and sounds.

"I do. The good Lord knows I do." She sighed as one who bears a great burden. "But William Yeomans is a fine cutler. Everyone says it. He works hard, long hours. They say that too. Maybe he doesn't have time for a wife. Or maybe he's got a temper. Can't have two like that under one roof, now can you?"

Tom shuddered. "I wouldn't want to live next to them." He took a bite of the pie. It was delicious, a work of art. With mince, everything depended on the quality of the vinegar.

"Perhaps that's why she left," Miriel said. "Though they seem on good enough terms, as far as anyone can see." She gave her head a world-weary shake. "You never know what goes on inside another house, now do you?"

"You never do, do you?" Tom mimicked the head shake.

Miriel nodded, satisfied they'd reached agreement on that deep question. "She's been visiting Mr. Poley for years now. Ten? Ten sounds about right. They met in prison, or so I heard. She used to visit prisoners, bring them bits of this and that to ease their time."

"That sounds charitable," Tom said. Not like the Joan Yeomans he'd encountered.

"Charitable!" Miriel blew out a lip fart. "Someone paid her to find out things is my guess." She bent forward, giving Tom a good look at her enormous bosom, and whispered, "*He* was there to spy on Catholics. That's what he does, or one of the things."

Tom grimaced. "I wouldn't want that job. Dangerous. And unwholesome, to my way of thinking."

"Mine too. Best to leave them be is what I say. But I hear Mr. Poley does right by both of them — the Yeomans, I mean. Nice gifts every now and again. *Costly.* They say he gave the husband a silver chalice."

Tom let out a low whistle. "High wages for the use of a man's wife." He winked at his new friend.

She swatted him on the shoulder with her rag. "You're a naughty one, aren't you?"

He made a pious face. "I may be a little naughty from time to time."

"Mm-hmm." She nodded at him, then left to serve some other patrons.

When she came back, he said, "I'm curious about this Mr. Poley. What's his story?"

She shook her head and wagged a finger. "You tread lightly around that man. I mean it, now. He doesn't like anyone meddling in his affairs. You'll regret it if you try."

"What does he do?"

"Well, I can tell you one thing." She shot glances from side to side, making sure the men at the other tables were minding their own business, then leaned down again to speak quietly. "Between you and me and the tabletop, he played a cruel trick on a gentleman in Southwark not so very long ago. Mrs. Yeomans had her eye on a property over there not far from the docks. The gentleman who owned it refused to meet her price. Probably way too low, knowing that woman and her hard ways. She got the place in the end though, and at the price she wanted." She paused, waiting for a comment.

Tom obliged. "How'd she manage that? House in Southwark, close to the docks. Must've been lots of other buyers."

"Not if they knew what was good for them. Mr. Poley informed the sheriff that the gentleman who owned it had missed church three weeks running. They fined him forty shillings!"

"Ugh!" Tom recoiled as from a bad smell. "That's dirty. That's low."

"As low as can be," Miriel agreed. "And now he's on their list, isn't he? They don't care that he had a sick child and wanted to give his wife a turn out of the house."

Tom met her brown eyes. "That tells me everything I ever needed to know about Robert Poley. I thank you for the confidence. And I promise I won't share it."

"I knew you were the trusty sort from the moment you walked in." She flashed a saucy grin. "Even if you are too handsome for your own good."

Tom laughed. Before he could frame a suitable retort, she pointed out the window. "Speak of the devil and there he appears."

"And that's me, off after him. I have a few questions for that man." Tom gulped down the last of his ale, rose, and stuffed the cheese pie in his pocket. He laid some coins on the table, then bent to drop a kiss on Miriel's cheek. "Thanks for the news — and the company."

Pink spots flared as she beamed at him. "Watch your back."

Tom hastened into the street, coming up alongside his quarry and matching his stride. He pointed his chin at the package wrapped in yellow linen that Poley clutched to his chest. "Perival & Sons, eh? Someone's having a good week. What is it, a silver platter? A mirror?" The mercer's shop in the Royal Exchange enjoyed a reputation for costly gifts, which it flaunted by wrapping them in quality cloth.

"None of your concern, Master." Poley cast a quick glance at Tom's clothes. Then he gave him a second look and stopped walking. "You were at the funeral last week. Friend of Mr. Walsingham?"

"A friend of Mr. Marlowe." Tom put a slight curve on his lips, but his eyes were hard.

"Ah." Poley poked his tongue into his taut cheek. "Well, I'm sorry for your loss, Mr. . . . ."

"You can call me Tom."

Poley nodded. "That would be Thomas Clarady, I'll wager. Mr. Frizer told me you and your friend — a Lady Dorchester, wasn't it? — were asking questions about the inquest." He chuckled, a genial sound. "Frizer told me you were something of a feather-wit."

"I can play the fool when it suits my purposes."

Poley nodded again. He seemed to be storing up small facts with each dip of his beak-like nose. "You were here yesterday asking questions with a green-eyed vixen. Lady Dorchester had green eyes, Frizer noted. Quite distinctive."

"They're common enough. Mr. Frizer didn't strike me as an observant man."

"More than you might think," Poley said, "though less than I might wish."

He seemed willing to let Trumpet's involvement go. A wise choice. No one stirs up an earl if he can help it, especially not by slandering his wife.

"I still have those questions." Tom tilted his head toward the tower at St. Mary's. "Could I beg a moment in the churchyard before you go home? I'm not eager to meet your landlady again." He gave his thigh a rueful rub.

Poley laughed, a touch of pride in his dark eyes. "She's a brave one, all right." He stood a moment with his package in his arms, looking up at Tom with a measuring gaze. Then he shrugged and said, "Why not? But only a moment, and I don't promise answers."

They walked to the narrow yard and stopped underneath an ancient ash tree. Tom leaned on a mossy gravestone, but Poley stood balanced on his feet with his package in his arms. He looked as if he could stand in that pose all day. Tom remembered Kit telling him once that half of intelligence work was riding and the other half was waiting, with a slice of talking in between.

"I just want to know what happened to my friend," Tom said. "Mr. Walsingham told me about the inquest, but things don't quite make sense to me."

"Which things?" Poley asked, as mildly as if Tom had asked about the selection of mirrors at Perival's.

"The moment of truth." Tom gave him an up-and-down look, taking his time, from the black hair streaked with gray to the stocky frame supported by stout legs. Something over forty years old, judging by the extra stone around Poley's waist and the thinning hair. Past his prime, but by no means frail.

"Now that I've met you, Mr. Poley, I find it even harder to believe you could sit there on that bench doing nothing while a furious struggle went on beside you. I'd have jumped up to get away or grabbed at their arms. I would've done something."

"Would you? Two men younger than yourself, cursing and spitting, grappling over possession of a sharp knife?" Poley held out his hands, palms up. "You're a braver man than I am, Mr. Clarady. Perhaps you could have prevented that tragic accident. You Inns of Court men take training in the arts of combat, from what I hear. I myself am not a

251

man of violence. On the contrary. I was stunned by their fury, just as if you'd struck me on the head. By the time my wits revived, it was all over."

Tom grunted. He didn't believe it. This steely eyed knave hadn't lost his wits or his nerve since the day of his birth. At least he'd used different words this time.

Tom's heart sank as he accepted the fundamental truth that he would never learn exactly what had happened in that fateful moment. No one would. The only men who knew would lie about it to their graves.

He moved on. "Mr. Walsingham told me he arranged a meeting with you and Kit — Mr. Marlowe. Mrs. Bull told me you two spent most of the day walking about the garden together, talking. What were you talking about?"

"My, my. You are the dogged little hound, aren't you?" Poley's lip curled as every trace of geniality vanished. "Sniffing about here and there, prying into matters that don't concern you. You should know better. Frizer told me you claimed to be the confidential clerk of Francis Bacon. If that's true, then you must know his brother, Anthony Bacon. In which case, you've probably already guessed what sorts of things a man like Marlowe might want to talk about at a lodging house in Deptford."

The sudden shift in humor set Tom on his guard. But the man's pridefulness, which showed in his stance and the tilt of his head, might yet trip him up. "I know Marlowe was hoping for a new assignment. One that would take him north, for a change, instead of east."

"He wasn't up to it. I knew that after five minutes. The man couldn't control himself. He couldn't stop his fat mouth from flapping." Poley spoke those last words in a taunting tone, then thrust his chin out as if inviting a blow.

What good would that do him? Give him an excuse to draw his knife?

The belligerence was an act, meant to provoke a rash response. It wouldn't work. Marlowe had taught Tom not to let himself be baited. "Is that why you killed him? Because he liked to poke at men's beliefs? Kit was a philosopher as well as a poet. A great one, on both counts."

Poley shrugged, not caring one small fig about the quality of the life he'd cut short. "The choice was his. Continue to make a braying ass of himself all across London or shut his noisy clapdish and do the work he claimed to want. He brought this on himself. One way or another, his days were numbered."

It wouldn't qualify as a confession in a court of law, but it was good enough for Tom. Poley had gone to Deptford ready to lower the axe if his masters commanded it. That must have been the real purpose of the meeting, for him to question Kit about his plays, his plans, and his fatal, boasting blasphemy. Poley chose the lodging house so no one would connect that quiet interrogation with anyone in authority.

The report went off to Nonsuch. *He can't be stopped, and he knows too much.* When the order came back to silence the offender, Poley made Frizer and Skeres do the foul deed, using some combination of threats and bribery.

Poley watched Tom think it through, his lip still curled in that superior sneer. "I'd let it go if I were you, Mr. Clarady. There are worse things than a knife in the eye."

Was that a threat? Of what? Not violence, not here. Poley hadn't shifted his stance an inch and still held his costly trinket in his arms. He couldn't very well report him for non-attendance at church. Tom planted his well-clad backside in the pew at Gray's Inn Chapel every Sunday morning. First, because he had to try twice as hard to overcome his father's lack of gentility, and second, because you didn't work for Francis Bacon without becoming a keen judge of sermons.

He'd learned all he could here. "I had to know. Kit was a friend. And he was murdered for his imagination."

Poley shook his head as if chiding a wayward pupil. "You know better than that. Marlowe was a soldier in a great battle. He made himself an enemy when he refused to silence himself, so someone had to do it for him."

"A battle for what?" Tom asked, still flailing at the futility of it all.

Poley puffed a dismissive breath past his moustache. "I never ask that question."

TWENTY-FIVE

Francis sat in the library at Nonsuch studying some of Anthony's intelligence reports. His task was to analyze them and write a summary that might ultimately be shown to the queen. This small desk in the farthest corner of one of the largest libraries in the land afforded him as much privacy as he was likely to find in the crowded palace. If any prying eyes loomed over his shoulder, he could slide the papers back into his writing box.

A shadow fell across his desk, startling him into shaking a blot of ink onto his page. He'd have to copy that out again. He pulled a sheet of paper facedown over the rest and looked up to find an usher in palace livery standing a respectful four feet away.

"If it please you, Mr. Bacon, two gentlemen of the Privy Council request your attendance upon them in the council chamber."

"Who?"

"Sir Thomas Heneage and Lord Keeper Puckering."

What could they want? A breath of hope whispered that they might want to express their support — limited, of course, at this early stage — for his candidacy for Attorney General. A vote of confidence from the Lord Keeper would be helpful indeed.

"I suppose they want me now."

"And it please you, Master." The usher spoke in subservient tones, but his posture told a different story. He would wait, staring implacably, until his quarry had been flushed and sent scurrying in the desired direction.

"Very well." Francis blew on the inkblot, though it had already dried, and stacked his papers together. He stoppered his inkpot and stowed everything into his carved box, locking it with a small brass key. He rose and picked it up. He'd just have to carry the thing with him. He could hardly leave confidential papers, even locked in a stout oak box, lying about.

He followed the usher to the council chamber, a paneled room with a high ceiling built for the purpose by King Henry. A huge square table dominated the space, even though it stood below a dais with a throne set ready for the queen. She attended few sessions but could appear at any time. Clerestory windows set into deep stone niches lit the room on bright days like this one. Wheels of candles could be lowered over the table when the sky turned gray.

Only two men sat at the vast table on this beautiful Saturday afternoon — men like Francis, who would rather work than ride, shoot, or play at bowls. Both were dressed in solemn black, their dark beards jutting over plain linen ruffs. Both wore black hats with tall crowns and black silk bands. There the resemblance ended.

Puckering's fleshy features made him look older than his fifty-odd years, as stolid as a prosperous merchant. Heneage, on the other hand, retained the clean lines of a once-handsome face in spite of the deep wrinkles around his eyes. He'd been one of Her Majesty's Gentlemen of the Privy Chamber in his youth. Those men were chosen for beauty as well as family connections. Gossip said she'd been wont to flirt with him to make Lord Leicester jealous. She had a long memory for a handsome face, continuing to favor her favorites over the years.

They exchanged the briefest of courtesies while the usher removed himself from the chamber. Francis set his writing box on the table and took a seat opposite the two councilors.

Heneage spoke first. "We hear your name is being pushed forward for the Attorney General position."

Francis didn't like the word "pushed." "I am honored by my Lord Essex's good opinion."

"Given your performance at Parliament," Puckering said with a curled lip, "you'll need all the backing you can get."

Francis was taken aback by the overt hostility. Was this why they'd summoned him — to barter their favor? Whatever could he offer them in exchange? "I've only just heard about it myself."

Heneage said, "It's never too early to show your support for the great work of our time."

"What work is that?" Francis asked, though he had an inkling.

Puckering took up the call. "Rooting out dissension in whatever form it takes, wherever it arises, once and for all."

An ambitious program unlikely to succeed, given the disposition toward contrariness that seemed to be part of human nature. But they wouldn't like that answer. Francis offered a stock response. "As both you good gentlemen know, I and my family have always stood firm on behalf of the Church of England, through both advocacy and practice."

"That's not enough!" Heneage pounded his fist on the polished oak. "We must take the battle to the streets, to seek out those who oppose our religion through rebellion and mockery. Those clever, self-styled wits who use a public platform to spread doubt and dissension. They must be stopped."

Francis's heart sank. He was talking about Christopher Marlowe. "You're the ones to whom Robert Poley sent his message from that house in Deptford. You're the ones who gave him permission to execute the poet."

Puckering bristled. "He was given every chance to recant and promise to reform his ways."

"Why not just put him in prison for a few months or years to repent his folly?"

"Rack him and turn him loose, like Thomas Kyd?" Heneage demanded, as if Francis had ordered that futile travesty. "That was meant to serve as an example. A warning to the others. But it only seems to have inspired pity for the man. It had no effect whatsoever on his heartless chambermate."

It had some effect. It had deepened Marlowe's opposition to the authority view and sacrificed the goodwill of Kyd's friends in the writing trade.

"I understand the importance of religious unity," Francis said. "I advocate it. It creates peace and builds faith in place of corrosive skepticism. But we must take care that our efforts to achieve unity do not deface the laws of charity. Let not the punishment exceed the crime."

"If you are not with us, Mr. Bacon," Heneage said, "you are against us."

He seemed to mean it as a threat, but Francis did not fear these men or their zealotry. Not with Lord Essex standing in front of him and his renowned parents behind. But there was little to be gained from arguing with men in so intransigent a humor. "What would you have me do?"

"Your servant has been questioning the coroner's report," Heneage said. "He has gone so far as to interrogate our confidential agent. We will not tolerate such interference."

Puckering twisted his thick lips in a scowl. "Call off your dog, if you value him."

A chilling choice of terms. But Francis merely nodded. This request he could fulfill in good conscience. "My clerk is grieving over the sudden death of a friend. He heard a secondhand report from the inquest and found himself unable to accept it. I shall write to him at once advising him to rest content with the official verdict. The courts are adjourned until Michaelmas. It's time for him to go home for the summer."

He'd had a letter from Tom that morning reporting on his conversation with Robert Poley. The spy had more or less admitted his crime. Now Francis knew who had authorized it. The questions raised by the oddities in the coroner's report had been resolved, including the motive for murdering a talented young man who had yet to reach the pinnacle of his achievements.

But nothing could be done about it. The queen approved such harsh measures in the quiet war against dissension, at least tacitly. Lord Essex wouldn't stand up for more conciliatory methods. He had other battles to fight.

There could be no justice for Christopher Marlowe. Francis's concern now must be to protect Tom from the reckless hand of zealotry.

* * *

He returned to his shared chamber to write an urgent letter to Tom warning him to desist. He'd barely started it when an usher in the orange-and-white livery of the Earl of Essex knocked on his door.

"Mr. Bacon?" The man bowed shortly, causing the white plumes in his tall hat to dance. "His Lordship wishes to see you at once in the Presence Chamber."

"The Presence Chamber?" Francis blinked at him uncomprehendingly. He had yet to receive permission to approach Her Majesty, even so near as the outermost of her reception rooms.

"If you would please follow me, Mr. Bacon. His Lordship awaits."

Francis shrugged. His day for unexpected summonses, it would seem. "Lead on."

His Lordship beamed at him as he entered the richly paneled and painted room. Indeed, the young earl fairly bounced on his toes in eagerness. "Today, we press our suit, Mr. Bacon. I tried to catch her yesterday after her hunt, but she was too greedy for her supper to listen. She's ready now." He rubbed his hands together. "She won't deny me today."

The earl led the way down the thick rush matting that ran from the outer door of the Presence Chamber all the way to the anteroom of the queen's bedchamber. They stepped off the royal pathway several yards before the throne under its red canopy. Sir Francis Knollys, Treasurer of the Royal Household, was waved away at their approach. His gaze lingered on Francis as he passed, his stoic expression revealing nothing.

Francis inhaled the imaginary aroma of power carried on the real scents of musk perfume and coal ashes from this morning's fire. He blinked at the splendor of the tapestries covering the walls with scenes of hunting and courtly life from the time of Charlemagne. It had been over a year since his eyes had had the honor of gazing upon these royal works of art.

He followed three steps behind the earl, bowing head-to-knee at the same time as His Lordship. He lingered in that posture for a moment longer to express his uttermost humility in the presence of his sovereign. She liked these little gestures, even while seeing through their designs. Such was the complexity of Elizabeth Tudor. A lesser monarch would enjoy the adulation without the insight.

Essex began with a summary of Francis's qualifications. He'd been called to the bar at the tender age of twenty-two, becoming the youngest barrister in history. He'd been made a bencher of Gray's Inn, if only a probationary one, at the age of twenty-six. He'd given an exemplary reading — an essential rite of passage for men on a legal career — only two years later. He'd been Dean of the Chapel at Gray's for several years now.

The queen listened patiently to the recital, though with a small quirk upon her lips. "I know all that, my Lord Essex. How not, since half those honors came from me?"

That wasn't entirely fair, though Francis would fling himself out the window onto the pavement below before saying it. A goodly share of the credit went to his father, who had been much loved and admired during his long years of membership in Gray's. A portion surely went to his own abilities. He had done the preparation for his reading, after all, and no one else had delivered it. The members of Gray's Inn had made him dean — hardly a desirable position, but still an honor of sorts.

"Nevertheless," Essex said, "they merit repetition under the current circumstances. I should note that Mr. Bacon is also considered a pre-eminent scholar of the law by everyone who understands such matters. His *Twenty-Five Maxims* have done more to clarify the common law than any other work."

Her Majesty's august gaze lit on Francis. Did he perceive the slightest touch of friendly regard in the depths of her eyes? "We are aware of Mr. Bacon's qualifications. But you left out his many years of service as a Member of Parliament."

The pleasure of seeing his queen's face and the momentary thrill of that elusive hint of friendliness turned to dust. His speeches against the triple subsidy still rankled, nearly two months later.

"Served ably and well," Essex said, taking a step closer and squaring his shoulders. Few men in the world dared adopt such an assertive posture in the royal presence, but then that was part of why she loved him. "He must speak his mind, or what use is he?"

"Better use when his mind bends closer to mine," the queen retorted. "I prefer a tool that fits my hand. And you pass over his other lacks, my lord. His youth, for example. Mr. Coke has ten years' advantage, to say nothing of a year of active practice as my Solicitor General."

"A single year tells you nothing, my liege," Essex said. "Leave him in that post, say I, to prove his worth more clearly."

"Jump a man with no experience over one with a full year?" The queen laughed — a short, sharp bark, but her eyes were merry. She loved sparring with her favorites. It kept them on their toes. "You say nothing of Mr. Coke's many cases in the courts. How many has Mr. Bacon argued? A great throng, one would expect, having been pulled across the bar so long ago?"

Francis looked at his feet, wishing a hole would open beneath them so he could plummet into the service chamber below. He hadn't bothered to take any cases in the Westminster courts. They tended to turn on mundane matters such as prior commitments and moveable boundaries. They were boring, in other words, and the clamor in Westminster Hall raised a deafening echo that afflicted his ears.

Essex boldly stood his ground. "A trivial oversight readily repaired, Your Majesty, when the courts reconvene in the autumn."

"But what of the youth, my lord?" The queen's smile now held a challenge. "Should we not prefer maturity for so important a post as Attorney General?"

"Youth is no obstacle." Essex bristled, as Francis knew the queen had intended. "Rather it is an advantage." The earl, four years Francis's junior, embarked on a prideful review of his own achievements. He had led men to the aid of King Henri the Fourth in France — an expedition whose results were ambiguous at best.

They bickered for a while in a familiar fashion, Essex and the queen, over the interpretation of his deeds. Brave or foolhardy? Successful or disastrous? Francis kept his gaze on his shoes, which could have been better polished. He could have worn a better hat and had Pinnock brush his doublet more thoroughly.

A palpable shock rolled through him every time a voice rose. At least Her Majesty seemed to be enjoying herself, playing her young favorite like a well-tuned lute. She poked at his pride, and he leapt to his own defense. It might have been amusing at a greater distance and without Francis's own future at stake.

The earl gave up on France and switched to the Low Countries, where he had once again led men to fight for the Protestant cause.

"Yet the Duke of Parma sits at his ease in Brussels," the queen observed, "peering almost into my chamber windows. You've come full circle, my good lord. Because the Duke of Parma is the reason I required that triple subsidy, which Mr. Bacon so loftily sought to deny me."

Francis returned his full attention with a start. "Your gracious Majesty, I was only ever thinking of my duty to your august —"

"Silence!" she snapped. "I did not give you leave to speak."

He pressed his lips together and blinked to stem a spurt of frightened tears.

"A counterpoint can be offered for the sake of fruitful debate, I should think." The earl allowed anger to color his tone — a grave mistake.

Francis braced himself, knowing where the blow would fall.

The queen raised a jeweled finger to point directly at him while continuing to address the earl. "This man holds more fault than any of the rest in Parliament for obstructing my requests, which always express the urgent needs of my realm. Those whom I look to for support betray me at their cost."

She turned her painted face to Francis, bending her elbow to stab the finger at him for emphasis. "I expect fealty, Mr. Bacon. I expect compliance. If it had been in the king my father's time, you would find yourself banished from my presence forever."

"You are mercy itself, Your Highness." Francis bowed so low his head nearly reached his ankles. He continued to bow as he backed away from the throne. At a suitable distance, he turned and scurried out with as much dignity as he could muster.

TWENTY-SIX

By Monday morning, Tom was ready to wrap up his affairs in London and go home. He had one last chore to complete — bringing in the author of the Dutch Church libel so he could claim his hundred crowns. He'd had a letter last week from Martin Younge saying that he'd found a ballad printer who specialized in bawdry and libels. Younge would be glad to take Tom around to the man's shop any afternoon.

Tom had answered at once begging a delay, being preoccupied with Marlowe's murder. But now he'd answered his nagging questions and accepted Mr. Bacon's counsel not to expect public justice. He'd think of something to do about Poley somewhere down the road.

Shortly before dinner, a boy brought him a letter from Trumpet. Tom had sent her a full report of his conversation with Poley on Saturday. They could discuss the details when they met, either in London, if she could manage one more visit in the next week, or perhaps in that hunting box near Nonsuch. He could take a detour on his way home.

Trumpet's letter said she could shake loose from her duties at court on Tuesday to help him find the libeler. She would be at Dorchester House by noon at the latest. "Wait for me!" she commanded.

Much as he loved kicking around the city with Trumpet and Catalina, Tom had no intention of knocking on Younge's door with her at his side. Clara was the only one of Tom's former *amours* that Trumpet had met. She was also by far the most beautiful. He could imagine the jealous tauntings he'd be forced to listen to for the rest of the day.

Better to get the hundred crowns today and treat Her Ladyship to a feast at the Antelope tomorrow. They'd make it a farewell supper — or farewell for now. They always found a way to meet again in Dorset.

Tom sent a note to Martin Younge asking for the favor of his time that afternoon. Then he had dinner in the empty hall, stubbornly downing the second under-cook's mutton stew rather than spend his own coin for a decent meal in a tavern. Besides, the undercook clearly needed the practice.

He noticed more houses boarded up on his way through the city. No one jostled him as he came through Newgate. No heedless drivers forced him to leap over the gutter to get out of the way. People kept their faces turned stiffly toward their destinations, as if the plague could leap from eye to eye. The June sunshine beat down on their heads, raising steam from puddles of muck.

Plague loved the summer, they said. Time for him to be gone.

Clara answered the door with baby Gerrit in her arms and Hanna half-hidden in her skirts. She smiled her ethereal smile and stepped back to let Tom in. "He's in back." She tilted her head to show the direction.

Tom thanked her, patting each child on the head. He liked seeing her — what man wouldn't? — but felt no tug of desire. He was glad for the second test and gladder for passing it. Trumpet owned him now, body and soul. Time had changed Clara into a pleasant reminder of youthful adventures long left behind.

Younge leaned against a typesetting table, wiping ink from his fingers with a rag. The smell of ink assaulted

Tom's nose the moment he walked through the door — tangy copper and nose-curling sulphur. The three men working in the crowded shop seemed oblivious to the stink. A man could get used to anything, in time.

"Mr. Clarady." Younge greeted him with a tilt of his head. "Got your note. Let's step outside. Wouldn't mind stretching the legs."

The rear door opened into a cobbled yard that smelled of the privy shared by several houses. A narrow alley led them into the yard around the Dutch Church. Younge adopted the patient pace of a man accustomed to walking with toddlers, making what appeared to be an accustomed circuit of the grass paths winding between tombs and headstones.

"I found your printer," he said without preamble. "Fellow named Jack Mullens. He's the lowest sort, if you want my judgment. Specializes in libels and bawdry — the hotter, the better, in both cases."

"How does he get away with it?" Tom couldn't help but grin at the knave's audacity.

"He doesn't, if you mean avoiding fines. He reckons the fines he pays are a regular expense, like ink and paper. They don't add up to much. Money's not worth what it was when the fines were set. Makes sense, if you have no conscience. The lewd stuff always sells best."

"Sad but true." Tom liked ballads as much as the next man but favored the fantastical and the romantic over other types. His friend Ben loved anything satirical. They both liked a little saucy byplay here and there, and no one could resist court gossip, but neither cared for the crude stuff. He couldn't remember seeing any such works, much less hearing them cried on street corners. He supposed only certain stalls carried the more unsavory works and only showed them to known customers.

"Mullens didn't know about the libel posted on our church door," Younge said, "but I told him what I

267

remembered of it. He said he had a writer who liked nothing better than that sort of thing — verses that stir up anger and ill-will. Name of Richard Cholmeley."

"We guessed as much, Mr. Bacon and me. But you can't have a man arrested on a guess. I'm grateful for the confirmation."

"Still something of a guess," Younge said, "but a good one. Mullens said you can find Cholmeley at the Angel most afternoons. That's where he picks up his commissions."

"That tavern off Cheapside you sent me to." Tom met Younge's gaze as the clear memory of the man he'd met there formed in his mind. "Don't tell me — he's a gentleman, barely. Long face, square chin?" Tom made a slicing gesture across his beard.

Younge nodded. "That's what Mullens said. Can't miss him, he said, but it seems you've already met the man."

"We didn't trade names." Tom shook his head ruefully. "I could've saved us both a deal of work if I'd asked. Though it wouldn't have meant anything to me back then."

"Funny how things work out." Younge waved at a sexton coming through the gate and turned back toward his shop. "You'll get him this time. I'd bring a friend if I were you. A man who would write such wicked stuff won't fear a few hard blows."

"Good advice." Tom stopped at the entrance to the alleyway. He didn't need to go back through Younge's house. "You've earned a share of the reward as well as my thanks."

Younge waved that off. "Get that villain off the streets before he stirs up real harm to my family. That's reward enough for me."

"I'll do it," Tom promised.

They shook hands, two men in good accord, and took their separate ways. Tom grinned as he emerged onto Broad Street. He'd made a new friend.

And now he needed another kind of friend — the kind who would back you up in a fight. He hoped to avoid a scuffle, but he couldn't march a grown man down Lothbury to the Guildhall by himself. He could use a couple of stout lads who would appreciate a chance to take revenge for Thomas Kyd.

He walked through Bishopsgate and on to the Goose and Gall. He had wondered why writers spent so much time in their favorite taverns until he saw the squalor men like Robert Greene and Thomas Nashe lived in. They didn't have an oak-paneled hall lit by clerestory windows like he had at Gray's. Anytime he tired of his own small room, he could cross the yard to work in the company of his fellows in a warm room with a cup of decent ale.

The Goose and Gall served that function for the scribbling tribe, especially those who wrote for the theater. The place wasn't well populated in the middle of the afternoon, but a dozen or so men and women sat at tables in the large front room. Fewer patrons meant less tobacco smoke — easier on the nose and eyes. And a lower volume of talk to shout through.

Tom got a mug of beer from the tapster and raised it high to draw attention. "Anyone here count himself a friend of Thomas Kyd?"

Some men's eyes narrowed, but several answered, "Here!" "Aye!"

One of those was none other than Anthony Munday. Short but stocky, he wore his gray-streaked beard a little longer than the current style. His dark brown doublet and galligaskins had also seen better days, though they fit him well and were made of good cloth. His soft round cap bespoke a man who cared nothing for fashion. The lines on his forehead and cheeks spoke of many years of hard work — or a habitually sour humor. Knowing what he knew of the man, Tom suspected time and temper had both left their marks.

His eyes met Munday's, who shrugged. "I've filched some of my best ideas from Kyd."

That raised a soft laugh. The mention of Kyd's name had sobered the room.

Nashe didn't like Munday, but Tom had nothing against him other than a general distaste for the work he did to supplement his writing income. Munday was a pursuivant — a man who traveled around the shires collecting lists of Catholics from local sheriffs and justices of the peace. Sometimes he'd serve warrants for the arrest of someone suspected of harboring priests or passing along banned books. Tom wouldn't do that work himself, but someone had to do it.

Now it occurred to him that Munday might know other kinds of informers, given his not-so-secret trade. He walked over to Munday's table. "Ever heard of a man called Cholmeley?"

"I have," a man behind him said.

Tom turned to see a rangy-looking fellow with light brown curls on his head and chin. "And you are?"

"Henry Porter." The man got to his feet to shake Tom's hand. "I write comedy when I can, bits for other men's plays." He nodded at Munday, who nodded back. "You know the stuff — farts and secret lovers, fat men getting stuck in windows."

Tom grinned. He liked that sort of stuff, in small doses.

"I wrote the clown scenes in *Doctor Faustus*," Porter bragged.

"You worked with Marlowe." That impressed Tom, though the instigator was most likely the theater owner and not the playmaker.

"I've worked with everybody," Porter said. "And written my share of ballads. The bawdier, the better, for the good of my purse. Which is how I know Cholmeley. We sell to the same printer. A man called Mullens."

"Do you know him by sight?" Tom asked. "Cholmeley, I mean?"

"That I do."

"So do I," Munday said, "but not from ballads. Not a nice man, Cholmeley. What do you want him for?"

"A hundred crowns." Tom bent his head, causing the others to lower theirs toward him. "I have it on good authority that he wrote the Dutch Church libel."

"Ho, ho, ho!" Munday said, sitting back. "You have some interesting sources, Mr., ah . . ."

"Clarady. Thomas Clarady. And yes, I do. Reliable ones. I'm sure I've got the right man."

"Then let's go get him," Porter said. "You'll give us a share, I assume."

"Ten crowns apiece." Tom had worked it out on his way here. Twenty to Mr. Bacon plus twenty to these assistants still left him sixty crowns the richer.

They left the tavern and walked down to Cheapside, making no effort to walk together. They found Cholmeley sitting in the same place at the back of the Angel's front room, crowded even at this hour. He'd changed his clothes, but he had the same squat nose and the square beard over a square chin. Not a handsome fellow, though not ugly enough to turn heads.

Cholmeley's gaze lit first on Munday. Recognition creased his brow. He flicked a glance at Porter, and the crease deepened. Then he noticed Tom and laughed. "Well, well, well. If it isn't my Inns of Court man, with a couple of round dogs nipping at his heels."

That drew a sharp look from Munday and a couple of barks from Porter. "Woof, woof!"

Tom nodded at his quarry. "You could've saved me some trouble if you'd introduced yourself a month ago."

"Nah." Cholmeley shook his head. "Too much fun watching the curs chase their tails." He jerked his blunt chin at Munday. "Don't tell me these churls solved the riddle for you."

"I solved it," Tom said. "They're here to help me deliver you to the sheriff."

Cholmeley growled in the back of his throat and stared into his cup, as if seeking a way out. He didn't find one. He drained the drink — bitter ale, by the smell of the place — and stood up. "They won't keep me long. I didn't write that thing for my health."

"I know why you wrote it." Tom took one arm, and Munday took the other. Porter led the way out of the tavern and back through Cheap to the Guildhall.

Tom had been here several times over the years, but he always felt the same sense of awe as he entered the square bounded by the wings of the ancient building. Whitehall, center of the queen's government, consisted of a jumble of houses both simple and grand. Gray's Inn contained the wonder of the English common law within its bounds. But the Guildhall, with its tiers of arches and graceful small towers, displayed London's pride in centuries of craftsmen.

They walked across the cobbled square and into the entry hall. Several men stood in one corner, questioning an urchin. The men were dressed like ordinary workmen in short-skirted doublets and long slops, but they bore constable's badges on their hats. A clerk stood behind a counter in the center of the hall. He watched Tom and the others hustle Cholmeley toward him with an air of infinite boredom.

"This," Tom announced, "is the man who wrote the libel posted on the door of the Dutch Church on the fifth of May. I'm here to collect the reward."

"How do you know he's the one?"

Tom explained the chain of discovery, emphasizing the printer's judgment as the most authoritative. "I can't name my sources or give you any specifics here in this public hall, but I can assert that this man has done this sort of work before."

"Oh, that's convincing." The clerk tossed a laugh toward the constables in the corner. "Who are you, if you don't mind my asking?"

"I'm Thomas Clarady, gentleman of Gray's Inn."

The constables turned to look at him. Two of them smiled. Tom smiled back. No one had expected the libeler to be identified. It had taken him a solid month, but he'd succeeded.

"I'll tell the whole story to the sheriff," Tom said. "And only to the sheriff."

The clerk sighed. "If you must." He left through an inside door, returning in a few minutes. He beckoned at Tom's group and led them back to a stuffy room where Sheriff Gerard sat in a large oak armchair. Some fifty years old, he was impeccably dressed in severe black with a wide white ruff framing his round face and black beard.

Tom stood before him with his hands behind his back to deliver his report. The sheriff listened with a skeptical quirk on his lips until Tom mentioned Francis Bacon. That name perked him up. He glanced at Anthony Munday several times too, as if gaining confirmation from the pursuivant's stony face.

In less time than Tom had expected, he'd shaken the sheriff's hand and watched a clerk count out a hundred crowns in stacks of five. Tom slid ten of the silver coins toward Munday, who bit one to test its quality before dropping them into his purse. "Easiest money I've earned this week."

Another ten went to Henry Porter, who grinned. "The only money I've earned this week." He clapped Tom on the back. "Anytime you need help, Clarady. I'm your man."

Munday bade them good-bye at the door and walked north. Tom turned south, planning to go home by way of his money box in Blackfriars. Porter walked beside him with a spring in his step and a happy grin on his face. He lived on Lambert Hill and was keen to get home to his quills.

He shot Tom a sly glance. "As good as money — almost — I had an idea back there for a set of comic interludes. Have to be a play like *Arden of Faversham*, with everyone rushing about conspiring against everyone else. I'd have a balladeer standing down left between scenes spouting some scurrility about one of the players. Or better — about all of them. No one in the play knows who the knave is, but he causes a lot of trouble."

Tom grinned. "Sounds funny. I'd pay to see that."

He was willing to hear more, but as they crossed Cheapside, two of the men from the Guildhall loomed up and laid their hands on Tom, one on either side.

"Thomas Clarady?" the taller one asked. He didn't wait for an answer. "You're wanted for questioning at Bridewell."

A deep chill shook Tom from head to toe. "Wanted by whom?"

The shorter one shrugged. "Reckon you'll find out when you get there. We've a warrant right and proper, so don't think about running."

"I won't run." Tom caught Porter's worried eyes. "You have to help me. You're all I've got. My master's name is Francis Bacon. He's a bencher at Gray's Inn, but he's currently attending upon the queen at Nonsuch Palace."

One of the constables gave an audible gulp but kept his grip on Tom's arm.

Tom kept his eyes on Porter. "I'm begging you, man. Do me this favor and I'll be forever in your debt. Ride to Nonsuch as fast as you can. Tell Mr. Bacon I've been arrested for questioning in Bridewell — those very words. He'll know what to do."

"I don't have a horse." Porter sounded almost as frantic as Tom felt.

274

"Hire one." Tom worked a hand into his doublet and pulled out the purse with his reward. He gazed at it sadly for a moment, then cried, "Bah!" and tossed it to the playmaker.

The short constable reached for it, but Porter caught it first. He shifted a few feet away.

The tall constable scolded his fellow. "We were supposed to get the purse back."

The short one shrugged. "Too late now."

"How do I get there?" Porter asked Tom.

"Take a wherry to Lambeth. Hire a horse. The stabler will give you directions from there. Lots of traffic coming and going. You'll find your way easily enough. Use what coin you need and give the rest to Mr. Bacon."

Porter hefted the purse in his hand with a look of wonder on his face. "Will they know this Francis Bacon at the guardhouse?"

"They'll know him. And they'll know where to find him. If they have any trouble, tell them to ask the Earl of Essex's steward." He looked the taller constable right in the face as he pronounced those last words.

The constable's sneer wilted. Then he blew a rude breath past his brushy moustache. "Funny how every knave in London is the best of chums with an earl. But it's nigh on four o'clock. Whoever you know or think you know, you'll enjoy the hospitality of Bridewell's interrogators tonight."

Tom willed himself not to quail. "Go," he told Porter. "Make haste, I beg you." He watched the playmaker — a man he had just met — walk away with ninety crowns in his pocket and Tom's hopes riding on his shoulders.

May God make him the man I need for him to be this day!

TWENTY-SEVEN

Francis hooked up the front of his doublet while Pinnock laced his hose under the peplum in back. He had broken his fast in bed, basking in the quiet after the two barristers who shared the room dressed their grunting selves and went down to the hall. He, in contrast, chose his clothes carefully this morning. The queen had relented shortly after Saturday's debacle and granted him access to the Privy Chamber again. He meant to spend every minute of every day in that hallowed room from this point forward.

He chose a three-inch ruff with an inch of lace — neither too gaudy, nor too plain. After Pinnock brushed his hat, he tied a lavender ribbon around the crown. Not a royal purple — he would never presume! He wore the softer purple of Gray's Inn, his greatest source of pride and achievement thus far. Leave the unappreciated Parliamentarian aside and let the legal scholar step forward.

He had no sooner exited his humble lodgings when a messenger ran up to stand before him, panting. "Well?" Francis asked.

"You've a messenger from London at the gate. He says it's urgent."

"What's it about?" He didn't want to walk all the way to the gatehouse only to hear that one of Anthony's clerks had been censured by the steward at Gray's for coming in after hours.

"He says your clerk's been arrested. They've taken him to Bridewell for questioning."

"God's bones!" A tremor of fear shook Francis from head to toe. "Why didn't you say that first?" He strode quickly toward the gatehouse, leaving the messenger to catch up. This was no coincidence, Tom being arrested two days after Heneage and Puckering had issued their oblique threats. It would take that long for the constables to locate their target.

The messenger got ahead of him as they neared their goal. He gestured with both hands to connect Francis to a tall, lean man in the rusty black of a gentleman scholar. He wasn't a member of Gray's. Tom must have been in the city when they took him.

The man had been leaning against the wall near a horse whose reins were looped through an iron ring. Now the man stepped forward to meet him. "Mr. Bacon? Francis Bacon?" When Francis nodded, he removed his hat and made a courteous bow. "I'm Henry Porter. A playmaker and balladeer, also a gentleman of Oxford. I met your clerk Mr. Clarady only yesterday, but I happened to be with him when he was arrested. He begged me bring the message to you, so here I am."

Francis thanked him. "What happened?"

Porter told him about bringing Richard Cholmeley, a vile knave if ever there was one, to the Guildhall, where Tom collected the prize for identifying the Dutch Church libeler. They'd seen constables idling about the entry talking to a boy. Porter now guessed the boy had been following Tom. Just his good luck that the prey had led him into the lion's den.

Francis shook his head. Tom should have left for Dorset on Monday morning instead of continuing to pursue matters best left undisturbed. But he couldn't have known a warrant had been issued for his arrest. Francis had told him all would be well if the Marlowe inquiry were dropped. He'd forgotten about the libel which had started it all and those irresistible hundred crowns.

"Clarady said you'd know what to do," Porter said. "Oh, and he told me to give you this." He fished a fat purse from his commodious slops and handed it over. "That's the Lord Mayor's reward. I think they meant to take it back, but Clarady was too quick for them." Porter scratched the edge of his curly beard. "He gave me ten crowns for helping with Cholmeley. Another ten went to the other fellow who came along. Didn't seem fair for me to spend my own money on this errand. I spent the night in Lambeth so I could get an early start. So I dipped in for another ten crowns."

"I see." It didn't cost twenty shillings to spend a night at an inn and hire a horse for one day, but never mind. One didn't haggle in a time of crisis. Besides, Francis intended to extract the thirty percent Tom had promised Anthony before returning the purse.

Porter deserved credit for turning over any of the money and for delivering this vital message. Francis noted the excited gleam in the playmaker's eyes as he scanned the busy palace yard, the delicate towers with their fanciful crenellations, and the painted walls. He'd been given more than twenty crowns this day, and he'd set his feet inside the halls of power. He'd acted in good faith and been fully rewarded for it.

"Should we go straightaway?" Porter asked, sounding reluctant.

"Yes," Francis said. Then he held up a finger. "Not quite." He walked under the gatehouse and found his messenger. He gave the man a shilling to tell Pinnock that his master was off to London for a day and a night. Then the messenger should find any secretary of the Earl of Essex and give him the same message, adding that Clarady had been arrested for no reason other than to threaten Francis. That might summon greater help than a mere barrister could supply.

He turned back to Porter, intending to have him walk around to the stables with him, when a sudden thought made him gasp. *Trumpet!* She would flay him alive if he left without telling her what had happened. He wasn't sure of the time, but Her Ladyship was probably still in the queen's bedchamber, doing whatever the ladies did there.

Should he wait for her to emerge? That could be an hour or more. Francis stared blankly over Porter's shoulder while he considered the arguments *pro* and *contra*.

His every instinct told him time was of the essence. Questioning was the excuse Puckering had given for arresting Thomas Kyd. But surely the Lord Keeper would never go so far as to rack Bacon's confidential secretary. On the other hand, Kyd's arrest had been completely egregious — a wanton abuse of power.

Then again, what excuse could Trumpet make to leave her duties? The queen wouldn't want to hear about some clerk, whoever his master, being arrested. She would assume her officers knew what they were about. She expected her ladies to make her their sole concern, at least while they were in her presence. Access was the greatest concession, after all.

And then there was Porter, standing by his horse with a bemused expression on his face. Dare he introduce this observant playmaker to the unpredictable Lady Dorchester? What if Trumpet insisted on stopping at her hunting box to transform herself into a man?

But no. She wouldn't take the time, not when Tom's well-being was at stake. She was far more familiar with these theater people than he was. She could manage Porter. Also, she had more courage than most men and would move heaven and earth to rescue Tom.

He raised his finger at Porter again and entered the gatehouse to roust out another messenger. He gave him instructions for approaching the queen's bedchamber to deliver a message, giving him more coins to pass along to Her Majesty's Gentlemen when he got there. He should wait for an answer and then come straight back.

Realizing that would take a minimum of half an hour, he sent a third messenger to Pinnock, bidding him to pack a bag and bring it, with both their horses, to the northern gatehouse. Then he sighed and went to stand beside the wall with Porter.

He gave half an ear to the man's detailed description of a play he'd been working on for some years. A comedy of the lowest sort, though it did indirectly advocate marital fidelity. Before the chapel bell could toll twice, Trumpet came hurrying across the paved yard, taking small, quick steps under the great wheel of her farthingale. The wide skirts seemed to hover just above the ground as she glided forward.

Porter bowed so deeply to her he nearly tipped over. "I thought Clarady was boasting about knowing an earl."

"I'm a countess," Trumpet snapped. "Tell me everything, but hurry. I'll have to change clothes."

Porter told his story without hems or haws. Francis attempted to reassure her — and himself — that these supposed questioners, if they existed at all, would undoubtedly leave Tom alone for at least a couple of nights. "They like to build fear. He'll be miserable, but not harmed."

"You don't know that. They want to teach someone a lesson. You, him, other friends of Marlowe's. We must hurry." Then she threw her hands in the air. "But I can't ride in this gown! Come with me." She pointed at Porter. "You wait here."

Francis followed her, stepping lively to keep up. They reached her bedchamber, which she shared with another countess, who must still be waiting on the queen. "How did you get away?" he asked.

She gave him a coy look. "I'm with child, as it happens." Her eyes narrowed at whatever she saw on his face. "It's Stephen's. But I puke every morning. This time I let Her Majesty catch wind. She sent me away with a snap of her fingers. I'll make a better excuse later."

She went behind a screen with her Spanish maidservant to deconstruct her elaborate court costume.

Speaking of excuses . . . "May I use your desk?" Permission granted, Francis sat and wrote a quick note to the Earl of Essex. Verbal messages could be garbled and he would hate for His Lordship to feel slighted. Besides, the earl ought to know to what depths his rivals on the council would stoop.

He folded the letter and sealed it with his ring, then handed it to one of the grooms Trumpet had summoned.

Trumpet emerged in sensible traveling clothes and took a turn at the desk, dashing off three notes while Catalina bundled costly fabrics into two large, flat bags. Trumpet followed Francis's questioning look as she handed her letters to yet another palace servant. "I mean to go straight to the warden when we get to Bridewell and remind him of my husband's earlier visit. That gown will speak more loudly than an army of heralds."

She had summoned grooms, ordered servants, donned a fresh costume while considering the effects of another, and written letters to three persons, who must be important individuals here at the palace, without batting an emerald eye. Her face was drawn and pale, but her voice had never quavered, nor had her posture stooped.

The dread in Francis's heart abated under the force of her command. A smile stole across his lips. The Duke of Parma could count himself most fortunate that this woman had not been born a boy.

TWENTY-EIGHT

Tom awoke with a jerk, shivering, and tried to pull his bedclothes up over his shoulders. Only there weren't any covers, nor any bed. He lay on a heap of moldy straw wearing nothing but his shirt. He blinked at the weak light, breathed in the dank smell of wet bricks, and remembered. He was in Bridewell Prison — and not on the upper floors that housed drunkards and vagrants.

He was in the basement, where they brought prisoners for interrogation.

His chest tightened with fear. His legs curled up in a protective pose, hoarding what warmth his body could supply. He could barely feel his numb toes, and great shivers rolled through him, like waves on the open sea. He remembered Thomas Kyd, cold and filthy after only a week in this shuddering hell. He tried not to look at the pulley attached to the high ceiling or the ropes that ran through it, gathered into neat loops on a hook in the wall. A pair of iron manacles dangled from one end.

The guards had stripped him of his clothes, commenting gleefully on their quality, when they'd first brought him down here. He'd rattled off the names and titles of every great person he knew — not a short list — but they'd only laughed.

"You'd be amazed at how many men are the closest of dear friends with the Earl of Northumberland. Or even the queen. They have cousins who are nephews of a neighbor whose father once waited upon Great Harry himself. 'She'll remember me,' they cry." That brought another round of harsh guffaws.

He'd begged them for his stockings, pleading in pathetic tones that now rang mockingly in his ears, adding humiliation to cold, hunger, and dread. They'd brought him a jug of stale water and a hunk of bread last night. He'd drunk the water — he couldn't help himself, his thirst was so great. But the bread had crawled with weevils. He'd pushed it through the bars on the tiny window in the door. Now his stomach growled, and he found it hard to think about anything else.

At least they'd given him a chamber pot.

He heard a clanking — of keys, perhaps — coming toward him. He remembered walking down a long brick-lined corridor in which every sound echoed, knowing misery waited at the end. He'd heard wails and whimpers all through the night. He hadn't expected to sleep at all, shivering in the scratchy, inadequate straw, listening to sounds he might be making himself before long. But exhaustion had taken him sometime after dawn.

Now he heard footsteps too, more than one man. Then he heard a key thunking into the lock and forced himself to sit up.

The door opened, and Robert Poley walked in with the air of a man visiting a sick friend. "How are we this morning, Clarady? I trust you slept well."

Terror closed Tom's throat. Poley worked for the Lord Keeper, and the Lord Keeper had ordered Kyd's torture. He struggled to work some spit into his mouth.

Poley watched him with a little smile of satisfaction. "You'll find your voice soon enough. They say screaming loosens the tongue something wonderful."

"God rot you, Poley," Tom managed. "You'll never get away with this."

"Oh, I'll get away. I always do. And yes, someone will come for you sometime, I have no doubt. Tomorrow, if you're lucky. That's a long time down here."

Tom pulled himself up to sit with a straight back against the wall. He tucked his shirt tails between his legs to preserve some shred of dignity. "Why are you doing this? All I did was talk to you."

"You poked your prying nose into my affairs. I don't like that, Tom. And neither do my masters. I'm going to teach you to be less inquisitive. That's a lesson you sorely need."

Tom couldn't think of anything but Kyd, huddled aching in the straw. Mr. Bacon would come for him, but when? What if Porter had run off with the money? Eighty crowns was a powerful temptation. Or even if he'd done the right thing and gone to Nonsuch, what if Mr. Bacon had gone to Twickenham? How long would it take to find that out and ride there instead? He wished he'd told him to find Lady Dorchester, but he'd scrupled to speak her name out in the open street.

Trumpet would be here today, this afternoon, at her house on the Strand. Less than a quarter mile away, but she didn't know where he was. She couldn't know unless Mr. Bacon was still at Nonsuch and caught her before she left.

Too many *ifs*. Too many hours. He glared balefully at Poley as his empty stomach clenched. If he'd been given a meal he could eat, he'd be spewing it into the straw right now.

Poley nodded. He smiled that knowing smile again. Unlike Tom, he'd done this before. He went to the door and spoke through the bars. "Call the men to work the manacles. And I'll need a desk and a writing box."

Tom watched the preparations, fighting for his sense of himself as a man. He clambered to his feet, drawing himself up to his full height and lifting his chin. "What in God's name do you mean to ask me? Marlowe's gone.

Even if I had evidence against him, which I don't, it wouldn't do you any good."

"It might," Poley said. He sat on the stool they'd brought with the desk and opened the writing box, as calm as a lawyer preparing to take a deposition. "There are others in his atheist school worth pursuing. Men my masters consider rivals. You'll tell me everything you know or can imagine about them before we're through. I'll make you wish you never heard the name of Christopher Marlowe."

Two guards came at Tom with hands ready to seize him. "Don't fight us," one of them advised. "You'll need your strength."

They gripped his arms, holding him still while another guard pulled his ankles together and began to strap weights to his feet. Tom got one good kick in. The weight-strapper grunted like an overburdened laborer, got to his feet, and drove his meaty fist into Tom's belly. He finished his work while Tom retched and groaned, still caught between the other two.

The strapper then took the loops of rope from the hook on the wall, shaking one end toward a corner, ready for pulling. He brought the manacles over to Tom. "Hands in front."

Tom struggled, resisting, knowing it was useless. But his body refused to stand meekly waiting for punishment.

The cold iron rings closed around his wrists with echoing clicks. Tom swallowed hard as the guards lifted him into position under the pulley, standing on the block tied to his feet, facing his tormentor.

Poley sat writing on a clean sheet of paper, uninterested in the tedious process of readying a prisoner for questioning. When the strapper said, "All set," he looked up and smiled. "Ah, good. Let's begin, shall we?"

One guard took up a position at Poley's side. The other two went behind Tom and took hold of the rope. They pulled together, hand over hand, in a practiced rhythm, hauling Tom into the air, suspended by his wrists. He felt his spine and his sinews lengthen and flexed his biceps, stretching his fingers high in hopes of something to grip, something to pull on to relieve the growing pressure in his shoulders.

All the blood in his body seemed to rush upward. His head hung forward, weighting his neck. A great ache arose in his chest as sweat sprang out on his clammy skin. He wanted to endure it in dignified silence with a contemptuous sneer on his lips. He tried to summon Kit's face as a model but couldn't find anything in his mind but pain. A groan escaped him.

"I don't know anything," Tom pleaded. "I'm just a clerk."

"Ah, but whose clerk?" Poley jerked his chin at the man beside him, who came over to clasp Tom around the knees. He tugged, and Tom wailed in agony.

Poley dipped his quill in the ink. "So tell me, Tom. What's Anthony Bacon interested in these days?"

TWENTY-NINE

"I won't forget the service you've done us today, Mr. Porter." Trumpet couldn't manage a smile, but she meant her words. They'd stopped in the yard at the Lambeth inn where the playmaker had hired his horse. Trumpet and Mr. Bacon would ride on to the wharf.

"I only wish I could've reached you yesterday. I hope Clarady's night in prison hasn't done him too much harm."

Henry Porter removed his hat and bowed to her, then walked toward the inn with a bounce in his step. He'd done his best to maintain a somber mien on the ride from Nonsuch, but his excitement at being thrown into the company of such important persons had leaked out through his shining eyes and irrepressible smiles.

Trumpet couldn't blame him. He had repaid Dame Fortune's gift by honoring Tom's trust in him.

Now Trumpet turned her mount to face the road. "What's our plan, Mr. Bacon? We should go to the prison together, don't you think? But I need to change clothes. And we'll want stronger supports to demand Tom's release, if we're to counter an order from a Privy Councilor."

Bacon nodded. "I'll go straight home to write a letter to my uncle. I can't put it in so many words on paper, but I can hint that Lord Keeper Puckering is behind this. My uncle won't like that, not in the least. He'll send me something — a writ or a signed note."

"Writer your letter at my house. Your costume is adequate for your role. One of my servants will dust you off." Trumpet clucked at her mare, and the group moved forward at walk. "I fear your letter may not be enough. Your uncle might be too ill to receive letters or away from home. And I'm not certain he will recognize the urgency. We need someone more forceful, more righteous. I shall write to your aunt."

* * *

At Dorchester House, Trumpet led Bacon to the library and pointed him toward paper and ink. She sat at her usual desk and penned a swift note to Lady Russell, Tom's legal guardian. Trumpet had lived under Her Ladyship's roof for one year, during which they'd forged an alliance. Each recognized the other as a woman who knew her worth and intended to make sure everyone else knew it too.

She wrote that Tom had been arrested on suspicion of atheism. That would rouse the militant heart of the Calvinist lady like nothing else could. The threat of torture was imminent. Speed was required. Trumpet would call at Blackfriars in half an hour. Could Her Ladyship have a letter ready that would set the fear of God's wrath in the heart of the prison warden?

Trumpet ordered her carriage to be readied and brought around to the front. Then she sent a servant to bring a brush to spruce up Bacon's doublet and hat. She had food and drink sent to him as well. She and Catalina fairly ran up to her bedchamber to change clothes again. The minute the servant dropped her cases and closed the door, Trumpet burst into tears, standing in the middle of the room clutching her belly while deep sobs wracked her body.

Catalina stroked her shoulders, murmuring soothing words in Spanish until the storm subsided. Then she said, "We will save him, my lady. And he will still be Tom. Nothing can change that."

Torture could. Trumpet had never seen the results herself, but Tom had told her about Thomas Kyd. His voice had trembled with pity and disgust at what had been done to the man.

She couldn't think about that now. She had work to do. She tilted her head back and screamed at the ceiling, expelling all her doubt and dread. Then she filled her lungs with wrath, shaking herself from head to toe.

They got her out of her traveling suit and back into her court gown — shimmering ivory silk embroidered with red roses. The wheel around her waist extended a full foot on either side. It dipped lower in front to accommodate the pointed hem of her boned bodice, elongating her torso and drawing the eye up to the cleft of her breasts. Her thickly padded sleeves added width to her slender shoulders, and the high circle of her lacy supportasse framed her head like a halo.

Catalina draped a strand of pearls around her neck and fixed another strand into her hair. "Shall we paint, my lady?"

"Paint away," Trumpet said. "I want the master of Bridewell to fall flat on his face when he sees me coming."

So her face was whitened, her cheeks rouged, and her eyebrows plucked to a narrow line. Thus armored, they went down to the library, where Bacon was slitting the seal on a letter.

"It's from my uncle." He displayed two pages. "His house is just across the street, and luckily, he's sitting at his desk. He agrees the offense against me is great, whoever ordered the arrest. The enclosure reads simply, 'Release

Thomas Clarady at once, without further prejudice or penalty.' It bears both his seal and his signature."

"Good," Trumpet said. "We'll collect another letter from your aunt on the way."

Bacon nodded at her costume. "I doubt the master has many visits from ladies of your rank."

"He'll wish he had none."

Lady Russell met them at the door of her house in Blackfriars. Her letter covered a full sheet of foolscap. She was among those who appointed members to the prestigious board of governors of Bridewell and Bedlam. She had personally supported three successful candidates who would leap at the chance to return the favor by discharging an irresponsible ignoramus unable to recognize a good Christian gentleman when he was dragged illegally through the doors.

If the warden wished to avoid prison himself, she had written, he would release Mr. Clarady at once, restoring to him every article of clothing and any other possessions, such as coins or jewelry, that he might have had on his person when he arrived. She would know if anything were omitted. She expected immediate compliance and would know if there were any delay. Retribution would be swift and certain.

Trumpet thanked her briefly. They turned the carriage around. They had to drive back up to Fleet Street to cross the bridge and come back down to the riverside prison. It would have gone faster in a wherry but would have been less impressive on arrival. Few things spoke of wealth and privilege like a gilded and painted carriage pulled by a matched pair of high-stepping black geldings.

People stopped and stared as they pulled into the yard. This wasn't the Tower. Bridewell's usual guests arrived on foot, in rags. Men bowed from the waist as if tugged by strings when Trumpet emerged from the coach. She and her two attendants strode into the hall, where a liveried servant bowed himself toward her. He begged to know what Her Ladyship desired.

"I desire to speak with the warden. At once. He's holding a friend of mine whom I wish to be released."

The servant bowed himself away, returning with a stout man with a bristling gray-streaked moustache under a fleshy nose. The warden didn't fall on his face, but he nearly fell on his round arse, staggering as he spotted a court lady in full rig standing in his hall. He bowed as deeply as his belly would allow.

She demanded Tom's immediate release. "I believe you met my husband recently on a similar errand. My Lord of Dorchester will wonder why we are compelled to rectify your abuses yet again."

The warden spluttered excuses, falling mute as Bacon stepped forward to read out both letters in Parliamentarian tones. Trumpet glared at the paunchy knave, tapping her foot, barely able to contain her overwhelming bodily need to find Tom.

When the warden took precious seconds to blink at the letters' content, she leapt at him with her hands extended like claws. "Where is he?" she growled through bared teeth.

The warden jumped back, then snapped his fingers at two guards beside an inner door. They trotted over to exchange mumbles with their master. The warden turned toward Trumpet. "Will you wait here, my lady?"

"I will not." Trumpet strode toward that inner door. She would shout the place down until she heard Tom's answering call.

The guards trotted forward again, trying to get ahead of her. One slithered past her skirts with his back pressed against the wall. He led the group to a staircase lit by two meager torches, leading down into a well of stink and dampness. Trumpet shivered, but not from the sudden cold.

She heard a wail and began to run, pushing the guard in front of her. "Where is he? *Where?*" She had turn and run back when the guard knocked on a door behind her.

She pushed past him into a filthy cell where Tom — beautiful, brave, beloved Tom — hung from the ceiling with only a sweat-soaked shirt covering his naked form. His head hung on his chest, and his face was drawn in lines of pain.

His eyes were closed, but at the bustle coming through the door, he cracked one open. Then, from somewhere in the depths of his gallant heart, he summoned half a smile. "Ah, Lady Dorchester! How good of you to come. I fear we haven't any refreshments to offer —"

"Shut up, you fool!" To Catalina, she cried, "Catch him!" Then she raised her claws at the guards holding the long rope, roaring at them. "I'll have you whipped till your bones are bloody!"

They dropped the rope and ran from the room. Tom fell into Catalina's strong arms, nearly driving her to the floor. Trumpet whirled on her toes in the little room and reached past her skirts to wrap her padded arms around him. It took both women to hold him up. He sagged heavily against them as they helped him sink down to the cold stone floor. He groaned as they lowered his arms. The poor limbs lay limp in his lap, his hands still trapped in those horrible bands of iron.

Trumpet couldn't bend very far forward in her long whalebone stays, so she gathered Tom's sweet head to her side, stroking the lank hair from his brow with a soothing hand. He sighed, closing his eyes. "I wasn't sure this time," he whispered.

"That I would come for you?" Trumpet blew out a dismissive breath. "Fiddle-faddle."

"How would you know, if Porter proved faithless? Or if Mr. Bacon had been in Twickenham or if —"

"Shh. I will always find you. You know that. If my message failed to find you at Gray's, I would've gone to the Goose and Gall. Someone there would've told me about you leaving with Porter and Munday. I would've tracked you from the Guildhall here. I would use everything in my power to reach you." She bent sideways with some effort to kiss his forehead. "You're lucky I'm a countess now and not just another law student."

"I'm lucky you're you," Tom said. "You were fairly unstoppable as a boy too."

Tears filled her eyes. "Always find you," she whispered, straining down for another kiss. She straightened, sniffed, and blinked her eyes clear.

Catalina knelt to untie the weights binding Tom's feet. Trumpet noticed for the first time a gentleman with a round face and thinning blond hair standing behind a small desk. She recognized him from the church in Deptford — Robert Poley. His calculating eyes shifted between her, Tom, and Francis Bacon, who stood between him and the door.

He'd seen her kiss Tom. Dangerous hands to hold that secret. Well, it couldn't be undone. She'd have to hope her status would supply some protection.

For now, she'd let Bacon deal with him. The guards who led her down here had fled along with the rope-pullers. She commanded the only one left to unlock the manacles. He obeyed, turning the key and opening the rings. Then he too ran out the door. Catalina pulled the bracelets off and threw them against the wall. She began chafing Tom's wrists and forearms, murmuring to him in Spanish.

Poley studied Trumpet as if planning a portrait, assessing her clothes and her painted face. His eyes lingered on the hand resting on Tom's bare head. He nodded as if confirming something, then turned to Bacon. "You can't keep me."

"I wouldn't try. I'll have those papers though." Bacon stepped forward to place a hand on the pages loosely stacked upon the desk. His eyes widened as he read something written on the uppermost sheet. He said to Poley, "You won't dare speak of what you've seen or heard in this cell to anyone, not even the Lord Keeper. He can't protect you from the queen's favorite, who happens to be my patron, or the Lord Treasurer — my uncle. Who do you think will bear the blame if word of what you've done today gets out?"

Poley glared at him, his tongue poking into his cheek. Then he shrugged. "I'll be difficult to find for the next year or so. But don't worry. Your man didn't tell me much. That's a list of items in your brother's wardrobe, in Latin, interspersed with some kind of barbarous babel that must be Law French." With that, he left.

Bacon lifted a sheet of paper to read and barked a short laugh. He shook his head at Tom with a fond smile. "These are my legal maxims."

Tom managed a weak smile. "It went easier when he was writing." Then he closed his eyes again, leaning his head against Trumpet.

"His clothes?" she asked Bacon.

He nodded and leaned out the door, shouting for a guard. When one came, he issued orders in the crisp tones of a man bred in the upper echelons of government.

Catalina began rubbing Tom's feet and ankles, provoking another long groan. She stopped. "Do I hurt you?"

"No, please," he said. "Keep going. I'd forgotten I had those." He rolled his eyes to look up at Trumpet and whispered, "They really hurt me." He would never admit that to anyone else.

"I'll kill them all," she promised. "Each and every one. Might take a while."

He chuckled, or tried to. It ended in a cough, which turned into a groan.

His clothes came, and they helped him into them, all three of them. Tom was beyond shame. He sighed as their gentle hands soothed him. By the time Bacon knelt to buckle his shoes, Tom could stand on his own, with one hand on Catalina's shoulder. They made their way slowly back up to the hall, where a servant in livery shuffled forward in a half bow, extending a letter toward Trumpet.

"It's from Lady Russell," she said, slitting the seal with her thumbnail. "She wants me to bring Tom to her to recuperate. She claims Gray's is a desert at this time."

"She's right about that," Bacon said. "He can't manage on his own."

"Well, he's not going to her house." Trumpet clapped her hands to have paper, ink, and a flat surface brought to her. The swift obedience made Tom smile — a reward beyond rubies for the bother of moving about in these enormous clothes.

She penned a note to Her Ladyship declaring that she was taking Tom to Dorchester House. "He's been racked," she wrote. "He needs a physician. He needs a hot bath. My husband's ushers will guard him against further assault, and I have an excellent cook. I will brook no argument on this score, though I will send him to visit you as soon as he is able. And, of course, you are always welcome in my house."

She sealed it with her ring and bade the messenger run all the way to Blackfriars.

Bacon and Catalina leant their shoulders to support Tom on either side. Trumpet walked beside Bacon, wishing she weren't so hindered by her clothes, even though the costume had won the day.

"What will you tell the queen?" Bacon asked her in a low voice.

"She doesn't want a pregnant woman in her bedchamber. Too much mess. I'll write to tell her I'm on my way to join my husband in Dorset. She'll be glad for it."

"What about your lord husband?" His tone made clear the true import of that question.

"Stephen would insist that I stay to tend to his friend. When Tom's ready to travel, we'll ride together. We'll be the very souls of discretion, never fear, but after this nightmare, I intend to deliver him to his mother's house in Dorset myself."

They reached the carriage. A groom jumped down from the bench to help Catalina load Tom inside. While they waited, Bacon gave Trumpet a doubtful smile. "My lady aunt considers herself more effective than any physician. And she considers Tom part of her estate. She'll never relinquish him to you."

"Mr. Bacon," Trumpet said, arching her narrow brows, "you astonish me. I should think a legal scholar of your eminence would know that possession is nine-tenths of the law."

THIRTY

"No dancing," the surgeon said, holding Tom's gaze with a stern look. He'd just untied the slings that had supported Tom's injured shoulders for the past two weeks. "No fencing for two months. No tennis. No wrestling. And God forbid, no archery!" He fingered his short beard as if trying to guess what other mischief Tom might get into. "You can ride, if you must, but only at a walk. No galloping. No jumping. No racing of any kind."

"I promise." Tom gave each shoulder a tentative roll. Still tender, but not too bad. He couldn't imagine fencing or racing at the moment. He was glad for the permission to ride though. As comfortable as Trumpet had made him and as much as he loved seeing her face every day, he wanted to go home. He just had one more thing to do.

He'd spent most of the past two weeks lying in this well-appointed bed, where servants attended upon his every need. Trumpet had bundled him into this room directly from the carriage. She'd given orders for a fire to be lit and a tub to be brought up with vessels of hot water and loads of clean towels. She'd directed the steward to supervise Tom's bath and gone off with Catalina to change clothes.

Meanwhile, Mr. Bacon had sent for his own physician, who took a sample of Tom's urine and declared it free of faults. He prescribed poppy juice for the pain — which had been considerable that first week — and left after pocketing his fee. Then the surgeon came to examine Tom's joints. That knave's job seemed to consist of twisting and bending each of Tom's limbs until he screamed. He reckoned Tom hadn't been hung up for more than half an hour, judging by the damage done. It had felt longer, but then Tom remembered Poley glancing at the door as if expecting to be interrupted.

The surgeon left. A few minutes later, a short rhythm rapped on the door heralded Trumpet's appearance.

"Intro!" Tom called. He pressed his hands gingerly into the mattress to push himself up and swing his legs down from the bed.

"How is it?" Trumpet asked, studying his shoulders as if she'd never seen such things before.

"Not bad. Look." He raised both arms to shoulder height, slowly, but without wincing. Then he got to his feet and wrapped both arms around her, pulling her close to his chest and breathing in the lavender scent of her hair.

She wrapped her arms around his waist. A small sound emerged, followed by a snuffle.

"Are you crying?" Tom demanded.

"Of course not." But another snuffle betrayed her.

Ah, well. She'd rescued him from the worst ordeal of his life. She could snuffle all she liked. He released her, then took her hand to lead her to the window seat overlooking the garden. They'd spent most afternoons in that garden, talking. Best friends as well as lovers, they never lacked for topics.

They argued about the uses of torture and the relative merits of small and large estates. They discussed the themes and plot devices of every play they'd ever seen. They agreed that Henry Porter was a man of parts who deserved their consideration.

They talked about the baby. Tom had thought about that a lot while staring at the underside of the brocaded tester. He'd fumed about Trumpet's betrayal in the dark hours of the night, working up a hearty sense of outrage. Then she'd come to check on him in the morning. She'd plump his pillows and kiss his forehead, and his righteous wrath would melt away like thin autumn snow. After a week of that, he'd accepted both the baby and her reasons for making it.

"When I stopped thinking like a jealous oaf," he told her one afternoon in the garden, "and considered your daily life, I realized that you couldn't put him off forever. One son is all very well, but children die every day, from a hundred causes. You need spares — the more, the better. Furthermore, if we keep doing what we like to do, which I hope we do, you're bound to fall pregnant again one of these days. If you never allowed Stephen to, er, to —"

"Exercise his marital rights?" Trumpet was smiling at him with so much affection in her sparkling eyes, Tom could barely finish his thought.

But he had to get it all out. "He'd know it couldn't be his, and then things would go badly for you. Once I understood that, I knew I could live with the rest." He gave her a wry smile. "If Steenie can love mine, knowingly or not, I can love his. Besides, they're both yours. That's all that matters."

Tears filled her eyes. Tom nodded, satisfied. Stephen couldn't touch her like that. She still belonged to him, deep down where it mattered.

They talked about Tom's future, though that raised more questions than it answered. They agreed he would pass the bar without difficulty. They also agreed that if it came down to it, which it probably would, he should mortgage his estate to attain his livery. Neither could countenance the idea of a barrister who continued to be a ward of the state.

Trumpet made a gallant attempt to contemplate Tom's eventual marriage, proposing an assortment of undesirable gentlewomen she knew from court as potential wives. Tom couldn't look at her — her heart-shaped face and green eyes, always lively with expression and intelligence — and think about other women. His mind simply wasn't big enough.

"I took care of those guards," Trumpet said.

"What?" Tom pulled his gaze away from the garden. "Which guards?"

"The ones who hurt you." She sounded indignant.

He frowned at her. "You didn't — surely you wouldn't —"

She laughed in his face. "Kill them? I wanted to, but no, my better angels prevailed. I had them snatched off the street outside of Bridewell last night and dropped off some fifteen miles out into the countryside. They had the long walk back to consider the consequences of their deeds. And to wonder where they might find other work. Bridewell won't be taking them back."

"Well done!" Tom hoped the dark roads contained many a rut and rock, so the varlets' legs would hurt as much his shoulders had.

Trumpet basked in his approval for another minute, then asked, "When will you be ready to travel?"

"In two days, if that suits you. I'll go to Gray's and pack my things this afternoon. Mr. Bacon wrote that he'd be there today."

She nodded. "I'll be glad to put London behind me this year."

Tom cocked his head at her. "We have one more thing to do. Roydon sent me a note this morning. He has a plan to catch Ingram Frizer after a guild dinner tomorrow evening. Are you with us?"

"I wouldn't miss it."

* * *

Tom walked back to Gray's Inn — a quarter mile, all by himself — to pack up his things. He'd send to Dorchester House for a cart when he was ready. Tom knocked on Bacon's door and found him alone.

"I never thanked you," he said.

Bacon waved that off. "You saved my life once. Besides, Lady Dorchester did most of the work. She's becoming a force to be reckoned with." He sounded somewhat alarmed.

"Good thing she likes us, then." Tom grinned and sat on the stool behind his desk. It seemed to have shrunk since he'd sat there last. He gave his master a somber look. "I fear the Lord Keeper's message was meant as much for you as for me."

"If so, they miscalculated. They can't threaten me that way. No one can tolerate their retainers being made vulnerable to such abuses. If it becomes known, Heneage and Puckering will lose support for anything they might propose in future." Bacon chuckled. "In fact, if I agree to hold my peace, I may be able to guarantee their approval of my bid for Attorney General."

"Happy to be of service." Tom laughed. It didn't hurt. Another sign of returning strength.

Bacon shook his head. "Words cannot express how sorry I am that you were caught in those terrible coils."

"I have only myself to blame. I'm the one that poked the bear. But I had to do it. I owed it to Kit. Now that I know what happened to him and why, I can rest content."

"Even though no one will be punished?"

"Someone might be." He noted the question in his master's eyes but answered it with only a bland smile.

Bacon didn't press. "Poley took a grave risk assaulting a man with your connections."

"He didn't believe me when I warned him." Tom grinned. "He certainly didn't know about Lady Russell. I poked a bear. He waked a dragon."

Bacon laughed at that. "I hope you thanked her."

"Never fear. I gave her exactly what she wanted most." He shot Bacon a broad wink.

And got the desired response. "Tom!" Bacon's eyes and mouth went wide with shock.

"Now, now. None of that. What a mind you have!" Tom savored the effect for a moment before relenting. "I let her catechize me in the library at Dorchester House all afternoon last week. She wanted to be certain no trace of deadly atheism lurked within my breast. None does, never fear. I loved Kit like the brother I never had, but I learned early on not to fall into his theological traps. As for Her Ladyship, I know my Bible almost as well as she does, thanks to those months in Cambridge."

Tom paused, his gaze turning inward as he thought back. Then he said, "Ironic, isn't it? Those were five of the hardest months of my life, but they laid trails that led me all the way to Bridewell — and out again."

Bacon nodded. "Irony, or something else. God's mill grinds slowly, you know."

* * *

Tom, Trumpet, and Catalina met Mathew Roydon, George Peele, and some other poets at an alehouse with a view of the Drapers' Hall. The women had dressed like young gentlemen down on their luck. Tom marveled at the way Catalina could transform one suit of doublet and slops into testimonials of status and relative wealth. A spot of mustard here, a patch sewn discreetly — yet visibly — there. Each woman's coloring might be distinctive, but their clothes were the clothes of a hundred ordinary men.

"Where's Porter?" Tom asked as he accepted a mug of beer from the wench.

"He came into some money somehow." Roydon winked at Tom. "He's gone back to Oxford to wait out the plague. He said he'll look you up when he gets back."

"Good," Tom said. "I owe him my thanks."

"What's the plan?" Trumpet asked. "We can't grab the man off Broad Street. Can we?"

"Not in daylight," Peele said. He had peered at her with his weak eyes as if wondering if he'd seen her before, then given up with a shrug. "We're guessing he's still enjoying Walsingham's largesse in Scadbury. He'll have to catch a wherry to get home."

"Eating Kit's bread and sleeping in Kit's bed," someone grumbled.

"Hopefully not that," Peele said. "We'll follow him down to the docks. He'll pick a quay east of the bridge, probably Lyott or Somers."

"Billingsgate, if we're lucky," another said. "The streets aren't safe there for an honest man."

"No," Roydon agreed. "Nor for a lying, murdering knave."

Trumpet nodded. "So we stalk him into a dark alley and thrash him within an inch of his life."

"Precisely," Peele said.

"Seems a little unfair." Tom counted with his finger around the table. "Seven of us against one of him. He can't be much of a fighter, by the looks of him. Skeres probably held Kit down."

"We'll catch up with him later," Roydon promised.

"I'll hold Frizer down," one of the men offered. "Fair's fair."

Peele grinned. "How about if we each take one good punch? We want it to hurt."

Tom thought about it, then nodded. "I can live with that."

They watched as drapers spilled out of the hall, laughing loudly, staggering as they clapped each other on the shoulders. Frizer came out with them, shaking hands right and left. How many deals had he made over the rabbit with red currant sauce?

Tom watched him with a deep and icy loathing. His companions were silent too, mugs forgotten as they aimed their silent fury across the street. Frizer finally left the group, walking down toward Gracechurch Street, swinging his arms like a man without a care in the world.

The Friends of Marlowe rose as one and went out to follow him. As they neared the river, they saw him enter an alley. Tom told Roydon to take another man and run around the next street to come up the far end. "It's a short one," he said. "We can box him in."

The sun had sunk below the tops of the three- and four-story houses looming over the narrow strip of packed dirt. Lines of drying sheets hung overhead, high enough for a man on a horse to pass without losing his hat. Shadows lurked under jettied first floors. People had drawn their curtains against the coming night.

Tom stepped forward and shouted, "Ingram Frizer!"

Frizer turned full around, startling when he saw four men blocking the way back to the main street. "Who are you?"

"We're friends of Christopher Marlowe."

Roydon, coming up behind Frizer, said, "You remember Kit. The man you murdered three weeks ago in Deptford."

"That was an accident!" Frizer cried. "The jury agreed. An accident, nothing more."

"We don't believe you," Trumpet said. "Your story had more holes than a poor man's stockings."

Frizer babbled the same weak lies in the same weary words he'd used before. Tom had had enough. "Who's first?" he asked the others. He raised a fist and took a few steps toward Frizer.

"Go ahead," Roydon said. "I'm next."

They each took a turn, pounding a fist into Frizer's face or midsection. He tried to escape, but they caught him each time and pushed him back into the circle. Each man said, "For Kit," or "This is for Marlowe," as he landed his blow. When everyone had his turn, Roydon said, "Speak of this to anyone and we'll do it again."

"And twice on Fridays," Peele quipped.

Tom whirled the whimpering man around three times and pushed him off toward the river. They watched him stagger to the end of the alley and disappear into the gloom. Tom looked at his companions' faces, pale in the lowering light. "Have any of you been to Deptford to visit Kit's grave?"

None of them had. They walked down to Somers Kay, made sure Frizer wasn't standing there, and caught the first wherry that could hold them all. As they passed the King's Head, Trumpet said, "Wait here a minute." She and Catalina dashed inside, returning with a big basket held between them filled with bottles and cups.

They walked up to St. Nicholas and found Kit's grave, marked with a small stone shallowly etched with his name and the dates 1564 - 1593. Too few years for so marvelous a man. They sprawled around the grave, passing the cups and bottles around. Each proposed a toast to the greatest poet of them all. Then they drank and spouted bits of Marlovian magic at each other until the cock crowed.

It was enough, almost.

HISTORICAL NOTES

Find <u>maps for the Francis Bacon mystery series</u>.

I can't stop grieving for Christopher Marlowe, though he died over four hundred years ago. He was a brilliant poet, a challenging dramatist, and a handsome young man with a questing mind. To die at age twenty-nine, before he had a chance to grow into his gifts, is tragedy enough. Compound that with a puzzling inquest report of his last day and his death becomes impossible to accept. Everyone who writes about this period ends up writing about Kit's death. It's one of those historical conundrums that task our minds.

The best nonfiction book about Marlowe's death is *The Reckoning* by Charles Nicholl (Harcourt, Brace, 1992). Nicholl explores everything and everyone who impinged in any way on Marlowe around the day of his death. It's a great book, beautifully written with breathtaking scholarship. But in the end, the conclusion he draws remains pure speculation. How not, when the facts are so sparse and so hard to connect? Read the book and form your own theory about what happened. If you want a good biography of Marlowe, I like Park Honan's *Christopher Marlowe: Poet & Spy* (Oxford University Press, 2007). He offers a theory of his own.

I grieve for Marlowe, but I feel a deeper sorrow for Thomas Kyd. I didn't know much about him until I started the research for this book. Hugely popular in his day, he's all but forgotten now. Being tortured destroyed him. He wrote six plays before that wrongful arrest, all produced to great acclaim. Afterward, he only managed to translate one French play. He died in 1594 at the age of thirty-six. Kyd was tortured merely for knowing Marlowe. Worse for a writer, his plays are no longer performed. Marlowe's are. I saw *Doctor Faustus* at the Barbican Centre in London a few years ago and *Edward II* by candlelight at the Sam Wanamaker Playhouse at Shakespeare's Globe (beyond awesome). History can be so unfair.

Nobody, as far as I know, has been able to come up with a good way to connect the Dutch Church libel to the arrest of Christopher Marlowe. I puzzled over it for a week and finally had to follow Nicholl's line, more or less, that it was commissioned as an excuse to drum up anti-atheist fervor. If so, the commissioner hired the wrong guy. The connection between the libel and atheism is as thin as wet silk.

Read it for yourself, if you feel inspired. This page will come up first if you google it or try: www.lesliesilbert.com/churchlibel.html. Then go read Baines's *Note* and Cholmeley's *Remembrances*, conveniently provided by the British Library:
www.bl.uk/collection-items/accusations-against-christopher-marlowe-by-richard-baines-and-others

The notes in their description are drawn from Nicholl's book. Both the *Note* and the *Remembrances* are great examples of the kind of thing that rattled people in those days. They had as much trouble with fake news as we do, only far fewer literate people.

Nearly everyone in this book is real. I think the only ones I made up are my usuals: Tom, Trumpet, Catalina, and Pinnock. Oh, and Stephen, Clara, and Mrs. Sprye. I found all the real people in Nicholl's book. I did a little consolidating to keep the number of shady characters down. I got what I could from Nicholl and Wikipedia (which draws on the Dictionary of National Biography), but I had to make up appearances and manners for everyone. They were all too cheap to buy portraits, I guess. (I think a lover paid for the portrait of Marlowe [presumed] that appears on the cover.)

Here are the real people who appeared in this book, including our regular cast for completeness:

- Mr. Francis Bacon
- Mr. Anthony Bacon
- Queen Elizabeth I
- Robert Devereux, 2nd Earl of Essex
- Sir Robert Cecil, Francis Bacon's cousin
- Christopher Marlowe (1564 - 1593)
- Sir Thomas Heneage (1532 - 1595). Nicholl claims he was Robert Poley's employer. It's plausible. Even commissioning that crazy libel in order to catch Marlowe is plausible for the time. 'Struth, it's plausible for our time, if you think about Russian meddling in American elections or Nigerian princes fishing for money.
- Lord Keeper John Puckering (1544 - 1596). He has a portrait, viewable at Wikipedia. I've completely taken against him, so I can't say anything positive about his life. Puckering and Heneage were apparently hand-in-glove on the anti-atheist campaign. I focused on Puckering because I like his name better and his office makes things more poignant for Francis Bacon.

Poor Thomas Kyd was still writing letters to Puckering swearing his innocence and asserting his good Christian character a year after his release. I can never forgive Puckering for that. Never.

- Thomas Walsingham (1561 - 1630). He and his wife successfully cultivated James VI of Scotland throughout the 1590s. Even so, Thomas is chiefly remembered for having been a friend of Christopher Marlowe. That tells what lasts in the long run.

- Audrey Walsingham (1568 - 1624). I could not find a date for their marriage. I doubt they really were married as early as 1593, but I'm always on the lookout for interesting female characters, so I pulled her in. She was the power in that couple. She became a favorite of Queen Elizabeth, who knighted her husband in 1596. Audrey was also a favorite of James's wife, Queen Anne, who made her Mistress of the Robes. She bore a son and a daughter. The daughter died young, but the son outlived his parents and prospered.

- Robert Poley (fl. 1568– aft. 1602). Everything we know about the three men present when Kit died is thanks to Nicholl's research. Poley was old enough to have participated in the Babington Plot. He's last mentioned in the historical record in 1602. He was a sizar at Clare College, Cambridge, which means his father was too poor to support him at university and he wasn't clever enough to win a scholarship like Marlowe.

- Joan Yeomans. She and Poley met in prison. He was there to inform on Catholics. She was carrying messages or something. They really did live together in her mother's lodging house, which she inherited, in spite of her being married to

William Yeomans, cutler. I made up all the stuff about how that worked. I also made her a shrew. Who else would live with an evildoer like Poley?

- Ingram Frizer (d. 1627). He lived long and prospered, the rat. Audrey continued to favor him, helping him win King James's favor too.

- Nicholas Skeres (1563 - 1601). He seems to have been a professional coney-catcher — an Elizabethan con man. He was the son of a merchant who died when Nick was a child. Not much of an excuse, considering the average life spans of the day.

- Mrs. Eleanor Bull (1550 - 1596). A respectable widow operating a respectable lodging house in the busy port of Deptford. If it weren't for Christopher Marlowe, she would have vanished into the mists of time. Did she ever travel across the river to see one of his plays, I wonder?

- Thomas Kyd (1558 - 1594). *Arden of Faversham* is attributed to Kyd, with possible assists from Marlowe and Shakespeare, then a newcomer to London. I saw that play here in Austin in 2019, performed by the Hidden Room Theater troupe. Hilarious!

- Mathew Roydon (d. 1622). Another poet more honored in his day than ours. In fairness, not much of his work survives. The discussion of his works on his Wikipedia page makes his stuff look fairly pointy-headed.

- George Peele (1556 - 1596). Now I can't remember where I got the bit about his nearsightedness. Nicholl, probably. There's a collection of Peele's work out there. He wrote comedies, dramas, and poetry. He knew everybody. He died of the pox.

- Anthony Munday (1560? - 1633). He worked for Sir Richard Topcliffe catching Catholics. He wrote a dozen or so plays, which were appreciated in his time but not in ours. He also wrote poetry and pamphlets on many themes and devised pageants for the guilds.
- Henry Porter (d. 1599). Why make up a writer when there are so many of them to choose among? He probably studied at Oxford for a time and wrote several comedic plays. *The Two Angry Women of Abington* seems to have survived. One of these days, I may read it.

ABOUT THE AUTHOR

Anna Castle holds an eclectic set of degrees: BA in the Classics, MS in Computer Science, and a Ph.D. in Linguistics. She has had a correspondingly eclectic series of careers: waitressing, software engineering, grammar-writing, a short stint as an associate professor, and managing a digital archive. Historical fiction combines her lifelong love of stories and learning. She physically resides in Austin, Texas, but mentally counts herself a queen of infinite space.

BOOKS BY ANNA CASTLE

K eep up with all my books and short stories with my newsletter: www.annacastle.com

The Francis Bacon Series

Book 1, *Murder by Misrule.*

Francis Bacon must catch a killer to regain the queen's favor. He recruits Thomas Clarady to chase witnesses from Whitehall to the London streets. Everyone has something up his pinked and padded sleeve. Even Bacon is at a loss — and in danger — until he sees through the disguises of the season of Misrule.

Book 2, *Death by Disputation.*

Thomas Clarady is recruited to spy on the increasingly rebellious Puritans at Cambridge University. Francis Bacon is his spymaster; his tutor in both tradecraft and religious politics. Their commission gets off to a deadly start when Tom finds his chief informant hanging from the roof beams. Now he must catch a murderer as well as a seditioner. His first suspect is volatile poet Christopher Marlowe, who keeps turning up in the wrong places.

Dogged by unreliable assistants, chased by three lusty women, and harangued daily by the exacting Bacon, Tom risks his very soul to catch the villains and win his reward.

Book 3, *The Widow's Guild.*

London, 1588: Someone is turning Catholics into widows, taking advantage of armada fever to mask the crimes. Francis Bacon is charged with identifying the murderer by the Andromache Society, a widows' guild led by his formidable aunt. He must free his friends from the Tower, track an exotic poison, and untangle multiple crimes to determine if the motive is patriotism, greed, lunacy — or all three.

Book 4, *Publish and Perish.*

It's 1589 and England is embroiled in a furious pamphlet war between an impudent Puritan and London's wittiest poets. When two writers are murdered, Francis Bacon is tasked with ending the tumult once and for all. But can he and his assistants stop the strangler without stepping on any very important toes?

Book 5, *Let Slip the Dogs*

It's 1591, Midsummer at Richmond Palace, and love is in the air — along with the usual political courtships and covert alliances. Secret trysts, daring dalliances, and a pair of pedigreed hounds keep Francis Bacon and his gallant team busy while trying to catch one devilishly daring murderer.

Book 6, *The Spymaster's Brother*

Anthony Bacon is home from France. An invalid, his gouty legs never hinder his agile mind. He's built the most valuable intelligence service in Europe. Now the Bacon brothers are ready to offer it to the wealthiest patron.

Then Francis finds the body of a man who's been spreading dangerous rumors about Anthony. Clues point to his private secretary. Can they sort through the lies before disaster strikes?

Book 7, Now and Then Stab

London, 1593. An anonymous ballad calls for violence. The mayor offers 100 crowns for the author's name. Thomas Clarady wants that money and drags Francis Bacon in to help.

Then the authorities turn on two popular playmakers. One is tortured. Another is killed in a brawl. The official story seems plausible, but Tom doesn't buy it. He refuses stop digging, uncovering a plot best left buried.

Bacon and his team hazard their lives to find the truth. Whether justice can be obtained is another matter.

The Professor & Mrs. Moriarty Series

Book 1, Moriarty Meets His Match

Professor James Moriarty has one desire left in his shattered life: to stop the man who ruined him from harming anyone else. Then he meets amber-eyed Angelina and his world turns upside down. Stalked by the implacable Sherlock Holmes, he's tangled in a web of murder and deceit. He'll have to lose himself to save his life and win the woman he loves.

Book 2, Moriarty Takes His Medicine

Professor and Mrs. Moriarty help Sherlock Holmes investigate a case he can't pursue alone: a doctor who may be committing murders for hire, ridding husbands and sons of their fussy, wealthy wives and mothers. When Angelina defies James to enter the lion's den, he must abandon his scruples and race the clock to save her — and himself.

Book 3, *Moriarty Brings Down the House*

An old friend brings a strange problem to Professor and Mrs. Moriarty: either his theater is haunted or someone's trying to ruin him. The pranks grow deadlier, claiming the first victim; then someone sets Sherlock Holmes on their trail. The Moriartys must stop the deadly pranks threatening a West End Christmas play before someone they love is killed.

Book 4, *Moriarty Lifts the Veil*

Professor and Mrs. Moriarty each take on a small case to fill the time before their next play opens. They place a bet on who will finish first. James will find out if three old soldiers have been cheated of their discharge pay. Angelina must find a missing servant, presumed to have been poached. But as they start asking questions, things take a dark turn. They uncover corruption at the heart of a circle of Army officers. A man is murdered, a friend is blamed, and Sherlock Holmes is sent to catch him. The Moriartys must use all their courage and ingenuity to save their friend, stop the loathsome crimes, and put the killer behind bars.

The Jane Moone Cunning Woman Series

Book 1, *The Case of the Spotted Tailof*

Cunning woman Jane Moone must defend her apothecary father from a murder charge with the aid of a talking cat, a fairy frog, and a skeptical - but very handsome - barrister.

Made in the USA
Las Vegas, NV
10 February 2022

43642229R10192